WKF

tennis. ~~~~~~~~~~~~~~
Twitter, @bjdanielsauthor

New York Times and *USA TODAY* bestselling author
Caridad Piñeiro is a Jersey girl who just wants to write
and is the author of nearly fifty novels and novellas. She
loves romance novels, superheroes, TV and cooking.
For more information on Caridad and her dark, sexy
romantic suspense and paranormal romances, please
visit caridad.com

Also by B.J. Daniels

Steel Resolve
Iron Will
Ambush Before Sunrise
Double Action Deputy
Trouble in Big Timber
Cold Case at Cardwell Ranch
Hard Rustler
Rogue Gunslinger
Rugged Defender

Also by Caridad Piñeiro

Cold Case Reopened
Trapping a Terrorist

Discover more at millsandboon.co.uk

MURDER
GONE COLD

B.J. DANIELS

DECOY
TRAINING

CARIDAD PIÑEIRO

MILLS & BOON

First Published in Great Britain 2022
by Mills & Boon, an imprint of HarperCollins*Publishers* Ltd
1 London Bridge Street, London, SE1 9GF

www.harpercollins.co.uk

HarperCollins*Publishers*
1st Floor, Watermarque Building,
Ringsend Road, Dublin 4, Ireland

Murder Gone Cold © 2022 Barbara Heinlein
Decoy Training © 2022 Harlequin Books S.A.

Special thanks and acknowledgement are given to Caridad Piñeiro for her contribution to the *K-9s on Patrol* series.

ISBN: 978-0-263-30333-9

0322

MIX
Paper from
responsible sources
FSC™ C007454

This book is produced from independently certified FSC™ paper to ensure responsible forest management.

For more information visit: www.harpercollins.co.uk/green

Printed and Bound in Spain using 100% Renewable electricity at CPI Black Print, Barcelona

MURDER GONE COLD

B.J. DANIELS

This new Heroes series is dedicated to all my fans who have followed my books from Cardwell Ranch to Whitehorse and back again. I hope you like these wild Colt brothers and Lonesome, Montana.

Prologue

Billy Sherman lay in his bed trembling with fear as the thunderstorm raged outside. At a loud crack of thunder, he closed his eyes tight. His mother had warned him about the coming storm. She'd suggested he might want to stay in her room now that his father lived somewhere else.

"Mom, I'm seven," he'd told her. It was bad enough that he still slept with a night-light. "I'll be fine." But just in case, he'd pulled out his lucky pajamas even though they were getting too small.

Now he wished he could run down the hall to her room and crawl into her bed. But he couldn't. He wouldn't. He had to face his fears. That's what his dad said.

Lightning lit up the room for an instant. His eyes flew open to find complete blackness. His night-light had gone out. So had the little red light on his alarm clock. The storm must have knocked out the electricity.

He jumped out of bed to stand at his window. Even the streetlamps were out. He could barely see the house across the street through the pouring rain. He tried to swallow the lump in his throat. Maybe he should run down the hall and tell his mother about the power going off. He knew she would make him stay in her room if he did.

Billy hated being afraid. He dreamed of being strong

and invincible. He dreamed of being a spy who traveled the world, solved mysteries and caught bad guys.

His battery-operated two-way radio squawked, making him jump. Todd, his best friend. "Are you asleep?" Todd's voice sounded funny. Billy had never confided even to his best friend about his fear of the dark and storms and whatever might be hiding in his closet. But maybe Todd was scared sometimes too.

He picked up the headset and stepped to the window to look out at the street. "I'm awake." A bolt of lightning blinded him for a moment and he almost shrieked as it illuminated a dark figure, walking head down on the edge of the road in the rain. Who was that and...? He felt his heart leap to his throat. What was it the person was carrying?

Suddenly, he knew what he had to do. He wasn't hiding in his room being scared. He would be strong and invincible. He had a mystery to solve. "I have to go," he said into the headset. "I saw someone. I'm going to follow whoever it is."

"No, it's storming. Don't go out. Billy, don't. Billy?"

He grabbed his extra coat his mother kept on the hook by his door and pulled on his snow-boots. At the window, he almost lost his nerve. He could barely see the figure. If he didn't go now he would never know. He would lose his nerve. He would always be afraid.

He picked up the headset again. "The person is headed down your street. Watch for me. I'll see you in a minute." Opening his window, he was driven back for a moment by the rain and darkness. Then he was through the window, dropping into the shrubbery outside as he'd done so many other times when he and Todd were playing their game. Only the other times, it hadn't been storming or dark.

He told himself that spies didn't worry about a thunderstorm. Spies were brave. But he couldn't wait until he reached Todd's house. Putting his head down he ran through the rain, slowing only when he spotted the figure just ahead.

He'd been breathing hard, his boots slapping the pavement, splashing through the puddles. But because of the storm the person hadn't heard him, wouldn't know anyone was following. That's what always made the game so much fun, spying on people and they didn't even know it.

Billy realized that he wasn't scared. His father had been right, though he didn't understand why his mother had gotten so angry with his dad for telling him to face his fears and quit being such a baby. Billy was facing down the storm, facing down the darkness, facing down all of his fears tonight. He couldn't wait to tell Todd.

He was smiling to himself, proud, when the figure ahead of him suddenly stopped and looked back. In a flash of lightning Billy saw the face under the hooded jacket—and what the person was carrying and screamed.

Nine years later

Chapter One

Cora Brooks stopped washing the few dinner dishes she'd dirtied while making her meal, dried her hands and picked up her binoculars. Through her kitchen window, she'd caught movement across the ravine at the old Colt place. As she watched, a pickup pulled in through the pines and stopped next to the burned-out trailer. She hoped it wasn't "them druggies" who'd been renting the place from Jimmy D's girlfriend—before their homemade meth-making lab blew it up.

The pickup door swung open. All she saw at first was the driver's Stetson as he climbed out and limped over to the burned shell of the double-wide. It wasn't until he took off his hat to rake a hand through his too-long dark hair that she recognized him. One of the Colt brothers, the second oldest, she thought. James Dean Colt or Jimmy D as everyone called him.

She watched him through the binoculars as he hobbled around the trailer's remains, stooping at one point to pick up something before angrily hurling it back into the heap of charred debris.

"Must have gotten hurt with that rodeoin' of his agin," she said, pursing her lips in disapproval as she took in his limp. "Them boys." They'd been wild youngins who'd grown into wilder young men set on killing themselves by riding anything put in front of them. The things she'd seen over the years!

She watched him stand there for a moment as if not knowing what to do now, before he ambled back to his pickup and drove off. Putting down her binoculars, she chuckled to herself. "If he's upset about his trailer, wait until he catches up to his girlfriend."

Cora smiled and went back to washing her dishes. At her age, with all her aches and pains, the only pleasure she got anymore was from other people's misfortunes. She'd watched the Colt clan for years over there on their land. Hadn't she said no good would ever come of that family? So far her predictions had been exceeded.

Too bad about the trailer blowing up though. In recent years, the brothers had only used the double-wide as a place to drop their gear until the next rodeo. It wasn't like any of them stayed more than a few weeks before they were off again.

So where was James Dean Colt headed now? Probably into town to find his girlfriend since she'd been staying in his trailer when he'd left for the rodeo circuit. At least she had been—until she'd rented the place out, pocketed the cash and moved back in with her mother. More than likely he was headed to Melody's mother's right now.

What Cora wouldn't have given to see *that* reunion, she thought with a hearty cackle.

Just to see his face when Melody gave him the news after him being gone on the road all these months.

Welcome home, Jimmy D.

JAMES HIGHTAILED IT into the small Western town of Lonesome, Montana. When he'd seen the trailer in nothing but ashes, he'd had one terrifying thought. Had Melody been in it when the place went up in flames? He quickly assured himself that if that had happened, he would have heard about it.

So…why hadn't he heard about the fire? Why hadn't Melody let him know? They'd started dating only a week before he'd left. What they'd had was fun, but definitely not serious for either of them.

He swore under his breath, recalling the messages from her that he hadn't bothered with. All of them were along the line of, "We need to talk. Jimmy D, this is serious. Call me." No man jumped to answer a message like that.

Still, you would think that she could have simply texted him. "About your trailer?" Or "Almost died escaping your place."

At the edge of the small mountain town, he turned down a side street, driving back into the older part of town. Melody's mother owned the local beauty shop, Gladys's Beauty Emporium. Melody worked there doing nails. Gladys had been widowed as long as James could remember. It was one reason Melody always ended up back at her mother's between boyfriends.

He was relieved to see her old Pontiac parked out front of the two-story rambling farmhouse. A spindly stick of a woman with a wild head of bleached curly platinum hair, Gladys Simpson opened the door at his knock. She had a cigarette in one hand and a beer in the other. She took one look at him, turned and yelled, "Mel… Someone here to see you."

Someone? Lonesome was small enough that he could easily say that Gladys had known him his whole life. He waited on the porch since he hadn't been invited in, which was fine with him. He'd been toying with the idea that Melody was probably mad at him. He could think of any number of reasons.

But mad enough to burn down the double-wide out of

spite? He'd known some women who could get that angry, but Melody wasn't one of them. He'd seen little passion in her before he'd left. He'd gotten the impression she wasn't that interested in him. If he'd had to guess, he'd say she'd been using him that week to make someone else jealous.

Which was another reason he'd known their so-called relationship wasn't going anywhere. In retrospect though, leaving her to take care of the place had been a mistake. It hadn't been his idea. She'd needed a place to stay. The double-wide was sitting out there empty so she'd suggested watching it for him while he was gone.

Even at the time, he'd worried that it would give her the wrong idea. The wrong idea being that their relationship was more serious than it was. He'd half hoped all the way home that she'd moved back in with her mom or a friend. That the trailer would be empty.

He just never imagined that there would be no place to come home to.

"Jimmy D?"

From the edge of the porch, he turned at the sound of her voice. She stood behind the door, peering around it as if half-afraid of him. "Melody, I was just out at the place. I was worried that you might have gotten caught in the fire."

She shook her head. "I wasn't living there anymore when it happened."

"That's good." But even as he said it, he knew there was more story coming. She was still half hiding behind the door, as if needing a barrier between them. "I'm not angry with you, if that's what you're worried about. I'm just glad you're okay."

He watched her swallow before she said, "I'd rented your trailer to some guys." He took that news without reacting badly. He figured she must have needed the money and he *had* left her in charge of the place, kind of.

"Turned out they were cooking meth," she said. "I didn't know until they blew the place up."

James swallowed back the first few words that leaped to his tongue. When he did find his voice, he said, "You didn't know."

She shook her head. "I didn't." She sounded close to tears. "But that's not all I have to tell you."

He held his breath already fearing that the news wasn't going to get better. Before his grandmother died, she'd explained karma to him. He had a feeling karma was about to kick his butt.

Then Mel stepped around the edge of the door, leading with her belly, which protruded out a good seven months.

The air rushed out of him on a swear word. A million thoughts galloped through his mind at breakneck speed before she said, "It's not yours."

He felt equal parts relief and shock. It was that instant of denial followed by acceptance followed by regret that surprised him the most. For just a second he'd seen himself holding a two-year-old little girl with his dark hair and blue eyes. They'd been on the back of the horse he'd bought her.

When he blinked, the image was gone as quickly as it had come to him.

"Who?" The word came out strangled. He wasn't quite over the shock.

"Tyler Grange," she said, placing her palms on the stretchy top snug over her belly. "He and I broke up just before you and I..." She shrugged and he noticed the tiny diamond glinting on her ring finger.

"You're getting married. When?"

"Soon," she said. "It would be nice to get hitched before the baby comes."

He swallowed, still tangled up in that battle of emotions. Relief was winning by a horse length though. "Congratulations. Or is it best wishes? I never can remember."

"Thanks," she said shyly. "Sorry 'bout your trailer. I'd give you the money I got from the renters, but—"

"It's all right." He took a step toward the porch stairs. After all these years in the rodeo game, he'd learned to cut his losses. This one felt like a win. He swore on his lucky boots that he was going to change his wild ways.

From inside the house, he could hear Gladys laughing with someone. He caught the smell of permanent solution.

"Mama's doing the neighbor's hair," Melody said. He nodded and took a step off the porch. "Any idea where you're going to go?"

Until that moment, he hadn't really thought about it. It wasn't like he didn't have options. He had friends he could bunk with until he either bought another trailer to put on the property or built something more substantial. He and his brothers, also on the rodeo circuit, used the trailer only to stay in the few times they came home to crash for a while—usually to heal up.

Not that he was planning on staying that long. Once he was all healed up from his last rodeo ride, he'd be going back. He'd left his horse trailer, horse and gear at a friend's.

"I'm going to stay at the office," he said, nodding to himself. It seemed the perfect solution under the circumstances.

"Uptown?" she asked, sounding surprised. The word hardly described downtown Lonesome, Montana. But the office *was* at the heart of town—right on a corner of Main Street.

"Don't worry about me," he said. "You just take care of yourself and give my regards to Tyler." He tipped his hat and headed to his pickup.

As he drove away, he realized his heart was still pounding. He'd dodged a bullet. So why couldn't he get that image of him holding his baby daughter out of his head? Worse was how that image made him feel—happy.

The emotion surprised him. For just that split second, he'd had to deal with the thought of settling down, of having a family, of being a father. He'd felt it to his soul and now he missed it.

James shook his head, telling himself that he was just tired, injured and emotionally drained after his homecoming. All that together would make any man have strange thoughts.

Chapter Two

James reached high on the edge of the transom over the door for the key, half-surprised it was still there. He blew the dust off and, opening the door, hit the light switch and froze. The smell alone reminded him of his father and the hours he'd spent in this office as a child after his mother had died.

Later he'd hung around, earning money by helping any way he could at the office. He'd liked hanging out here with his old man. He chuckled, remembering how he'd thought he might grow up and he and Del would work together. Father and son detective agency. Unfortunately, his father's death had changed all that.

He hadn't been here since the funeral, he realized as he took in his father's large oak desk and high-backed leather office chair. More emotions assaulted him, ones he'd kept at bay for the past nine years.

This was a bad idea. He wasn't ready to face it. He might never be ready, he thought. He missed his father and nine years hadn't changed that. Everything about this room brought back the pain from the Native American rugs on the floor and the two leather club chairs that faced his dad's desk and seat.

He realized he wasn't strong enough for this—maybe especially after being hurt during his last ride and then coming home to find his home was gone. He took one final look and started to close the door. He'd get a motel room for the night rather than show up at a friend's house.

But before he could close the door, his gaze fell on an old Hollywood movie poster on the wall across the room. He felt himself smile, drawn into the office by the cowboy on the horse with a face so much like his own.

He hadn't known his great-grandfather Ransom Del Colt. But he'd grown up on the stories. Ransom had been a famous movie star back in the forties and early fifties when Westerns had been so popular. His grandfather RD Colt Jr. had followed in Ransom's footprints for a while before starting his own Wild West show. RD had traveled the world ropin' and ridin' until late in life.

He moved around the room, looking at all the photographs and posters as if seeing them for the first time. The Colts had a rich history, one to be proud of, his father said. Del Colt, James's father, had broken the mold after being a rodeo cowboy until he was injured so badly that he had to quit.

Del, who'd loved Westerns and mystery movies, had gotten his PI license and opened Colt Investigations. He'd taught his sons to ride before they could walk. He'd never stopped loving rodeo and he'd passed that love on to his sons as if it was embedded deep in their genes.

James limped around the room looking at all the other posters and framed photographs of his rodeo family. He felt a sense of pride in the men who'd gone before him. And a sense of failure on his own part. He was pushing thirty-six and he had little to show for it except for a lot of broken bones.

Right now, he hurt all over. The bronc he'd ridden two days ago had put him into the fence, reinjuring his leg and cracking some of his ribs. But he'd stayed on the eight seconds and taken home the purse.

Right now he wondered if it was worth it. Still, as he stood in this room, he rebelled at the thought of quitting. He'd made a living doing what he loved. He would heal and go back. Just as he'd always done.

In the meantime, he was dog tired. Too tired to go look for a motel room for the night. At the back of the office he found the bunk where his father would stay on those nights he worked late. There were clean sheets and quilts and a bathroom with a shower and towels. This would work at least for tonight. Tomorrow he'd look for something else.

LORELEI WILKINS PULLED into her space in the alley behind her sandwich shop and stared at the pickup parked in the space next to it. It had been years since she'd seen anyone in the building adjoining hers. She'd almost forgotten why she'd driven down here tonight. Often, she came down and worked late to get things ready for the next day.

Tonight, she had brought down a basketful of freshly washed aprons. She could have waited until morning, but she'd been restless and it was a nice night. Who was she kidding? She never put things off for tomorrow.

Getting out, she started to unload the basket when she recognized the truck and felt a start. There were rodeo stickers plastered all over the back window of the cab, but the dead giveaway was the LETRBUCK personalized license plate.

Jimmy D was back in town? But why would he… She recalled hearing something about a fire out on his land. Surely, he wasn't planning to stay here in his father's old office. The narrow two-story building, almost identical to her own, had been empty since Del Colt's death nine years ago. Before that the structure had housed Colt Investigations on the top floor with the ground floor office rented to a party shop that went broke, the owners skipping town.

Lorelei had made an offer on the property, thinking she would try to get a small business in there or expand her sandwich shop. Anything was better than having an empty building next door. Worse, the owners of the party-planning store had left in a hurry, not even bothering to clean up the place, so it was an eyesore.

But the family lawyer had said no one in the family was interested in selling.

As she hauled out her basket of aprons, she could see a light in the second-story window and a shadow moving around up there. Whatever James was doing back in town, he wouldn't be staying long—he never did. Not that she ever saw him. She'd just heard the stories.

Shaking her head, she tucked the basket under one arm, unlocked the door and stepped in. It didn't take long to put the aprons away properly. Basket in hand, she locked up and headed for her SUV.

She couldn't help herself. She glanced up. Was she hoping to see the infamous Jimmy D? Their paths hadn't crossed in years.

The upstairs light was out. She shook her head at her own foolishness.

"Some women always go for the bad boy," her step-mother had joked years ago when they'd been uptown shopping for her senior year of high school. They'd passed Jimmy D in the small mall at the edge of town. He'd winked at Lorelei, making her blush to the roots of her hair. She'd felt Karen's frowning gaze on her. "I just never took you for one of those."

Lorelei had still been protesting on the way home. "I can't stand the sight of Jimmy D," she'd said, only to have her stepmother laugh. "He's arrogant and thinks he's much cuter than he is."

"Don't feel bad. We've all fallen for the wrong man. And he *is* cute and he likes you."

Lorelei had choked on that. "He doesn't like me. He just enjoys making me uncomfortable. He's just plain awful."

"Then I guess it's a good thing you aren't going to the prom with him," Karen said. "Your friend Alfred is obviously the better choice."

Alfred was her geek friend who she competed with for grades.

"Jimmy D isn't going to the prom," she said. "He's too cool for proms. Not that I would go with him if he asked me."

Lorelei still cringed at the memory. Protest too much? Her stepmother had seen right through it. She told herself that all that aside, this might be the perfect opportunity to get him to sell the building to her. But it would mean approaching Jimmy D with an offer knowing he would probably turn her down flat. She groaned. From what she'd heard, he hadn't changed since high school. The only thing the man took seriously was rodeo. And chasing women.

FORMER SHERIFF OTIS OSTERMAN pulled his pickup to the side of the street to stare up at the building. Lorelei Wilkins wasn't the only one surprised to see a light on in the old Colt Investigations building.

For just a moment, he'd thought that Del was still alive, working late as he often did. While making his rounds, Otis had seen him moving around up there working on one of his cases.

The light in that office gave him an eerie feeling as if he'd been transported back in time. That he could rewrite history. But Otis knew that wasn't possible. One look in the rearview mirror at his white hair and wrinkled face and he could see that there was no going back, no changing anything. But it was only when he looked deep into his own eyes—eyes that had seen too much—that he felt the weight of those years and the questionable actions he'd taken.

But like Del Colt, they were buried. He just wanted them to stay that way. Blessedly, he hadn't been reminded of Del for some time now. He'd gone to the funeral nine years ago, stood in the hot sun and watched as the gravedigger covered the man's casket and laid sod on top. He told himself that had been the end of a rivalry he and Del had fought since middle school.

He watched the movement up there in Del's office. It had to be one of Del's sons back from the rodeo. Small towns, he thought. Everyone didn't just know each other. Half the damned town was related.

Otis drove down the block, turning into the alley and cruising slowly past the pickup parked behind Del's narrow two-story office building.

He recognized the truck and swore softly under his breath. Del Colt had left behind a passel of sons who all resembled him, but Jimmy D was the most like Del. Apparently, he was back for a while.

The former sheriff told himself that it didn't necessarily spell trouble as he shifted his truck into gear. As he drove home though, he couldn't shake the bad feeling that the past had been reawakened and it was coming for him.

Chapter Three

James woke to the sun. It streamed in the window of his father's office as he rose and headed for the shower. Being here reminded him of the mornings on his way to school that he would stop by. He often found his father at his desk, already up and working. Del Colt's cases weren't the kind that should have kept his father from sleep, he thought as he got dressed.

They were often small personal problems that people hoped he could help with. But his father treated each as if it was more important than world peace. James had once questioned him about it.

They may seem trivial to you, but believe me, they aren't to the people who are suffering and need answers, Del had said.

Now, showered and dressed, James stepped from the small room at the back and into his father's office. He hesitated for a moment before he pulled out his father's chair and sat down. Leaning back, he surveyed the room and the dusty window that overlooked Main Street.

He found himself smiling, recalling sitting in this chair and wanting to be just like his dad. He felt such a sense of pride for the man Del had been. His father had raised them all after their mother's death. James knew that a lot of people would have said that Del had let them run wild.

Laughing, he thought that had been somewhat true. His father gave them free rein to learn by their mistakes. So, they made a lot of them.

Everything was just as his father had left it, he realized as he looked around. A file from the case his father had been working on was still lying open on his desk. Next to it were his pen and a yellow lined notepad with Del's neat printing. A coffee cup, the inside stained dark brown, sat next to the notepad.

A name jumped out at him. Billy Sherman. That kid who'd been killed in a hit-and-run nine years ago. *That was the case his father had been working on.*

He felt a chill. The hit-and-run had never been solved.

A knock at the door startled him. He quickly closed the case file, feeling as if he'd been caught getting into things that were none of his business. Private things.

He quickly rose, sending the chair scooting backward. "Yes?"

"Jimmy D?" A woman's voice. Not one he recognized. He hadn't told anyone he was coming back to town. He'd returned unannounced and under the cover of darkness. But clearly someone knew he wasn't just back—but that he was here in Del's office.

He moved to the door and opened it, still feeling as if he were trespassing. The light in the hallway was dim. He'd noticed last night that the bulb had burned out sometime during the past nine years. But enough sunlight streamed in through the dusty window at the end of the hall to cast a little light on the pretty young woman standing before him.

"I hope I didn't catch you at a bad time," she said, glancing past him before settling her gaze on him again. Her eyes were honey brown with dark lashes. Her long chestnut brown hair had been pulled up into a no-nonsense knot that went with the serious expression on her face. She wore

slacks, a modest blouse and sensible shoes. She had a briefcase in one hand, her purse in the other. She looked like a
woman on a mission and he feared he was the assignment.

LORELEI LOOKED FOR recognition in the cowboy's eyes and
seeing none quickly said, "I'm sorry, you probably don't
remember me. I'm Lorelei Wilkins. I own the sandwich
shop next door." When he still hadn't spoken, she added,
"We went to school together?" She realized this was a
mistake.

He was still staring at her unnervingly. When he finally
spoke, the soft timber of his low voice surprised her. She
remembered the unruly classmate who'd sat next to her
in English, always cracking jokes and acting up when he
wasn't winking at her in the hall between classes. She realized that she'd been expecting the teenaged boy—not
the man standing before her.

"Oh, I remember you, Lori," he drawled. "Hall moni-
tor, teacher's assistant, senior class president, valedicto-
rian." He grinned. "Didn't you also read the lunch menu
over the intercom?"

She felt her cheeks warm. Yes, she'd done all of that—
not that she'd have thought he'd noticed. "It's *Lorelei*,"
she said, her voice coming out thin. She knew her reputation as the most uptight, serious, not-fun girl in the class.

"I remember that too," he said, his grin broadening.

She cleared her throat and quickly pressed on. "Look,
Jimmy D. I saw your light on last night and I—"

"It's James."

"James…?" she repeated. She suddenly felt tongue-tied
here facing this rodeo cowboy. Why had she thought talking directly to him was a good idea? She wished she'd tried
his family lawyer again instead. Not that that approach
had done her any good.

She took a breath and let it out, watching him wince as he shifted his weight onto his obviously injured leg. Seeing that he wasn't in any shape to be making real estate deals, she chickened out. "I just wanted to welcome you to the neighborhood."

"I'm not staying, in case that's what you're worrying about. I mean, not living here, exactly. It's just temporary."

She suspected that most everything about his life was temporary from what she'd heard. She was angry at herself for not saying what she'd really come to say. But from the look on his bruised face and the way he'd winced when he'd shifted weight on his left leg, she'd realized that this wasn't the right time to make an offer on the building. He looked as if he would say no to her without even giving it a second thought.

From her briefcase, she awkwardly withdrew a ten percent off coupon for her sandwich shop.

He took it without looking at it. Instead, his intense scrutiny was on her, making her squirm.

"It's a coupon for ten percent off a sandwich at my shop," she said.

He raised a brow. "Who makes the sandwiches?"

The question was so unexpected that it took her a moment to respond. "I do."

"Huh," he said and folded the coupon in half to stuff it into the pocket of his Western shirt.

What had made her think she could have a professional conversation with this…cowboy? She snapped her briefcase closed and turned to leave.

"Thanks," he called after her.

Just like in high school she could feel his gaze boring into her backside. She ground her teeth as her face flushed hot. Maybe she'd been wrong. Maybe some things never changed no matter how much time had gone by.

JAMES SMILED TO himself as he watched Lorelei disappear down the hall. He hadn't seen her in years. As small as Lonesome was, he'd have thought that their paths would have crossed again before this. But she didn't hang out at Wade's Broken Spur bar or the engine repair shop or the truck stop cafe—all places on the edge of town that he frequented when home. Truth was, he never had reason to venture into downtown Lonesome because he usually stayed only a few days, a week at most.

Seeing Lorelei had made him feel seventeen again. The woman had always terrified him. She was damned intimidating and always had been. He'd liked that about her. She'd always been so smart, so capable, so impressive. In high school she hadn't seemed to realize just how sexy she was. She'd tried to hide it unlike a lot of the girls. But some things you can't cover up with clothing.

What surprised him as he closed the door behind her was that she still seemed to be unaware of what she did to a man. Especially this man.

He sighed, wondering what Lorelei had really stopped by for. Not to welcome him to the neighborhood or give him a sandwich coupon. It didn't matter. He knew that once he found a place to stay, he'd probably not see her again.

Something bright and shiny caught his eye lying on the floor next to his father's desk. He moved toward it as if under a spell. He felt a jolt as he recognized what it was. Picking up the silver dollar money clip, he stared down, heart pounding. Why hadn't his father had this on him when he was killed? He always carried it. *Always.*

James opened it and let the bills fall to the desktop. Two twenties, a five and three ones. As he started to pick them back up, he noticed that wasn't all that had fallen from the money clip.

He lifted the folded yellow lined notepad paper from

the desk. Unfolding it he saw his father's neat printing and a list of names. As was his father's habit, he'd checked off those he had interviewed. But there were six others without checks.

James stared at the list, realizing they were from Del's last case, seven-year-old Billy Sherman's hit-and-run. His father had stuck the list in his money clip? Had his father been on his way to talk to someone on that list? Why had he left the clip behind? He'd always had so many questions about his father's death. Too many. Ultimately, after what the sheriff had told him, he'd been afraid of the answers.

Moving behind the desk, he sat down again and opened the case file. His father's notes were neatly stacked inside. He checked the notes against the list. Everyone Del had interviewed was there, each name checked off the list.

But the list had stopped with a name that made his jaw drop. Karen Wilkins? Lorelei's stepmother? Why had his father wanted to talk to her? She lived a half dozen blocks from where the hit-and-run had happened.

Chapter Four

James glanced at the time. Almost one in the afternoon. He'd lost track of time reading his father's file on the hit-and-run. Finding Karen Wilkins name on the list had scared him. He couldn't imagine why Del wanted to talk to her.

He'd gone through everything several times, including all of his father's neatly handwritten notes. Del didn't even use a typewriter—let alone a computer. He was old-school through and through.

James realized that after everything he'd gone through, he still had no idea why Karen's name was on the list or why it might be important.

His stomach growled. He thought of the coupon Lori had given him. Pulling it from his pocket, he reached for his Stetson. It was a short walk next door.

As James entered the sandwich shop, a bell jangled over the front door. From the back, he saw Lori look up, her expression one of surprise, then something he couldn't quite read.

He walked up to the sign that said Order Here and scanned the chalkboard menu. His stomach rumbled again. He couldn't remember when he'd eaten—sometime yesterday at a fast-food place on the road. He'd been anxious to get home only to find he no longer had a home.

Lori appeared in front of him. "See anything you'd like?"

He glanced at her. "Definitely." Then he winked and looked up at the board again. He heard her make a low guttural sound under her breath. "I'll take the special."

She mugged a face. "It comes with jalapeño peppers and a chipotle mayonnaise that you might find too…spicy."

He smiled. "I'm tougher than I look."

She glanced at the leg he was babying and cocked a brow at that.

"It was a really big bronco that put me into the fence. For your information, it didn't knock me off. I held on for the eight seconds and came home with the money."

"Then it was obviously worth it," she said sarcastically. "Let me get you that sandwich. Is this to go?"

"No, I think I'll stay."

She nodded, though he thought reluctantly. When she'd given him the coupon, he could tell that she'd never expected he would actually use it. "If you'd like to have a seat. Want something to drink with that?"

"Sure, whatever's cold." He turned and did his best not to limp as he walked to a table and chair by the front window. This time of the day, the place was empty. He wondered how her business was doing. He wondered also if he'd made a mistake with what he'd ordered and if it would be too spicy to eat. He'd eat it. Even if it killed him.

What was it about her that he couldn't help flirting with her when he was around her? There'd always been something about her… He couldn't imagine how they could be more different. Maybe that's why she'd always made it clear that she wasn't in the least interested in him.

Fortunately, other girls and then women had been, he thought. But as he caught glimpses of her working back in the kitchen, he knew she'd always been an enigma, a puzzle that he couldn't figure out. Flirting with her sure hadn't worked. But, like his father, he'd always loved a good mystery and seldom backed down from a challenge.

Was that why he couldn't let this go? He needed to find out why her stepmother was on Del's list. Why the list was tucked in Del's money clip and why he hadn't had it on him that night. James knew he might never get those answers. Just as he might never know how his father ended up on the train tracks that night. So, what was the point in digging into Del's old unsolved case?

Wouldn't hurt to ask a few questions, he told himself. He wasn't going anywhere for a while until he healed. He had time on his hands with nothing to do—nothing but seeing about getting the wreckage from his burned trailer hauled away and replacing it with a place to live. He told himself he'd get on that tomorrow.

Lori brought out his sandwich and a tall glass of iced lemonade along with plastic cutlery and napkin roll. She placed the meal in front of him and started to step away. He grabbed her hand. She flinched.

"Sorry," he said quickly as he let go. "I was hoping since you aren't busy with customers that maybe you could sit down for a minute. Join me?"

"I guess I could spare a moment." She hesitated before reluctantly slipping into a chair across from him.

He smiled over at her. "I feel like you and I got off on the wrong foot somehow." He waited for her to say something and realized he could wait all day and that wasn't going to happen. She wasn't going to help him out. He took a sip of the lemonade. "Delicious. Let's start with the truth. What did you really come by for earlier? It wasn't to welcome me to the neighborhood."

She shook her head. "This isn't the time or the place." He raised a brow at that, making her groan. "You never change. Are you like this with every woman?" She raised a hand. "Don't answer that. I already know." She started to get up, but he stopped her.

"Seriously, you can tell me."

She studied him for a long moment before she asked, "Has your family lawyer mentioned that I've made several inquiries about buying your father's building?"

"Family lawyer?"

"Hank Richardson."

"Oh, him." James frowned. "He's our family lawyer? I guess I didn't realize that." She sighed deeply. "Why do you want to buy the building?"

"No one is using it. The place is an eyesore. I might want to expand into it at some point."

He nodded. "Huh. I'll have to give that some thought."

"You do that." She started to rise.

"Wait, I'm serious. I'll think about it. Now can I ask you something else?" She looked both wary and suspicious. "I was going through an old case file of my father's earlier. It was the one he was working on when he died. You might remember the case. Billy Sherman. Killed by a hit-and-run driver. So, I'm looking into it and—"

Her eyes widened. "What are you doing?"

He couldn't help but look confused. "Having lunch?"

"You're not a licensed private investigator."

"No, I'm not pretending to be. I just found the case interesting and since I have some time on my hands…"

She shook her head. "Just like that?" She sighed. "Are you living next door now?"

"For the moment. It's not that bad."

"Like your latest injury isn't that bad?" she asked, clearly upset with him.

"I'll heal, but if you must know my cracked ribs still hurt like hell." He took a tiny bite of his sandwich and felt the heat even though he'd mostly gotten bread. He knew instantly what she'd done. "This is good."

She was watching him as he took another bite. "I make my own bread."

"Really?" The heat of the peppers was so intense that they felt as if they would blow the top of his head off.

"You don't have to sound so surprised."

"Don't take this wrong, but back in high school, I never thought about you in the kitchen baking bread."

"Doubt you thought about me at all," she said and slipped out of her chair.

But as she started past, he said, "I thought about you all the time. But I was smart enough to know you were out of my league."

She'd stopped next to his table and now looked down at him. Her expression softened. "You don't have to eat that. I can make you something else."

He shook his head, picked up his sandwich and took another big bite. He'd eat every ounce even if it killed him, which he thought it might. The intense heat made its way down his throat to his chest. It felt as if his entire body was on fire. He sucked in his breath. Somehow, he managed to get the words out. "This isn't too spicy."

She shook her head. At least she was smiling this time as she walked away.

Chapter Five

James had a lot of time to think since his spicy lunch had kept him up most of the night. It was a small price to pay, he told himself. He wasn't sure exactly what he'd done to Lori in high school or since that had her so upset with him. He'd been the high school jock and goof-off who'd gotten by on his charm. She'd been the studious, hardworking serious student who'd had to work for her grades. Why wouldn't she resent him?

But he suspected there was more to it than even his awkward attempts at flirting with her. He felt as if he'd done something that had made her dislike him. That could be any number of things. It wasn't like he went around worrying about who might have been hurt by his antics back then. Or even now, he admitted honestly.

He kept going over the conversation at lunch though. She'd tried to pass off her anger as something from high school. But he wasn't buying it. She hadn't been a fan of his for apparently some time, but when she'd gotten upset was when he'd said he was looking into his father's last case, Billy Sherman's hit-and-run.

Add to that, her stepmother's name was on his father's list. Del Colt had been meticulous in his investigations. He'd actually been really good at being a PI. Karen Wilkins wouldn't have been on that list unless his father thought she knew something about the case.

James was convinced by morning that he needed to talk to Karen. He knew Lori wasn't going to like it. Best that he hadn't brought it up at lunch.

But first, he wanted to talk to the person who'd hired his father to look into the hit-and-run after the police had given up.

ALICE SHERMAN GASPED, her hand over her heart, her eyes wide as she stared at James. It seemed to take her a moment to realize she wasn't looking at a ghost. "For a moment I thought… You look so much like your father."

James smiled, nodding. "It's a family curse."

She shook her head as she recovered. "Yes, being that handsome must be a terrible burden for you, especially with the ladies."

"I'm James Colt," he said, introducing himself and shaking her hand. "I don't think we've ever met." Alice worked at the local laundry. "I was hoping to ask you a few questions."

She narrowed her eyes at him. "About what?" She seemed really not to know.

"I hate to bring it back up and cause you more pain, but you hired my father to look into Billy's death. He died before he finished the investigation."

"You're mistaken," she said, fiddling with the collar of her blouse. "I didn't hire your father. My ex did."

That caught him flat-footed. He'd seen several checks from Alice Sherman in his father's file and Alice had been the first on Del's list of names. He said as much to her.

Her expression soured. "When my ex's checks bounced, I paid Del for his time. But what does that have to do with you?"

"I'm looking into the case."

Alice stared at him. "After all these years? Why would you do that? You...? You're a private investigator?"

"No. It was my father's last case. I'm just looking into it."

"Well, I'm not interested in paying any more money." She started to close the door.

"Please, Mrs. Sherman," he said quickly. "I don't mean to remind you of your loss. I just want to know more about your son."

She managed a sad smile. "Billy is *always* on my mind. The pain never goes away." She opened the door wider. "I suppose I have time for a few questions."

As James took the chair she offered him, she walked to the mantel over the fireplace and took down a framed photograph of her son.

"This is my favorite snapshot of him." She turned and handed it to him. It was of a freckle-faced boy with his two front teeth missing smiling broadly at the camera. "Billy was seven," she said as she took a seat on the edge of the couch facing him. "Just a boy. He was named after my father who died in the war."

"You've had a lot of loss," James said as she brushed a lock of her hair from her face. After the accident, it was as if she'd aged overnight. According to his father's file, Alice would now be forty-five. Her hair was almost entirely gray and there were deep lines around her eyes and mouth. "I'm so sorry. I don't want to make it worse."

"Have you found new information on the case?" she asked, her gaze intent on him. He realized that he might have given her the wrong impression.

"No, not yet. I'm not sure where my father had left the case. Had he talked to you about his investigation before his death?"

"He called me that afternoon, asked if I was going to be home. He thought he might be getting close to finding the hit-and-run driver," she said. "I waited for him but he never showed up. I found out the next day about his pickup being hit by the train."

"He said he thought he might be close to solving the case?" He felt hope at this news. Maybe he wasn't playing at this. Maybe there was something he could find after all. "Did he tell you anything else?"

She shook her head. "Unfortunately, that's all he said."

This news had his heart hammering. He'd always wondered if his father's so-called accident had anything to do with the case. If he was that close to finding the hit-and-run driver… Sheriff Otis Osterman's investigation had ruled Del's death an accident due to human error on his father's part. Either Del hadn't been paying attention and not seen the train coming at the uncontrolled railroad crossing or he'd tried to outrun the train.

Neither had sounded like his father.

The autopsy found alcohol in his father's system and there had been an empty bottle of whiskey found on the floor of his pickup.

James had never accepted that his father had been drunk and hadn't seen the train coming. If he was close to solving the Billy Sherman case, there is no way he would have been drinking at all.

Alice had gotten up and now brought over more photographs of her son. He'd been small and thin. A shy boy, not an adventurous one. There'd been two theories of how Billy ended up outside on the street that night. The obvious one was that he'd sneaked out for some reason. The other was that he'd been abducted.

"Is there any reason Billy might have left the house that night after you put him to bed?" James asked cautiously.

"No, never. Billy would have never gotten up in the middle of the night and gone out for any reason. He was afraid of the dark. He hated admitting it, but he still slept with a night-light. He was also terrified of storms. There was a terrible storm that night. The wind was howling. Between it and the pouring rain you could hardly see across the street." She shook her head, her gaze unfocused for a moment as if she were reliving it. "He *wouldn't* have gone out on his own under *any* circumstances."

"So, you're still convinced that someone abducted him?"

"His bedroom window was wide open." Her voice broke. "The wind had blown the rain in. His floor and bedding were soaked when I went in the next morning to wake him up and found him gone." All of this he'd already read in his father's file. He could see it was a story she'd told over and over, to the sheriff, to Del, to herself. "I started to call the sheriff when Otis drove up and told me that Billy had been found a few blocks from here lying in the ditch dead." She made angry swipes at her tears. He could see that she was fighting hard not to cry.

"The sheriff said he didn't find any signs of a forced entry," James said. "According to my father's notes, you said you locked the window before tucking Billy in at nine. Maybe you forgot that night—"

"No, I remember locking it because I could see the storm coming. I even closed the blinds. It's no mystery. The only way Billy would leave the house was if his father came to his window that night. Sean Sherman. Not that he'll tell you the truth, but I know he took my boy. Have you talked to him?"

"Not yet." He was still working on the angle that Billy, like every red-blooded, American boy, had sneaked out a time or two. Having been a seven-year-old at one time, he asked, "Did Billy have his own cell phone?" She shook her head. "What about a walkie-talkie?"

"Yes, but—"

"Who had the other two-way radio handset?"

He watched her swallow before she said, "Todd. Todd Crane. But he swore he hadn't talked to Billy that night."

"I'm just covering my bets," James said quickly. He gathered that his father hadn't asked her this. "Did the sheriff talk to Todd?"

"I don't know. I think your father asked me about Billy's friends, but my son wouldn't have left the house that night even for his best friend, Todd."

James rose to lay a hand over hers as she gripped the stack of framed photos of her son. "Do you mind if I see his room?" Even before she led him down the hall, he knew Billy's room would be exactly like he'd left it even after nine years.

It was a classic boy's room painted a pale blue with a Spiderman bedspread and action figures lined up on the bookshelf.

Moving to the window, James examined the lock. It was an old house, the lock on the window old as well. Maybe Billy *had* been abducted and the sheriff had missed something. But wouldn't there have been footprints in the wet earth outside Billy's window? Unless he'd been taken before the storm hit and the prints had been washed away.

James left, promising to let Alice Sherman know if he discovered anything helpful. The look in her eyes was a stark reminder of what he'd set in motion. He'd gotten her hopes up and the truth was, he had no idea what he was doing.

KAREN WILKINS WASN'T HOME. Her car wasn't parked in front of her freshly painted and landscaped split-level. Nor was it in the garage.

Todd Crane, who would now be around sixteen, hadn't been on his father's list. But Del had talked to Todd's stepmother, Shelby Crane.

Since it was a Saturday, James figured the boy wouldn't be in school. He swung by the house only a few blocks from Alice Sherman's. The woman who answered the door was considerably younger-looking than Alice. Shelby Crane was a slim blonde with hard brown eyes.

"Yes?" The way she was holding the door open only a crack told him that Alice might have already called her.

"I'm James Colt and—"

"I know who you are. What do you want?"

"I'm guessing that you spoke with Alice," he said. "I'd like to talk to your son."

"No." She started to close the door, but he stopped her with his palm.

"Your son might know why Billy Sherman was outside that night," he said, his voice growing harder with each word.

"Well, he doesn't."

"If that's true, then I can't see why he can't tell me that himself."

"He doesn't know. He didn't know nine years ago. He doesn't know now." Again, she started to close the door and again he put a hand on it to stop her.

"Did he and Billy talk on walkie-talkies back then?"

"My son had nothing to do with what happened to that boy. You need to go. Don't make me call the sheriff." She closed the door and this time he let her.

As he started to turn and leave, he saw a boy's face peering out one of the upstairs windows. Then the curtain fell back, and the boy was gone. He wondered why Shelby was so afraid of him talking to her son.

His phone rang as he was getting into his pickup. Melody? He picked up.

"I just got a call from the sheriff's department," she said without preamble. "Carl said you have to get a permit to remove the burned trailer from your land."

"Why would he call you?"

Silence, then a guilty, "I might have tried to hire someone to haul it away before you got back."

James shook his head. Did she not realize he would have noticed anyway? The missing double-wide and the burned area around it would have been a dead giveaway. "No problem. I'll swing by and pick up a permit. Thanks for letting me know."

He was still mentally shaking his head when he walked into the sheriff's department.

Sheriff Carl Osterman, younger brother of the former sheriff Otis Osterman, was standing outside his office with a large mug of coffee and the family sour expression on his face. A short stocky man in his late fifties, Carl believed in guilty until proven innocent. Word was that he'd arrest his own grandmother for jaywalking, which could explain why he was divorced and not speaking with his mother or grandmother, James had heard.

"Wondered when I'd be seeing you," the sheriff drawled. "Suppose you heard what happened out at your place."

"It was fairly noticeable."

Carl took a long moment to assess him over the rim of his mug as he slurped his coffee. "You know those meth dealers?"

"Nope. I was on the road. I didn't even know Melody had rented the place."

The sheriff nodded. "You need a permit to haul that mess off."

"That's why I'm here."

"What are you planning to do out there?" Carl asked.

James shook his head. "I don't have any plans at the moment."

"Heard you were staying in your father's old office."

News traveled fast in Lonesome. "My family still owns the building."

Carl nodded again, still eyeballing him with suspicion. "Margaret will give you a form to fill out. Could take a few days, maybe even a week."

"I'm in no hurry."

"That mean you're planning to stay for a while?"

James studied the man. "Why the interest in my itinerary, Carl?"

"There's a rumor circulating that you've reopened your father's office and that you're working one of his cases. Last I heard you weren't a licensed private investigator."

He hid his surprise, realizing that Shelby Crane had probably called. "No law against asking a few questions, but now that you mention it, I worked for my father during high school and when I was home from college and the rodeo so I have some experience."

"You need a year and a half's worth before you can apply for a license under state law."

He pretended he always knew that. "Yep, I know. Got it covered. Application is in the mail." It wasn't. But damn, he just might apply now.

The sheriff put down his coffee cup with a curse. "Why would you do that unless you planned to stay in town?"

James smiled. He *wasn't* planning to. "Just covering my options, sheriff."

"The state runs a criminal background check, you know."

He laughed. "Why would that concern me?"

"If you have a felony on your record—"

"I don't," he said with more force than he'd intended.

"Good thing they don't check finances or your mental health."

James laughed. "Not worried about either." With a shake of his head, he turned and walked over to Margaret's desk. Without a word, she handed him the permit application.

"You'll need to pay twenty-five dollars when you return that permit," Carl called after him.

OTIS HAD JUST gotten through mowing the small lawn in front of his house. The summer air smelled of cut grass and sunshine. He turned on the sprinklers and, hot, sweaty and tired, went inside. He'd only just opened a can of beer and sat down when Carl called.

"You know what that damned Colt boy has gone and done now?" his brother demanded. James Colt was far from a boy, but Carl didn't give him a chance to reply. "He's been going all over town asking questions about his father's last case. He thinks he's a private eye."

He didn't have to ask what case. Otis was the first one on the scene after getting the call about the boy's body that was found in the ditch next to a house under construction in the new subdivision near where the Shermans lived. The memory still kept him awake some nights. He'd been a month away from retiring. Carl had been his undersheriff. The two of them had worked the case.

"Legally, James can't—"

"He's applied for a state license!" Carl was breathing hard, clearly worked up. "He says his experience working with his father should be enough. It probably is. It's so damned easy to get a PI license in this state, he'll get it and then—"

"And then *nothing*," Otis said. "He's a rodeo cowboy. I heard he's hurt. Once he feels better, he'll be back in the saddle, having put all of this behind him. Even if that isn't the case—which it is—he's inexperienced, the Sherman case is ice cold and we all know how hard those are to solve. And let's face it, he's not his father. I'll bet you five bucks that he quits before the week is out."

Carl sighed. Otis could imagine him pacing the floor of his office. "You think?"

"You know I don't throw money around."

His brother laughed. "No, not Otis Osterman." He sighed again. "I just thought this was behind us."

"It is," he said even though he knew it might never be true. Billy Sherman's death was unsolved, justice hadn't been meted out and what happened that night remained a mystery. There were always those who couldn't live with that.

Unfortunately, Del Colt had been one of them. Him and his damned digging. He'd gotten into things that had been better off left alone.

But Otis had five dollars that said James Colt was nothing like his father. For the young rodeo cowboy's sake, he certainly hoped not.

Chapter Six

After leaving the sheriff's office, James drove aimlessly around town for a while. He knew he should quit right now before he made things any worse. What had he hoped to accomplish with all this, anyway? Was he so arrogant that he thought he could pick up where his father had left off on the case and solve it just like that?

So far all he'd done was stir up a wasp's nest that was more than likely going to get him stung. If he hadn't left Melody in his trailer, if she hadn't rented it, if the renters hadn't blown it up, if he'd gone to a motel and never gone to his father's office…

He reminded himself that getting involved with Melody was all on him. He thought of one of his father's lectures he and his brothers had been forced to endure growing up.

Life is about consequences, Del would say. *Whatever you do, there will be a repercussion. It's the law of nature. Cause and effect.*

What are you trying to say? one of his brothers would demand, usually himself most likely. *'Cause the effect I'm getting is a headache.*

His father would give him a reprimand before adding, *Don't blame someone else when things go wrong because of something stupid you did. Take responsibility and move on. It's called growing up.*

He and his brothers had made fun of that particular lecture, but it had never seemed more appropriate than right now.

His stomach growled. He looked at the time. Two in the afternoon. He hadn't had breakfast or lunch. He drove downtown. There was a spot in front of the sandwich shop. He took that as a sign.

"Tell me you aren't going to make a habit of this," Lori said when he walked in, but she smiled when she said it.

He smiled back at her. Distractedly he studied the chalkboard. The special today was a turkey club. He shifted his gaze to her. "I'll take the special and an iced tea."

"Do you want that on white, wheat or rye?"

"White." He hadn't been *that* distracted that he hadn't noticed her. Today she was dressed in a coral blouse and black slacks. The blouse was V-necked exposing some of the freckled skin of her throat and a small silver heart-shaped locket that played peekaboo when she moved. Her hair was pulled up again, making him wonder if it would fall past her shoulders if he let it down. "With mayo."

"It will be just a few minutes," she said, straightening her blouse collar self-consciously before hurrying into the back.

He took his usual seat. His leg was better today but his ribs still hurt. He kept thinking about his father's case, wishing he hadn't opened up this can of worms. Now that he had, what choice did he have?

Which meant he would have to talk to Karen Wilkins. Her stepdaughter wouldn't like it. Of that, he was certain. He just hoped that neither was involved. He liked Lorelei. He always had. Her stepmother owned a workout studio in town. Widowed, Karen was active in the community and had been as long as James could remember. He used to think "stepmother like stepdaughter." So why did Del have Karen on his list?

Deep in thought, he started when Lorelei set down the plate with his sandwich in front of him. She gently placed the glass of iced tea, giving him a worried look.

"You all right?" she asked. "You seem a little skittish."

He smiled at that. "I've been better."

"Is it true?"

"That's a wide-open question if I've ever heard one."

"Are you really applying for a private investigator's license?"

He chuckled. Thanks to the sheriff, he was. Probably also thanks to the sheriff everyone in town now knew. "Yep. How do you feel about that?"

She seemed surprised by the question. "It has nothing to do with me."

He nodded, hoping it was true. "Still, you seemed to have an opinion yesterday."

Lori looked away for a moment, licked her lips with the quick dart of her tongue, and said, "I was going to apologize for that."

"Really?" he said as he picked up his sandwich and took a bite. He chewed and swallowed before he said, "And I thought you were going to apologize for trying to kill me with that sandwich you made me yesterday."

Her cheeks flushed. "You didn't have to eat it," she said defensively.

He held her gaze. "Yes, I did."

The bell over the front door jangled. She looked almost relieved as she went to help the couple that came in.

Chapter Seven

After James finished his sandwich and iced tea, he wrote a note on the bill Lori had dropped by on her way past his table. The shop had gotten busy. He could see her through the small window into the kitchen. She was making sandwiches in her all-business way. It made him smile. Whatever she did, she did it with so much purpose.

He wondered what would happen if she ever let her guard down. He wished he could be there when she did.

As he left, he pulled out the list of names. It was time to talk to Karen Wilkins and relieve his mind. She couldn't be involved. He had to find out why she was on the list.

James was surprised how young Karen looked as she opened the door. A small woman with chin-length blond hair and large luminous brown eyes, the aerobics instructor was clearly in great shape. In her late forties, Karen and her stepdaughter could have almost passed for sisters rather than stepmother and stepdaughter.

From the expression on her face though, she wasn't glad to see him. He wondered if it had anything to do with him taking over his father's old case. Or if it was more about his reputation. Would he ever live down his misspent youth?

"I hope I haven't caught you at a bad time," he said. She was dressed in leggings, a T-shirt and sneakers as if on her way to her exercise studio. "Do you have a few minutes? I'd like to ask you a few questions."

The woman chuckled, reminding him of Lorelei for a moment. "Whatever you're selling Jimmy D—"

He raised his hands. "Not selling anything. I've taken over my father's old private investigative business temporarily. I'm looking into the last case he was working on before he died."

She raised an eyebrow and he saw her expression turn both serious—and wary.

"I'm here about Billy Sherman's hit-and-run."

Her eyes widened. "Wasn't that almost ten years ago?"

"It was. Please, I promise not to keep you long."

She didn't move. "Why would you think I would know anything about that?"

"Because you were on my father's list of people he wanted to interview."

Her face paled and he saw the fear. She quickly looked away. "I can't imagine how I could possibly help even if I didn't have a class in a few minutes." Her gaze shifted back to his but only for a second. "I was just leaving. I'm sorry. This really isn't a good time." With that, she closed the door.

He stood for a moment feeling shaken to his core. He knew from experience what guilt looked like. Fear too. Turning, he walked out to his pickup and had just slipped behind the wheel when Karen Wilkins's garage door gaped open, and her car came flying out. She barely missed the front bumper of his pickup before she sped away.

She seemed to be in an awful hurry to get to her class, he thought as he gave it a moment before he followed her.

"WHAT'S WRONG?" LORELEI felt panicked at the fear she heard in her stepmother's voice the moment she'd answered her phone.

"It's…nothing, I'm sorry."

"It's not nothing. I can hear it in your voice. Mom—" Lorelei's mother died when she was three. Both her parents had been young—her mother twenty-two when she died, her father twenty-four. She barely remembered her mother. After her mother died, her father went for ten years before even dating.

It had been a shock when he'd come home from an insurance conference with Karen who had looked like a teenager at twenty-five. Lorelei had been thirteen, Karen only twelve years older. People said they could be sisters. At the time, the comment had made her sick to her stomach. How could her father do this to her?

Lorelei hadn't accepted the woman into their lives for a long time, refusing to call her mom. But at some point, her stepmother had won her over and she'd begun calling her mom since she'd never really had a mother before Karen.

The only time she called her Karen had been when she was angry at her like for grounding her or mentioning that she had a boyfriend when her father had said she was too young to have one. Most of the time though, she and Karen had been as close as biological mother and daughter.

"I'm just being silly," Karen said now. "I had a little bit of a scare, for no good reason really. Let's forget it. Tell me how you are doing."

Lorelei looked to the ceiling of her shop kitchen. "I'm doing fine. Had a busy lunch crowd and now I'm prepping for tomorrow." Just like she did every day. "Mom, tell me what's wrong. You never call me at work."

"I shouldn't. I know how busy you are."

"I'm not busy right now. Talk to me."

Silence, then finally, "James Colt is back in town. Apparently, he's taking over his father's investigations business?"

"I don't know. Maybe. Mom, why—"

"That boy is trouble. He always has been. I just don't like the idea of him being in the same building as you."

"He's not in the same building," she said, unable to understand why her stepmother was so upset over this. "He's staying next door in his father's office."

"So, you've seen him?"

"He's stopped by for sandwiches a couple of times." She realized that her stepmother was calling from her car. "Are you in your car? Where are you going?"

"Nowhere. I mean…to the store. I'm out of milk."

Her stepmother didn't drink milk. Nor did she hardly eat anything but fruit and vegetables. Her stepdaughter owned a sandwich shop and her stepmother didn't eat even gluten-free bread. "Are you sure you're all right?"

"Sometimes I just need to hear my daughter's voice. I didn't mean to scare you."

Scare her? Lorelei realized that was exactly what she'd done. Scare her. This wasn't like Karen. Whatever had upset her… She realized that it seemed to be James Colt and his plan to take over his father's PI business. It had upset her too, but Lorelei had her reasons going all the way back to middle school. She couldn't imagine first how her stepmother had heard and second why that would upset her unless…

"Mom," she said as a bad feeling settled in her stomach. "Did James come by to see you?"

"I'm at the store about to check out," her stepmother said. "I have to go. Talk to you later." She disconnected.

Lorelei held the phone feeling a wave of shock wash over her. Her stepmother had just lied to her. She wasn't in the store checkout. Karen had still been in her car driving.

She'd heard the crunch of tires on gravel. Where had her stepmother gone? Not the store with its paved parking lot.

She quickly called her back. But got voice mail straight away. She didn't leave a message.

AT FIRST KAREN WILKINS seemed to be driving aimlessly around town. James had finally pulled over on a side street with a view of Main Street near her exercise studio and waited. She pulled in front of the studio and he'd thought she was going to get out.

But a few minutes later, she took off again without getting out of the car. If she'd had a class, someone else was now teaching it apparently. This time, she headed out of town. James waited until another car got behind Karen Wilkins's car before he pulled out and followed.

A few miles out of town, he saw her brake lights come on ahead of him right before she turned down a gravel road and disappeared into the pines. He caught up, turned and followed the dust trail she'd made, wondering if she was finally going to park somewhere.

He didn't have to wonder long. Around a curve in the road, he saw her car stop in front of a large house set back in the pines. Pulling over, he watched her exit her car and hurry up the steps. As she rang the doorbell, she looked around nervously, before the door opened a few moments later.

The man in the doorway quickly pulled Karen Wilkins into his arms, holding her for a moment before he wiped her tears and then kissed her passionately. As he drew her inside, he glanced around—giving James a clear view of his face—before he quickly closed the door.

James felt as if he'd touched a live wire. He let out a low curse. He'd been hoping that he was wrong about Lorelei's stepmother. He'd hoped there was a simple explanation for her being on his father's list. James still didn't want to believe it, but there was no doubt that he'd upset Karen Wilkins on his visit to her house. Since then she'd been running scared.

And look where she'd run. Straight into the arms of Senator Fred Bayard.

Chapter Eight

James drove back into town, stopping in at the local hardware store that his friend Ryan owned. He found him in the back office doing paperwork. "What is Senator Bayard doing in Lonesome?"

His friend looked up and laughed. "You don't get out much, do you? Fred had a summer home built here about ten years ago. He's one of my best customers, always building something out there on his property."

James didn't follow politics. The only reason he'd recognized the man was because his face had been in so many television ads before the last election. "Why here?"

Ryan leaned forward, his elbows on his desk. "His family's from here. It isn't that unusual. What has got you so worked up? I didn't know you were back in town, let alone that you cared about politics."

"Wait, the senator's from Lonesome?" That couldn't have been something he'd missed.

"His mother was Claudia Hanson, the postmistress. Fred grew up here. He was your father's age. Claudia moved them to Helena at some point when she married Charles Bayard, also a senator, and Bayard adopted Fred."

"I never knew that."

"His great-grandfather started the original sawmill here in Lonesome about the time the railroad was coming through. Heard he made a bundle making and selling railroad ties to the Great Northern. Did you pay any attention at all during Montana history class?"

"Apparently not." He vaguely remembered this, but it had been out of context back then. "You've met him then?"

"Fred? He's a good old boy. Like I said, he stops in when he's in town, which isn't often. Most of the time he's in DC. The rest of the time, he's building corrals or barns or adding onto the summer house, even though he spends so little time here during the year."

James sank into the chair across from Ryan's desk, thinking about what he'd just seen. Karen in the man's arms. "Doesn't he have a wife?"

"Mary? I don't think I've ever seen her. She doesn't spend much time here. They have a big place outside of Helena. I think she stays there most of the time doing her own thing. Why the interest?"

He shook his head. "Have you ever seen him with another woman?"

Ryan looked surprised. He leaned back in his chair. "I'm guessing you have. Someone I know?"

"I'm probably mistaken." He quickly changed the subject. "I'm back for a while. I supposed you heard about Melody and my trailer." His friend nodded. "I'm staying at my dad's old office for the time being." He chewed at his cheek for a moment. "I'm thinking about getting my PI license."

"Seriously?"

"I need to heal up before I go back on the rodeo circuit. I thought it would give me something to do."

Ryan narrowed his gaze. "If I didn't know you so well, I might believe that. What's really going on?"

He sighed. "I'm kind of working Del's last case, Billy Sherman's hit-and-run death. It's never been solved."

"Like a tribute to your old man?"

"Maybe."

"And you think Senator Bayard is involved?"

He shook his head. "I was following a lead that made me aware of Bayard. You said he had his summer home built about ten years ago? So, he might have been here at the time of Billy Sherman's accident."

Ryan gave him a wary look. "Where are you going with this?"

James pulled off his Stetson and raked a hand through his hair. "I have no idea. I'm probably just chasing my own tail."

His friend laughed. "I'd be careful if I were you. Bayard carries a lot of weight in this state. Talk is that he might run for governor."

"Don't worry. I'm just following a few leads. I hate that Del didn't get to finish the case." He thought about mentioning what Alice had told him. That Del said he was close to solving it—and was killed that very night.

But he knew what it would sound like and Ryan knew him too well. Conspiracy theory aside, he had his own reasons for fearing what he might find if he dug into his father's death. His father had been acting strangely in those weeks—or was it months—before his death. Something more than the case had been bothering him.

"How's things with you?"

Ryan motioned to the paperwork stacked up on the desk. "Busy as usual. More people are finding Lonesome. I bought the lumberyard a few years ago. Quite a few new houses coming up, so that's good. You thinking about building out there on your place?"

"I'll see what my brothers want to do when they get back after the rodeo season."

"You can't see yourself staying long-term?"

A fleeting image of Lorelei popped into his head, followed by the little girl on the horse. He shook his head. "Nope, can't see myself staying."

LORELEI CLOSED THE shop right after her last customer left. She usually stayed open until six, but tonight she was anxious to leave. She'd tried to call her stepmother numerous times, but each call had gone to voice mail. After how frantic Karen had sounded earlier…

She parked out front. No sign of her stepmother's car. As she started toward the front door, she checked the garage and felt a surge of relief. Her car was parked inside. At the front door she knocked. Normally she just walked right in. But nothing about earlier had felt normal.

"Lorelei?" Her stepmother seemed not just surprised to see her but startled. True, Lorelei hadn't stopped over to the house for a while. She'd been so busy with the sandwich shop. "Is something wrong?"

"How can you ask that?" Lorelei demanded. "You called me earlier clearly upset and when I tried to call you back, my call went straight to voice mail. I've been worried about you all afternoon."

"I'm so sorry. I guess I turned my phone off. Come in." She moved out of the doorway.

As she stepped in, she tried to breathe, admitting to herself just how scared she'd been and how relieved. Her stepmother seemed okay. But Karen wasn't easily rattled. Instead, she'd always taken things in her stride. In fact, she'd seemed really happy for a long while now. Except for the way she'd sounded on the phone earlier.

She turned to study her stepmother and saw something she hadn't before. How had she not noticed the change in her? Karen Wilkins was practically glowing. She was always slim and trim because she often led classes at her studio. But she appeared healthier and happier looking.

"You look so...good," she said, unable to put her finger on what exactly was different about her stepmother.

Karen laughed, brown eyes twinkling, clearly pleased. "Why, thank you."

"Has something changed?"

Her stepmother's smile quickly disappeared, replaced by a frown. "Why would you ask that?"

"I don't know. You just seem...different."

Brushing that off, Karen headed for the kitchen cupboard, saying over her shoulder, "I made some granola. I was going to call you and see if you—"

"Mom. Stop. Why were you so upset earlier when you called me?"

Her stepmother froze for a moment before turning to face her. "I feel so foolish. I got worked up over nothing." Lorelei put her hands on her hips, waiting.

Finally, Karen sighed and said, "James Colt paid me a visit."

Which explained her stepmother's reaction to him staying in the building next to the sandwich shop. "He came here? Why would he—"

"He's taking over one of his father's old cases apparently and was asking questions about something that happened years ago."

Lorelei noticed that her stepmother was twisting the life out of the plastic bag with the granola in it. "What case?"

"That hit-and-run... The boy, Billy Sherman."

"Why would he ask *you* about that?" But she was thinking, why would that upset her stepmother so much?

Her stepmother turned back to the cupboard. Lorelei watched her busy herself with fixing a bag to send home with her. "I have no idea. He's probably asking a lot of people in the neighborhood."

Lorelei frowned. The accident had happened probably a half mile from her stepmother's house. "I'm sure that's all it was," she said, even though her pulse was spiking. She knew her stepmother. Something was definitely wrong. "It still doesn't explain why you were so upset."

Karen sighed. "I was just sorry to find out that he's back in town and in the office next to you given the crush you had on him in high school."

"I didn't have a crush on him in high school!" she protested, no doubt too much.

"Lorelei, I was there. I saw your reaction to that boy. You're doing so well with your business. I'm just afraid you're going to get mixed up with him."

"I'm not getting mixed up with him. He's come over to the shop a couple of times. I don't know where you got the idea I had a crush on him."

Her stepmother merely looked at her impatiently before she said, "Here, take this home." Karen thrust the bag of granola into her hands and looked at her watch. "I'm sorry I have a class I'm teaching this evening. I wish you could stay and we could watch an old movie." She was steering her toward the door. Giving her the bum's rush, as her father would have said.

She wanted to dig her heels in, demand to know why she was acting so strangely. Was it really because she was worried about Lorelei and James Colt, her new neighbor, the cowboy impersonating a PI?

That was ridiculous.

JAMES HAD BEEN at his father's desk, head in his hands, when the pounding at his door made him jump. What the— "Hold your horses!" he called as he rose to go to the door. "What's the big—" He stopped when he saw Lori standing there.

Her face was flushed, her brown eyes wide, her breathing rapid as if she'd run up the stairs. She was still wearing what she'd had on earlier.

"Is there a fire?" A shake of her head. "Are you being chased by zombies?" A dirty look. "Then I give up." He leaned against the doorjamb to survey her, giving her time to catch her breath. He had a pretty good idea what had her upset, but he wasn't going to bring it up unless she did.

"Why are you questioning my stepmother about the hit-and-run accident?" she demanded.

"Why don't you step in and we can discuss this like—"

"Do you have any idea how much you upset her?"

He nodded slowly. "Actually, I do. Which makes me wonder why, and now why you're even more upset."

Lori took a breath then another one. Her gaze swung away from him for a moment. He watched her regain control of her emotions. She swallowed before she looked at him again. "Why did you question her?" Her voice almost sounded in the normal range.

He moved aside and motioned her into the office. With obvious reluctance, she stepped in, stopping in the middle of the room.

"I love what you've done with the place," she said derisively.

James glanced around, seeing things through her eyes. "I've been meaning to buy a few things to make it more… homey. I've been busy."

"Yes," she said turning to glare at him. "Intimidating my stepmother."

"Is that what she told you?"

A muscle jumped in her jaw. "I will ask you again. Why my stepmother?"

"She was on my father's list."

Lorelei stared at him. "What list?"

He stepped around behind the desk, but didn't sit down. "My father had a method that worked for him. Did you know he solved all of his cases? He was methodical. I wish I was more like him." He could see her growing more impatient. "He would write down a list of names of people connected to the case that he wanted to talk to. He'd check off the ones as he went. Your stepmother was on the list. He hadn't gotten around to questioning her before he was killed. I decided to take up where he left off and ask her myself."

"And?"

"And nothing—she got upset, said she had a class and threw me out."

"Maybe she did have a class."

He gave her a you-really-believe-that look? He watched all the anger seep from her. She looked close to tears, her back no longer ramrod straight, her facial muscles no longer rigid.

"Why would she know anything about Billy Sherman?" she asked quietly.

He shrugged and stepped around the desk to dust off one of the leather club chairs. She moved to it as if sleep-walking and carefully lowered herself down. Behind the desk again, he opened the bottom drawer, took out the bottle of brandy his father kept there and two of the paper cups.

After pouring them each a couple of fingers' worth, he handed her a cup as he took the matching leather chair next to her. He noticed her hand trembled as she took the drink. She was scared. He was afraid she had good reason to be.

He waited until she'd taken a sip of the brandy before

he asked, "Can you think of any reason your stepmother would be so upset about talking to me about the case?"

She shook her head, took a gulp and looked over at him. "You can't really think that she is somehow involved." When he didn't speak instantly, she snapped, "James, my stepmother wouldn't hit a child and keep going."

"I'm not saying she did. But she might know who did."

Lori shook her head, drained her paper cup and set it on the edge of his desk as she rose. "You really think she would keep a secret like that?"

"People keep secrets from those they love all the time," he said.

She glared at him. "What is that supposed to mean?"

"Just that she might be covering for someone."

Her eyes flared. "If you tell me that you think she's covering for me—"

He rose, raising both hands in surrender as he did. "I'm not accusing you. I'm just saying…" He met her gaze, surprised at how hard this was. He and Lori had gone through school together and hardly said two words the entire time. It wasn't like that much had changed over the past few days, he told himself even as he knew it had. He liked her. Always had.

"I think your stepmother knows something and that's why she got so upset." He said the words quickly.

Her reaction was just as quick. "My stepmother wouldn't cover for *anyone*. Not for such a horrible crime. You're wrong. She doesn't keep secrets." She started toward the door.

"You might not know your stepmother as well as you think you do." All his instincts told him she didn't.

She reached the door and spun around to face him, anger firing those brown eyes again. "What are you trying to say?"

"That your stepmother might have secrets. Maybe especially from you."

She scoffed at that, and hands on her hips demanded to know what he was talking about.

"After I questioned her about Billy Sherman's death, your stepmother headed for her studio, saying she had to teach a class. But instead of teaching, she drove out of town and into the arms of Senator Fred Bayard."

He saw the answer as the color drained from her face. She hadn't known. "I'm sorry." He mentally kicked himself for the pain in her eyes before she threw open the door and stormed out.

He swore as he heard her leave. How did his father do this? He had no idea, but he suspected Del was a hell of a lot better at it than he'd been so far.

Chapter Nine

For the next few days, James avoided the sandwich shop and Lori. He felt guilty for exposing her stepmother. But he'd hoped that Karen Wilkins might be honest with her stepdaughter. He needed to know what the woman was hiding—other than the senator.

He'd called out-of-town body shops and left messages for them to call if they had a front end–damaged car from hitting something like a deer after the date of Billy Sherman's death. He didn't have much hope, given how much time had passed. He also assumed his father had done the same thing nine years ago without much success.

While he waited to hear back, he mulled over the case as he cleaned up the office and back bedroom. He bought a few things to make the place more comfortable by adding a couch, a couple of end tables, a coffee table, a large rug and some bookshelves for more storage.

For the bedroom, he'd bought a new rug for the hardwood floor and all new towels, rug and shower curtain for the bathroom. He'd even replaced his father's old vacuum with a new one and dusted and washed the windows. By the time he was through with all the hauling and cleaning his leg hurt and his ribs ached worse.

But when he looked around the place, he felt better. He'd also sent in his application for his private investigator license and dropped off his permit at the sheriff's office to have the burned-out trailer removed from the property. Margaret had suggested a company that did that kind of work. After a call to them, he was told the work would be done this week.

James had to admit he was pretty impressed with what he'd accomplished. But he was no closer to finding Billy Sherman's killer. Also, he realized that he missed Lori's sandwiches and the time he spent with her. He'd been hitting the local In-N-Out, but had pretty much gone through the fried food menu over the past few days. He found himself craving the smell of fresh-baked bread—and the sweet scent of Lori.

He just wasn't sure what kind of reception he would get so he decided to do some real work first. After pulling out the list of names, he grabbed his Stetson and headed for the door.

Maybe he'd get a sandwich to go, he thought as he locked and closed the office door behind him. He'd worried about Lori since he'd dropped the bombshell. All she could do was throw him out if she really couldn't stand the sight of him, right?

LORELEI HAD DRIVEN straight to her stepmother's house the evening after James had told her about her stepmother's relationship. She'd seen a light on and movement behind the kitchen curtains. Her stepmother's car was in the driveway, which was odd. She'd slowed and was about to pull in when she saw a second shadow behind the kitchen curtains.

She'd quickly pulled away, feeling like a coward. Why hadn't she confronted her stepmother and whoever was in the house with her? She told herself she needed to be calm before she did. That it would be better if she spoke about this with her stepmother when she was alone.

When she'd run out of excuses, she'd driven home and looked up Senator Bayard online. There were publicity photos of him and his wife, Mary, and their three daughters—all adults, but all younger than Lorelei.

James had to be wrong. He'd misunderstood. Although she couldn't imagine what had made him think that her stepmother would have an affair with a married man—let alone keep it from her only stepdaughter.

She knew that was the part that hurt. She and Karen had been close, hadn't they? And yet, the other night when she'd driven by, her stepmother hadn't been alone. Could have been a neighbor over, but Lorelei knew it wasn't true. The shadows had been close, then moved together as if one before breaking apart and disappearing from view. Her stepmother did have secrets.

The bell over the front door of the sandwich shop jangled and she looked up to see James Colt come in. He was the last person she wanted to see right now. Or ever. Emotions came at her like a squad of fighter jets. Mad, angry, embarrassed, upset, worried, resigned and at the same time her heart beat a little faster at the sight of him.

"Any chance of getting a sandwich to go?" he asked almost sheepishly.

"I suppose," she said, still battling her conflicting emotions.

He glanced from her to the chalkboard. She studied him while he studied it. He was wearing a blue paisley-patterned Western shirt that matched his eyes. She wondered if he'd bought it or if it was purchased by a girlfriend. It was tucked into the waist of his perfectly fitting jeans. One of his prizewinning rodeo buckles rounded out his attire. He shifted on his feet, taking her gaze down his long legs to his boots. New boots? She'd heard him hauling stuff in and out the past few days and knew he'd been shopping.

"I'll take the special on a roll," he said.

After all that, he'd chosen the special? "Iced tea?"

"How about a cola?"

"Fine. Have a seat. I'll bring it to you."

He nodded and met her gaze. "Lori—"

Whatever he planned to say, she didn't want to hear it. Turning on her heel, she hurried into the kitchen to make his sandwich and try to calm her pounding heart. What was it about the man that had her hands shaking? He just made her so…so…so not her usual controlled self.

Lori. No one had ever called her anything but Lorelei. Leave it to James to give her a nickname. Leave it to James to say it in a way that made her feel all soft inside.

JAMES COULDN'T GET a handle on Lorelei's mood. He hated to think what she was putting in his sandwich. Maybe coming here hadn't been his best idea. But he was hungry, and at least for a few minutes he got to breathe in the smell of freshly baked bread and stretch out his legs.

He didn't have to wait long. When he saw her coming, he started to get up but she waved him back down.

"I thought you'd prefer I take it to go."

She shook her head. "Barbecued pork is hard to eat in your pickup, though I'm sure you've managed it before," she said as she sat down in a chair opposite him.

He wasn't sure the last was a compliment so he simply unwrapped his sandwich and carefully lifted the top piece of bun to see what was inside.

"It's just pulled pork, my fresh coleslaw and house special barbecue sauce," she said, sounding indignant.

"It's your special sauce that I'm worried about," he said.

"It's not too spicy. A tough cowboy like you should be able to handle it." Her gaze challenged him to argue.

He put the sandwich back together and took a bite. "Delicious." He took another bite. He really was starved.

"Do you have to keep sounding surprised that I can make a decent sandwich?" she demanded.

"Sorry, it's just that you're so…so…" He waved a hand in the air, wishing he hadn't opened his mouth.

"So? So what? Uptight? Too good to do simple things?"

He took a bite, chewed and swallowed, stalling. "You're so…sexy." He held up a hand as if expecting a blow. "I know it's a cliché that a sexy woman can't cook. Still…"

"Sexy?" She shook her head and let out an exasperated sigh, but she didn't leave his table. He continued eating. He could see her working through a few things. But when she finally spoke, her words took him by surprise. "I need to know why my stepmother is on your father's list."

He wiped his mouth with a napkin and took a drink of the cola. "I don't know. That's why I went to talk to her."

He could see she was struggling with the next question and decided to help her out. "After she got so upset I followed her. She drove all over town, at one point made a couple of phone calls and then drove out of town. I didn't even know the senator had a house here until he opened the front door."

"Just because she went to his house— Isn't it possible they're just good friends?"

He shook his head. "He took her in his arms and kissed her. It was passionate and she kissed him back. They both seemed nervous, worried that someone was watching and hurriedly closed the door."

"Someone *was* watching," she said under her breath. She looked sick to her stomach.

"I'm sorry to be the one to tell you. I was surprised to see her name on the list. I went there hoping she'd tell me why. It was a shot in the dark. But then when she got so upset before I even had a chance to ask her…"

She nodded. "Refill?" she asked, pointing at his cola.

He shook his head. "You haven't talked to her?"

"I haven't wanted to believe it. I was hoping you were wrong." Her gaze came up to meet his. "I suppose if anyone knows a passionate kiss when he sees one, it would be you though."

He laughed, leaning his elbows on the table to close the distance between them. "You give me a lot more credit than I'm due." She harrumphed at that. "Why do I get the feeling that I did something to you back in grade school or high school or this week and that's why you're so angry with me?"

"You didn't. It's just that I know what kind of man you are."

"Do you?" he asked seriously before shaking his head. "I thought you were smarter than to believe everything you hear. Especially about me." He dropped his voice. "I've kissed a few women. But I'm still waiting to kiss the one who rattles me clear down to the toes of my boots."

She raised a brow. "You've been in town for a few days. I'm sure you have one in your sights already."

"Oh, I do," he said, realizing it was true. He just wondered if he'd ever get the chance to kiss her.

LORELEI CALLED HER stepmother after James left. "I was thinking we could have dinner together tonight if you don't have any plans. I could pick up—" She was going to suggest something vegan for her stepmother, when Karen interrupted her.

"You don't have to pick up anything. I can make us a nice salad for dinner."

She felt off balance. She'd been half expecting her stepmother to make an excuse because she was seeing her... lover again tonight? "Sure, that would be great."

"Good, then I'll see you about six thirty," Karen said.

"See you then."

She disconnected, telling herself that James was wrong. That what she'd seen last night might not even have been the senator. That her stepmother's name being on Del Colt's list meant nothing.

When she arrived at the house a little after six, her stepmother answered the door smiling and seeming excited to see her. She ushered her into the kitchen where she'd made a pitcher of lemonade. "I thought we could eat out on the patio. It's such a beautiful evening."

Lorelei had planned to question her after they ate, but she realized she couldn't sit through chitchat for an hour first. She watched her stepmother start to pour them each a glass of lemonade over ice.

"Are you having an affair with Senator Bayard?"

Her stepmother's arm jerked, lemonade spilling over the breakfast bar. Without looking at her, Karen slowly set down the pitcher, then reached for a dishcloth to clean up the mess. Without a word, she'd already admitted the truth.

"I can't believe this," Lorelei cried. "When did this happen? *How* did this happen? He's *married*!"

Her stepmother turned to her, her face set in stone. "He's getting a divorce and then we're going to get married."

"That's what they all say," she snapped. "Don't you watch daytime talk shows?"

"He's separated and has been for some time. He's been staying at the family's summer home here when he isn't in Washington." Karen looked down at the dishcloth in her hands. "We've been seeing each other for a while now." She looked up.

"Before he and his wife were supposedly separated." It wasn't a question.

"I'm not proud of it. It just happened."

Lorelei shook her head. *"It just happened?"*

"I love him and he loves me."

She bit her tongue, thinking how different this conversation would have been if she'd been the one having the affair. Her stepmother would be hitting the roof right now. Look how upset she'd supposedly gotten over James Colt being in the building next door to her stepdaughter. "You haven't said how you met him."

"Our paths crossed a few times while he was here building his summer home," she said. "We found we had a lot in common."

Lorelei wanted to ask what, but she wasn't ready to hear this. "You're serious." Of course her stepmother was. That glow she'd noticed. Karen was in *love*. That her stepmother would even consider an affair with a married man told her how head over heels she was with this man.

"With him possibly running for governor, the timing isn't good, but we're going to get married once the fallout from his divorce settles."

She couldn't bring herself to say that she wasn't holding her breath and neither should her stepmother. But she was so disappointed and angry right now that she couldn't deal with this. Karen had cautioned her about men since she was thirteen.

"Let me get the salad and we can go out on the deck and—"

"I'm sorry," she said. "I've lost my appetite." With that she turned and started for the door.

"Lorelei, wait."

She stopped at the door, closing her eyes as she heard her stepmother come up behind her. She thought of all the tantrums she'd thrown as a teen, all the arguments she and Karen had had over the years. They'd always made up and gotten through it.

"I'm sorry I've disappointed you."

"I am too, Karen." She started to open the door, felt her stepmother tentatively touch her back and flinched.

Her stepmother quickly removed her hand. "Disappointed in me or not you have to understand, I'm an adult. I get to make my own decisions, right or wrong." Her voice broke. "I'm still young. I've been lonely since your father died. Can't you try to be happy for me?"

Lorelei felt herself weaken, her love for her stepmother a constant in her life. Karen was right. She was still young and she'd been a widow for years now. Of course she was lonely; of course she wanted a man in her life.

"I'm trying," she said and turned to face her. "Tell me you aren't involved in what happened to the Sherman boy. Swear it on my life."

Her stepmother looked shocked. "Why would you ask—"

"Because I know you. For you to get so upset over James's questions about the case that you'd run to your lover and be seen, you must have something else to hide. Tell me the truth."

Her stepmother took a step back. "So, it was James who saw us and ran right to you to tell you. I should have known."

"He didn't run right to me. I cornered him, demanding to know why he would question you. But you still haven't answered my question," Lorelei said, that knot in her chest tightening. "Swear. On my life."

"Don't be ridiculous," Karen snapped and took another step back. "I would never swear to anything on your life. You're upset and don't know what you're saying. You should go before either of us says something we'll regret."

Lorelei felt tears burn her eyes. "You already have." With that, she opened the door and left.

Chapter Ten

After leaving the sandwich shop, James had felt at loose ends. He drove out to his family's ranch. *Ranch* was a loosely used term since no one had raised much of anything on the land. It was close to a hundred acres covered with pines. Some of it was mountainous while a strip of it bordered the river.

He and his brothers had talked about selling some of it off since they didn't use it, but Willie, their eldest brother, talked them out of it.

"Land doesn't have to do anything and someday you're going to be glad that it's there and that it's ours," Willie had said.

The remains of the double-wide trailer had been removed leaving a scorched area of ground where it had been. But James could see where grass was already starting to grow. It wouldn't be long before nature healed the spot.

James stood looking at the rolling hillsides, towering pines and granite bluffs. He was glad Willie had talked them out of selling even a portion of it. This land was all that brought them back here. It was the one constant in their lives. The one tangible in their otherwise nomadic lives.

That and the office building. He thought about Lori

wanting to buy it. He still thought of the place as Del's and felt himself balk at the idea of ever giving it up.

Back at the office, he found several notes tacked to his back door. Word had gotten out that he was in business. One was from an insurance company offering him surveillance work if he was interested. The other was from someone who wanted her boyfriend followed. He laughed, delighted that he had several new PI jobs if he wanted them.

But first he had to finish what he'd started. He drove out to Edgar Appleton's house some miles from town. Edgar owned a heavy equipment construction company. He and his crew had been working near where Billy Sherman's body had been found. One of his employees, Lyle Harris, had been operating a front loader that morning. He was about to dump a load of dirt into the ditch when a neighbor woman spotted the body and screamed—stopping him.

Edgar lived on a twenty-acre tract. His house sat off to one side, his equipment taking up the rest of the property. Several vehicles were parked in front of the house when James climbed the steps to knock. He could hear loud voices inside and knocked again.

A hush came from inside the house a moment before the door opened. Edgar filled the doorway. He was a big man with a wild head of brown hair that stuck up every which way. He was wearing a sweatshirt with his business logo on it and a pair of canvas pants. It appeared he'd just gotten home from work.

"If this is a bad time..."

"James Colt," Edgar said in a loud boisterous voice. "Bad time? It's always a bad time at this house. Come in!" He stepped aside. "Irene, put another plate on the table."

She yelled something back that he didn't catch just a moment before she appeared behind her husband wiping her hands on her apron. "You'd think I'm only here to cook and clean for this man." She smiled, her whole face lighting up. "Get on in here. I have a beef roast and vegetables coming out of the oven. I hope your table manners are better than Ed's. I could use some stimulating conversation for once." Her laugh filled the large room as she headed back to the kitchen.

"The meanest woman who ever lived," Edgar said so she could hear it. Her response was swift, followed by the banging of pots and pans. "I don't know what I would do without her."

"That's for sure!" she called from the kitchen.

"I can't stay for dinner. I probably should have called first," James said.

"Sorry, but you have no choice now," Edgar said as he looped an arm around his shoulders and dragged him in. "She'll swear I ran you off and I'll have to hear about it the rest of the night."

He had to admit, Irene's dinner smelled wonderful. He heard his stomach growl. So did Edgar. The man laughed heartily as he swept him into the dining room off the kitchen.

"I didn't come for dinner, but it sure smells good," he told Irene as she brought out a pan of homemade rolls. "Let me help you with that." He grabbed the hot pads on the counter and helped her get the huge pot out of the oven. It was enough food to feed an army, he saw. "Are there other people coming?" he asked as she directed him to a trivet at the head of the large dining room table.

"At this house, you never know," Irene said. "I like to be prepared. As it is, Ed didn't bring home half the crew tonight so I'm glad you showed up."

"Me too," Ed said as he sat down at the head of the table and began to slice up the roast. Irene swatted him with the dishtowel she took from her shoulder before she sat to his right and motioned James into the chair across from her.

"James, I want to hear it all," she said smiling as she reached for his plate and Edgar began to load it up with thick slices of the beef. "You know what I'm talking about," she said, seeing his confusion. "Is it true? You've taken over your father's private investigative business? We'll get to Melody and what happened to your trailer later."

"Sorry, I should have warned you," Edgar said with a laugh. "The woman is relentless." As he said it, he reached over and squeezed her arm.

For the rest of the meal, they all talked and laughed. James couldn't recall a time he'd enjoyed more. Seeing how these two genuinely cared about each other was heart-warming and Irene's dinner was amazing.

"I know you didn't come by for dinner," Edgar said when they'd finished and Irene got up to clear the table. James started to rise to help her but she waved him back down.

He explained that he was looking into his father's last case, the hit-and-run that killed Billy Sherman.

"We were working in that subdivision. You know Lyle, my front-end loader operator, was working that morning," Edgar said. "He was getting ready to fill in that ditch we'd dug when a neighbor lady came over with some turnovers she'd made for the crew. She saw Billy lying there and started screaming." He shook his head. "It wrecked us all." Irene came from the kitchen to place her hand on the big man's shoulder for a few moments before taking the rest of the dirty plates into the kitchen.

"That was a new neighborhood nine years ago, new pavement," James said. "Did you see skid marks, any indication that whoever hit him had tried to stop?"

Edgar wagged his big head. "The sheriff, that was Otis back then, said the driver must have thought he hit a deer and that was why he didn't stop. Plus it was raining hard that night. I reckon the car was going so fast when it hit the boy—he was pretty scrawny for his age—that the driver hadn't known what was hit."

"But the driver had to have known it wasn't a deer, even if he didn't stop," James said. "There would have been some damage to the car, a dent or a broken headlight." Edgar nodded. "I would think the car would have had to have been repaired."

"You're assuming the driver was local, but even if that was the case, he wouldn't have had it repaired in town."

James thought of the next name on his list that his father hadn't gotten to: Gus Hughes of Hughes Body Shop in town. But Edgar was right. If it had been a local, then the driver would have gotten the car repaired out of town.

Irene came in and changed the subject as she served coffee and raspberry pie with a scoop of ice cream.

"I can't tell you how much I've enjoyed this meal," James told her before Edgar walked him to the door.

"I hope you find out who killed that boy," the big man said, patting him on the shoulder. "It's time he was put to rest."

LORELEI WOKE FEELING exhausted after a night of tossing and turning. She kept thinking about her stepmother and going from angry to sad to worried and regretful for the things she'd said. Her stepmother couldn't know anything about Billy Sherman's death. So why hadn't she sworn that? Why had she gotten even more upset and basically thrown Lorelei out of her house?

After a shower, she dressed for work. Owning her own business meant she went to work whether she felt like it or not. She had a couple of women she hired during the busiest seasons to help out, but she'd never considered turning the place over to one of them before this morning.

She reeled her thoughts back. What had she been doing nine years ago when Billy Sherman died? Working in a friend's sandwich shop in Billings, learning the business. Before that she'd had numerous jobs using her college business degree, but hadn't found anything that called to her. She'd always known that she wanted the independence of having her own business.

And what had her stepmother been doing nine years ago? Karen had her exercise studio and had been teaching a lot, as far as Lorelei could remember.

Frowning now, she tried to remember if it had been her stepmother who'd told her about Billy Sherman's hit-and-run or if she'd heard it on the news. Didn't she remember a phone conversation about it? Her stepmother being understandably upset since it had happened not that far from her house in that new adjoining subdivision.

Lorelei felt sick to her stomach and more scared than she'd ever been. She had to know the truth. But if she couldn't get her stepmother to tell her...

It was still early. She called her friend Anita and asked her if she wanted to fill in today, apologizing for the short notice. Anita jumped at the opportunity, saying she had nothing planned and could use the money.

"I had already made a list of the specials," Lorelei told her. "Everything you need is in the cooler. You just have to get the bread going right away. I'll be in to help as soon as I can."

Anita said she was already on her way out the door headed for the shop, making Lorelei smile. Her business would be fine. Grabbing her purse, she headed for her car.

WITH THE RISING SUN, James had awakened knowing he was going to have to talk to former sheriff Otis Osterman at some point. He had too many questions about how the sheriff had handled the investigation. According to his father's notes, Otis had refused to give him any information. James suspected it was one reason his father had taken a case that had still been active.

Del hadn't gotten along with the former sheriff and James had a history with Otis due to his wayward youth. So, he wasn't expecting the conversation was going to go well.

After getting ready for his day, he decided he would talk to Gus Hughes first, then swing by Otis's place out by the river. His father had already talked to Gus, but James thought it wouldn't hurt to talk to him again.

However, when he went downstairs to where his pickup was parked out back of the office building, he found Lorelei Wilkins leaning against his truck waiting for him.

He braced himself as he tried to read her mood. "Mornin'," he said, stopping a few safe feet from her.

She looked as if she didn't want to be there any more than he did. For a moment, he thought she would simply storm off without a word. "I want to hire you."

Of all the things that he'd thought might happen, this wasn't one of them. "I beg your pardon?"

"You heard me," she snapped, lifting her chin defiantly. "What do you charge?"

Good question. He had no idea. Legally, he wasn't a private investigator yet. The application and money had been sent in. He was waiting for his license. "If we're going to talk money, we should at least go somewhere besides an alley. Have you had breakfast?"

"I couldn't eat a thing right now."

"Could you watch me eat? Because I'm starved!" He gave her a sheepish grin. Even after that meal he'd had last night, he was hungry. He figured she might relax more in a public place. She also might not go off on him in a local cafe filled with people they both probably knew.

Because, he suspected before this was over, she would want to tell him what she thought of him.

LORELEI ADMITTED THIS was a mistake as she watched James put away a plate of hotcakes.

"You sure you don't want a bite?" he asked between a forkful.

"I'm sure." The smell of bacon and pancakes had made her stomach growl, reminding her that she hadn't eaten dinner last night. But she still couldn't swallow a bite right now, she told herself. She just wanted to get this over with.

"So, are you going to do it or not?" she demanded.

He finished the hotcakes, put down his fork and pushed the plate aside. She watched him wipe his mouth and hands on his napkin before he said, "What exactly is it you want me to do?"

"I just told you," she said between gritted teeth. Leaning forward and dropping her voice even though there wasn't anyone sitting near them in the cafe, she said, "Find out the truth about my…" She mouthed, "Stepmother."

He seemed to give that some thought for a moment before he said, "Wouldn't the simplest, fastest approach be for you to ask her yourself?"

"I already tried that," she said and sighed.

"And she denied any knowledge?"

She looked away under the intenseness of those blue eyes of his. "Not exactly. She asked me to leave her house."

"Come on," James said, tossing money on the table before rising. "Let's go."

It wasn't until they were in his pickup that he said, "What is it you think I can do that you can't?"

"I thought you had some…talent for this."

"Like what? Throw my magic lariat around her so she tells the truth? Or use my brawn to beat the truth out of her?"

She mugged a face at him. "Of course not. I thought maybe you could break into her house and look for evidence."

Now they were finally getting somewhere, James thought. He disregarded the illegal breaking and entering part and asked, "What kind of evidence?"

She swallowed before she said, "A diary maybe. She used to keep one. Or...maybe a bill from like, say a...body shop for car repairs."

"What would make you think I'd find something like that even if nine years hadn't passed?"

"Because," she snapped, clearly losing patience with him. "If she was the one who hit Billy, then she would have had to have her car repaired, right? Has this thought really not crossed your mind?"

"My father already talked to Gus Hughes at his body shop."

She waved a hand through the air in obvious frustration. "Are you just pretending to be this dense? She wouldn't have taken it to the local body shop. She's smarter than that. She would have taken it out of town. It's not like she could keep it hidden in her garage for long."

"But she also couldn't simply drive it out of town either without someone noticing," he said.

"Maybe she did it at night."

He shook his head. "Still too risky. And how does she explain no car for as long as it was in the body shop?"

"It was summer. She always rides her bike to work in the summer. There must be some way she could get the car out of town to a body shop and get it brought back without anyone being the wiser."

"I have a couple of thoughts on the matter. In fact, I'm talking to someone on my list today about just that. I've already made inquiries of a half dozen body shops within a hundred-mile radius."

She sat back, looking surprised. "So, you *have* thought about all of this?" He didn't answer, simply looked at her. She let out a breath and seemed to relax a little. "You still haven't told me what you charge."

"Let's see what I turn up first, okay?"

Lorelei nodded and looked uncomfortable. "I'm starved. Would you mind stopping at a drive-thru on the way back to your office?"

He chuckled and started the engine. Out of the corner of his eye he watched her. She was scared, and maybe with good reason, that her stepmother was somehow involved.

He'd wanted to solve this case for his father. Also to prove something to himself. But right now he wanted to find evidence to clear Karen Wilkins more than anything else because of her stepdaughter. He wanted to put that beautiful smile back on Lori's face, even as he feared he was about to do just the opposite.

Chapter Eleven

After James dropped Lori off at her shop, telling her he'd think about what she'd asked him to do, he drove out to the river. It was one of those clear blue Montana summer days so he decided to quit putting it off and talk to former sheriff Otis Osterman. He'd save Gus Hughes for later, when he'd be glad to see a friendly face.

He put his window down and let the warm air rush in as he drove. He could smell the pines and the river and sweet scent of new grass. It reminded him of the days he and his brothers used to skip school in the spring and go fishing down by the river. One of his favorite memories was lying in the cool grass, listening to the murmur of the river while he watched clouds drift through the great expanse of sky overhead. His brothers always caught enough fish for dinner that he could just daydream.

The former sheriff lived alone in a cabin at the edge of the water. Otis's wife had died of cancer a year before he retired. He'd sold their place in town and moved out here into this two-room log cabin. His pickup was parked in the drive as James knocked. He knocked louder, and getting no response walked around to the back where he found the man sitting on his deck overlooking the river.

"Hello!" he called as he approached the stairs to the

deck. He didn't see a gun handy, but that didn't mean that there wasn't one.

Otis jumped, his boots coming down loudly on the deck flooring.

"Didn't mean to startle you," James said as he climbed the steps and pulled up a wooden stool to sit on since there was only one chair and Otis was in it.

"Too early for company," the former sheriff growled, clearly either not happy to be startled so early—or equally unhappy to see a member of the Colt family anytime of the day.

"I'm not company," he said. "I'm here to ask you about Billy Sherman's hit-and-run."

Otis gave him a withering glare. "Why would I tell you anything?" As if his brother Carl hadn't already told him.

"My father was working the case when he died. I've decided to finish it for him."

"Is that right? You know anything about investigating?"

"I worked with Del from the time I was little. I might have picked up a few things."

Otis shook his head. "You always were an arrogant little bastard."

"That aside, I'm sure you must have had a suspect or two that you questioned."

"Would have come out to your place and talked to you and your brothers but you felons were all too far away at some rodeo or other to have done it."

"Technically, none of us are felons," James said. "What about damage to the vehicle that hit him? You must have tried to find it."

"Of course we tried. Look, we did our best with what we had to work with. Your father thought he could do better. But he didn't find the person, did he?"

"He died before he could."

"To keep his record intact."

James shook his head. He'd known this would be ugly. "My father didn't kill himself."

"You really think his pickup stalled on the tracks with a train coming and he didn't have time to get out and run?" Otis shook his head. "Unless there was some reason he couldn't get out." He mimed lifting an invisible bottle to his lips.

Bristling, James warned himself to keep the temperature down. If things got out of control, Otis would have his brother lock him up behind bars before he could snap his fingers. "Del did have a shot of blackberry brandy on occasion, but according to the coroner's report, he wasn't drunk."

"But he could have been trying to get drunk after the argument he had with a mystery woman earlier that day in town," Otis said. "At least, that's the story I heard. The two were really going at it, your father clearly furious with her."

James pushed off the stool to loom over the man. "If anyone started that lie, it was you to discredit my father. The only reason he would have taken an open case like Billy Sherman's was if he thought you and your brother were covering something up. If he hadn't died, what are the chances that he would have exposed the corruption in your department?"

"I'd be careful making wild accusations," Otis warned.

"Why?" He leaned closer, seeing that he'd hit a nerve. "It's never stopped you."

Otis held up his hands. "You've got your grandfather Colt's temper, son. It could get you into a whole pack of trouble."

James breathed hard for a moment before he took a step back. That was one of the problems of living in small-town

Montana. Everyone didn't just know your business, they knew your whole damned family history.

"I'm going to find out the truth about Billy Sherman's death. And while I'm at it, I'm going to look into my father's death as well. You make me wonder if they aren't connected—just not in the way you want me to believe."

"You're wasting your time barking up that particular tree, but it's not like you have anything pressing to do, is it? You should be looking for the mystery woman."

James smiled. Otis's forehead was covered with a sheen of sweat and his face was flushed. "You would love to send me on a wild goose chase. Are you that worried that I might uncover the truth about how you and your brother handled the Sherman case? You're wondering if I'm as smart as my father. I'm not. But maybe I'll get lucky."

"Get off my property before I have you arrested for trespassing."

"I'm leaving. But if I'm right, I'll be back, only next time it will be with the real law—not your baby brother."

LORELEI COULDN'T BELIEVE what she'd done. Now that she was away from James, she regretted hiring him and planned to fire him as soon as she saw him. The man didn't even have a private investigator's license. What had she been thinking? He was worse than an amateur. He thought he was more trained at this than he was because he'd run a few errands and done some filing for his father.

It had been a spur-of-the-moment stupid decision and not like her at all. She usually thought things through. She blamed James for coming back and turning her life and her upside down.

Worse, as the day stretched on, she'd also had no luck reaching her stepmother. By almost closing time, she'd already sent Anita home and was prepping for the next day, angry with herself. Not even rock and roll music blasting in her kitchen could improve her mood.

She felt so ineffectual. Had she really suggested to James that he break into her stepmother's house and search for incriminating evidence against her? She groaned at the thought that he might have already done it.

If she really believed he would find such evidence, then why didn't she simply look herself? She had an extra key to the house and she knew when her stepmother should be at the studio.

But she also knew the answer. She was afraid she *would* find something damning and do what? Destroy it?

The front doorbell jangled. She looked up to see the very pregnant Melody Simpson waddle in. "Hey," the young woman called. "Am I too late to get a sandwich?"

She hurriedly turned down the music as she realized she'd forgotten to lock the front door. This was exactly the kind of behavior that was so unlike her.

"Not if you want it to go," Lorelei said, even though she was technically closed.

"Sure." Melody waddled up and studied the board. "White bread, American cheese, mustard and no lettuce."

Lorelei nodded. "Twelve inch?" A nod. "Anything to drink? I have canned soda to go."

The young woman shook her head and stepped to the closest table to sit down. "My feet are killing me."

Not knowing how to answer that, Lorelei hurried in the back to make her a cheese sandwich. It felt strange seeing James's pregnant former girlfriend. Not that they had dated long before he'd left town. Still...

"I heard about you and Jimmy D," Melody called back into the kitchen.

"Pardon?"

"Breakfast at the cafe this morning early, whispering

with your heads together. The two of you were the talk of the town before noon."

Lorelei gasped as she realized the rumors that would be circulating. She groaned inwardly. Because it had been so early, people might think that she and James had spent the night together!

That thought rattled her more than she wanted to admit. She could just imagine Gladys's Beauty Emporium all atwitter. The place was rumor mill central. She started to tell Melody that it wasn't what it looked like, but the explanation of her early morning meeting with James was worse.

"I just wanted you to know that I'm not jealous," Melody added.

That stopped Lorelei for a moment. Melody wasn't jealous? Why would she be jealous? She finished wrapping up the sandwich, bagged it and went back out front to find the woman had kicked off her shoes and was rubbing her stocking-covered feet.

She put the bag on the counter along with the bill. After a minute, Melody worked her shoes back on and limped over to her. As she dug a wad of crumpled bills from her jacket pocket, Lorelei said, "Why would you be jealous? I heard you were marrying Tyler Grange and having..." Her gaze went to Melody's very distinct baby bump. "His baby."

Melody continued to smooth out singles on the countertop, her head bent over them with undue attention.

Lorelei felt a start. *It was Tyler's baby, right?* "Have your plans changed?" she asked, finding herself counting the months by the size of Melody's belly. What if it was James's? And why did that make her heart plummet?

"Naw, my plans haven't changed. Tyler's going to marry me," Melody finally said as she finished. Lorelei realized Melody had been counting the bills. She took the fistful of ones. "It's just that I really cared about James. I want him to be happy. I guess if you can make him happy…" She sounded doubtful about that.

"Sorry, but it isn't like that between me and James."

Melody picked up the sack with her sandwich inside. "If you say so. Just don't hurt him. He's real vulnerable right now." With that, she turned and left.

Lorelei followed her to the door and locked it behind her. James vulnerable? That was a laugh. But as she headed back to finish up in the kitchen, she wondered why Melody would even think that.

Shaking her head, she tried to clear James Colt out of it. She hadn't seen him since this morning. She'd checked a few times to see if his pickup was parked out back. It hadn't been. She could have tried calling him—if she'd had his cell phone number.

She told herself she'd fire him when she saw him. She just hoped he hadn't done anything on her behalf and, at the same time wishing he had, but only if he hadn't found anything incriminating.

"Sounds like you had quite the day," Ryan said when James stopped by the hardware store. "I can't believe that you threatened Otis. Wish I'd seen that."

They were in the back office, Ryan's boots up on the desk as he sipped a can of beer from the six-pack James had brought. After his visit with Otis, James had driven around trying to calm down. He'd stopped at a convenience store, picked up the beer and headed for Ryan.

The two of them had roomed and rodeoed together in college. Ryan always knew he would come back and run his father's hardware store. James hadn't given a thought to what he would do after he quit rodeo.

"You'd better watch your back," Ryan was saying. "Otis hates you and his brother is even less fond of you."

"I'm not afraid of that old fart or his little brother." He took a drink of his beer. "I'd love to nail Otis's hide to the side of his cabin."

"I wouldn't even jaywalk if I were you until you leave town again. You know how tight he is with his younger brother. What all did Otis say that has you so worked up?" his friend asked.

James chewed at his cheek for a moment. "He insinuated Del killed himself possibly over a broken heart because of a mystery woman or because he couldn't solve the Billy Sherman case or because he was a drunk and couldn't get out of his pickup before the train hit him."

Ryan raised a brow. "What woman?"

"According to Otis, my father was seen arguing with a mystery woman earlier in the day before he was killed. Apparently not someone from around here since Otis didn't have a name."

"Seriously?"

"He was more than serious. He suggested I should find that woman. It was obvious that he's worried what I might find digging around in the Sherman case—and my father's death. I'm just wondering why he's so worried."

His friend took a long drink and was silent for a few minutes. "I've always wondered about your old man's accident."

"Me too. What was Del doing out on that railroad track in that part of the county at that time of the night? There are no warning arms that come down at that site. But the lights would have been flashing…" He shook his head. "I've always thought it was suspicious but even more so since I found out that Del told someone that he was close to solving Billy Sherman's case."

Ryan let out a low whistle. "Now you're a private investigator almost, investigate."

He smiled. "Just that simple?"

"Why not? Sounds like it's something you've thought about. Why not set your mind at ease one way or another?"

"Just between you and me? This is a lot harder than I thought. But you're right. I've already got half the town upset with me. Why not the other half?" He looked at his phone and, seeing the time, groaned. "I'd planned on stopping by Gus Hughes's garage. If I'm right, someone had to pay to get their car fixed out of town nine years ago."

"You're thinking it might have been Terry," his friend said. Terry Durham worked for Gus. "Now that you mention it, Terry bought that half acre outside of town a little over nine years ago and put a camper on it. Could be a coincidence. Not sure how much he would charge to cover up a hit-and-run murder vehicle. But since he's usually broke…"

James drained his beer, arced the can for a clean shot at the trash in the corner and rose to leave. "Thanks. I think I'll stop by his place and have a little talk with him."

"Thanks for the beer. Best take these with you." Ryan held up the other four cans still attached to the plastic collars.

James shook his head. "I figure you'll need them if the rumors are true. Are you really dating the notorious Shawna Collins?"

Ryan swore as he hurled his empty beer can at him.

James ducked, laughing. "And you're warning *me* to be careful." He stepped out in the hall before his friend found something more dangerous to throw at him.

Although Del Colt had talked to Terry Durham according to his list—and checked him off—James wanted to ask him where the money had come for his land and trailer.

Terry lived outside of town on a half-acre lot with a trailer on it. James pulled into the woods, his headlights catching the shine of a bumper. In the large yard light, he recognized Terry's easily recognizable car and parked behind it. The souped-up coupe had been stripped down to a primer coat for as long as James could remember seeing it around town.

Getting out of the pickup, he started toward the camper. But stopped at the sight of something parked deep in the pines. A lowboy trailer. The kind a person could haul a car on.

The lowboy trailer was exactly what he wanted to talk to the man about and he felt a jolt of excitement. Maybe he could solve this.

Whoever had hit Billy Sherman would have had some damage to their vehicle or at the very least would have wanted to get the car out of town and detailed to make sure there was no evidence on it. One way to get the car out of town was on the lowboy. Terry Durham always seemed to need money. Add to that his proven disregard for the law and the huge chip on his shoulder, and you had someone who would look the other way—if the price were right.

Moving toward the camper again, he saw that there appeared to be one small light behind the blinds at the back. He knocked on the door. No answer. No movement inside. Was it possible Terry had come home and left with someone else?

James was debating coming back early tomorrow when he started past Terry's car and caught a scent he recognized though the open driver's side window.

He stopped cold, his guts tightening inside him as he glanced over inside the car.

Terry was slumped down in his seat behind the wheel, his eyes open, his insides leaking out between his fingers.

Chapter Twelve

It was daylight by the time James had told the sheriff his story a dozen times before losing his temper. "I've told you repeatedly, I went out there to talk to Terry about a car he might have been paid to haul to another town."

"Whose car?" Sheriff Carl Osterman asked again.

James sighed. "Billy Sherman's killer whose name I don't know yet."

"You're back in town for a few days and now we have a murder. As I recall, you and Terry never got along. I recall a fistfight my brother had to break up out at the Broken Spur a couple years ago."

"That was between Terry and my brother Davey. I had nothing against Terry and I certainly had no reason to kill him. So, either believe me or arrest me because I'm going home!"

When the sheriff didn't move, James pushed out of the chair he'd been sitting in for hours and headed for the door.

"Don't leave town!" Carl called after him.

He held his tongue as he strode out of the sheriff's department to take his first breath of fresh air. It was morning, the sun already cresting the mountains. He felt exhausted and still sick over what he'd seen earlier.

After he'd called 911 and the sheriff had arrived, he'd been ordered to wait in the back of Carl's patrol SUV while an ambulance was called along with crime techs. Eventually Terry Durham's body had been extricated from the car and hauled off in a body bag.

Even now, it took him a moment to get his legs under him. The last time he'd seen anything like that had been when a bull rider had been gored. He still felt sick to his stomach as he made his way to his pickup. He tried not to think about it. He'd wanted to ask Terry if someone paid him to take their damaged car out of town on that lowboy trailer of his nine years ago.

He'd been hoping the answer wasn't going to be Karen Wilkins. Terry wouldn't have done it for just anyone—unless the price was right.

Now he was dead. James feared it was because of the questions he'd been asking about Billy Sherman's death.

As he pulled up behind the office building, he saw that Lorelei's SUV was already parked behind her shop. He got out and was almost to his door, when she rushed out.

"I need to talk to you," she said. She smelled like yeast, her apron dusted with flour. There was a dusting of flour on her nose. He couldn't imagine her looking more beautiful.

But right now, he just needed some rest. He held up his hands. "Whatever it is, can we please discuss it later." He opened his back door and started to step in when she grabbed his arm.

"Are you sick or drunk?" she demanded.

He turned to look at her. She sounded like the sheriff because he'd had beer on his breath earlier. "I'm not drunk, all right? Lorelei, it's just not a good time. Whatever it is, I'm sure it can wait until I get some sleep."

"Rough night?" she mocked.

"You could say that."

Her gaze suddenly widened. "Oh, no. You found something. You went to my stepmother's and—"

He sighed, realizing why she'd been waiting for him to return. "I didn't go to your stepmother's." She'd hear about this soon anyway. "I went out to Terry Durham's and found him…murdered. I've been at the cop shop ever since."

She let go of his arm. "I'm sorry."

He nodded. "Now I just need a shot of brandy and a little sleep. I've spent hours answering the sheriff's questions. I can't take any more right now." She nodded and stepped back. "Later. I promise. We'll talk then." He stepped through his door, letting it slam behind him as he slowly mounted the stairs.

It wasn't until he reached the office door that he saw the note nailed to it.

Tearing it off, he glanced at the scrawled writing.

Get out of town while you still can.

Inside the office, he unlocked his father's bottom drawer and pulled out the .45 he would be carrying from now on.

LORELEI STARTED AT the sound of her phone ringing. She pulled a tray of bread from the oven and dug her cell out of her apron pocket. "Hello?"

"I hope I didn't wake you." It was her stepmother.

"No. I'm at work. I've been here for hours."

"You must be expecting a big day." Her stepmother sounded almost cheerful.

Right, a big day, she thought remembering her encounter with James not long after sunrise. If that was any indication of how this day was going to go…

"I saw that you called yesterday," her stepmother said when Lorelei hadn't commented. "Sweetheart, I'm sorry about the way we left things. I had to get away for a while." With her lover? Lorelei didn't want to know. "I think we should get together this evening and talk. I'll make dinner. I thought you could come over after work." Her stepmother sounded tentative. "Please, Lorelei. You're my daughter. I love you."

She felt herself weaken. "Fine. But I need you to be honest with me."

"I am being honest with you. I don't know why seeing James upset me, but it had nothing to with Billy Sherman." A lie, she thought. "I was just worried that you were getting involved with him." Another lie? "He's all wrong for you." Yet another lie?

Lorelei closed her eyes to the sudden tears. "I'll see you this evening." She disconnected, hating this. They used to be so close. She feared everything had changed. Her stepmother had hidden a married lover. But that might not be the worst of it.

As she went back to work, she remembered what James had told her. Terry Durham had been murdered. She couldn't remember the last murder in Lonesome—then with a start, realized it would have been Billy Sherman's hit-and-run. James said he'd found Terry's body. He'd been so upset. Because he felt he might have caused it by asking questions around town from his father's list of people like her stepmother?

She felt a chill even in the warm kitchen. What if the two murders were connected? Hadn't she heard something about Terry getting beaten up after he tried to cheat during a poker game in Billings? But what if Terry was murdered because he worked at the local body shop and knew who killed Billy Sherman?

The thought shook her to her core. What if Billy Sherman's killer had felt forced to kill again? At the sound of a trash can lid banging in the alley, she quickly moved to the back door to look out in time to see James.

When she'd seen him coming in disheveled and exhausted she'd jumped to the conclusion that he'd been out on the town with a woman. It was reasonable given his reputation, but still she felt bad about how quickly she'd judged him. She'd been so ready to add this onto her list of reasons she couldn't trust the man. With a curse, she realized he'd probably thought she'd been jealous.

"Did you get some sleep?" she asked from the doorway.

"Some. Sorry I was short with you earlier."

She shook her head as if it had been nothing. As he joined her, she caught the scent of soap and noticed that his hair was still wet from his shower. He smelled good, something she wished she hadn't noticed. His wet dark hair was black as a raven's wing in the sunlight. It curled at the nape of his neck, inviting her fingers to bury themselves in it, something else she wished she hadn't noticed.

"You wanted to talk to me?"

"You look like you could use a cup of coffee," she said, stalling. "I have a pot on. Interested?"

He hesitated but only a moment. "Sure." He followed her into the kitchen at the back and leaned against the counter, watching her. She could feel the intensity of his gaze on her. She felt all thumbs.

Fire him. Just do it. Like ripping off a Band-Aid. Thank him and then that will be it. You can pretend that you were never so serious as to do something so stupid as hire him to investigate your own stepmother in the first place.

When she turned, he was grinning at her in that lazy way he had, amusement glinting in the vast blue of his gaze. His long legs were stretched out practically to the center of the kitchen as he nonchalantly leaned against her counter. "You want me to help you?"

She thought he meant the coffee and started to say that she had it covered.

"You aren't going to hurt my feelings," he said. "I figured you've changed your mind about hiring me. I don't blame you. Sometimes it's better not to know. And when it's your own stepmother—"

She bristled. "I didn't say I don't want to know if she's involved."

One dark eyebrow arched up. "So, what is it you're having such a hard time saying to me?" he asked as he pushed off the counter and reached her in two long-legged strides.

Lorelei swallowed the lump that had risen in her throat. The scent of soap and maleness seemed to overpower even the aroma of the coffee. Suddenly the kitchen felt too small and cramped. Too intimate.

She stepped around him to the cupboard where she kept the large mugs, opened the door and took down two. Her hands were shaking. "I didn't say I was going to fire you."

"No?" He was right behind her. She could practically feel his warm breath on the back of her neck.

She quickly moved past him with the mugs and went over by the coffee pot.

She heard him chuckle behind her.

"Do I make you nervous?" he asked as she filled both mugs shakily. When she turned around, he was back on the other side of the kitchen, leaning against the counter again, grinning. "I do make you nervous." He laughed. "What is it you're afraid I'm going to do? Or are you afraid I'm *not* going do it?"

"Sometimes you just talk gibberish," she snapped. His grin broadened. "I want to know when you're going to do what I'm paying you to do."

"Paying me?"

She stepped toward him, shoved one mug full of coffee at him and waited impatiently for him to take it. She wished she'd never suggested coffee. The less time she spent around this impossible man the better. Right now, she wanted him out of her kitchen.

Seeing that he had no intention of going anywhere, she said, "We can talk in the dining room." With that she turned and exited the kitchen, her head up, chin out and her heart pounding. She told herself with every step that she hated this arrogant man. Why hadn't she fired him?

She slipped into a chair, cupping the mug in her hands, her attention on the steam rising from the hot coffee.

He slid into a chair opposite her and turned serious. "Let's face it, Lori. You don't want to know about your stepmother. So let's just forget it and—"

She reached into her pocket, pulled out the key and slapped it down on the Formica table. "That opens the back door to her house."

He stared at the key for a moment before he raised his gaze to her again. "You don't have to do this." She merely stared back, challenging him at the same time she feared she would change her mind. "Fine." He picked up the key and put it in his jeans pocket. Then he took a sip of his coffee.

"What does Terry Durham have to do with Billy's hit-and-run?" she asked.

He looked up in surprise. "I didn't say—"

"You didn't have to." She had a bad feeling that Terry's death had nothing to do with a poker game gone wrong.

"He works at the body shop. As you pointed out yourself, the vehicle that hit Billy would have some damage to it. How would you get it fixed without anyone being the wiser? Get it out of town quickly. Terry had a car-hauling trailer and now he's dead. Add to that, after the hit-and-run, Terry bought a piece of property and a small camper." James shrugged. "It's all conjecture at this point, but it stacks up. I start asking questions and now he's dead."

"What is it you'll look for at my stepmother's?"

"The person who owned the damaged car might have left a trail. Either a receipt from the body shop that fixed it. Or a lump sum withdrawal from a bank account to pay Terry off. But that's if they kept a record from nine years ago."

Her heart pounded. "Give me the key back."

He hesitated only a moment before he dug it out of his jeans and handed it over. "So, I'm fired."

Lorelei shook her head as she pocketed the key again. "No, I'm going with you." He started to put up an argument, but she cut him off. "It will be faster if I go. I know where she keeps her receipts, and her bank account records. Karen keeps everything. Come on," she said, pushing away her unfinished coffee. "She'll be at her studio now."

"You sure about this?" he asked.

"Not at all, but I can't do this alone and I have to know."

He met her gaze. "If what we find incriminates her, I won't cover it up even to protect you."

"You come with integrity?"

"It costs extra," he said to lighten the mood for a moment. "But seriously, if you want to change your mind, now's the time, Lori."

She didn't correct him. In fact, she was getting to where she liked her nickname, especially on his lips. "I'm serious too." She knew she couldn't live with the suspicion. "I have to know the truth before tonight. I'm having dinner at her house."

"Great," he said under his breath as he downed his coffee and rose from the table as she called a friend to come watch the shop.

Chapter Thirteen

James parked in the alley behind the house after circling the block. Karen Wilkins's car wasn't in the drive. Nor had there been any lights on in the house. He could feel Lorelei's anxiety.

He was about to suggest she stay in his pickup, when she opened her door and climbed out. Her expression was resigned. He could tell that she was doing this come hell or high water. She looked back at him, narrowing her eyes and he was smart enough not to argue.

Lori produced the key as they walked through the back-yard. The sky overhead was robin egg blue and cloudless, the air already warming with the summer sun. A meadow-lark sang a short refrain before they reached the back door.

He watched her take a breath as she unlocked the back door and they stepped in. "Does she keep an office here?"

With a nod, Lori led the way. The office was a spare bedroom with multipurpose use. There was a sewing machine and table and containers of fabric on one side. A bed in the middle and a small desk with a standing file cabinet next to it.

James headed for the filing cabinet only to find it locked. He looked at Lori who still hadn't spoken. He suspected she was having all kinds of misgivings about this but was too stubborn to stop it.

She opened the desk drawer and dug around for a few moments before she picked up a tiny wooden box that had been carved out of teak.

"My father gave her this." She opened the lid and with trembling fingers removed a tiny key and handed it to him.

He unlocked the top drawer and thumbed through the folders. Then he tried the second drawer. Karen's bank was still sending back the canceled checks nine years ago. He dug deeper and found small check boxes all labeled. She was certainly organized. He looked for personal checks from nine years ago, found the box, handed it to Lori. She sat down at the desk and began to go through them.

"You're looking for a check to Terry Durham or a towing company after Billy Sherman's hit-and-run so after April 10th," James said. "Also, a check to a body shop in another town." She nodded and set to work.

He found Karen's monthly account statement in the third drawer and quickly began to sort through them looking for a large withdrawal after April 10 from nine years ago. He'd just found what he was looking for when he heard a car door slam.

They both froze. "I thought you said she was working," he whispered.

"She was supposed to be. Maybe it isn't her."

James heard a key in the front door lock. "It's her." He grabbed the months he needed of the checking account documents and carefully closed the file drawer. He saw Lorelei pocket a handful of checks and slip the box into the top drawer as he motioned toward the closet.

He opened the door as quietly as possible. It sounded as if Karen had gone to one of the bedrooms on the other side of the house. The closet was full of fabric and craft supplies. There was just enough room for the two of them if they squished together. He eased the closet door closed as the sound of footfalls headed in their direction.

A moment later Karen came into the room. He heard her stop as if she'd forgotten what she'd come in for. Or as if she sensed something amiss? He tried to remember if they had left anything out that could give them away. He didn't think so. But if she opened the desk drawer she would see the check box. As neat and organized as she was, she would know.

He held his breath. He could feel Lori, her body spooned into his, doing the same. Her hair smelled like a spring rain. He could feel the heat of her, the hard and soft places fitting into some of his. He tried to think about baseball.

With relief, he heard Karen leave the room. The front door slammed and he finally let out the breath he'd been holding. A few moments later, a car engine started up. James waited until the sound died away before he carefully opened the closet door.

Lori stepped out, straightening her clothing, looking flushed.

"Sorry about that," he said, his voice sounding hoarse. She pretended she didn't know what he was talking about, which was fine with him. "Let's finish and get out of here."

He went through the bank statements and then Karen's retirement papers. That's when he found it. A large withdrawal of ten thousand dollars.

"Lori?" He realized that she hadn't moved for a moment. She was staring down at a canceled check in her hand. All the color had drained from her face. "What is it?" Without a word, she handed him the check.

The check had been made out to the bank for ten thousand dollars. He flipped it over and saw that the money had been deposited into Lori's account. "I don't understand."

"Nine years ago I looked into getting a loan to open a

sandwich shop," she said, her voice breaking. "The bank turned me down. My stepmother had offered to cosign on the loan but I didn't want her risking it if I failed. I had no experience."

"And then you did get the loan," he said.

She nodded. "The president of the bank called, said he noticed I had applied for the loan and that he knew me and was willing to take a chance on me. He lied. It was all my stepmother."

She looked as if she might burst into tears at any moment as she put the check back in the box and opened the file cabinet to put the box away. He watched her relock the file cabinet and put the key back where she'd found it and close the desk drawer.

"I can imagine what you're feeling right now," he finally said.

"Can you?" She turned to face him. "I didn't trust my stepmother. I hired you and then I sneaked in here with you looking for dirt on her. Did we find anything? No. Instead, I find out that she took money out of her retirement to help me open my sandwich shop, the woman I've been at odds with for days because of you."

He didn't feel that was fair, but was smart enough not to say so. "I'm sorry. But we didn't find anything." Instead, he'd found a large withdrawal from a retirement plan but not to cover a crime. "No checks to Terry Durham or a body shop." He held up his hands. "So good news."

She merely glared at him before she pushed past him and headed out the back door. He double-checked the room to make sure they hadn't left anything behind and followed. By the time he reached the pickup, she was nowhere to be seen.

He climbed behind the wheel and waited for a few minutes, but realized his first thought was probably the right one. She'd rather walk back than ride with him. He started the engine and drove out of the alley.

Another great day as a private investigator, he thought with disgust.

CORA SWORE SHE had a sixth sense these days. She'd been in the living room knitting while she watched her favorite television drama when she had an odd feeling. Putting aside her knitting and pausing her show, she went into the kitchen and picked up her binoculars.

These special night vision binoculars had paid for themselves the first night she got them. It truly was amazing what a person could see especially since she lived on a rise over the river.

First she scanned the river road. Only one car parked out there tonight and she recognized it. The same couple that often parked out there on a weekday night. She thought for a moment, wondering if there was any way she could benefit from this knowledge and deciding not, scanned farther downriver.

Tonight not even a bunch of teenagers were drunk around a beer keg. Slow night, she thought, wondering why she'd thought something was going on.

Out of habit, she turned the binoculars on the Colt place. At first she didn't see anything since she wasn't really expecting to—until she saw a pickup coming through the woods on the Colt property with no headlights on. Had she heard the driver pull in? Or did she really have a sixth sense for this sort of thing?

She wondered as she watched the pickup stop on the spot where the burned-out trailer had once stood. James Colt? She waited for the driver to exit the rig. Western hat and a definite swagger, she thought, but she couldn't see the face because he kept his head down.

Following him with the binoculars, she watched as he went around to the back of his pickup and took out a box. It must have been heavy because he seemed to strain under the weight. To her surprise, he carried the box over to where the debris from the burned-out double-wide had been. He hesitated, then put down the box before going back to the pickup. He returned with a small shovel.

She watched, transfixed as he began to dig a hole into which he dumped whatever was in the box. Then he shoveled the blackened earth over the hole.

Shoving back his hat to wipe a forearm across his brow, Cora got her first good look at his face. She felt a start as she recognized him.

Her hand began to sweat because suddenly she was holding the binoculars so tightly, her heart racing in her chest. She watched former sheriff Otis Osterman carry his shovel and the empty box back to the pickup. A moment later he drove off.

LORELEI FELT ASHAMED and guilty and not just because of her stepmother. She'd blamed James for all this when she'd been the one who'd hired him. How could she possibly think her stepmother was involved in Billy Sherman's death? Worse, that her stepmother would try to cover it up? She hated too that she'd felt a wave of relief when they hadn't found anything incriminating. Had she been that worried that they would? She was a horrible stepdaughter. She promised herself that she would make it up to Karen.

The walk back to the shop helped. Fortunately, the moment she entered her kitchen, she had work to do. Anita had a lot done, but there was still more bread to be made before she opened at 11:00 a.m. She thanked Anita, paid her and sent her on home, needing work more today than ever.

When she'd come in the back way, she'd been thankful that James's pickup wasn't anywhere around. She recalled the two of them in the closet, her body pressed into his, and felt her face flush hot as she remembered his obvious...desire. Fortunately, he hadn't been able to feel her reaction to it. At least she hoped not.

"Lorelei?"

She spun around in surprise to see Karen standing in the kitchen doorway. She really needed to start locking the back door.

"Are you all right? You're flushed," her stepmother said as she quickly stepped to her, putting a hand on Lorelei's forehead.

"I'm baking bread and it's hot in here."

Her stepmother looked skeptical but let it go. "I hope you don't mind me stopping by."

She wiped her hands on her apron. "I'm glad you did."

"I know you're busy but I didn't want to do this over the phone. I'm afraid I have to cancel our plans for dinner tonight. I'm sorry. Something's come up."

Lorelei raised a brow, sick to the pit of her stomach at how quickly her suspicions had come racing back. "I hope it's nothing bad."

"No." Her stepmother looked away. "Just a prior engagement I completely forgot about." Lorelei nodded. "So, we'll reschedule in a few days." Karen let out a nervous laugh. "You and I are so busy."

"Aren't we though," she said, hoping the remark didn't come out as sarcastic as it felt. Her stepmother wasn't acting like herself. It wasn't Lorelei's imagination. She wanted to throw her arms around her and hug her although she couldn't thank her for the personal loan without telling her that she'd gone through her checks.

But at the same time, she wanted to demand her stepmother tell her the truth about what was going on. No matter what, she couldn't keep lying to herself. Something was definitely going on with her stepmother besides the affair.

"I'll call you." Her stepmother headed out of the kitchen.

"Mom!" Lorelei's voice broke. "Be careful."

Karen looked surprised for a moment. "You too, dear."

JAMES FELT AS if he'd been spinning his wheels. He knew no more about Billy Sherman's death than he had when he started this. Now he'd alienated someone he had been growing quite fond of since his return to town.

As he was passing a house in the older section of town, he recognized the senior gentleman working in his yard. James pulled up in front of the neat two-story Craftsman with its wide white front porch. Getting out, he walked toward the man.

Dr. Milton Stanley looked up, a pair of hedge clippers in his hands. His thick white eyebrows raised slightly under small dark eyes. "You're a Colt."

He nodded. "James."

"You look like your father."

"My father's why I stopped when I saw you. Could we talk for a minute? I don't want to keep you from your work."

"I was ready for a break anyway." Milton laid down his clippers, took off his gardening gloves and motioned toward the house. "Take a seat on the porch. I'll get us something to drink."

James followed the man as far as the porch and waited. He could hear the doctor inside the house. Opening and closing the refrigerator. The clink of glass against glass. The sound of ice cubes rattling.

A few minutes later, the screen door swung open with a creak and Milton reappeared. He handed James a tall glass of iced lemonade and motioned to two of the white-painted wooden rockers. Each had a bright-colored cushion. James could imagine the doctor and his wife sitting out here often—before her death.

They sat. James sipped his lemonade, complimented it and asked, "You were coroner when my father was killed. I need to know if you ran tests to see if he was impaired."

The doctor drained half of his lemonade before setting down the glass on one of the coasters on the small round end table between them. James watched him wipe his damp hands on his khaki pants.

Milton frowned. "Why are you asking this?"

"Because of the case he was working on at the time of his death. It was ruled an accident by the sheriff, but I've since learned some things that make me think he might have been murdered."

"Murdered?"

"I'm not sure how, but I've only been working my father's old case a few days and already someone I wanted to talk to has been killed," James said. "I've always questioned my father's death but never more so than now. I've learned that he was close to solving Billy Sherman's hit-and-run."

The doctor frowned. "There was no alcohol or drugs in your father's system at the time of his death."

James blinked, swamped with a wave of relief. "None?"

"None."

The relief though only lasted a moment. "Then how did it happen?" Why didn't he get out of the pickup before the train hit him? Surely, he saw the flashing lights. Did he think he could beat the train? That wasn't like his father. Del was deliberate. He didn't take chances.

Milton shook his head. "Any number of things could have led to it. He might have had something on his mind and didn't notice the flashing lights. The train hit him on the driver's side. He might not have had time to get out. The pickup engine could have stalled. He could have panicked. You can't see that train because of the curve until it's almost on top of you. Your father's accident wasn't the first one at that spot. The railroad really needs to put in crossing arms." He picked up his lemonade and drained the rest of it.

James drank his and placed the empty glass on a coaster on the table. He could tell the doctor was anxious to get back to his gardening. "Thank you for your help."

"I'm not sure I was much help," Milton said and followed him as far as the yard. The doctor picked up his clippers and went back to work.

CORA STEWED. HER favorite television drama couldn't even take her mind off what she'd seen. She tried to work it out in her mind. That was the problem. She wasn't even sure what she'd seen—just that Otis Osterman hadn't wanted to be caught doing whatever it was. Of that she was sure.

Putting her knitting aside again, she picked up her cell phone and muted the television. She let the number ring until she got voice mail. Then she called back. It took four times, one right after the other, before the former sheriff finally picked up.

"What the hell do you want, Cora?" he demanded.

"I bought myself one of those video recorders."

"What?"

"I was trying to learn how to use it and I accidentally videoed the darnedest thing. *You.* You're right there on my video."

"What. Are. You. Talking. About?"

"I couldn't figure out why you would be on the Colt property, let alone why you would dump a box of something into the ashes where the Colt's burned-out trailer had been, let alone why you would then cover it up with that little shovel you keep in your pickup."

She listened to him breathing hard and knew that she'd struck pay dirt. "I'm thinking James Colt would be interested in seeing my little video. Heck, I suspect he'd pay good money given how he feels about you. Trespassing and so much more. So how much do you think my video is worth? Maybe I should just take it to the FBI."

Otis swore and Cora smiled. She could tell by the low growl on the other end of the line that she had him. She didn't care what he'd planted on Colt property. It was no skin off her nose. But she could certainly use a little supplemental income.

"You addled old woman. I don't know what you think you saw—"

"That's why I'm having this young person I met put the video up on the internet. Technology is really something these days. I bet someone has a theory about what you were doing, don't you? Even your brother the sheriff won't be able to sweep this under the rug—not after I make sure everyone knows the man in the video is a former sheriff. That should make it go viral, whatever that is. My new young friend assures me it's good though."

"Maybe I should come out to your place and we should discuss this," Otis said through what sounded like clenched teeth.

"I wouldn't suggest that. I get jumpy at night and you know I keep my shotgun handy. I'd feel terrible if I shot you."

"What do you want?" he demanded angrily.

"Five thousand dollars."

Otis let out a string of curses. "I don't have that kind of money."

"Well, not *on* you. You'll have to go to the bank and when you do, you tell them you borrowed money from me and want to pay it back. Just have them put it into my account. It's a small town. They'll do it. As soon as I get confirmation, I'll drop the video by your cabin. Maybe you'll have something cold for us to drink."

He growled again. "How do I know you won't make copies and demand more money?"

"Shame on you, Otis. They do say crooks are often the most suspicious people. I wouldn't have a clue how to make a copy."

"I want the camera too."

"Well, now that's just rude. I'm still learning how to use it. But I'll bring it when I bring the video. We can discuss it. With that night vision thing, the camera won't be cheap. Tomorrow then. Have the bank call me. Look forward to seeing you, Otis." She laughed. "In person. I've already seen enough of you in the movies." She laughed harder and disconnected.

Then she went to check her shotgun to make sure it was loaded, putting extra shells in her pocket, before she locked and bolted all the doors.

Chapter Fourteen

When James returned to the office, he saw that it appeared someone was waiting for him. A bike leaned against his building in the alley with a young boy of about sixteen sitting on a milk crate next to it.

As he got out of his truck, the boy rose looking nervous. "Can I help you?" James asked.

"Are you the PI?"

He smiled. "I guess I am."

"I need to talk to you." He looked around to make sure there wasn't anyone else around. "It's about Billy."

In that instant, he realized who this boy must be. "Todd?" The boy nodded. "Does your mom know you're here?" The boy shook his head. "I'm not really supposed to talk to you without a parent present." Then again, he wasn't a licensed PI yet, was he?

"But I'll tell you what," he said quickly seeing the boy's disappointment. The kid had been waiting patiently. He couldn't turn him away especially when Todd might have valuable information. He glanced at the time. "What if we have another adult present who can advise you?"

Todd looked worried. "Who?"

"Hungry?" He asked the boy, remembering himself at that age. His father used to ask if he had a hollow wooden leg. Where else was all that food going?

Todd nodded but then hesitated. "What about my bike?"

"It's safe there." James pushed open the back door into the sandwich shop. Once that smell of fresh bread hit the kid there was no more hesitation.

LORELEI SAW JAMES first and started to tell him he was the last person she wanted to see—when she spotted the boy with him. Her gaze went from the boy to James in question.

"This is Todd. He's hungry." James turned to the kid. "What kind of sandwich would you like?"

"I suppose you don't have a hot dog?" the boy asked her sheepishly.

"Let me see what I can do. Would you like some lemonade with that?" The boy nodded and actually smiled. Her gaze rose to James.

He shook his head since he didn't have a clue what was going on. "We'll just have a seat. We're hoping you can join us. Todd wants to have a talk with us."

"With *us*?"

"You're going to be the adult in the group," James said.

She smirked. "I always am."

He smiled. "I knew I'd picked the right woman for the job. Mind if I go ahead and lock the front door while we talk so we aren't interrupted?" He didn't wait but went to the door and put up the closed sign and locked the door.

She did mind, even though it was past closing time. What was this man getting her into? She made Todd a mild sausage sandwich with a side of ketchup and mustard and poured three lemonades before bringing them out on a tray to the table. She put Todd's in front of him.

"So, what's this about?" she asked as she slid into the booth next to the boy. Todd had already bitten into his sandwich. He gave her a thumbs-up as he chewed.

"Todd was waiting for me behind my office. He wanted

to talk to the PI." She raised a brow. "I explained to him that we probably shouldn't talk without an adult present. It's kind of a gray area."

Lorelei shook her head. "I'm not sure I want to be part of this."

"I have to tell him about Billy," Todd said, putting down his half-eaten sandwich. He took a drink of lemonade. "I know what my mom told you when you came over to see her. She forgot that I did have Billy's other walkie-talkie headset that night and that after that, she threw it away."

"You and Billy talked on the two-way radios the night he died?"

Todd nodded, looking solemn.

"About what time was that?" James asked.

"He woke me up. The electricity had gone off but I looked at my Spiderman watch. It was almost ten thirty. I told him not to do it."

James shot her a look before shifting his gaze back to the boy. "Do what?"

"He said he had to go out. That he'd seen someone walk by his house in the rain and that he needed to follow whoever it was."

"His mom told me that Billy didn't like storms," James said. "Why would he go out and follow someone?"

He picked up his sandwich, took a large bite and chewed for a moment before swallowing. "Billy and I had this game we played. We pretended we were spies. We used to pick someone to follow. It was fun. They usually heard us behind them and chased us off. But sometimes we could follow them a really long way before they did."

"Who was he following that night?" James asked.

Todd shook his head. "He said he had to see what they were doing before he chickened out. I told him not to.

He said the person was headed down the street in my direction and that I should watch for him and come out. I watched from the window, but I never saw him and then I fell asleep. I just figured he chickened out, like he said. Or his mom made him go to bed and quit using the walkie-talkies."

"How did you pick the people you followed?" James asked.

The boy shrugged. "Sometimes we would just see someone who looked dangerous."

"Dangerous?" Lorelei repeated.

"Sometimes we just wondered where they were going, so we followed them."

"So, Billy just saw someone out the window and decided to go out into the storm to follow them?" she asked, unable to hide her incredulity.

"I guess. It might have been someone he'd been following before that."

"Was it a man or a woman?" Lorelei asked.

"Billy said, 'I just saw someone outside my window. I have to follow and find out what they're doing.' He sounded…scared." The boy looked down at his almost empty plate. "When I heard you asking my mom about Billy, I knew I had to tell you." He bit into what was left of his sandwich and went to work on it.

"Does your mom know about the call from Billy?"

The boy shook his head adamantly. "Billy and I took a blood oath not to ever tell our parents about our spy operations. But I think she was worried that I told Billy to go out that night and that everyone would blame me. I didn't. I swear. I tried to stop him." Todd's eyes shone with tears. Lorelei watched him swallow before he said, "I think he would have wanted me to tell you."

"Thank you, Todd. I'm glad you did," James said.

Lorelei touched the boy's shoulder. "You did the right thing."

He nodded, swallowed a few times and ate the last bite of his sandwich.

She looked across the table at James. He held her gaze until she felt a shudder at what they'd just heard and had to look away.

Chapter Fifteen

"Are you okay?" James asked Lori after Todd left. He'd helped her clear the table, then followed her back into the kitchen.

"Fine," she said, her back to him.

"I forgot about your dinner with your stepmother tonight. I'm sorry. I hope I'm not making you late."

She turned in his direction, avoiding eye contact. "She cancelled. Something came up." He said nothing. Finally, she looked at him. "She's scaring me."

He nodded. "But maybe it has nothing to do with Billy Sherman. At least now we know why Billy went out that night. We just don't know who he was following or why." He sighed. "I'm sorry. I feel like I never should have started this." She didn't exactly disagree with her silence.

"Hey," he said. "How do you feel about a big juicy rib eye out at the steak house? I'm buying."

She smiled and he could tell that she was about to decline when his cell rang. He held up a finger, drew out his phone and, seeing who was calling, said, "I need to take this. Hello?"

"Mr. Colt?"

He smiled to himself. No one called him Mr. Colt. "Yes?"

"My name is Connie Sue Matthews. I heard you have

taken over your father's private investigations firm and that you've been asking questions about Billy Sherman's death."

"That's right."

"You probably know I was the one who found the body that morning. Could I stop by your office? I know it's after hours, but it's the only time I'm free this week. I might have some information for you." She lowered her voice. "I don't want to get into it on the phone."

He shot a look at Lori. He'd been looking forward to that steak but had really been looking forward to dinner with her. He hesitated only a moment, hoping Lori would understand. If this woman had any information for him... "You know where my office is?"

"Yes, I can be there in a few minutes."

"Use the back entrance. I'll see you then." He disconnected and looked across the room at Lori. Only moments before he was mentally kicking himself for digging into his father's unsolved case and here he was cancelling his dinner plans because of it. What was wrong with him? "I'm afraid I'm going to have to postpone that dinner invitation."

"Bad news?" she asked, looking genuinely concerned.

"No, maybe just the opposite." He could only hope.

CORA SAT IN the house, the shotgun lying across her lap. All the lights were out and there was no sound except when the refrigerator turned on in the kitchen occasionally. She'd always been a patient woman. She'd put up with her no-account husband for almost fifty years. She could sit here all night if she had to.

But she knew she wouldn't have to. She knew Otis Osterman. He was a hothead without a lot upstairs. He'd stop by tonight and she would be waiting.

The fool would be mad, filled with indignation that

she'd called him out. He wouldn't be thinking clearly. She reminded herself to make sure he died in the house after he broke in. She didn't want any trouble with the law—especially Otis's baby brother, Carl. But an old woman like herself had every right to defend her life—and her property.

Otis should have taken her deal. He'd regret it. If he lived that long.

And to think back in grade school she'd had a crush on him. He'd been cute back then, blond with freckles and two missing front teeth. She shook her head at the memory. That was before high school when she found out firsthand about his mean streak. But she'd taken care of it—just as she'd taken care of everything else all these years. If he came around tonight, this time he would leave with more than a scar to remember her by. Or not leave alive at all.

CONNIE MATTHEWS WAS a small immaculate-looking woman in her late fifties. She was clearly nervous as she stepped into his office. He'd had just enough time to pick up the room and close the door to the bedroom before she'd arrived.

She sat on the edge of one of the leather club chairs, her purse gripped in her lap as he sat behind his father's desk. Idly he wondered how long it would take for him to think of this office as his own.

"You said you might have information on Billy Sherman's death?"

Connie looked even more uncomfortable. "Those boys, Billy and that Crane boy. I found them hiding in my bushes one day. They were always sneaking around, getting into trouble, stomping down my poor flowers. One day I caught them going through my garbage! Can you imagine? Billy said they were looking for clues. *Clues.* Clues to what, I'd demanded. And the Crane boy said, 'We know what you've been doing.' Then they laughed and ran off."

It sounded like typical boy stuff to James. He hated to think of some of the shenanigans he and his brothers had pulled. "Did you tell my father about this when he interviewed you?" James knew it wasn't in his father's notes.

She shook her head. "It seemed silly at the time because that young boy had lost his life. But what was he doing out in that storm in the middle of the night in his pajamas?"

"Since your house is the closest to where he was found, did you notice anyone outside that night? Hear anything?" He already knew the answer. *That* was in his father's notes. But Todd said that his friend was following someone.

"No, but I went to bed early. I don't like storms. I took some sleeping pills and didn't wake up until the next morning. By then the storm was over."

"What about your husband?"

"What about him?" Connie asked frowning.

"I wondered if he might have mentioned seeing anyone, hearing anything."

She shook her head. "George went to bed when I did so I'm sure he would have mentioned it, if he had seen someone or heard anything, don't you think? That's a busy road. Gotten even busier with all the houses that have come up. The mayor lives in the new section and I suppose you know that Senator Bayard lives just down the road from our place." She seemed to puff up a little.

That road was an old one used by a lot of residents who lived out that way. The subdivision had grown in the past nine years.

"Was there something more?" he asked. On the phone she'd sounded as if she might have new information. That didn't seem to be the case and yet she was still sitting across from him, still looking nervous and anxious. He waited, something he'd seen his father do during an interview.

"I hate to even bring this up, but I feel I was remiss by not doing it nine years ago," Connie finally said. "I think someone abducted that boy from his bed. Because what boy in his right mind would go out in a storm like that?" she demanded, clearly warming to the subject. "And I know who did it. It was the father." At his confused look, she said, "The *boy's* father, that ne'r-do-well, Sean Sherman. Weren't he and his wife arguing over the boy in the divorce? I think Sean snatched him out of his bed that night. That's why the mother didn't hear anything. The boy would have gone willingly with his own father otherwise he would have raised a ruckus, don't you think?"

"That is one theory. I wonder though how Billy ended up getting run over just blocks from his house?"

"Maybe the boy changed his mind, decided he didn't want to go with him and jumped out of the car. It would be just like his drugged-up father to run over the boy and then panic and take off."

James pretended to take notes, which seemed to please the woman. "I'll look into that," he told her, and she rose to leave, looking relieved.

"I wasn't sure if I should say anything or not," Connie said. "But you haven't been around much so you don't know a lot about this town and the people who live in it. I thought you should know." She let out a breath, nodded and headed for the door where she stopped to look back at him. "I'd be careful if I were you though. If Sean Sherman killed that boy, he thinks he's gotten away with it for nine years." She nodded again as if that said it all, but seemed compelled to add, "I hired Sean one time to do some landscaping. He made a mess of it. When I refused to pay him…" She shuddered. "The man has a terrible temper. He's dangerous."

"Thank you, Mrs. Matthews."

"I believe in doing my civic duty," she said primly and left.

CORA HEARD THE sound of shattering glass in the basement of her small house and smiled. Otis was just too predictable. What was he thinking he was going to do anyway? Kill her? The thought made her laugh. He was a nasty little bugger, but she couldn't see him committing murder. No, he'd come out here to scare her.

She shifted the shotgun in her lap and waited. Her chair was in a corner where she would see him when he came upstairs. She could hear him moving around down there. After tonight, Otis was going to replace that window he'd broken and anything else she wanted done around here.

Over the years, she'd collected a few people who were indebted to her after she'd caught them in some nefarious act. Some paid her monthly, others paid in favors. She didn't like to think of it as blackmail. She preferred to call it penitence for misdeeds done. She never asked for more than a person could afford.

But she didn't like Otis. She would make him pay dearly—if she didn't shoot him on sight.

Her cell phone rang, startling her. She glanced at the time. Almost one in the morning. The phone rang again—and she realized no sound was now coming from the basement.

"Hello?" she whispered into the phone, planning to give whoever was calling a piece of her mind for interrupting her at this hour.

"I got your money," Otis said. "I'll put it in your account

tomorrow. Why are you whispering?" He chuckled. "Oh, I hope I didn't wake you up."

She could hear what sounded like bar noise in the background. "Where are you?" she demanded.

"At Harry's as if that is any of your damned business," he snapped and disconnected.

She stared at the phone for a moment. Then she heard again a sound coming from the basement. Her blood ran cold. If Otis wasn't down there, then who was? Cora felt fear coil around her as she heard a sound she recognized.

A moment later, she smelled the smoke.

Chapter Sixteen

James was awakened some time in the night by the sound of sirens. Sheriff's department patrol SUVs and several fire trucks sped down Main Street and kept going until the sirens died away. He'd rolled over and gone back to sleep until his cell phone rang just after 7:00 a.m.

"Did you hear about the fire?" his friend Ryan asked. "That old busybody crossed the wrong person this time. Cora says someone set her house on fire, but I heard the sheriff's trying to pin it on her. Arson."

"You've heard all this already this morning?"

"The men's coffee clutch down at the cafe. You should join us. It's a lot of the old gang along with some of the old men in town. Pretty interesting stuff most mornings."

James shook his head and told himself he wouldn't be staying in town that long. His leg was better, and his ribs didn't hurt with every breath. It was progress. "Thanks for the invite," he said. "I'll keep it in mind."

"How is the investigation going?"

He was saved from answering as he got another call. "Sorry, I'm getting another call. Talk to you later?" He didn't wait for an answer as he accepted the call. At first all he heard was coughing, an awful hack that he didn't recognize. "Hello?" he repeated.

"I want to hire you." The words came out strained between coughs. "Someone tried to burn me alive in my own house last night."

"Cora?" The last time she'd said more than a few words to him, she'd been chasing him and his brothers away from her apple trees with a shotgun.

In between coughs, she said, "You're a private detective, aren't you?"

"Isn't the sheriff investigating?" he asked, sitting up to rub a hand over his face. It was too early in the morning for this.

"Carl? That old reprobate!" He waited through a coughing fit. "He thinks I set the fire, that's how good an investigator he is. I put myself in the hospital and burned down my own house? Idiot." More coughing. "You owe me, James Colt, for all the times you and your brothers trespassed in my yard and stole my apples."

He wanted to point out that she'd had more apples than she could ever use and let them waste every year. But they *were* her apples.

"The least you can do is prove that I didn't start the fire. Otherwise, the sheriff is talking putting me behind bars."

"I'll look into it," he said, all the time mentally kicking himself.

"Good. Don't overcharge me."

James disconnected. He lay down again, but he knew there was no chance he could get back to sleep. After Connie Matthews had left last night, he'd hoped Lori was still around. She wasn't so he'd gone out and gotten himself some fast food and then driven to Billy Sherman's neighborhood.

From there, he'd walked toward the spot where the boy had died. He'd tried to imagine doing the same thing in a violent thunderstorm at the age of seven. Whoever Billy had seen couldn't have been some random person like anyone he and Todd normally followed. The boy must have recognized the person. But then why hadn't he mentioned a name to Todd? Or maybe there was something about the person that had lured him out into the storm. James couldn't imagine what it could have been.

An image from a movie during his own childhood popped into his head of a clown holding a string with a bright-colored balloon floating overhead. It had given him nightmares for weeks. A kid afraid of the dark and storms wouldn't go after a clown—especially one with a balloon.

LORELEI HAD DRIVEN past her stepmother's house last night only to see all the lights were out and her car wasn't in the garage. She'd been tempted to drive out to the senator's house to see if she was there. Earlier this evening on the news she'd heard that the senator and his wife were officially divorcing.

"They reported that they've been separated for some time now and believe it is best if they end the marriage," the newscaster had said. *"Senator Bayard said the divorce is amicable and that he wishes only the best for Mary."*

It had sounded as if Mary was the one who'd wanted the separation and divorce. Maybe she had. Maybe Lorelei had been too hard on her stepmother.

The news had ended with a mention of Bayard being called back to Washington on some subcommittee work he was doing. She wondered how true that was. Maybe Fred and her stepmother had flown off somewhere together to celebrate the divorce.

What bothered Lorelei was that her stepmother felt the need to lie to her. Or at the very least not to be honest with her. Like providing the loan for the sandwich shop. Like falling in love without telling her. While Lorelei didn't approve of her stepmother's affair, she wanted her to be happy. She hated the strain in their relationship and promised herself that she would do what she could to fix it when she saw Karen again.

After a restless night, she'd gotten up and gone to work as usual. As she pulled in behind the shop to park, James was standing by the back door of his office grinning.

"My license came today. It's official—I'm a private investigator."

"Congratulations. You'll have to frame it and put it up on your wall."

"I know it seems silly being excited about it, but I am. It makes me feel legit. I also have a new client." She raised a brow. "I'll tell you all about it over dinner. I thought we'd go out and celebrate. I owe you a steak." She started to argue, but he stopped her with a warm hand on her bare arm. "Please? You wouldn't make me celebrate alone, would you?"

She knew he could make a call to any number of women who would jump at a steak dinner date with him. When she'd awakened this morning, she'd promised herself that she would see her stepmother tonight—if her stepmother was in town.

James waved the license in the air and grinned. "How can a Montana girl like you say no to a slab of grain-fed beef grilled over a hot fire?"

Lorelei laughed in spite of her sometime resolve to keep James Colt at arm's length. "Fine. What time?"

JAMES COULDN'T HELP smiling as he drove out to Cora's. Lori had agreed to have dinner with him. He hadn't been this excited about a date in... Heck, he wasn't sure he ever had been. That should have worried him, he realized.

Cora's house had sat on a hill. Smoke was still rising

up through the pine trees and into the blue summer sky as he pulled in.

After parking, he got out of his truck and walked over to the firefighters still putting out the last of the embers. One of the fears of living in the pine trees was always fire. But the firefighters had been able to contain the blaze from spreading into the pines. The small old house though seemed to be a total loss.

"I'm looking for the arson investigator," James said and was pointed to a man wearing a mask and gloves and a Montana State University Bobcats baseball cap digging around in the ashes.

"I'm Private Detective James Colt," he said introducing himself.

The man gave him a glance and continued digging. "Colt? That your property next door?"

"Yep."

"A lot of recent fires out here." He rose to his feet and extended a gloved hand before drawing it back to wipe soot onto his pants. "Sorry about that. Gil Sanders."

James couldn't help his surprise. "Gilbert Sanders?" he asked, remembering seeing the name on his father's list. But why would his father be interested in talking to an arson investigator as part of Billy Sherman's hit-and-run?

"Have we met before?" Gil asked, studying him. "You look familiar."

"My father, PI Del Colt, might have contacted you about another investigation."

The man frowned. "Sorry. Can you be more specific?"

"He was investigating the hit-and-run death of a local boy about nine years ago."

Gil shook his head. "You're sure it was me he spoke with?"

"Maybe not." Now that James thought about it, there hadn't been any notes from the interview in his father's file. "I'm here about another matter. Cora Brooks called me this morning. Anything new on the fire?"

"It was definitely arson. The blaze was started in the basement. The accelerant was gasoline. It burned hot and fast. She was lucky to get out alive."

James nodded. "The sheriff seemed to think Cora started the fire herself."

The investigator shook his head. "I've already reviewed the statements from the first responders. The property owner was in a robe and slippers carrying a shotgun and a pair of binoculars. That's all she apparently managed to save. She couldn't have outrun that fire if she started it. Not in those slippers. I'm told she is in her right mind."

"Sharp and lethal as a new filet knife."

Gil chuckled. "She told first responders that she'd heard someone breaking into her basement. That's why she had her shotgun. Not sure why the binoculars were so important to her, but I don't see any way a woman her age could have started the fire in the basement and hightailed it upstairs to an outside deck. Not with as much gas as was used downstairs. I'm not even sure she can lift the size gas can that was found."

Cora was apparently in the clear. "Thank you. If I figure out why I saw your name in my father's case file…"

"Just give me a call. But unless it pertains to a fire, I can't imagine why he had wanted to talk to me."

James shook the man's hand and nodded at Gil's cap. "Go Bobcats," he said and headed back to his pickup. Too bad all his PI cases weren't this easy, he thought. He headed for the hospital to give Cora the good news. This one was on him, no charge. He knew she'd like the sound of that.

OTIS STUMBLED TO his cabin door hungover, half-asleep and ticked off. Whoever was pounding on his door was going to regret it.

"What the hell did you do?" his brother Carl demanded, pushing past him and into the cabin. The sheriff turned to look at him and swore. "On second thought, I don't want to know."

"If this is about that fire out at Cora's—"

"What else? I saw you yesterday. You were going on about the woman and last night her house burns down." Carl raised a hand. "There's an arson investigator out there. I told him that I think Cora did it for the insurance money, but he sure as the devil isn't going to take my word for it."

"I didn't do it." Otis stepped past him to open the refrigerator. He needed the hair of the dog that bit him last night. Pulling out a can of beer he popped the top, took a long drink and looked at his brother.

"How deep are you in all this?" Carl demanded.

"I did something stupid."

His brother groaned. "I wouldn't be here if I didn't suspect that was the case."

"I took something out to the Colt place. I was going to make an anonymous call and let you find it. I know you'd like to get that arrogant little turd behind bars as much as I would."

The sheriff swore. "Tell me it isn't anything explosive. You get anyone killed—"

"No, just some illegal stuff. Doesn't matter now. I'll get it hauled away. It was stupid. Then Cora saw me, said she made a video of me dumping it…" He hung his head again.

"Otis, swear to me you didn't burn down Cora's house."

The former sheriff looked up, his expression one of disbelief and hurt. "I was at the bar. You can check. I was there until closing. Even better about the time it was catching fire, I called Cora from the bar. See I have an alibi so I'm gold."

His brother swore.

"What's wrong? There will be a record of the call—just before I heard the sirens. So it couldn't have been me."

Carl told himself that his brother had been at the bar to establish that alibi, which meant Otis had hired someone to set fire to the place. He wished he didn't know his brother so well. "If it wasn't you, any idea who might have wanted Cora dead?"

Otis chuckled. "Anyone who's ever crossed her path."

"Let's just hope Gil Sanders doesn't find any evidence out there that would make him think you had anything to do with this."

CORA TOOK THE news as would be expected. She nodded, told James he'd better not send her a bill and ordered him out of her room.

A near-death experience didn't change everyone apparently, he thought as he left chuckling.

He was still wondering if the Gilbert Sanders on his father's list was the arson investigator and if so what Del thought the man could offer on the hit-and-run case.

Meanwhile, he tracked down Sean Sherman. His call went straight to voice mail. He left a message asking Sean to call him and hung up. Sherman lived in a town not far from Lonesome. If he had to, James would drive over and pay the man a visit.

With that done, he considered his father's list again. Connie Matthews had said something in her original interview with his father that kept bothering him. Lyle Harris had been operating the front-end loader the morning Connie had seen the body and stopped him from covering it up.

James knew it was a long shot. His father had already

talked to the man and there wasn't anything in his notes that sent up a red flag. But he was running out of people to interview and getting worried that he'd missed something important.

At forty-five, Lyle Harris had quit his job with the local contractor after a work comp accident that had put him in a wheelchair. As James pulled up out front of his place deep in the woods, he noticed the ramp from the house through the carport to the garage. He recalled Ryan telling him that he'd donated the lumber and the men Lyle used to work with had donated their time to make the house more wheelchair accessible.

After parking, he got out and walked toward the house, changing directions as he heard the whine of an electric saw coming from the garage.

"Lyle!" he called. "Lyle, it's James Colt!" The sound of the saw stopped abruptly. He heard what sounded like a cry of pain and quickly stepped through the door into the large garage.

The first thing he saw was the wheelchair lying on its side. Past it, he caught movement as someone ran out the back door and into the pines. He charged into the garage thinking it had been Lyle who'd run out.

But he hadn't gone far when he saw that Lyle had left a bloody trail on the concrete floor where he'd crawled away from the wheelchair, away from the electric saw lying on the floor next to it, the blade dripping blood.

"What the hell?" he said, rushing to the man on the floor. He was already digging out his phone to call 911.

"No, don't. Please. Don't call. I'm okay," Lyle cried as he pressed a rag against the wound that had torn through his jeans to the flesh of his lower leg. "It's not fatal."

James stared at the man, then slowly disconnected before the 911 operator answered. "I just saw someone running out of here. What's going on?"

Lyle shook his head. "Could you get my chair?"

He walked over, picked it up and rolled the wheelchair over to the man, holding it steady as Lyle lifted himself into it.

"It looks worse than it is," Lyle said as he rolled over to a low workbench. He grabbed a first aid kit. "But thanks for showing up when you did."

"That blade could have taken off your leg," James said.

"Naw, it wouldn't have gone that far."

Lyle winced as he poured rubbing alcohol on the wound then began to bandage it with shaking fingers. From what James could tell, the man was right. The wound wasn't deep. "You want help with that?"

"No. I'm fine," he said, turning his back to him.

"You're in trouble." Lyle said nothing. "And whatever it is, it's serious." James took a guess on how many times he'd seen Lyle's rig parked in front of the casino since he'd been back in town. "Gambling?"

Lyle finished and spun the wheelchair around to face him. "I appreciate you stopping by when you did. Now what can I do for you?"

He sighed. His father used to say that you couldn't help people who didn't want to be helped. He knew that to be true. He chewed at his cheek for a moment, thinking. "Were you gambling nine years ago when Billy Sherman died?"

The question took the man by surprise.

James saw the answer in Lyle's face and swore. "Connie Matthews said that if she hadn't seen Billy Sherman's body lying in that ditch when she did, you would have dumped dirt on him with your front-end loader and he would never have been found. She also told my father that she'd been surprised that you were already working that morning since you usually didn't start that early. In fact, she'd been afraid you were going to get fired since she'd heard Edgar Appleton, your boss, warning you before that day about coming to work late so often. She thought that's why you were there so early that morning and that still half-asleep, you didn't see the boy and would have buried him in that ditch. You would have known that the concrete had been ordered for the driveway. It was going to be delivered that day. Had you covered Billy's body with dirt, it would have never been found."

Lyle stared him down for a full minute. "Like I said, thanks for stopping by."

"I don't believe you ran that boy down, but I do wonder if you weren't hired to get rid of his body. Maybe hired is the wrong word. Coerced into making Billy Sherman disappear?"

"You can see your way out," Lyle said, wheeling around and heading toward his house.

Chapter Seventeen

Lorelei couldn't believe that she'd agreed to have dinner with James. He'd caught her at a weak moment. The small table at the back of the steak house was dimly lit. A single candle flickered from a ceramic cowboy boot at the center. The candlelight made his blue eyes sparkle more than usual and brought out the shine of his thick dark hair.

If she had been on a real date, it would have been romantic. But this was James. A woman would be a fool to take him seriously.

James lifted his wineglass in a toast, those blue eyes taking her captive. "Thank you for indulging me tonight."

"My pleasure," she said automatically and realized she meant it as she lifted her own wineglass and tapped it gently against his. She couldn't remember the last dinner date she'd been on with a man. She took a sip of the wine. It was really good. "I'm surprised you know your wines."

He grinned. "You're impressed, aren't you?" He shook his head. "I called earlier and talked to the sommelier. I didn't want to look like a dumb cowboy."

"You could never be a dumb cowboy," she said, feeling the alcohol loosen her tongue. She'd have to be careful tonight. The candlelight, the soft music, the wine, the company, it made her want to let her hair down—so to speak. She'd pulled her hair up as per usual, but in a softer twist.

She'd worn a favorite dress that she'd been told looked good on her and she'd spritzed on a little perfume behind each ear.

She felt James's intent gaze on her a moment before he said, "You look beautiful." His tone sent a tremor through her that jump-started her heart.

Lorelei sipped her wine, fighting for a control she didn't feel. "Thank you. I could say the same about you." He'd worn all black from his button-up shirt to his jeans to his new boots. The outfit accented his long muscular legs and cupped a behind that could have sold a million pairs of jeans. The black Western shirt was opened just enough to expose the warm glow of his throat and make her yearn to see more.

There'd been a time when she'd dreamed of being with James Colt. When she'd fantasized what it would be like if he ever asked her out. But he never had. Until now. She had to remind herself that this wasn't a real date and yet it certainly felt real the way he was looking at her.

She was surprised to see that she'd finished her wine. James started to refill her glass—and not for the first time. She shook her head. Given the trail her thoughts had taken, the last thing she needed was more wine.

James suddenly got to his feet and reached for her hand. "Dance with me."

She took his hand before the words registered. Dance? She glanced at the intimate dance floor as he drew her to her feet. No one was dancing. But he was already leading her to it. He turned her to the middle of the dance floor and pulled her directly into his arms.

He drew her close and she let him. She pressed her cheek against his shoulder knowing she couldn't blame the wine. Their bodies moved in time to the music as if they were one of those older couples who'd danced together for decades.

Lorelei drew back a little to look into his eyes and wanted to pinch herself. Not even in her fantasies had she dreamed of James Colt holding her in his arms and looking at her like this. She'd been only a girl and, like her Barbie dolls, she'd long ago stored all that away. And yet here they were.

She pressed her cheek against his warm shoulder again, closed her eyes and let herself enjoy this moment. Because that's all it was. A moment. Just like in the closet with him. The memory made her smile. He'd actually been embarrassed by his reaction to her.

The song ended. There was that awkward moment when they stood looking into each other's eyes. She was certain that he wanted to kiss her, but the waiter came by with their salads. The moment gone.

Her heart was still triple-timing as James walked her back to the table, holding her hand, squeezing it before letting it go.

"You dance well," she said.

He grinned. "My brother Willie taught me."

She laughed and felt herself relax a little. He had been about to kiss her, hadn't he? Another awkward moment before they dug into their salads, both seemingly lost in their private thoughts.

By the time their meals came they were talking like friends who owned businesses next door to each other. They'd both grown up in Lonesome so it made it easy to talk about the past and stay away from the future. That moment on the dance floor had passed as if it had never happened. She suspected they both were glad of that. Otherwise, it could have made being business neighbors awkward. Neither of them wanted that.

ASKING LORI TO dance had been a mistake. Not that James hadn't enjoyed having her in his arms. He'd loved the sweet scent of her, nuzzling his way into her hair to get at its source behind her ears. She'd smelled heavenly. She'd felt heavenly.

He'd lost himself in the feel of her, wishing the song would never end. It was as if they'd called a truce, shared no uncomfortable past, had only this amazing few minutes moving together as one, in perfect sync.

And then the song ended and he'd looked at her and all he'd wanted to do was kiss her. She'd parted those lips as if expecting the kiss. He'd seen something in her eyes, a fire burning like the one burning inside him. And then the waiter had been forced to go around them to put their salads on their table and he was reminded of all the reasons he shouldn't get involved with this woman. He wasn't staying. Getting the PI license was a hoot, but he was a rodeo cowboy. If he solved this case, then it would make all of this worthwhile. But once he was healed, he would be leaving again. Long-distance relationships didn't work. Just ask Melody.

But all that aside, he'd mentally kicked himself for not kissing her when he had the chance. Maybe he'd known deep inside that once he kissed her there was no going back with this one. Lori wasn't like anyone he'd dated—if you could even call it dating. The others had known what they were getting into and had ridden in eyes wide open.

Lori was different. She expected more. Would want more from him. More than he had to give at this point in his life. One of these days he'd think about settling down, but he hoped those days were still a long way off.

Even as he thought it, he couldn't help looking over at Lori as he walked her to her door later that night. He felt the pull of something stronger than the road, maybe even stronger than the rodeo, stronger than even his resolve.

"Thank you for a lovely evening and congratulations again," she said as she pulled out her keys and turned to unlock her door.

He didn't feel like himself as he touched her arm and gently turned her back toward him. "Lori." It didn't feel like his arms that drew her to him. Or his lips that dropped hungrily to her mouth. Or his fingers that released her hair and let it fall in waves of chestnut down her slim back.

Her perfume filled his senses as her arms looped around his neck and he pushed his body into hers until the only way they could have been closer was naked in the throws of passionate lovemaking.

The kiss and that thought sent a bolt of desire rocketing through him. He had never wanted a woman like he did this one. He felt humbled with desire. He wanted to be a better man. He wanted to be her man. He wanted her. For keeps.

He felt her palms on his chest, felt her gentle push as she drew her mouth from his and leaned back to look into his eyes. He saw naked desire as well as the battle going on there. She was as scared as he was.

She shook her head slowly. Regretfully? And pulled free of his arms. He watched her straighten, brushing her long hair back as she lifted the keys in her hand and turned toward the door again.

He let her fumble with the key to the lock for a moment before he took the keys from her and opened her door. Then desire still raging through him, he handed her the keys and took a step back. He feared that if he took her in his arms again there really would be no turning back. He looked at her and knew he couldn't do it. He wouldn't let himself hurt this woman.

"Thanks again for tonight," he said, his voice rough with emotion. "I'll see you tomorrow." He turned and hurried down the steps to his pickup. He hadn't noticed the car that had gone by. Hadn't heard it. Only the taillights turning in the distance made him even aware that anyone had driven past. Nor did he give it more than a distracted notice as he climbed behind the wheel and, thinking of Lori, allowed himself to glance back at the house.

She was no longer standing there, thank goodness. The door was closed and a light glowed deep in the house. He sat for a moment, still shaken before he started the engine and headed toward home, knowing he wouldn't be able to sleep a wink.

But to his surprise, he fell asleep the moment his head hit the pillow only to be assaulted by dreams that wove themselves together in a jumbled pattern that felt too real and too frightening. In the dream, he'd known that it wasn't just him who was in danger. Lori was there and he was having trouble getting to her when the little blond-haired girl appeared on her horse. She was laughing and smiling as she cantered toward him. "Watch this, Daddy!"

He half woke in a sweat. The nightmare clung to him, holding him under even as he tried to surface. He was in uncharted waters on a leaky boat and it was impossible to swim with the concrete blocks that were tied to his ankles.

Chapter Eighteen

Lorelei woke and panicked for a moment, thinking she was late for work. She hadn't gotten to sleep until very late last night. It had taken her a while to process everything. James had kissed her. He'd called her Lori in a way that made her heart race. No one had ever given her a nickname. She hadn't been that kind of girl. Until James.

And that was the problem. He'd upset her orderly world. He'd made her burn inside with a need she knew only he could fulfill. He'd made her want to throw caution to the wind.

And then he'd been a perfect gentleman, unlocking her front door, handing her the keys and leaving.

She'd been shocked. But mostly...disappointed. She hadn't planned to invite him in. But he hadn't even tried. A man with his reputation? Surely, he had to know the power he had over women. He would know she was vulnerable after a kiss like that. So why hadn't he asked to spend the night?

Lorelei knew it was ridiculous that she was angry with him for not hitting on her. Everything the man seemed to do made her angry with him, even when he was well-behaved. Maybe it wasn't him. Maybe it was her who was the problem. Maybe he didn't find her attractive.

Those thoughts had her tossing and turning and losing sleep because of him. That too annoyed her with him.

She told herself that her life had been just fine before he'd showed up next door. Her stepmother was right. Having James Colt living next to her shop was a bad idea. The man was too…distracting.

As daylight crept into the room, she lay in bed staring up at the ceiling reliving the kiss, reliving the way he'd cupped the back of her neck, the way he'd buried his face in her hair, the way he said Lori.

"Oh, for crying out loud!" she snapped and swung her legs over the side of the bed. She was acting like a teenager.

The thought actually made her smile. She'd been so driven from middle school on that all she'd thought about was excelling in her school work so she could get into a good college. Then at college she'd worked hard to get top grades so she could get a good job. She hadn't let herself be a teenager and do what a lot of other teenagers did—like James Colt.

She'd missed so much. No wonder she'd never felt like this, she realized. Until now. Now she wanted it all. And she wanted it with James.

He had wanted her, hadn't he? That kiss… She'd seen the desire in his blue eyes. So why had he just walked away last night?

Because for the first time maybe in his entire life he was being sensible, something she'd been her whole life? Oh, that was so like him, she thought angrily as she stepped into the shower. *Now* he decided to be responsible.

James threw himself into work the next morning. His thoughts and emotions had been all over the place from the moment he'd opened his eyes. The cold shower he'd taken hadn't helped so he'd left the office early to avoid seeing Lori.

He knew it was cowardice, but after that kiss last night he didn't trust himself around her. That had been a first for him. Normally after a kiss like that, he would only avoid a woman if he didn't want to see her again. But Lori wasn't just some woman and that was the problem.

Because it was Montana, the drive to the next town gave him plenty of time to think—more than an hour and a half. In this part of the state, the towns were few and far between.

Alice Sherman's ex worked as a maintenance man at the local hospital. As it turned out, today was Sean's day off. A helpful employee told him that the man lived only a block away in a large apartment house.

James walked, needing to clear his head. On the drive over, he'd had plenty of time to think. Too much. He'd finally turned on a country station on the radio. Not that even music could get his mind off Lori Wilkins.

He went from wishing he hadn't come back to town to being grateful that he had because of her. He went from wishing he could get right back on the rodeo circuit to being too involved in not just this case to want to leave now. He knew the best thing he could do was give Lori a wide berth, but at the same time, he couldn't wait to see her again.

Now as he shoved open the front door of the large apartment house, he tried to focus on work. According to the mailboxes by the door, Sherman was in 322. He turned toward the large old elevator and decided to take the stairs.

The man who answered the door at 322 was tall and slim and nice-looking. He was nothing like James had been expecting. Nor was the man's apartment. It was neat and clean, much like the man himself. "May I help you?"

"I'm James Colt. I'm a private investigator in Lonesome."

"Did Alice hire you?"

"No. I believe my father, Del Colt, was hired by you to look into the death of your son. As you know, he died before he finished the case. I've taken it over. I'd like to ask you a few questions."

Sean Sherman seemed to be making up his mind. After a moment, he stepped back. "Come on in. I'm not sure how I can help," he said after they were seated in the living room. "Alice and I were separated at the time and in the middle of a divorce. I was fighting for joint custody, but I would imagine she already told you that." She hadn't, but James had read as much in his father's notes.

"Were you in Lonesome that night?"

The man hesitated a little too long so James was surprised when he finally answered. "Yes." That definitely wasn't what Sean had told Del.

"You were?"

Sean sighed before he said, "I lied to your father about that. I had my reasons at the time."

"Then why tell me the truth now?"

"Because if it will help you find out who killed my son, then nothing else matters."

"But that wasn't the case nine years ago?" James asked.

"Other people were involved. It was a very traumatic time in my life. The divorce, arguing over Billy. I don't know if Alice told you this or not." He met James's gaze and held it. "I was having an affair. Alice found out and our marriage was over. The affair was a mistake, one I will always regret. I didn't want all of that made public and having it thrown in Alice's face. We'd lost our son. We were both devastated. The rest of it wasn't important."

"I understand drugs were involved?"

"I'll be honest with you. I couldn't take the pain of what

I'd done, blamed myself for not being in the house with my family that night and I turned to drugs. It's taken me a long time to climb back out of that. Being honest is part of my recovery."

"If you were in Lonesome that night, but not at your house, where were you?" James asked.

Sean looked away for a moment before he said, "I was at Karen Wilkins's house."

He couldn't help his surprise. "She was the woman you were having the affair with?"

The man nodded. "I was in the middle of breaking it off with her."

"Were you there all night?" James asked.

"I think so. Things got very emotional. Karen left. She ran out into the storm. I started to go after her but turned back."

"She left on foot?"

He nodded. "But not long after that I heard her take her car and leave."

"What time was that?"

"I think it was about ten."

"You didn't go after her in your car?" Sean shook his head. "When did she come back?"

"I don't know exactly. I got into her booze, got disgustingly drunk and passed out; and when I woke up, she was standing over me distraught, screaming, crying and telling me to get out. It was daylight by then. I left and the only time I went back to Lonesome was for my son's funeral. I tried to mend things with Alice but…" He shook his head. "That's it."

James thought about it for a moment. "When you woke to find Karen home again what kind of shape was she in? I know she was upset. There was a thunderstorm that night. Was she still wet from being out in it?"

The man frowned. "No. Her clothes must have dried because they weren't wet. Stranger was the fact that she'd fixed her hair. She had to have been home for a while, I guess." He shook his head. "You can tell how out of it I was."

"She was wearing the same clothing though?"

"She was. She had to have been home for a while before she woke me up. I could tell that she'd had a shower." He shrugged. "I liked the smell of her shower gel."

James shook his head. If he knew anything about women who felt scorned, it was that they didn't calmly come home shower, fix their hair, put on the same clothing and then decide to wake you up to throw you out. So where had Karen been that she'd spent the night, taken a shower and gotten her clothes dried? He supposed it was possible that she'd gone to her exercise studio. They probably had showers there. Karen could even have a washer and dryer down there for all he knew. Still, it seemed odd.

"Did you hear any more from her?" he asked.

Sean shook his head. "That night pretty well ended everything in Lonesome for me."

"She's never tried to contact you?"

"Never. Nor did I ever contact her. It was over almost before it started. We both regretted it. I'm sure I could have handled it better than I did."

James thanked the man and showed himself out. He couldn't help being surprised about Karen. But at least now he knew why she was on his father's list. She'd been upset and out driving that night in the storm. Had she done something? Had she seen something?

He felt a start. But how had Del found out about her possible involvement in Billy's death? Sean hadn't told him and Karen certainly hadn't shared the information when James had tried to question her.

Had someone seen her that night?

LORELEI DID WHAT she always did on Sunday morning. She went to church; only today she was asked to help with the toddlers in child care during the service and jumped at it. She loved the job, especially toddler age. They were so much fun as they raced around, laughing and screaming and keeping her on her toes. Seriously, she later thought. What had she been thinking volunteering for this since she had thirteen toddlers between her and another volunteer? It was wonderful madness.

For several hours she forgot about everything, especially James.

Then it ended, parents picked up their children and she was facing what she did at home each Sunday after church: cleaning house. Today, the place got an extra good scrubbing even though it didn't need it. Her house was small— just the way she liked it since she spent so little time there.

She'd just finished when her doorbell rang. Her first thought was that it was probably her stepmother. They often did something together on a Sunday every month or so. But when she opened the door, it was James standing there. She blinked in surprise and then horror as she realized what she was wearing. Leggings and an oversized sweatshirt that hung off one shoulder. Her hair was pulled up in a high ponytail. She never wore much makeup, but now she wore none. And she smelled like cleaning solution.

"We need to talk," he said without preamble as he stepped in, seemingly not even noticing her appearance.

"Iced tea or beer?" she asked as she followed him into the kitchen.

"Beer." He looked around. "Nice house."

"Thanks." She took two beers from the refrigerator and handed him one as she led the way into the small living room and curled up on one end of the couch. He took the chair next to it, looking uncomfortable.

"If this is about last night—"

"No," he said too quickly. "I mean." He met her gaze. "No. It's about your stepmother." Lorelei groaned inwardly and thought, *Now what?* "I drove over to Big Timber and talked to Sean Sherman this morning."

She frowned. "Billy's dad?"

He nodded. "He told me something. Are you aware that your stepmother was seeing him nine years ago?"

James could have told her almost anything about her stepmother and she wouldn't have batted an eye. Karen had proven to her how little she knew about the woman who'd raised her.

"What do you mean 'seeing' him?" When James merely looked at her, she let out a cry and shot to her feet. "If you're trying to tell me that my stepmother is a serial philanderer with married men…"

"It might be worse than that," he said. "Sean told me he broke up with her that night. Upset, Karen left the house in the storm, at first on foot, but later came back for her car."

Lorelei had moved to the fireplace but now put her free hand over her mouth, her eyes filling with tears as her heart dropped like a stone, bottoming out.

"We don't know that she was the one who hit Billy—" he choked out. "But she went somewhere. When she returned to her house, she'd either gone straight to the shower, fixed her hair and dried her clothing and put on the same outfit before confronting Sean who'd passed out after being into her booze, or…"

She rolled her eyes. "Or what?"

"She'd been somewhere and showered and fixed her hair before returning to the house to make it look as if she'd been home longer than she had."

Lorelei removed her hand from her mouth and took a drink of her beer without tasting it. She thought she might throw up. "All you have is Sean's word for this, right?" she asked, already looking, hoping, for a way that none of this could be true.

"He's on the wagon, in a program that requires him to be honest, he said, which is why he was willing to talk now. I called Alice on my way back. It's true."

"What am I supposed to say?" she asked, her voice breaking.

"I'm worried about your stepmother. Do you have any idea where she is?" She shook her head. "I've been trying to reach her. From what I can tell she hasn't been home. Neither has the senator."

"Maybe they ran away together to celebrate his divorce," she said. "She thinks he's going to marry her."

"I hope she is with him. I would hate to think that she's alone. It might be my fault that she's left town. I need her side of the story."

Lorelei couldn't believe this and yet she could. It explained why her stepmother had gotten so upset that James was digging into the old hit-and-run case. Because she had a whole lot to hide. But Lorelei couldn't let herself think that her stepmother had killed that boy. She wouldn't.

"I'm sorry to be the one to tell you," he said, sounding as miserable as he looked. "I wish…" He shook his head. He didn't need to say it. She had her wishes too.

She put down her half-full beer. "I'll let you know when I hear from her."

James finished his beer, set the empty bottle on the small table by the chair and rose. He had taken off his Stetson when he'd come in. It now dangled in his fingers by the brim. She couldn't help but think about those fingers on her face, in her hair, last night as he'd kissed her. He'd been so gentle, his caress soft, his callused fingertips sending shivers through her.

He took a step toward her. She couldn't move, couldn't breathe, couldn't think. She felt her eyes widen as he leaned toward her and brushed his lips over hers. "About last night," he said, his voice low. "It was the best date I've ever had." He drew back, his gaze locking with hers before he turned and left.

Chapter Nineteen

James felt as if he'd been kicked in the gut by a bronc. But he'd come this far. He couldn't stop now. He had to finish his father's case. That meant finding Billy Sherman's killer—no matter where the path led him.

When his phone rang, he hoped it would be Lorelei. If not her, then her stepmother. But it was Lyle Harris.

"I've been thinking. I want to talk," Lyle said. "Can you come here?"

"I'm on my way." He turned and went back the way he'd come, turning and going east on a dirt road until he came to the small homemade sign that marked the way into Harris's place hidden in the pines.

James tried not to be anxious, but he'd known that there was more to Lyle's story. He'd just never thought he was going to hear it. Because Lyle was afraid of the person who'd hired him to cover up the body? Or out of loyalty to that person? Either way, James thought, he needed a break in this case. And this just might be it.

He parked, got out and checked the garage shop first before going up to the side door of the house. At his knock, Lyle called, "Come in."

Shoving open the door, he stepped first into a mud room, then a hallway with a lot of doors. "Lyle?" No answer. He felt his skin prickle as he realized belatedly that he might be walking into a trap. The garage had been large, easy to see if someone had been hiding to jump him.

You're getting awfully paranoid.

"In the kitchen," came Lyle's voice.

He headed slowly down the hall, pushing aside half-open doors on his way. True to his word, Lyle was in the kitchen, which had been remodeled to accommodate a man in a wheelchair.

"I was just making chili," Lyle said, his back to him. "My stepmother said no one eats chili in the summer." He turned then to look at James. "I do." Wheeling back to the pot on the stove, he stirred, turned down the heat, and putting down the spoon spun around. He looked nervous, which made James nervous too. "I called you at a weak moment. I'd just talked to my mom on the phone."

"Does that mean that you've changed your mind about telling me the truth?" James said, hoping that's all there was to this.

"Look, I know you're going to keep digging. I've heard around town. A lot of people are getting upset."

"They shouldn't be unless they have something to hide."

Lyle laughed. "Hey, in case you haven't noticed, Lonesome is a small town. It's tight, man. I don't think you realize the position you're in. This is dangerous because you've stirred things up after nine long years when everyone thought it was over."

"Why would they think that? Billy Sherman's killer was never found. Why would people not want the boy's killer to be found?"

"I'm going to level with you," Lyle said. "I think you're an okay dude. Well-meaning enough but treading where you shouldn't be treading unless you have a death wish. So, you're right. I *was* told to cover up the body in the ditch before anyone saw it—especially the neighbors' kids. But I was told it was a coyote."

"A coyote?"

"I saw the blood on the road where it had been hit that morning when I came to work. I had no reason to think otherwise. It was god-awful early in the morning. I was half asleep, half loaded too. I climbed up on my front loader—"

"You didn't go look at the coyote?"

"Why would I? I just loaded up the bucket and was about to dump it when that woman came out and started screaming. That's the truth."

James realized that he believed him. "There's just one thing you left out. Who told you it was a coyote?"

Lyle looked down at his feet for a long moment. "You see all these ramps out here? You see this kitchen? You think the state picked up the bill?" He shook his head. "My friends and the people I worked with did all this."

James felt an icy chill begin to work its way up his spine. "You ever think that the person who told you to bury the…coyote…was lying to you?"

Lyle met his gaze with an angry one. "No, I did not. Because I admire the hell out of the man who told me to do it. It's the kind of thing he would think to do if he saw a dead coyote in the road in a nice neighborhood where he thought it might upset the kids. You think he would have done that if it had been a little boy lying in that road?"

"I don't know. I guess it depends on who we're talking about." He watched Lyle's temper rise and fall before the man turned back to his chili. James thought he knew where this was headed. He didn't want it to be the man and his wife that he'd had dinner with a few nights ago. He didn't want to believe it and yet he knew that Lyle couldn't be talking about anyone else.

"Edgar told you about the coyote, didn't he? He's the one

who told you to come in early and cover it up. You didn't question it because you'd been coming in late and he'd been threatening to fire you. And like you said, you would do anything he asked you—even before your accident."

"It *was* a coyote," Lyle said as if trying to convince himself. "You say otherwise and you're going to destroy a good man. You don't want to do that in this town unless you're planning to leave and never come back. It might already be too late anyway."

James left the man to his chili, hearing the warning, knowing well enough how small towns worked. He suspected his father had made an enemy while working the case and it had gotten him killed.

He felt sick at the thought of Edgar Appleton being involved. He was thinking of the dinner that night, the love he saw between husband and wife, as he climbed into his pickup and started the engine. He didn't want to believe it. Worse, he didn't want to confront the man. Edgar and Irene were good people. But his father always said that even good people made bad decisions and ended up doing bad things sometimes.

Still… He'd turned around and driven through the dense pines toward the main road when he heard it. A rustling sound followed by the distinct rattle. His blood froze as his gaze shot to the passenger side floorboards of his pickup.

He hadn't noticed the paper sack when he'd gotten in. His mind had been on what Lyle had told him. Now though, it drew his attention like a laser as the head of the rattlesnake slithered out, its body coiling, the head rising as the rattles reached a deafening sound.

James slammed on the brakes, throwing the pickup into Park as he flung open the door and bailed out. Even as he did he felt the snake strike his lower calf, sinking its fangs into the top of his cowboy boot.

Chapter Twenty

As Edgar Appleton opened the door, James grabbed his hand and dropped eleven rattles into his palm. He saw the man's startled expression. "What the—"

"Someone put a rattlesnake in my pickup," James said and reached down to draw up his jeans pant leg to show where the snake had almost bitten through the top of his boot before he'd dragged it out and killed it, cutting off the rattles. "Want to guess why?"

The older man frowned. "If you're suggesting—"

"I was at Lyle Harris's house when the snake was put in my pickup. Nine years ago, you told Lyle Harris to bury the body."

Edgar blinked. "You should come in. Irene is out working in the garden. I can see that we need to talk." He turned and walked into the dining room.

Through the window, James could see Irene bent over weeding in the huge garden. He turned to Edgar, wishing this hadn't brought him to this house of all places. He waited, sick at heart.

The older man sighed and dropped into a chair, motioning for James to take one as well. But he was too anxious to sit. He stood near the window and kept waiting.

"Irene and I had been to a movie and stopped for milkshakes at the In-N-Out. We were headed back. It was pouring rain. Irene was driving. There was a car pulled off to the side of the road. Irene went around it and hadn't gone far when she hit something. She stopped, terrified of what she might have run over. We'd both been distracted by the car beside the road. Because of the storm, I had wanted to stop and see if the person needed help, but Irene was anxious to get home. She was worried that she'd left the oven on." He rubbed a hand over his face.

"You didn't check to see what she'd hit?"

"Of course I did," Edgar snapped. "I got out and ran back through the rain. I knew it hadn't been a person. It had been too small." He looked up at James, holding his gaze with a steady one of his own. "It was a coyote. I shoved it off the road. On the way home, I got to thinking about all those kids in that neighborhood seeing it on their way to school. Coyotes remind me of the dogs I've had over my life. So I called Lyle and told him to come in early and make sure it was buried before anyone got up."

"How did the coyote turn into a little boy's broken body?"

"I don't know." He lowered his voice, looked toward the garden. Irene still had her back to them. "I'm telling you the truth."

James didn't know what to believe. "What time was this?"

"A little after ten, I think."

"Did you see anyone else out that night? Did you see Billy?"

"No one other than the car pulled off the road."

"You didn't notice who was in the car or the make or model?"

"It was an SUV, like half the town drives. On top of that the night was pitch-black and with it raining hard… It was tough enough to see anything that night." Edgar swore. "Don't look at me like that. I can tell the difference between a coyote and a kid." His voice broke. "When I heard the news about Billy Sherman…" He looked out the window to the garden. "Irene was beside herself. My wife didn't even believe me. She really thought that I would cover up that child's death to protect her."

"I think you would too," James said. "But if you had, I think it would have eaten you up inside after all these years. I also don't think Irene would have let you."

The older man nodded, smiling sadly. "You're right about that. I'd hoped your father would find out who did it." He met James's gaze. "Find out who killed that boy. Do it for all our sakes."

He saw Irene headed back in. "About the snake—"

"I'll talk to my guys, if that helps, but Lyle has some of his own friends who I have no control over."

"Thanks. Give Irene my regards," he said and left.

LORELEI HAD ALREADY made up her mind that if she didn't hear from her stepmother today she was going to track her down. The day seemed to drag even though she was busy most of it. She was still reeling from what she'd learned from James about Karen and Sean Sherman. How could you think you knew someone so well, only to realize it was a lie?

All day long she'd thought James might stop in for a sandwich. He didn't. She wondered if he was avoiding her. Or just busy with his case. He'd already dug up so much about her stepmother, she feared it would get worse. So maybe not seeing him was good news.

That evening as she locked up, she noted that James's pickup wasn't parked out back. She felt a strange tremor of worry that something might have happened to him. Since he started asking questions about Billy Sherman's death, at least one person had been murdered.

She was almost to her stepmother's house when she saw her pull in. The garage door went up and her stepmother's car disappeared inside. Lorelei pulled in as the garage door closed. She didn't know what she was going to say now that she was here. Accuse Karen of yet another affair? Or of murder and covering it up?

Maybe all her stepmother had been hiding was her relationship with Billy Sherman's father and the divorce that followed. But was there more? Lorelei feared there was.

She climbed out of her SUV and walked to the front door. She didn't have to knock. The door opened and her stepmother was standing there with such a resigned look on her face that Lorelei wanted to cry.

Without a word, Karen stepped back to let her in. She followed her into the kitchen where her stepmother opened the refrigerator and pulled out a bottle of wine. Opening it, she poured herself a glass and, without asking, poured another. She set Lorelei's in front of her at the breakfast bar, then walked into the living room to sit down.

For a moment, Lorelei stared at the wine. Then impulsively, she picked it up and downed it before turning her phone to Record and walking into the living room. Even as she did it, she felt as if she was about to betray the woman who'd been her mother. But if Karen had killed that boy...

"I'm at a loss as to what to say to you," Lorelei said as she watched her stepmother sip her wine.

"And yet here you are." There was defiance in her words, in her look.

"You had an affair with Sean Sherman. You destroyed his marriage. Did you also kill his son?" She'd thought her words would get a quick and violent reaction.

Instead, her stepmother took another sip of her wine

and set the glass down on the end table next to her before she spoke. "I hate small towns. I told your father that when we moved here. It's like living in a fishbowl." She met Lorelei's gaze. "You were the best part of that marriage. I'd always wanted a child and couldn't have one of my own. I felt like you were my flesh and blood daughter, but I wasn't happy. I loved your father, but he definitely wasn't the love of my life. He couldn't…satisfy me."

"Could anyone?" She regretted the retort at once, sighed and sat down as a long silence fell between them.

"When Fred and I get married, I'm going to put this house up for sale," Karen said, looking around. "I'll sell the studio as well since we're going to get an apartment in Washington. We'll come here in the summer so it's not like I'm leaving forever, and you can always come visit us in Washington if you want to."

"What about Billy Sherman? You were upset and out driving that night."

Karen got a faraway look in her eye for a moment. "I loved Sean and he loved me. But he was determined to go back to his wife even knowing it would have never worked." She made eye contact again. "Remember when I told you that some women always go for the bad boys?" She chuckled. "That was me. And maybe you since I've seen the look in your eye whenever James Colt's name is mentioned."

"I'm nothing like you," Lorelei said, shaking her head.

Her stepmother chuckled again. "Sean had a wild side."

"What about Fred? Does he have a wild side?"

Karen looked away.

"It's all going to come out," Lorelei said. "Everything. James isn't going to quit, and neither am I."

Her stepmother looked at her again and she saw resignation in Karen's eyes. She felt her heart drop as her stepmother said, "That was one of the worst nights of my life."

When Lorelei spoke, it came out in a whisper. "What did you do?"

Karen took another drink of her wine. "I drove around. I was upset. I wasn't thinking clearly. I was crying and it was raining. I couldn't see anything so I pulled over beside the road. I knew I shouldn't be driving in the condition I was in and yet I couldn't stay in the house with Sean, knowing he was leaving me. My chance of happiness had been snatched away and right or wrong, I blamed Alice."

Lorelei lifted a brow. "After you stole her husband, you blamed her because her husband was going back to her?"

"You can't steal anyone's husband," she snapped with obvious disgust. "That's just what wives say so they don't have to take responsibility for their husbands being unhappy with them."

"I'm sorry, but that sounds like an excuse for what you did," Lorelei said and then quickly waved it away. "I don't care. Are we finally getting to what you did that night?"

"I was sitting in my car crying when this car went by. I heard this *thump-thump* and the brake lights came on and a man jumped out and ran back through the rain. The driver had run over something. I could see a small form lying in the road. The man kicked it off to the edge of the ditch with his boot, ran back and jumped into the car and they drove away."

Lorelei's heart had lodged in her throat. "You saw who killed Billy Sherman?"

"It wasn't Billy. I got out and went over to see. At first I thought it was a dog, then I realized it was a coyote. It was a young one. I picked the poor thing up. It was dead. I don't know where I planned to take it. As I said, I wasn't in my right mind. It doesn't make any sense now, but right then I felt this connection to that dead animal. I started walking down the road holding this dead animal in my arms and crying. I didn't know where I was going or what I was going to do with it."

Lorelei saw the pain in her mother's face, then the anger.

"I decided to leave it on Alice's front doorstep. She was killing me. I wanted her to suffer."

"As if she wasn't suffering enough?"

Karen looked away. "If you'd ever been in love—"

She thought of James and how he'd turned her life upside down. "So you left this dead coyote on her doorstep?"

"That was what I'd planned to do. But as I started by the house I saw her. She was out on her porch having a cigarette. She stubbed it out and went inside, slamming the door. I realized how small and cruel and juvenile my plan was so I turned around and headed back. I can't tell you how badly I felt about all of it, the affair, the people I'd hurt, but most of all the pain in my heart. I wanted so desperately to be loved like I felt I deserved." She glanced at Lorelei. "No offense to your father. He did the best he could, but he—"

"Back to Billy," she said, cutting her off.

Karen nodded. "I hadn't gone very far when I realized there was someone behind me. I turned and..." She swallowed, tears filling her eyes. "It was Billy. He'd been following me."

Chapter Twenty-One

James was headed back into town from the Appleton house when he got the call from Lori. He heard it at once in her voice. "What's wrong?"

"I need to see you." The quaver in her voice sent his pulse rocketing.

"Are you all right?" She had him scared.

"Just meet me at your office, okay?" Her voice broke. "It's important."

"I'm headed there right now," he said and sped up. "Just be careful." But she'd already disconnected.

As he pulled into the alley behind their buildings, she climbed out of her SUV and started toward him. The look on her face made him rush to her and pull her into his arms. She leaned into him for a moment, resting her head on his shoulder, before she pulled back.

He saw the plea in her eyes. Whatever was wrong, she needed to get it out. "Let's go upstairs," he said as he opened the door. He felt a draft, accompanied by a bad feeling. Slowly he began to climb upward, hesitating just before the top to peer down the hallway. Empty. But he could see the door to his office standing open.

Moving closer, he could see that the wood was chewed from where the lock had been jimmied. He wanted to send

Lori back to her car. Or into her shop, but he also didn't want to let her out of his sight.

"Stay behind me," he whispered as he pulled his weapon. A cone of light from inside the office shone golden on the hallway floor. He watched it as they moved quietly toward it. But no shadow appeared in the light. No sound of movement came from within the office.

At the door, he motioned Lorelei back for a moment before he burst into the office, his weapon raised and ready to fire. He saw no one and quickly checked the bedroom and bath. Empty.

Turning, he saw Lori framed in the ransacked office doorway. "Who do you think did this?"

"Someone worried about what I've discovered in the case," he said without hesitation as he holstered his gun and, ushering her in, locked the office door and bolted it. Turning to her, he said, "Tell me what's happened. I can see how upset you are."

She reached into her pocket and pulled out her phone. A moment later, he heard Karen Wilkins's voice—and her stepdaughter's.

WHEN THE RECORDING ENDED, Lorelei turned off her phone. At some point, she'd taken the chair James had offered her along with the paper cup of blackberry brandy.

"So, when Billy came face-to-face with your stepmother he screamed and ran into the storm. She didn't go after him. She didn't see him again."

She nodded. "You heard her. She swears it's true. She took the dead coyote into the trees and then she walked back to her car and drove home."

"Billy was killed in the same block from where your stepmother said she'd pulled off the road. I have a witness who saw her car there. Unfortunately, there were no video cameras in that area because of the empty lots and construction going on at the time. The witness killed the coyote just after ten that night. I need to know what time she saw Billy. And what time it was when she returned to her car and where she went after that. She didn't go home until daylight. Sean was at her house waiting for her. He said that she'd fixed her hair and wasn't wet from the storm. So where had she been?"

Lorelei shook her head, drained her blackberry brandy and rose. "I need to go home and try to get some rest. I have to work early tomorrow."

"I'm sorry you got dragged into this," James said as he got to his feet as well. "You look exhausted."

"I am. I knew she was hiding something." She met his gaze. "I honestly don't know what to believe. I thought she and my father had a good marriage. I was wrong about that. I was wrong about so many things. I thought I knew her. Now… I'm not even sure she's telling me the truth. What will you do now?"

"I'll talk to her. I'll tell her what you told me. I won't tell her about the recording. If I can establish a time sequence…"

"You think she did it, don't you?"

"I think she might have blotted it out of her memory. As she said, she wasn't in her right mind. Picking up a dead young coyote and carrying it down the street to play a mean joke? Clearly she wasn't herself."

"But upset enough to run over a little boy on her way home and not remember?" Lorelei shook her head. "We've already established that she's dishonest about at least her love life. We both know there is a part of her story that she's leaving out."

He stepped to her and took her shoulders in his big hands. His touch felt warm and comforting. She wanted to curl up in his arms. "I'm going to find out who killed Billy. Please, I need you to be careful. Someone doesn't want me to know the truth. I doubt they found what they were looking for in my office. I'm afraid of how far they might go to cover up their crime. I don't want you involved."

She smiled sadly. "Too late for that."

"But promise me you won't do any more investigating on your own."

She was too tired and drained and discouraged to argue.

"I'll see you tomorrow?" he said, meeting her gaze.

She nodded numbly and he let her go but insisted on walking her down to her car. He'd wanted to follow her home, except she wasn't having it. It was flattering that James cared, but she wasn't some helpless woman who relied on a man. She wasn't her stepmother. Lorelei wanted a man in her life, but she didn't need one.

"I'm fine," she assured him. "I'm more worried about you."

"Indulge me. Please. Call me when you get home, so I know you made it okay. Promise me?"

JAMES DIDN'T CARE what Lori said. He was going to follow her home to make sure she was safe. He felt as if he'd dragged her into this. Just being associated with him could be bad enough. Add in her stepmother...

As she drove away, he reached for his keys and swore. He'd left them upstairs in his shock at finding his office broken into and ransacked, not to mention the information Lori had gotten on her stepmother.

He turned and rushed upstairs in time to hear his phone ringing. The phone and his keys were on his desk. He scooped up the phone, thinking it might be Lori. It was Gilbert Sanders, the arsonist investigator. He glanced at the time and had a feeling the man wouldn't be calling now unless it was important.

He picked up the call on his way out the door.

"I was thinking about what you said about your father wanting to talk to me about a hit-and-run case he was working on," Gilbert said after a few pleasantries were exchanged. "I couldn't imagine why he'd want to talk to me about anything but a fire. But then I remembered. I *did* talk to him. He told me he was working on a case about a young boy who'd been killed, right?"

"Right. Billy Sherman."

"But that wasn't why your father called me. He wanted to know about a house fire. One fatality. The wife."

James frowned. "Whose fire?"

"His own. Del Colt wanted to know about the fire that killed his wife."

"I don't understand," James said as he reached his pickup and stopped. "My mother died of cancer."

"It was his first wife."

James couldn't speak for a moment. "His *first* wife."

"I'm sorry, you didn't know that your father had been married before?"

"No. What did you tell him about the fire?"

"Just that it had been ruled an accident, a faulty lamp cord. But I wasn't the one who handled that investigation. It was my uncle, the man I was named for, Gilbert T. Sanders, who did the investigation. Your father asked me to look into it for him. Something must have come up in his investigation of the hit-and-run that made him believe the fire that killed his first wife had been arson and was somehow connected to his case."

This made no sense. "Did you look into the fire?" James asked as he climbed into his pickup. Lori would probably be home by now and probably trying to call him.

"I did. I think your father might have been right."

"Wait, right about what?"

"The fire that killed his first wife," Gilbert said. "My uncle suspected it was arson, but there were extenuating circumstances. An eyewitness swore he saw the lamp ignite the living room."

"Who was the eyewitness?"

"Sheriff Otis Osterman. He was the first person on the scene. But I saw in my uncle's notes on the case that there was a string of small fires that summer around Lonesome. There was a suspect at the time."

James felt all the air rush from his lungs as Gilbert said, "Freddie Bayard, now Senator Fred Bayard. Freddie had apparently been a firebug since he was little. But there was no proof and his father, also a senator, made Freddie untouchable. The boy was sent away to a private school where his father promised he would get him the help he needed. In the report, there was also mention of Del and Fred being at odds, some rivalry that went back years."

"How is that possible?" James asked. "I didn't think Fred moved here until about ten years ago."

"His grandparents lived here and he stayed with them more than he stayed with his parents. His father was in DC a lot of the time and he and his mother weren't close. I'm not sure how any of this will help with your investigation."

"Me either, but thank you for letting me know." James pulled in front of Lori's house. No lights on. No Lori. She hadn't come straight home or she would be here by now. Fred Bayard was involved with Karen Wilkins and Lori was involved because of it.

He felt a tremor of fear. Why hadn't Lori gone straight home like she'd planned? Had her stepmother called? Had something happened?

He started to call Lori's cell when he knew where she'd

gone. Making a sharp U-turn in the middle of the street, he headed toward her stepmother's house.

As he drove, he couldn't get what Gilbert Sanders had told him out of his mind. He called his brother Davey only to get voice mail. He tried his brother Tommy. Same thing. He was about to give up when he realized the brother he needed to ask was his eldest brother, Willie.

"What's up?"

"Did you know Dad was married before?" he demanded.

Willie hesitated before saying, "Who told you that?"

"You just did! And you never said anything?" James couldn't believe this.

"Why would I? It had nothing to do with our family," Willie said. "Also, it was too painful for Dad. I wanted to protect him. They were married less than a month when she was killed. Luckily, he met our mom."

"Protect him from what?" James demanded.

"Heartbreak. He blamed himself for her death. Like us, he was on the rodeo circuit all the time. He'd left her alone in a house that had bad wiring. He didn't need to be reminded of the past. That's why I didn't tell you or the others."

"How did you find out?" he asked as he pulled up in front of Lorelei's stepmother's house.

"Otis Osterman told me. He was the cop who investigated the fire. He threw the fact that Dad left his wife in a house with faulty wiring in my face the first time he hauled me in on some trumped-up charge. I told him that if he ever said anything like that to me or my family again, I'd kill him. Apparently, he believed me."

"I'm getting another call," James said, hoping it would be Lori. "We'll talk about this soon." He disconnected from Willie and said, "Lori?"

Silence. He realized that the other call had gone to voice mail. He listened, still hoping it had been Lori. It was one of the out-of-town body shops he'd called inquiring about a vehicle being brought in from Lonesome nine years ago after Billy Sherman's death. He didn't bother to listen to the message. Right now he only cared about Lori. He couldn't shake a bad feeling that she was in trouble.

LORELEI HAD GRUDGINGLY promised to go straight home and call James when she arrived. Her intentions had been good when she'd left him. Until her stepmother called crying and hysterical.

"What's wrong?" Karen didn't answer, just kept crying. "Mom."

Calling her mom seemed to do the trick. "We broke up."

It took Lorelei a minute to realize that she must be talking about the senator.

"Why?"

More awful sobbing, before her stepmother said, "It was all based on a lie. How could I have ever trusted that he was really in love with me? Or that he wasn't just marrying me so I couldn't testify against him?"

At those words, Lorelei felt shaken to her soul. Marry her so she couldn't testify against him? "What are you talking about?"

"That night on the road. Billy." She was sobbing again. "I left out that part. When I was walking back to my car, Fred picked me up. On the way to my car…" More sobbing. "He ran over something in the road. It didn't seem like it was anything. I told him about the coyote… He didn't stop to check but he did look back in his side mirror. I saw his expression. I knew it wasn't a coyote."

Lorelei felt her blood run cold. Her stepmother was sobbing.

"I was so upset and freezing and there didn't seem to be any damage to his vehicle."

"He took you to his house," Lorelei said, seeing now how it had happened with her mother and the senator.

"He was so kind, so caring. I wanted to believe in him." More uncontrollable bawling.

She didn't need her stepmother to tell her what had happened after that night. Fred had been afraid that Karen could come forward with what she knew. He must have seen how much she'd needed a man in her life. He became that man to protect himself. Until Karen finally admitted the truth—and not just about the night Billy Sherman had died.

Lorelei had known women her own age who went from one man to the next, desperate to have someone in their lives. She'd felt sorry for them. She felt sorry for her stepmother. Karen would have been flattered at the senator's attention. She'd been lonely, had needed a man so desperately, that she would rather live a lie than admit the truth about her relationship with Fred Bayard.

Until now.

"You told him what you told me," Lorelei said.

"I knew you were right," her stepmother wailed. "James was going to find out. Fred became so angry. It's over." She began to cry harder.

Why hadn't she noticed how unhappy Karen had been? Why hadn't she known what her stepmother had been going through? Because Karen had seemed happy. And because Lorelei had been busy living her own life, seeing what she wanted to see.

"Mom, I'm almost to your house." But she didn't think Karen heard her. "Mom?" She kept hearing her stepmother's words. *I knew it wasn't a coyote.*

She could hardly make out her stepmother's next words, "Someone's at the back door. It can't be Fred. He's promised to go to the sheriff…" Then Karen's voice changed, and Lorelei knew her stepmother was no longer talking to her. "What are you doing here? I thought—"

Lorelei heard what sounded like the phone being knocked out of Karen's hand. It made a whishing sound as it skittered across the hardwood floor.

She couldn't make out the words, but it sounded like Karen and a man arguing. Then to Lorelei's horror, she heard her stepmother scream followed by a painful cry an instant before she heard the sound of what could be a body hitting the floor.

"Mom?" she cried into the phone. Silence. Then footfalls. The line went dead.

Her hands were shaking so hard on the wheel that she had to grip it tightly. She was calling 911 as her stepmother's house came into view and she saw the smoke.

Chapter Twenty-Two

The smoke seemed to be coming from the back of the house. The man had come in the back door. Lorelei knew who the man was, knew what he'd done and why. But as she made a quick turn and swung down the alley, she was surprised to see him jump into his large dark-colored SUV. She sped toward him as he ducked behind the wheel and took off in a hail of gravel. But not before she'd seen his license plate number. The senator had vanity plates.

She hit her brakes behind the house and bailed out of her vehicle. She could see smoke rolling out of the open back door. She was running toward the house when James came running around the side of the house toward her.

"My stepmother's inside," she screamed over the crackle of the blaze. "The senator was here. I heard him attack her, then set the house on fire." She could see flames rising at the kitchen windows.

"Stay here," James ordered as he pulled off his jean jacket, and putting it over his head ran into the open back door and into the smoke and flames.

Lorelei stood there, feeling helpless. She could hear sirens growing closer. The fire trucks would be here soon. But soon enough? She wanted to race into the house through the smoke and flames and find James, find Karen.

She felt her panic building. James was here because of her. He couldn't die because of her.

She began to cry tears of relief as she saw him come out of the smoke carrying Karen. She ran to him as the first of the fire trucks pulled up out front along with an ambulance and the sheriff.

"She's unconscious," James said, coughing. "But since she was on the floor, I don't think she breathed in much smoke."

Lorelei wiped at her tears as she ran to keep up with him as he carried Karen toward the waiting ambulance. James had risked his life to save her stepmother. She loved this man. The thought whizzed through her mind as they reached the sidewalk and were immediately surrounded by frantic activity as James handed over Karen and the EMTs went to work on her.

"Want to tell me what's going on here?" the sheriff asked as he sauntered up to Lorelei.

"My stepmother was attacked and left in a burning house to die," she snapped. "That's what happened. I saw the man who assaulted her and started the fire. I was on the phone with her when he attacked her. I was only a block away so I saw him running away as I drove up. I took down his license number. But I also saw his face. It was Senator Fred Bayard."

Carl started to argue that she had to be mistaken. "Fred is a godsend to this community. Without him and the donations he'd made—"

Karen, now conscious, pulled off her oxygen mask. She narrowed her gaze on the sheriff, stopping the EMTs from loading her gurney into the back of the ambulance.

"Senator Fred Bayard tried to kill me and then he set my house on fire," her stepmother said through coughing fits. "He also killed Billy Sherman. I know because I was in the car with him. He didn't stop to see what he'd run over. He just kept going. He would have killed me too."

The EMTs got the oxygen back on Karen as she gasped for breath.

"If you don't arrest the senator," Lorelei said, turning to the sheriff, "I will call the FBI and tell them that you refused to pick up the man who assaulted my stepmother, started the fire and left her to die. I don't think you want them looking into the other things you and your brother have done over the years to cover up crimes in Lonesome."

The EMTs loaded Karen into the ambulance. "I have to get to the hospital," she said and pushed past the sheriff.

"I'll take you," James said, suddenly at her side. He put his arm around her as they hurried to his pickup. She leaned into him, for once happy to have someone to lean on.

As she climbed in and he slid behind the wheel, she told him what her stepmother had told her on the phone before she'd heard Karen being attacked.

"When I drove up, I saw him running from the back of the house," she said. "He tried to kill my stepmother to cover up his crime." She fought tears, fearing that Fred would get away with it. The sheriff certainly didn't have the guts to arrest him.

SHERIFF CARL OSTERMAN swore as he watched the ambulance leave, siren blaring and lights flashing. James Colt and Lorelei Wilkins took off behind it. When had those two become so tight, he wondered. He'd thought Lorelei had more sense. Shaking his head, he watched the firefighters trying to put out the blaze and then sighing, climbed into his patrol SUV and headed out to the senator's place.

He knew how this was going to go down so he was in no hurry. It would come down to the senator's word against the woman he'd just broken up with and Lorelei, a younger woman protecting her stepmother. Not the best witnesses especially if all this had been caused by a domestic disagreement between the senator and Karen Wilkins. He certainly didn't want to take the word of a hysterical woman.

As he pulled up in the yard in front of the large summer house, he slowly got out. He wasn't surprised when Fred came out carrying a small suitcase and walked toward his helipad next to the house in a clearing in the pines.

Carl followed him. "If you have a minute, Fred?"

"Sheriff, good to see you. Actually, I don't. Something's come up. My chopper should be here any minute. I need to get to the airport. Government business."

The senator smelled as if he'd taken a quick shower, so quick that there was still that faint hint of smoke on him. "We have a problem," Carl said.

Fred smiled. "I'm sure it's nothing that you can't handle, Sheriff. It's one of the reasons I backed your campaign. Please don't tell me I supported the wrong man."

He could hear the sound of the helicopter in the distance. "You did back the right man," Carl said, bristling. "But money can only buy so much. This time I'm going to have to take you in for questioning, Fred. Lorelei Wilkins saw you leaving her stepmother's house. You stepped over a line. What you did can't be undone."

The senator shook his head. "I was at her house. I'm not sure what happened after I left, but I had just broken up with her stepmother. Karen was overwrought, threatening to kill herself. Of course Lorelei is going to blame me if the woman did something…stupid."

"It's more serious than that, I'm afraid, Fred. Karen regained consciousness. She says you assaulted her and set her house on fire. Lorelei was on a phone call with her stepmother and heard it all. Karen also says that you killed

Billy Sherman—that she was in the car that night and will testify in court that you didn't even stop."

"She's lying. I told you. I broke it off. She'd say anything to get back at me." The helicopter came into view.

Carl pulled out his handcuffs. A part of him had known that this day was coming and had been for years. Fred had gotten away with numerous crimes over the years since he was a boy. Back then he'd been a juvenile, his father a respected senator, his grandparents churchgoing people. But now that the man's house of cards had started to tumble, the sheriff suspected a lot more was about to come out.

Worse, Carl knew that he and Otis would be caught in the dirt once it started flying. He laid his hand on his weapon and slowly unsnapped the holster. Fred saw the movement, his eyes widening. The senator had to know that there was an easy way out of this for Carl, for his brother. If Fred were dead there would never be a trial, a lot of old cases wouldn't come to light.

"I hope you'll come peacefully, senator," Carl said. "But either way, you're going to have to come down to the station for questioning." He met the man's gaze and held it for a long moment.

Fred swore. "All the things I've done for your two-bit town." He angrily pulled out his phone and called his attorney.

"I'll tell the helicopter pilot that you won't be going anywhere for a while," Carl said, then turned back to the senator. "By the way, I heard from Gilbert Sanders, the state arson investigator, earlier today. He told me that he's reopening the Del Colt fire case. He thinks he has some new evidence." He watched Fred's spray-on-tanned face pale. "He was especially interested in talking to you."

"The statute of limitations on arson is five years."

"I guess you forgot. Del's first wife died in that fire. There is no statute of limitations on murder."

Chapter Twenty-Three

Lorelei found her stepmother to be in good spirits when she stopped by the hospital the next morning. Karen had a concussion from the blow the senator had dealt her and a mild cough from the smoke, but she was going to be fine.

"The prosecutor said he didn't think I would be arrested for withholding evidence," Karen said. "I'm just glad to be alive. But I can't stay in Lonesome. I should have left a long time ago."

She took her stepmother's hand. "You stayed because of me."

Karen smiled. "You always did give me the benefit of the doubt. I will miss you, but you need to get on with your life. You need not worry about me anymore."

She wasn't sure about that. "You put up the money for my shop from your retirement account."

"It was the right thing to do. I inherited the house and your father's money. It's what your father would have wanted me to do."

"I'm sorry things didn't work out for you," Lorelei said.

"I chose the wrong men for the wrong reasons." She shook her head. "I've learned my lesson. Don't look at me like that. Even old dogs can learn new tricks."

Lorelei laughed. "You're still young. There's someone out there for you."

"I hope so." She took a ragged breath. "What's going on with you and James Colt?"

She shrugged. "We had a moment, but now he's done what he set out to do. Solve his father's case. I'm sure he'll be going back on the rodeo circuit."

"I'm sorry."

"I'm sure it's for the best," Lorelei said. "I heard you're getting out of here today."

"I'm thinking of going to Chicago. I'll be back for the trial, if Fred's case goes to trial. But first I have to tie up some loose ends with the insurance company and the house. I've had an offer for the exercise studio and I've decided to take it. I'm looking forward to a fresh start in the big city."

She squeezed her stepmother's hand. "Please keep in touch."

"You know I will. You're my daughter." They hugged and Lorelei left before she cried. She would miss Karen. Her stepmother had been the last link she had with her father and the last reminder of her childhood. With Karen gone, she had no family left here.

The thought made her sad as she drove to her shop. Anita had volunteered to come in and work, which Lorelei had happily accepted. Given everything that had happened, she needed a little time off. Karen thought she was like her because of James Colt. Was he her bad boy? He had played that part in high school and for some time after, but she no longer thought of him that way. He was her hero. But he was also a rodeo cowboy at heart. The circuit would be calling him now.

As she got out of her SUV, James drove up. Just seeing him made her heart soar. Yesterday evening he'd gone to the hospital with her, but she'd sent him home after the doctors checked him over. He had smoke inhalation and she could tell he needed rest. He'd called to make sure she and Karen were both all right late last night. She hadn't had a chance to talk to him since.

He got out of his pickup and sauntered toward her. Had she really not noticed how good-looking he was that first day when she'd seen him again after all the years? She could laugh about it now. She'd thought his hair was too long, that he dressed like a saddle tramp, that he was too arrogant for a man who obviously lacked ambition. So why did he seem perfect now? He hadn't changed, but the way she saw him definitely had, she realized. She'd gotten to know the man inside him and fallen in love with him.

The thought struck her at heart level like a blow. She'd had the thought yesterday after he'd gone into a house on fire to save her stepmother. This time the thought carried no raw emotion. It just happened to be the truth.

And now he would be leaving Lonesome, leaving her.

"I'm starved," he said, grinning as he joined her.

"You're always starved," she said with a laugh.

He put his arm around her as they headed into the back of her sandwich shop. He did it casually and yet it sent a jolt through her. "What's the special today?"

"Pulled pork. Your favorite."

He looked over at her and smiled. "You know me so well. Anita must be working. Thank goodness since I don't want you going anywhere near my sandwich."

She thought of that day when she'd added hot sauce and sliced jalapeños to his sandwich—and he'd eaten every bite of it. "I'm still sorry about that."

"Sure you are," he said with a laugh as he headed for his usual table. "Have an early lunch with me?"

Lorelei nodded, fighting tears. She didn't want to think about the days he would no longer stop by. When his pickup wouldn't be parked in the alley next door. When she wouldn't see him. "Let me place our orders. I'll be right back. Iced tea or lemonade?"

"Both." He looked so happy. He'd solved his father's last case. Why wouldn't he be happy? But she feared it was more about going back on the rodeo circuit.

JAMES TOOK HIS usual seat at the booth and looked out on the town. Funny how his attitude toward Lonesome had changed. It had been nothing more than a stopover on his way somewhere else for so many years. He realized that he hadn't appreciated it.

Now he felt more a part of the place. It was a good feeling, one he would miss if…when he went back on the rodeo circuit. He'd done what he'd set out to do. Solve his father's last case. Still, it felt unfinished. There was the question of his father's death. He thought the truth about it still might come out—if as he suspected Otis had something to do with Del Colt's death.

The senator's arrest had a domino effect. The feds had stepped in and taken over the case. Gilbert Sanders turned over new evidence to the prosecutor regarding the Del Colt case along with other fires that were quickly attributed to Fred. He was being held without bail.

A small-time criminal Otis Osterman had arrested back when he was sheriff was picked up and charged for drug possession. He copped a plea, giving up Otis as the one who'd hired him to burn down Cora Brooks's house. The prosecution, closely watched by the feds, began looking into how other investigations had been handled by both Carl Osterman and his brother Otis. Under pressure, Carl had resigned, and the reign of the Osterman's was over. More of their misdeeds would be coming out, James knew.

He dragged himself out of his thoughts as Lori appeared

with a tray full of food and drinks. "I'm sorry. I could have helped you with that."

She gave him a dismissive look. "I do this for a living. I can handle it."

He watched her slide into the chair across from him and take everything off the tray. He'd never imagined he would have these kinds of feelings for Lorelei Wilkins and yet he did. Once, it had been flirting. Now... Now it was so much more. She had a pull on him stronger than gravity.

"What will happen now with the case?" she asked after they'd tucked into their sandwiches in companionable silence.

"Probably the most Fred will go down for will be assault, arson and manslaughter even if the prosecution can prove he set the fire that killed my father's first wife. He might get some time in prison, but probably not much. But his career is over. He'll be a felon. He won't even be allowed to vote, own a gun or hold office in most states and there are countries that won't allow him in."

She put down her sandwich. "It's not enough. What about Billy?"

James shook his head. "I doubt a jury will convict him on that because of lack of evidence. Karen says he ran over something. All Fred has to do is lie and say he didn't. It's her word against his. There apparently wasn't any damage to his large SUV."

"He's in a position where he can lie and there will be people who will believe him over my stepmother."

James couldn't argue that. "Taking away his career and ruining his reputation will hurt the most. He'll lie, say he was railroaded by a scorned woman. That he was innocent of all of it. But he ran from your stepmother's house after assaulting her and setting her house on fire. Add to that the other fires... His reputation is toast."

He watched her pick at her sandwich as if she'd lost her appetite. "Do you think he would have married Karen?"

She shook her head. "I think she realized there was no happy ending with the lie between them. She would have always questioned his love for her."

James reached across the table to cover her hand with his own. "People disappoint us but ultimately we're all human. That's what my dad used to say. We do what we have to do to survive. For some, that's lying, cheating, stealing and even killing. For others it's small lies and secrets. My dad was good at uncovering them and finding a little justice or at least peace for those in pain. I understand now why he loved doing this."

"So you're hooked on the PI business?" She'd said it jokingly, but he knew at the heart of her question what she was asking. This year's rodeo season was in full swing. He was healed. There was nothing to keep him from getting back to his life. He'd accomplished what he'd set out to do. Solve his father's last case—with Lori's help. If he didn't go soon…

Lori. He looked into her face, saw her compassion, her spirit, her desire that mirrored his own. How could he leave her for months to go back on the rodeo circuit? But then how could he not? He wasn't getting any younger. He didn't have that much time left in the saddle and there were a lot of broncos he'd yet to ride.

LORELEI STOOD IN the kitchen of her shop after James left. He'd said there were some things he had to take care of and that he would see her later. She and her friend Anita were prepping for the next day and getting ready for the lunch crowd. It was Saturday and a beautiful summer day. There would be a lot of picnickers coming for her special weekend basket.

"I keep thinking about everything that happened," she said, voicing her doubts out loud. "It doesn't feel over."

"I'm sure it's going to take a while to process everything." She and Anita had been good friends in high school. While Lorelei had gone to college, Anita had married her childhood sweetheart, had babies and settled in Lonesome. Lorelei looked up to her since Anita had definitely had more life experience because of it.

"I keep thinking about something Karen said. She heard a car go by moving fast when she was in the trees getting rid of the coyote. She hid, so she didn't see the car or the driver. She said that's when she realized that she couldn't do what she'd been doing anymore. That she needed to find a man who appreciated her and wanted to marry her and that things were really over between her and Sean."

Anita stopped to plant one hand on her hip. "Where are you going with this?"

"I'm not sure. Right after that, she stepped back on the highway in the pouring rain and was picked up by the senator," Lorelei said. "Of course, Karen thought it was fate."

"Until the senator hit Billy."

"That's just it. Karen said he ran over *something* in the road. Not that he *hit* something."

"I'm not sure I see the difference."

"That car that sped by too fast while Karen was hiding in the trees, what if that's the driver who actually hit and killed Billy Sherman?"

"But you don't know who it was."

"No. Minutes later the senator would pick up Karen and run over something in the road and not bother to stop." She grimaced. "He must have seen the boy lying on the road in his rearview mirror."

"Well, you know what kind of man he is already," Anita said.

"But what if Billy was already dead? What if the senator panicked, thinking he had killed the boy and believing Karen would know he'd done it? When he looked back in his side mirror, he would have seen the boy's clothing. From that moment on, he had to keep my stepmother from ever telling so he seduced her that night."

Anita shuddered. "And when he realized he could no longer trust her, he tried to kill her and burn down her house."

"Maybe that's what he planned all along. I really doubt he would have married her and yet he couldn't break up with her for fear of what she might do. He must have felt trapped. How ironic would it be if he was innocent?"

"Innocent is not a word I would use with him, but I see what you mean," Anita agreed. "But how can you prove that Billy was already dead, hit by the car before the senator's vehicle drove over the remains?"

"I have no idea," Lorelei said. "But I'm going by Alice Sherman's today. My stepmother was going to stop by her house, but I talked her out of it. Karen wanted to send her a card to tell her how sorry she was about everything. She's now decided that to change she needs to apologize to those she hurt."

"Not a bad idea."

"No, but I think Karen showing up there might not be a great idea. So I said I'd drop off the card she wrote instead. I wanted to see if Alice might remember a car flying past that night. My stepmother said Alice had been outside smoking a cigarette when she'd seen her but had gone back inside. I would imagine she'd been at the window making sure Karen kept going past."

Anita looked skeptical. "Are you sure she'll want to talk to you? I mean, you are Karen's daughter. But what's the worst that can happen? She'll throw you out."

"That's a pleasant thought," she said as she tossed her apron in the bin and headed for her SUV parked outside. But she had to try.

She noticed that James's pickup was still parked in the alley. She considered sharing her theory with him but decided otherwise. There was a good chance that the senator had been the one to hit Billy in that big SUV of his with the huge metal guard on the front. Questioning Alice Sherman probably wouldn't go anywhere anyway.

On top of that, she could see a shadow moving around in the upstairs apartment. Was James packing? Would he tell her goodbye?

JAMES HAD LOOKED around the office, his gaze lighting on his private investigator's license. He'd taken Lori's advice. He'd framed it and put it on the wall next to his father's. It had felt presumptuous. But he liked the look of it there.

He knew he should start packing. He needed to pick up his horse and trailer. He turned and saw the Colt Investigations sign in the front second-story window. He should take that down. He'd already had several calls from people wanting to hire him as the news had swept through Lonesome.

The crazy part was that he would never have solved it without Lori's help. He still didn't know what he was doing. He was playacting at being a PI. But it had given him some experience. Maybe with more…

The worst part was that something was still nagging at him about the case. He told himself that the FBI would get to the bottom of any questions he might have. Everything was in good hands.

He turned to look at his framed PI license hanging on the wall over the desk next to his father's again. He felt torn about leaving. When he thought about Lori he wasn't sure he could leave. But would he regret it later if he didn't go at least one more year on the circuit? It would probably be his last.

His cell phone rang. "Congrats," Willie said. "You're all over the news. Dad would be proud."

"Thanks."

"I suppose I know what you're doing. Packing. Did I hear you might catch up to us in Texas?"

"Thinking about it."

"What? You aren't already packed? What's going on?" James knew he had to make a decision. He still didn't know how or why his father had died that night on the railroad tracks. He feared that he never would.

He'd been offered more cases since the senator's arrest. Maybe he could make a living at this PI thing. He and Lori had found Billy Sherman's killer. They'd made a good team.

"I'm packing," he told his brother. "I'll let you know, but probably Texas." He disconnected. But something was still nagging him. About the case? About leaving?

He stepped over to the desk and sat down. Earlier, he'd filed the case away. Now he pulled it out. There were his own notes in with his father's. Would his father be proud?

What was bothering him? He flipped through the file, stopping on the coroner's report. He'd read it over when he'd first started the case. Billy's injuries had been consistent with being hit by a vehicle. Numerous bones had been broken but it was a massive head injury that was listed as cause of death.

Numerous bones had been broken, he read again and looked through the list. Billy's right arm had been shattered and was believed to have been run over by the vehicle's tire after initial impact.

He picked up his phone and called Dr. Milton Stanley.

He figured the man would be out working in his yard and was surprised when he picked up. "This is a bit unusual, but I was looking at the coroner's report on Billy Sherman. I need to know if this is consistent with a small boy of seven being struck by a large vehicle."

"It would depend on the size of the car. If it was a large SUV or pickup or a small car, the injuries would be different. The state medical examiner did this autopsy. Send me the report and I'd be happy to give you my opinion."

James glanced around the office and spotted his father's old fax machine. "I can fax it to you. I don't have a copy machine."

The doctor laughed. "How about a computer? No? If you're going to stay in business, son, you need to get into at least the twentieth century. Just take a photo of it with your phone and send it to me."

He'd just hung up, wondering what it was he was looking for when his cell phone rang. When he saw it was one of the out-of-town body shops he'd called, he remembered that one of them had called him back but he'd never listened to the message or returned the call. He'd forgotten about it with everything else that had been going on.

"You still looking for a vehicle that might have been involved in a hit-and-run?" a man asked.

He wasn't and yet he heard himself say, "What do you have?"

"I saw the message you left about looking for a damaged vehicle after April 10th nine years ago. I killed the message before my boss saw it," the man said. "Otherwise, no one would be calling you right now."

Did the man want money? Was that what this was about? "So why are you calling me?"

"After that date you mentioned, we had a car come in. It was late at night on a lowboy trailer. My boss had it dumped off. He pushed it into one of the bays. He didn't know I was still in the garage. I was curious so after he left I took a look at it. It wasn't the first car that rolled in that was…questionable. This one bothered me because there was blood on it and…hair."

Even as James told himself that this wasn't Billy's hit-and-run, he felt his heart plummet. This vehicle had been involved in a hit-and-run somewhere. Unless this guy was just leading him on. "Why didn't you report it?"

"My boss was an ass but I needed the job. My old lady was pregnant."

"You don't work there anymore?" He waited for the man to ask for money.

"I won't after this. I was suspicious so I bagged the hair and a scrap of clothing that was stuck in the bumper. Now I find out that the clothing matched the description of what that boy was wearing. I also took a piece of clean cloth and I wiped up some of the blood and put it into the bag for insurance. Look, I could get in trouble for this in so many ways. But now I've got a kid and when I heard about the trial of that senator for running over that boy… I want to see him hang."

So did James. "The FBI is going to want that bag with the evidence in it and your statement. Will you do it?"

Silence, then finally, "What the hell. My old lady says it's bad karma if I don't. It's been bothering me for the past nine years."

"They'll also want the make and model of the car."

"No problem. I even took down the license plate number." He rattled it off and James wrote it down. He was frowning down at what he'd written, when the man said, "It was a mid-sized sedan. I took a photo. Hold on, I'll send it to you."

A few moments later, the photo appeared on James's

phone. By then he knew deep down what he'd been fearing. The car wasn't Senator Fred Bayard's large black SUV. The license plate number had been wrong as well.

Heart in his throat, he stared at the car in the photo and remembered where he'd seen it. Parked in front of Alice Sherman's house.

Chapter Twenty-Four

Lorelei was about to give up. After ringing the doorbell several times and finally knocking at Alice Sherman's door, she still hadn't been able to raise anyone. She'd seen the car in the garage so she suspected the woman was home. There had been a news van parked outside when Lorelei had driven up, but it left after she hadn't gotten an answer at the door.

She was about to leave the card from her stepmother when the door opened a crack.

"What do you want?" Alice wore a bathrobe and slippers. Her hair looked as if it hadn't been washed in days. The woman stared at her, clearly not having a clue who she was.

"Mrs. Sherman, I'm—"

"It's not 'Mrs.' You're a local. I've seen you before. You one of those reporters?"

"No," she quickly assured her before the woman could close the door. "I'm Lorelei Wilkins. I own the sandwich shop in town. I just stopped by to—"

"Wilkins?" She grabbed hold of the door as if she needed it for support. "You're related to Karen?"

"She's my stepmother. She's in the hospital—"

"Like I care." Tears welled in Alice's eyes. "I hate her. I hope she dies."

"I'm sorry." Lorelei was still holding the card in her hand. "What's that?"

"It's a note from my...from Karen."

Alice's eyes widened. "She sent you with a card for me? How thoughtful after what she did to my life," she said, her voice filled with rancor. Suddenly the woman opened the door wider. "You should come in."

That had been her hope originally, using the card as an excuse. But now she wasn't so sure. "I don't want to disturb you—"

"Too late for that. Come in."

Lorelei hesitated for a moment before stepping in. As she did, Alice Sherman snatched the card from her hand.

"Sit." She tore into the envelope. "Did she tell you what she did to me?" Alice didn't wait for an answer. "She destroyed my life and now everyone is going to know and she and her boyfriend are going to pay. It's just too bad my ex-husband isn't going to prison too."

"The senator's not her boyfriend anymore," Lorelei said as Alice motioned her into a chair. This was clearly not the best time to be asking questions about Billy's death, she thought. But then again she couldn't imagine a time that would be. The senator's arrest and Karen's part in it had obviously opened the old wounds—wounds Lorelei suspected hadn't ever started to heal.

"But he *was* her boyfriend," Alice said, showing that she had been listening. "Karen lied to protect him and herself after they killed my boy."

Lorelei took a seat. She watched her read the card not once, but twice before she ripped it up and threw it into the fireplace.

Alice reached into a container on the hearth, drew out a match, struck it and tossed it into the shredded paper.

Flames licked through the card in a matter of seconds before dying out.

"What did you really come over here for?" Alice asked, turning to face her. "It wasn't to bring me a card from your mother."

She didn't correct her. She thought of Karen as her mother. "You're right. I had wanted to ask you about the night Billy died."

Alice looked surprised. "Why? The cops have Billy's killers."

"I was hoping you could help me with something. Karen was in the pines not too far from here when she heard a car go racing past."

The woman's eyes narrowed. "The senator."

Lorelei shook her head. "He didn't drive by until minutes later when Karen was walking back up the road toward her car. I was wondering if you saw the vehicle go by? If you might have recognized it."

"I had other things on my mind besides looking out the window."

She couldn't help her surprise or hide it. Alice was looking at her expectantly, waiting as if almost daring Lorelei to call her a liar. "It's just that you saw my stepmother."

"I don't know what you're talking about." Alice rubbed the back of her neck as she turned to look at the ashes in the fireplace, her back to Lorelei.

"My mother had been headed for your house but when she saw you and when you saw her, she changed her mind."

Alice picked up the poker and began jabbing at the charred remains of the card lying in the bottom of the fireplace. "I just told you I didn't look out the window."

Lorelei felt a chill move slowly up her spine. One of them was lying and this time, she believed it wasn't Karen. A thought struck her as she watched the woman's agitation increasing with each jab of the poker. "She said you quickly disappeared from the window. Not long after that, she heard the car go racing by." The chill moved through her, sending a wave of goose bumps over her flesh.

In that instant, she knew. Worse, Alice knew that she'd put it together. Lorelei shot to her feet, but not quickly enough. Alice spun around, the poker in her hand, getting between Lorelei and the door.

Brandishing the poker, the woman began to make a wailing sound. Lorelei took a step back and then another as she shoved her hand into her pocket for her phone and looked for a way out.

The wailing stopped as abruptly as it had started. Alice got a distant look in her eyes that was more frightening than the wailing. "I saw her out there through the rain. She'd taken my husband, destroyed my family. I knew Sean had broken it off with her. I knew that was why she was out there in the rain. I hated her. I just wanted her dead. Then I saw her turn and head back up the road toward her house."

Lorelei felt her phone in her pocket, but she didn't dare draw it out as Alice advanced on her, brandishing the poker.

"I went into the garage and got into my car. I opened the garage door, hoping it wouldn't wake Billy. I planned to be gone for only a few minutes. I knew exactly what I had to do. She'd asked for it and now she was going to get what she had coming to her."

Lorelei bumped into the kitchen table. She glanced toward the back door, but knew she'd never reach it in time. Alice stopped a few feet away. Her eyes looked glazed over as if lost in the past, but Lorelei didn't dare move as she took in her surroundings—looking for something she could use for a weapon.

When Alice spoke, her voice had taken on a sleepwalking kind of sound effect. "It was raining so hard, the night was so dark. I saw the figure running down the road. I hit the gas going faster and faster. The rain was coming down so hard, the wipers were beating frantically and…" Alice stopped talking, her eyes wide with horror. She began to cry. "I didn't know. How could I know? It was so dark, the rain… I didn't know." The poker wavered in her hands. "What was he doing out there in the storm? I thought he was in bed. I thought…" She looked at Lorelei, her gaze focusing and then hardening as her survival instincts took over. "I thought I killed Karen. She took my husband and then my son.

"And now I'm going to take her daughter."

Lorelei's cell began to ring, startling them both.

JAMES TRIED LORELEI'S cell on his way over to Alice's. At lunch, he remembered their discussion. Something had been nagging at Lori too, he realized. The same thing that had been bothering him.

Karen had said that the senator ran over something. Not hit something. That had been the clue the whole time. When the call to Lori went to voice mail, he called Karen. She said she'd just gotten home from the hospital after being released.

"Have you see Lorelei?" he asked, trying not to sound as worried as he was.

"She was going over to Alice Sherman's house. I had a card I wanted her to deliver."

James swore. "Call 911 and tell them to get over there. I'm on my way. Lorelei could be in trouble."

He sped toward Alice Sherman's house. He remembered Karen saying that she'd heard a car go racing past while she was in the pines getting rid of the coyote. That was after seeing Alice—and after Alice saw her walking down the road in the rainstorm. He desperately wanted to be wrong.

Just the thought of what Alice might have done, what she'd been living with… If he was right, she'd killed her own son and then covered it up. What would she do if forced to face what she'd done? That was what terrified him. If Lorelei asked too many questions…

He was almost to Alice's house. He could see Lori's car parked in the driveway. He just prayed he was wrong, but all his instincts told him that she was in trouble. He just prayed he could reach her in time.

Chapter Twenty-Five

Alice ran at her, swinging the poker, aiming for her head. Lorelei had only a second to react. She grabbed the back of the wooden chair next to her at the table and heaved it at the woman. The chair legs struck the poker, knocking it out of Alice's hands and forcing her back. The poker clattered to the kitchen floor and then skittered toward the refrigerator away from both of them.

Shoving the fallen chair aside, Alice came at her like something feral. "You and your boyfriend just couldn't leave it alone. Billy is buried. Why can't you let him rest in peace?"

"Alice, you don't want to do this," Lorelei cried as she managed to get on the other side of the kitchen table. "It was an accident. You didn't know it was Billy."

But the woman was shaking her head as she suddenly veered to the right. She thought Alice was going for the poker on the floor in front of the refrigerator deeper in the kitchen. She decided to make a run for it. She had just come around the end of the table and was headed for the living room and the front door beyond it at a run when she heard the gunshot. Sheetrock dust and particles fell over her, startling her as much as the loud report of the gun.

"Take another step and the next bullet will be for you," Alice cried.

Lorelei turned slowly to look back. The woman held the gun in both hands, her stance a warning that she was no novice at this.

"We're going to go for a ride," Alice said and motioned with the gun toward the door to the garage.

Lorelei had seen enough movies and read enough thrillers to know that you never wanted to be taken to a second location. That was where someone would eventually stumble over your shallow grave. Or their dog would dig up your remains. It was how you made the headlines.

But she also thought that as desperate as Alice appeared, maybe she should take her chances. From the look in the woman's eyes, she would shoot her here and now—just as she'd warned. Maybe during the drive Lorelei might see an opportunity to get the upper hand.

Out in the garage, Alice ordered her behind the wheel. As she climbed in, Alice got in the other side and ordered, "Start the car. I will shoot you if you do anything but what I tell you."

The key was in the ignition. As Alice hit the garage door opener, Lorelei snapped on her seatbelt, started the car and drove out of the garage.

"Go left."

She turned onto the street, her brain whirling. So far Alice hadn't buckled up. Lorelei was debating what to do when she saw James's pickup racing up the other side of the street. She swerved in front of him hoping to get his attention.

"What do you think you're doing?" Alice demanded, shoving the gun into her face as they sped past James. Had he seen her? Had he seen Alice and the gun pointed at her head?

"You called him!" Alice screamed. "I told you not to do

anything stupid, but you did." She had turned in the seat and was looking back.

In her rearview mirror, Lorelei saw James make a U-turn and come after them. He had seen her, but Lorelei realized it had been a mistake to draw his attention. James couldn't save her. Alice would kill her before that.

Worse, Alice had put down her window and was now shooting at James. In the rearview mirror, she saw the pickup's windshield shatter.

Lorelei swerved back and forth as she tried to keep the woman from getting a clean shot at James. He'd knocked out the rest of the windshield and was still coming up fast behind them. She swerved again and Alice banged her head on the window frame.

"You silly fool," the woman screeched, turning the gun on her. "I told you. Didn't I tell you? You've left me no choice."

Lorelei hit the gas again. She knew she had to act fast. Alice was too close to the edge. It would be just like her to pull the trigger and then turn the gun on herself. She slammed her foot down hard on the gas. The car jumped forward, the speed climbing quickly.

"What are you doing?" Alice cried. They were on the straightaway almost to the spot where Billy had died.

Alice was screaming as if she'd realized where they were. "No! No!" She took aim and Lorelei knew what she had to do.

Keeping the gas pedal to the floor, she suddenly swerved to the right. The car bounced down into the shallow ditch. Alice, still not belted in, was slammed against the door, throwing her off balance in the seat as she tried to aim the gun at her.

But Lorelei didn't let up on the gas as she pointed the

vehicle toward the stand of pines in the empty lot across from where Billy died.

"I should have killed you at the house!" Alice screamed as she took aim at Lorelei's head.

The car bucking and bouncing across the field, she let go of the steering wheel with one hand to try to grab for the gun. The shot was deafening, but nothing like the sound when the car hit the trees.

JAMES COULDN'T BELIEVE what he was seeing. He'd never felt more helpless as he watched Alice's car leave the road. It roared down into the ditch then headed for the pines. He hit his brakes, barely getting his pickup stopped before the car crashed into the pines.

He leaped out and ran toward the wrecked car. Steam rose from the engine. He could see that the front end of the car was badly damaged—mostly on the passenger side. Lori had been behind the wheel. As he raced to that side, Connie Matthews came out of her house.

"Call 911. Hurry!" he yelled at her as he reached the driver's side door and saw that the window had been shot out. He felt his heart drop. Had Alice shot her? Is that why the car had left the road, why it had crashed into the pines?

Inside he could see Lori. Her airbag had gone off and was now deflated over the steering wheel with Lori draped over it. There was blood dripping onto the deflated airbag.

He noticed it all in a split second as he tried unsuccessfully to open her door. Past her, he could see Alice. She'd gone through the windshield and now lay partly sprawled across the hood. She hadn't been wearing her seatbelt. Nor had her airbag activated.

James could hear sirens headed their way. He put all his weight into opening the door, surprised when he looked down and noticed his own blood. He'd taken a bullet in his arm but hadn't even realized it.

The door groaned and finally gave. In an instant he was at Lori's side. He felt for a pulse, terrified he wouldn't find one. There it was. Strong, just like her. He felt tears burn his eyes as relief rushed over him.

"Lori?" he said as he knelt beside the car. "It's going to be all right, baby. It's all going to be all right now. You're a fighter. Don't leave me. Please, don't leave me."

Soon he heard the EMTs coming, telling him to step aside. He rose and moved away, running a hand over his face as he watched them go to work. One of the EMTs noticed he was bleeding and pulled him aside.

More sirens and more rigs pulled up. Workers rushed past with a gurney for Lori. He turned away as he saw them checking Alice. It had been clear right away that she was gone.

He didn't remember going back to his pickup and following the ambulance to the hospital. Just as he didn't remember calling his brothers. Just as he didn't remember the doctors taking care of his gunshot wound or giving his statement to a law enforcement officer. All he'd thought about was Lori.

Hours later, he was walking the floor in the waiting room, when Willie arrived, followed soon after by Davey and Tommy. The surgeon had come in shortly after that to tell him that Lori had survived and was in stable condition.

"You should go on home and get some rest," the doctor told him. "You won't be able to see her until later today anyway."

He hadn't wanted to leave, but his brothers had taken him under their capable wings. When he'd awakened hours later in his bed, he'd gotten up to find them sitting in their dad's office. His arm ached. He'd looked down at the bandage, the horror of what had happened coming back to him.

"I just called the hospital," Willie said as James walked into the room. "I talked to a nurse I know. Lorelei's good. If she keeps improving as she has, you can see her later today."

James's knees felt weak with relief as he dropped into his father's office chair his brother Tommy had vacated for him.

"Now tell us what the hell has been going on here," Willie said. "Tommy went out to get us something to eat and came back with newspapers. You're a famous detective?"

"Not quite or Lori wouldn't be in the hospital right now," he said.

"Lori, is it?" Willie asked, grinning. "We saved you something to eat and made coffee. You fixed up the place pretty nice. But I think you'd better tell us what's been going on."

When he finished telling them between bites of breakfast washed down by coffee and a pain pill, his brothers were staring at him.

"You're good at this?" Davey said and laughed.

"Not quite," he said. "I almost got myself and Lori killed."

"You solved the case," Willie said.

James shook his head. "I almost got Lori killed."

"It's pretty clear to me what's going on here," Davey said. "James is in love."

His three brothers looked at him as if waiting for him to deny it. But he couldn't. It was true. He loved Lori. He repeated it out loud. "I love Lori."

His brothers all laughed, stealing glances at each other

as if they couldn't believe it. James was the last one they'd have expected to get serious about anyone.

"Wait, what are you saying? You're giving up rodeo?" Tommy said.

LORI OPENED HER eyes and blinked. She thought she was seeing double. No, not double, quadruple. Four men dressed in Western attire standing at the end of her bed. All tall, dark and handsome as sin. One in particular caught her eye. She smiled at James and closed her eyes again.

When she woke up again, James was sitting by her bed. "I dreamed that there were four of you," she said, her hoarse voice sounding strange to her. "Four handsome cowboys."

He rose quickly to take her hand. "My brothers."

"I haven't seen them in years. They're…gorgeous."

James grinned down at her. "You're still drugged up, aren't you."

She nodded, smiling. "I can't feel anything but this one spot on my head." She reached up to touch her bandage. "Alice shot me."

"Fortunately, the bullet only creased your scalp, but it did give you a concussion and bled a lot. The doctors had to stitch you back up, but you're going to be fine." He squeezed her hand. "You scared the hell out of me, Lori. I thought for sure…" She saw him swallow. "I wish you would have told me you were going to see Alice."

"You were busy packing."

It was true. He'd planned to leave. He'd put the case behind him even though something had been nagging at him. "You hadn't been gone long when I got a call from one of the auto body shops that had fixed her damaged car after the hit-and-run. When I saw the photo of the car…"

"The senator didn't kill Billy," she said.

"No, he did apparently run over part of his body though and he didn't stop. Not to mention what he did to your mother. So he's still toast."

She nodded and felt her eyelids grow heavy. "I thought you might have already left."

He shook his head. "I'm not going anywhere. You rest. I'll be here."

Lorelei closed her eyes, hoping the next time she woke he wouldn't be gone and that this would have been nothing more than a sweet dream.

WILLIE COLT STOOD in the small second-floor office about to propose a toast. James had dug out a new bottle of blackberry brandy and paper cups.

"To my brother James," Willie said. "The first of the brothers to take his last ride."

There was laughter followed by rude remarks, but as James looked around the room at his brothers he'd never been happier. It had been so long since they'd all gotten together. "I've missed you guys." He still couldn't believe that they'd dropped everything and come running when he'd needed them.

The four of them had always been close, but definitely lived their own lives. They'd see each other at a rodeo here and there, but often went months without talking to each other. But when the chips were down, they always came through. They would squabble among themselves as boys, but if anyone else got involved, they stood together.

"You're really doing this?" Davey said, throwing an arm around his brother. "You're going to marry this woman?"

James nodded, grinning. "I really am. Well, I'm going to ask her to marry me. She hasn't said yes yet. I thought I should wait until she's not doped up on the drugs they're giving her for the pain."

He'd been to the hospital every day. Lori was getting better. She was strong, just as he knew. She had bounced back fast and would be released from the hospital today.

"When are you going to ask her?" Davey wanted to know.

"I'm not sure. Soon, but I want to do it right, you know." He looked over at Tommy who'd wandered behind their father's desk and was now inspecting both James's and their father's private investigator licenses.

"You'll miss the rodeo," Davey predicted.

He couldn't deny it. "Not as much as I would miss Lori. I don't expect you to understand. I wouldn't have understood myself—until I fell in love."

Davey laughed. "I've been in love. It comes and goes. Mostly goes."

"I'm talking about a different kind of love other than buckle bunnies on the circuit," he said. "I can't even explain it. But you'll know it when it happens to you."

"So you're sticking with this PI gig?" Willie asked. "It sounds even more dangerous than bronc riding."

James chuckled. "Sometimes it definitely is. But I like it. I see why Dad liked it. Lori has her sandwich shop. Not sure what we'll do when we have kids."

"Wait a minute. *Kids?*" Davey said before the others could speak.

"She's not pregnant."

Willie chuckled. "You haven't even…"

"Nope. We literally haven't gotten that far." He grinned. "But I know she'll want kids. I'm just hoping she'll want to start trying right after the wedding."

Willie was shaking his head. "Boy, when you fall, you fall hard. You sure about this?"

"I've never been more sure of anything," he said. He couldn't describe what it had felt like when he'd leaped out of his pickup and run toward Alice Sherman's car. The driver's side window had been blown out. There was blood everywhere. His knees had threatened to buckle under him when he'd realized that Lori had been shot.

"I'm thinking about building out on the ranch," he said. "There's plenty of room for all of us. As long as there are no objections." There were none. He knew that right now his brothers couldn't see themselves settling down. Eventually they would and the land would be there for them all.

"You going to keep the name, Colt Investigations?" Tommy asked. It was the first time he'd spoken since they'd come back from the hospital.

James studied him. "I guess, why?"

"Any chance you might want a partner?" his brother asked. Everyone turned to look at Tommy.

"Are you serious?" Davey sounded the most surprised. "You just turned thirty. You have a lot of rodeo ahead of you."

Tommy shook his head. "I've been thinking about quitting for some time now. I guess I was waiting for someone to go first." He smiled at James.

"You have even less experience at being a private investigator than James," Willie pointed out. "No offense."

"It can't be that hard," Davey joked. "If James can do it."

"Right, nothing to it. James and Lorelei both almost got killed," Willie said, sounding genuinely worried.

But Tommy didn't seem to be listening. "Look at this office. I could start by getting it up to speed technologically." He continued, clearly warming to the subject. "We could invest in computers, an office landline, equipment and even filing cabinets."

James realized that his brother was serious. "You've given this some thought."

Tommy nodded. "I didn't work with Dad as much as you did, but I could learn on the job while I helped do whatever you needed done. Didn't you say a lot of the jobs you've been offered were small things like Dad used to do, finding lost pets, tracking cheating husbands and wives, filming people with work comp injuries Jet Skiing, that sort of thing. What do you say?"

"I actually think he's serious," Davey said with a shake of his head.

Willie had been watching them. "It sounds like a pretty good deal. We all know we can't rodeo forever."

"I say great," James said, surprised and yet delighted. He stepped to his brother and started to shake his hand, but instead pulled him into a bear hug. "Let's do this."

Willie was smiling broadly. "You could change the name to Colt Brothers Investigations."

"I like that," James said and looked to his brother. Tommy smiled and nodded. He looked at Willie and Davey. "That way if the two of you ever—" Before he could get the words out, Davey stopped him.

"Not happening," Davey said. "I have big plans. None of them include getting myself shot at unless it's by an irate boyfriend as I'm going out a bedroom window."

They all laughed. Willie had been quiet. As James looked at him, his older brother winked at him. "Let's just see how it goes, but I know one thing. Dad would have loved this," he said, his voice breaking. He lifted his paper cup. "To Dad." They all drank and James refilled their cups.

"There is one more thing," James said. "One of the investigations I'll be working on involves Dad. I don't think his death was an accident." As he looked around the room at each of his brothers he saw that they'd all had their suspicions. "Maybe we can find out the truth."

"I'll drink to that," Davey said, and the rest raised their paper cups.

Chapter Twenty-Six

Lori looked forward to James's visits each day at the hospital. And each day she'd waited for him to tell her he was leaving. She knew she was keeping him in town and hated that he felt he had to stay because of her.

I'm fine, she'd told him yesterday when he'd come by. *I know you're anxious to get back on the rodeo circuit. Please don't stay on my account.*

I'm not going anywhere, he'd said. *I just spoke to the doctor. Told me that you're going to be released tomorrow. Which is good because I have a surprise for you.*

A surprise?

Yes, a surprise and no I'm not giving you any clues.

She'd been allowed to dress but had to wait for a wheelchair to take her down. She'd begun to worry that James wouldn't show up. Maybe that was the surprise, she'd been thinking when he walked in. She felt a wave of relief wash over her and felt herself smiling at just the sight of him.

He grinned. "Ready to blow this place?"

She nodded, a lump in her throat. He'd stayed for her. He had a surprise for her. She tried not to, but her heart filled like a helium balloon even as she warned herself that this was temporary. James never stayed anywhere long, and he'd been here way past time. Those boots of his would be itching to make tracks.

He wheeled her down to his pickup and helped her into the passenger seat. "I want to show you something," he said as he started the engine. "You feel okay, comfortable, need anything?"

She laughed. "I'm fine," she said as she buckled up her seat belt and settled in, wondering where he was taking her. "Still no clue as to this surprise of yours?"

James shook his head, still grinning. The radio was on to a Western station. Lorelei felt herself relax. She breathed in the warm summer air coming in through the open window. She was alive. Suddenly the world seemed bigger and brighter, more beautiful than she remembered—even the small town of Lonesome.

When she voiced her euphoric feeling out loud, James laughed and reached over to take her hand.

He gave it a squeeze, his gaze softening. "It sure seems brighter to me too, being here with you."

Lorelei felt her heart fill even more and float up. She felt giddy and as hard as she tried to contain her excitement, she couldn't as he headed out of town. She glanced over at him, again wondering where he was taking her.

He turned off onto a dirt road back into the pines and kept driving until the road ended on the side of a mountain overlooking the river. He stopped, cut the engine and turned toward her.

She wasn't sure what surprised her more, that he'd brought her here or that he seemed nervous.

"Do you like it?" he asked, his voice tight with emotion. She must have looked perplexed because he quickly added, "The view. I'm thinking about building a house on this spot. What do you think?"

She looked out at the amazing view. "It's beautiful." He was thinking about building a house here? This was the surprise? "How long have you been thinking about building here?"

"For a while now," he said. "Do you feel up to getting out? There is a spot close by I wanted to show you."

JAMES HAD NEVER been so nervous in his entire life. He'd climbed on the back of rank horses without breaking a sweat. He'd even ridden a few bulls he shouldn't have in his younger days. He'd been stomped and almost gored and still, he'd never hesitated to get back on.

But right now, as they walked through the wildflowers and tall summer grass toward his favorite spot, he felt as if he couldn't breathe.

He couldn't help being nervous. He'd planned out his life and Lori's and he wasn't even sure she wanted to marry him. They'd been through a lot in a short time. They'd gotten close. But they'd had only one date. One kiss.

It had been one humdinger of a kiss though, he thought with a grin.

As he walked, he reached into his pocket and felt the small velvet box. The engagement ring was an emerald, Lori's birthstone. The moment he'd seen it, he'd known it was perfect for her. He just hoped she liked it.

He took his hand out of his pocket, leaving the ring in its box. He had to do this right, he thought as he glanced over at her. Her bandages had been removed all except for one. The headaches were only occasional and minor. The doctor had said that she was good to go.

"This isn't too much for you, is it?" James asked, his voice sounding tight.

Lori laughed. "I'm fine, James. Are you sure you're all right though?"

His laugh sounded even more nervous than he felt. He

was glad when they reached the outcropping of rock. "This is my favorite spot."

"I can see why," she said, smiling up at him. "It's beautiful."

He reached down and picked a couple of wildflowers, held them in his fingers for a moment before he offered them to her. As she took them, he watched her expression soften. Her brown eyes seemed to turn golden in the summer sun. She was so beautiful that she took his breath away.

"Lori." He swallowed.

"James?" she asked, suspicion and concern in her voice.

"I'm in love with you." He spit out the words so quickly that he had to repeat them. "I'm madly in love with you." He waited for her reaction.

LORELEI COULDN'T HELP being shocked. He was looking at her as if he couldn't believe she really hadn't seen this coming.

"I brought you here because this is where I want to build our house. I know this is fast," he added quickly.

"And maybe out of the blue," she said, unable not to smile. "We've never even been on a real date."

"You didn't think dinner at the steak house was a real date? How about when we danced?"

She nodded and felt her cheeks warm. "That did feel like a date."

He grinned as if not as nervous as he'd been before. "How about when we kissed?"

She nodded as she felt color rising to her cheeks.

He cocked his head as he looked at her. "We packed a lot into a few weeks time, you and me. We solved a mystery together and almost got killed."

Chuckling, she said, "I suppose you could say we got to know each other."

His grin broadened. "I remember being in the closet with you."

She flushed and had to look away. "If that's your idea of courtship—"

"My idea of courtship is to spend every day loving you for the rest of my life."

"James, I know you feel responsible for what happened to the two of us and that's why you're saying this. But what about the rodeo?" she asked.

"I'm not asking you out of guilt, although I do feel responsible. I jumped into my father's case not realizing how many lives I was risking—especially yours. But over this time, you've changed me."

She couldn't help her skeptical look.

He laughed. "Changed me for the better. You've made me see what it is I want out of life. I want to be with you. When I almost lost you—"

"You didn't lose me. Once you realize that I'm fine, you can go back to the rodeo—"

"I'm not leaving. I figured I had maybe another year or two max. It was time, Lori. I love rodeoing, but I love you more."

Lorelei watched him drop to one knee. Reaching into his pocket, he came out with a small velvet box. "James?" She felt goose bumps ripple across her skin.

"Lorelei Wilkins? Will you marry me and make me the proudest man in the county?" he asked, his voice breaking.

"James."

"I want to go on dates with you, dance, kiss and make love. But I want to do it right. I want to do all of it with my wife. Say yes. You know you love me."

She laughed. "I do love you, Jimmy D."

He opened the small velvet box. "I saw this ring and it reminded me of you. One of a kind."

"My birthstone," she said. "Oh, James, it's beautiful." She met his gaze as tears filled her eyes. "Yes. Yes, I want to do all those things with you. As your wife."

He slipped the ring on her finger and rose to take her in his arms. The kiss held the promise of many days living on this mountainside overlooking the river. She could hear the laughter of their children, smell the sweet scents of more summers to come and feel James's arms around her always, sheltering her, loving her.

Chapter Twenty-Seven

Lorelei wanted to pinch herself as she stared into the full-length mirror at the woman standing there.

"You look beautiful," her stepmother said as she came up beside her. They smiled at each other in the mirror. "Such a beautiful bride."

"I'm doing the right thing," she said. "Aren't I? I know it's sudden. James and I hardly know each other."

"Hush," Karen said as she turned to her. "I've never seen anyone more in love than the two of you. You know James. And he knows you. I could see this coming for years. He was always trying to get your attention back in high school. You used to blush at just the sight of him."

"I still do," Lorelei confessed with a laugh. "It's the way he looks at me."

Her stepmother laughed. "I've seen it. It's the way every woman wants to be looked at. The way every woman wants to feel. You're very lucky."

"He makes me happy."

"I can see that." Karen looked at the time. "Ready?"

Lorelei took one last look at the woman in the mirror. She was glowing, radiating happiness and excitement. Life with James would never be dull. Anita had offered to buy the sandwich shop. At first Lorelei had been surprised that her friend would think she wanted to sell it.

I just assumed you'd be working with James in the PI business until the babies start coming, Anita had said with a wink.

She'd laughed at the thought, but only for a moment. *James mentioned the same thing. He says he can't do it without me.*

When she'd mentioned selling the sandwich shop to James, he'd been excited to hear that she was going to do it. *We'll change the name of the business to Colt Investigations.*

No, Lorelei had said. *I think it should be Colt Brothers Investigations. I won't be working there. I'll be too busy. We have a wedding to plan, a house to build and decorate to get ready for the babies we're going to make.*

I do like the sound of that last part, he'd said with a laugh. *Let's get on that right after the wedding.* And he'd kissed her.

"Shall we do this?" her stepmother asked, bringing Lorelei out of her reverie.

Lorelei nodded. She couldn't wait.

The church was full to overflowing. Her three bridesmaids were ready. So were the three Colt brothers, but all she saw was James standing at the end of the aisle, waiting for her. The look in his eyes sent heat rocketing through her. Last night he'd told her about this vision he'd had of a little girl of about two on a horse.

I know she's ours, he'd said. *Our little girl.*

She'd had the same dream. *I've seen her. She has your blue eyes.*

Lorelei took a step toward James and their future. She wanted to run to him, to throw her arms around him, to tell him again and again how much she loved him, how much she wanted him.

But instead, she took another slow step and then another. There was no reason to run. They had the rest of their lives together.

* * * * *

DECOY TRAINING

CARIDAD PIÑEIRO

To my daughter Samantha and her amazing creativity! Thank you for dragging me into TikTok and for being my best PR person. I am so proud of *Seoul Searching* and all the exciting things you're doing with Korean From Context. Saranghae, ttal.

Chapter One

The "Welcome to California" sign mocked him as it became increasingly smaller in his side-view mirror.

Shane Adler shot a quick look at the Lab/hound mix sitting in the bucket chair of his pickup. "What do you think about leaving Cali, Decoy? Are you excited, boy?"

Decoy looked at Shane and cocked his head, his brown-eyed gaze almost human. Questioning.

"Yeah, I'm not sure either, but what the heck," he said and wondered if he was losing it by treating the dog as if he were human. But Decoy had been his constant companion since arriving in the States a few weeks ago from Afghanistan. He had befriended the stray pup while on assignment, feeding it scraps and letting it follow him around while he trained his fellow soldiers. They had become inseparable after Decoy had found him in the rubble left by the explosion of a car bomb.

Shane reached out to rub the dog's head, but his shoulder painfully spasmed, making his hand shake violently, courtesy of the shrapnel from the blast, which had damaged his shoulder and ended his career as an Army sharpshooter trainer.

Upon his return to his home base at the Fort Irwin National Training Center, Shane had been at loose ends, and staying near the center only brought daily reminders of what he could no longer be: a soldier. It had been his dream since he'd been a little child and now that dream was done.

Deciding he needed a change of scenery, he'd packed up his things and bought an RV to transport him from his old life in the Army to somewhere else.

Anywhere else.

First stop: Boise, Idaho. In a little over twelve hours and nearly eight hundred miles, he'd visit an old Army pal who'd been honorably discharged a couple of years earlier. Shane hoped that with some time and distance from California, he could decide what he and Decoy would do with the rest of their lives.

The open road stretched out ahead of him, the white stripes on the black asphalt and sound of the wheels on the pavement creating an almost lulling rhythm. Between much-needed coffee and bathroom breaks, they didn't arrive in Boise until dusk was settling over the area.

He had no sooner parked his pickup and the RV on the street when his friend threw open the door of his home and wheeled down a wooden ramp to greet him.

He slipped out of the pickup, bent to bro-hug his friend and gripped his hand tightly. When he straightened, Shane said, "You're looking great, Gonzo." His friend appeared fit with thicker muscle across his upper body, but more importantly, his whole attitude was relaxed. There was a happy gleam in his green-eyed gaze that relieved Shane of worry about how his friend was doing.

"Feeling great, Shane. You're looking a little…tired," Gonzo said, never one to mince words. As Decoy sidled next to Gonzo, he rubbed the gold-brown fur around the dog's floppy ears. "Who's your little friend?"

"Name's Decoy. Saved my butt in Afghanistan so I couldn't leave him behind," Shane said and glanced at the dog, who barked and wagged his head as if to agree.

"No man or dog left behind," Gonzo said with a broad smile, then executed a perfect 180 and wheeled himself back up the ramp.

Shane and Decoy followed him into the modest ranch home, and once inside, Gonzo spread his arms wide. "Welcome to my home. *Mi casa es su casa.*"

"*Gracias, amigo.* I appreciate you letting me chill with you for a little bit," Shane said, his tone heartfelt. He and Gonzo, Gonzalo to his Lopez family members, had been teammates until the bullet that had nearly taken Gonzo's life had stolen his legs and Army career.

"My pleasure. My *mami* is looking forward to seeing you, too," Gonzo said and gestured to a nearby sofa.

"Please don't tell me your mom is already matchmaking," Shane said as he sat and Decoy circled around a couple of times before settling at his feet, head tucked onto his large paws.

Gonzo held his hands up as if in surrender. "I told her that you're just here for a few days, but you know *Mami.*"

Shane did. Every time that they'd gotten together here in Boise, Gonzo's mom had tried to find a girlfriend for Shane, hoping he'd settle down. Only Shane hadn't been sure back then and he was even more unsure now about what his future might entail. Changing the subject, he said, "How are *you* doing?"

Gonzo shrugged. "Dealing, *mano.* Getting strong," Gonzo said and flexed the hard muscles of his arms. "I've also been volunteering with a group that helps troubled teens. Demanding, but I understand them. The first few months after this were really hard to accept," he said and slapped the arms of the wheelchair.

"I wish I could have been here for you," Shane said, but he'd been deployed and unable to visit his friend until his short breaks between missions.

"You helped more than you know. I hope I can do the same, *mano*. How's the shoulder?"

Shane did a little roll with his injured arm and held his hand out. Only a small tremble, but it was enough to make it impossible to handle a weapon precisely. "Working. Not much pain, but some moves are hard," he said. It was the other things, like nightmares about the explosion and being trapped beneath the debris, that still rattled him more often than he liked. But he wasn't ready to share that with anyone, even a good buddy like Gonzo.

Gonzo narrowed his gaze, clearly assessing him. "Calling you out on that, but not going to push 'cuz I know how hardheaded you can be. Are you hungry?"

In answer, his stomach rumbled, and he splayed his hand there to quiet it. "Starving. I'm hoping your mom loves me enough to have made her world-famous tamales," he said, optimistic.

Gonzo's smile was easygoing and lit up his green eyes with happiness. "She did. I just have to crank up the steam to warm them. How about a beer while we wait?"

"I'd love one," he said and followed Gonzo to the kitchen, where he noted how the space had been adapted to make it more accessible for his friend. Counters had been dropped for easier reach and were free of any lower cabinets in many sections, allowing Gonzo to slip his wheelchair beneath to work. The upper cabinets were open-shelf mechanisms that pulled down for access.

"This is cool, bro," Shane said as he looked around the kitchen, which had been remodeled since his last visit.

"It's made my life easier, but my girlfriend finds it a little challenging," he said as he took a pot and placed it on a cooktop whose height had also been adapted.

"Girlfriend? Is it serious?" Shane asked, surprised because Gonzo had always been a player before his injury.

His friend's shrug provided an answer, but also questions. "I guess it is serious," Shane said and got another awkward shrug.

"It's tough, with me being like this and all, but she's amazing. I'm a lucky man," Gonzo said as he turned the heat up under the pot with the tamales.

Shane clapped his friend on the back. "If she's amazing, don't lose her, bro."

Gonzo shot him a look over his shoulder, a broad smile on his face. "I won't, but that's funny advice coming from you."

Shane dipped his head in acknowledgment. "It is," he said because he couldn't disagree. He had no clue about lasting relationships, so telling his buddy what to do was... ironic.

But he kept silent as the two of them worked in the kitchen to finish preparing the meal and set the table. While they ate, they shared beers and chatted about how Gonzo's mother was doing, his girlfriend and his work with the troubled teens.

As he had before, Decoy took a spot at Shane's feet and Gonzo didn't fail to notice. "You guys *are* inseparable."

Shane nodded and glanced down at his dog, whose gaze perked up with the attention. "We are. I owe him big-time," he said and offered Decoy a treat from the table. Decoy eagerly snapped up the piece of tamale and sat up, anxiously awaiting another bite.

Gonzo delayed for a moment and then said, "Some of my troubled teens spend time at a dog training facility. It helps them learn discipline by taking care of the dogs and doing chores in the kennels and barn."

"Sounds like it works for them," Shane said and forked up another piece of tamale, enjoying the tasty mix of the sweet corn masa and flavorful pork.

"It does. I'm impressed by how much they change after only a few weeks, but you know, Decoy looks like a Lab/hound mix and might be great at something like search and rescue. I mean, he saved you, right?" Gonzo said and gestured to Decoy with his beer bottle.

Shane glanced down at the dog, who peered up at him with love and trust. Much like Decoy had saved his life, he had rescued Decoy and maybe that had been for a reason, he thought, intrigued by Gonzo's idea.

"He is a smart dog and great at finding things," Shane said, thinking about how much Decoy loved it when they played hide-and-seek and how he'd found Shane in the wreck of what had once been their training building.

"What's the name of this place?" he asked.

"Daniels Canine Academy. I know the owner. Emma Daniels. You interested?" Gonzo said, although he suspected his friend already knew what the answer would be.

"Yes, I am. Can you make the connection?"

"I'd love to, *mano*. Here's to new beginnings," Gonzo said and raised his beer bottle as if in a toast.

Shane wasn't quite sure it was a new beginning, but it was definitely something worth exploring, he thought, and clinked his beer bottle against Gonzo's.

PIPER LAMBERT SAT beside her best friend, Emma Daniels, as the two of them listened to the Jasper police chief explain about their newest recruit, Ava Callan.

"Ava is a good cop. We're lucky to have snagged her from Chicago PD. She's got great skills, but I think she's having a little trouble fitting in with all the men and small-town life in Jasper," Chief Walters said. He was a sixty-something man with broad shoulders and thick muscle that was starting to go soft around his midsection. His brown-eyed gaze was warm and caring as it settled on Emma and he said, "I know you understand, Em."

"I do, Chief," Emma said. The chief had been the man who had taken Emma under his wing after her adoptive father, a K-9 police officer, had died in the line of duty and Emma had lost her way.

Much like Piper had lost her way when her Marine sergeant husband had been killed in Iraq four years earlier. Luckily, Emma had offered her home and her business as a way to rebuild her life. *So far things are going well,* she thought. She'd learned so much to become a dog trainer and loved sharing that knowledge with others.

"I think that pairing Ava with a dog and working with the two of you will help her develop a sense of belonging on the force and in town," he said and ran a hand through his receding gray hair.

"We'd be happy to have her with us, Chief. Let us know when she's coming and Piper and I will pick a dog for her so we can start her training," Emma said.

Chief Walters smiled and slowly got to his feet, grimacing a little as he did so.

"You okay, Chief?" Piper asked.

The older man smiled and nodded. "Just a touch of arthritis" he said playfully, but she and Emma knew the chief was counting down to when he would retire and ride off into the sunset to fly-fish with his retired K-9 partner, Buddy, who had been peacefully resting at the chief's feet during their meeting in Emma's living room. Emma normally met with clients in her office, but the chief was family.

Emma slipped her arm through the older man's, who was almost like a second dad to her. "It was nice seeing you today, even if it was for work. Hopefully you'll come around more often when you retire."

"Count on it, Emma. I love seeing what you're doing here and I'm so proud of you," he said and hugged her before facing Piper.

"You, too, Piper. You've been doing some amazing things with the K-9s for our department," he said and left Emma's side to embrace her.

"It's my pleasure, Chief. It's great to work with everyone on the force," she said, but the older man saw through her words.

"Except Captain Rutledge," he said as they strolled out of Emma's house and to the large driveway area where the police chief had parked his white Durango. The police force's emblem, a shield honoring the area's mountains, woods and the nearby Salmon River, was emblazoned on the door, his badge and a patch on the sleeve of his black uniform shirt.

"Except Captain Rutledge," Emma repeated. "It's obvious he's not a fan of the K-9 partners you've added to the force."

Chief Walters paused by the vehicle, arms akimbo. "Rutledge is an issue, and not just because of the K-9s. I keep on hoping he'll learn to play well with others, but..."

He didn't need to finish since both she and Emma were aware of the issues the chief had with his second-in-command and the other officers in the department.

"It'll work out," Piper said, hoping that no matter what happened when the chief retired, it would not impact the business her friend had worked so hard to build.

"It will," Emma said with a bob of her head as they watched the chief get into his SUV and drive away. After, Emma slipped her arm through Piper's, and with a tug, led her toward the facility that held the offices for the DCA, a small indoor training room, runs for the dogs and climate-controlled kennels.

"Did I mention we have a new client? Gonzo recommended him to us," Emma said and tilted her head to
glance at Piper. Strands of sun-streaked light brown hair
had escaped the ponytail Emma usually wore, and her
blue-eyed gaze sparkled with joy.

"Any friend of Gonzo's is a friend of ours," she said.
The Army vet's program with troubled teens had been a
success and when combined with Emma's program for
local at-risk teens, like the three young men currently at
work in the kennels and barn, she felt like she was making a real difference in people's lives.

"Great. I was hoping you'd work with him and his dog.
It's a Lab/hound mix and he's thinking they might go on to
work with a search and rescue group," Emma said.

"Labs and hounds are wonderful for SAR, so hopefully
his dog will be good for that," Piper said, remembering
some of their clients with similar animals who had gone
on to do search and rescue in various groups throughout
the country.

"I hope so, too. He's just left the Army and he sounded…
I'm not sure what to call it," Emma said as they walked
into her office, where she snared a manila folder from her
desktop.

Military. Great, Piper thought. She had nothing but the
utmost respect for those who served and their families, but
she had her own issues because sometimes military men
reminded her way too much of her dead husband. Those
were memories she'd rather keep buried to avoid the pain
they brought.

Piper took the file for their new client and opened it,
but barely skimmed through the paperwork before handing it back to her friend. "Are you sure I'm the right trainer
for him?"

Emma arched a brow. "Positive, Piper. You know, sometimes a trainer can learn things as well when they're working with a client."

She knew she wasn't perfect, far from it, but as for what she needed to learn...

"I'll do my best," she said and shot a quick glance at her smartphone as it vibrated to remind her of an upcoming meeting.

"Something wrong?" Emma asked, eyes narrowed as she glanced at her.

Piper held up her phone. "Just a reminder to see Tashya about the puppies that Jasper PD found last week. I was thinking of maybe picking one for myself."

"Good to hear. You've wanted your own dog for a long time," Emma said and clapped her hands happily.

"I have and those cute puppies Macon brought over may be perfect," she said, and didn't fail to notice the little wince at the mention of Emma's former client before her friend schooled her emotions. It had been clear to everyone that there had been a spark between Macon and Emma when he had been training with them.

"They may be," she said and gestured to her desk. "I've got a few calls to make before I quit for the day. Feel like meeting me at Millard's Diner for dinner?"

"I never say no to one of their burgers," Piper said, but thought it funny that Emma would choose a spot that was a hangout for the local police officers, including Macon Ridley. But the diner was a fun place to eat with red vinyl booths, bright blue counters and even a jukebox that gave it a very retro '50s vibe.

"Six sound good?"

"Six is perfect," she said and rushed out to meet Tashya, the young vet tech who had been one of many foster children Emma had taken in over the years, much like the Danielses had fostered Emma after she was removed from a home plagued by domestic violence. Thanks to the life insurance money left to her by her foster mom, Emma had been able to turn the Daniels homestead into the DCA and had fostered a number of children over the years to honor her adoptive parents.

As she neared one of the kennels, she heard Tashya's playful laughter, and it brightened the pall cast over her by the prospect of having to work with her new client.

Shane Adler. Ex-Army sharpshooter and instructor. Wounded vet.

A dangerous mix for a variety of reasons.

But at the sight of Tashya laughing and surrounded by over half a dozen playful pups that jumped up and climbed all over her, her worries fell away.

When she entered the kennel, one little dog bounded away from Tashya and sauntered over to her, a jaunty smile on her white-and-tan face. The puppies were a corgi/pit mix and would need little grooming thanks to their short hair, but a lot of attention since pits could be needy and very active.

She scooped up the pup, who wriggled in her arms and licked doggy kisses all along her jaw. "Easy, girl. I love you, too," she said with a laugh, but didn't release her as she walked to Tashya.

"That one is a handful," the young vet tech said as she finished examining the last puppy and shot to her feet.

"Is she ready to be adopted?" Piper asked, eager to start training the little dog.

"Dr. Beaumont said you can take her home tomorrow after the last of her shots."

"How is Marie doing?" Piper said. She hadn't seen the vet in weeks since she'd been so wrapped up with work at the DCA.

"She's busy. Her vet business is doing well. Any idea

what you'll name your pup?" Tashya asked as she rubbed the puppy's head.

Piper peered at the little dog, and the pup immediately gave Piper her attention. With her perpetual corgi smile, she radiated cheer, which prompted Piper to say, "Chipper." The dog yipped, almost as if approving of Piper's choice.

Tashya threw her head back in laughter, her smile bright against the creamy brown of her skin. "I'll round up what you'll need to take her home."

"Thank you so much. I'll come by after work tomorrow," she said and hugged the young woman before heading home.

She walked away into the gap between the barn where Emma kept two rescue horses and the building that held their offices and kennels. Behind the buildings was an open gap in the surrounding tree line and a small path through a nearby meadow to her tidy ranch house. She and Emma had worn down that path with the many times they'd used it. It was barely a ten-minute walk and when the weather was nice, as it was today despite a slight April chill, she loved to do the hike to stretch her legs and appreciate the beauty of the nature around them, especially since in the winter three or four feet of snow might blanket the ground, making the trek difficult unless she hauled out her cross-country skis. Emma often did the walk over to Piper's house as well for a girls' night.

The ground was a little soft from an earlier rain and the air still had that rain-fresh smell tinged with the scent of pines and fir from the nearby evergreens. The first spring wildflowers were beginning to blossom, painting the ground with shades of yellow, purple and white. After the April rains, the meadows would burst to life with the white and pink of woodland stars, purples of clematis and shooting stars, and the bright yellows of arrowleaf balsamroot and heartleaf arnica.

In the distance, the mountains rose up, snow frosting the highest peaks, but most of the snow would melt in the next few weeks and the flowers would start to blossom at those higher elevations.

But today the beauty of the nature around her didn't bring as much calm as it usually did, maybe because she had a niggling sense something wasn't right as she neared the backyard of her home.

Piper looked around, searching for the source of that disquiet, but didn't see anything when she walked to the front door. A weird feeling came to her, as if she was being watched, only after another quick look around, she didn't see anyone or anything, like the occasional black bear that sometimes wandered out of the woods. Then a smell wafted to her: cigarette smoke. Only there was no other home around for at least a couple of hundred feet.

Hands on her hips, she did a slow pivot once again, searching for the source of the odor, but couldn't find a thing.

Maybe I'm imagining it, or the smell came from a passing car, she thought, but that feeling of being watched chased her into her home, making her feel uneasy until she closed the door behind her and double-locked it. Only then did she feel relief.

She hoped that relief would last with the arrival of their new client.

Shane Adler. From the brief look she had gotten at his paperwork in the file Emma had passed to her, she knew he was a wounded vet and bound to have his demons, but so did she.

Maybe together they could find a way to exorcise those demons and move on with their lives.

Chapter Two

Shane stood by the firepit and stared at the Salmon River as it wound past the campground where he'd parked his RV. The air was frosty and scented with the fresh fragrance from a nearby stand of pines and the smoky remnants of last night's fire. Decoy sprawled beside him on the rug he had spread out on the smooth stones all around the living area for his camping space.

He'd arrived in the early morning the day before, eager to get settled before his first day at the Daniels Canine Academy. It had been a short drive from Gonzo's in Boise, just over three hours. That had given him time to stop in Jasper for groceries and other supplies.

The town was the kind of peaceful and picturesque small town that 1950s Hollywood would adore. Quaint shops, restaurants and well-kept older homes lined one side of Main Street and led to a central park with a gazebo. A vet's office, the fire and police departments and town hall were at the west side of the square. A library, shops and professional offices surrounded the park while the west end of Main Street led in the direction of the Salmon River and his campground.

After the chaos of life as a soldier, Jasper might be just what I need, Shane thought and with a low whistle at Decoy, headed to his pickup for the drive to the training center. The DCA was only twenty minutes away, but he didn't want to be late.

His parents had always told him that being late was a sign of disrespect and the military had only reinforced the importance of timeliness.

As he drove, he took note of the older but nicely maintained homes on large-sized properties along the road. A newer gray and stone ranch home sat at the corner where his GPS told him to turn for the final half-mile drive to the DCA.

He stopped in the driveway where two large poles held up a wooden sign that read Daniels Canine Academy next to the silhouette of a German shepherd. Beyond the sign was a long driveway leading to a trio of buildings.

"What do you think, Decoy? Looks good, right?" he asked and shot a quick peek at his dog as Decoy sat in the passenger seat.

The dog cocked his head to the side and peered at Shane, but then Decoy surprised him with a quick bark as if to say, "Get a move on."

"Sure thing, boss," he said with a laugh and wheeled his pickup down the drive to the parking spaces opposite a rambling, green-roofed ranch house. When he exited his vehicle and leashed Decoy, he noticed the three women working with a litter of puppies in a fenced-in area in front of a large agility course.

He approached quietly, not wanting to interrupt the training, but also wanting to get a feel for the women. Two of the women seemed to be of a similar age, late twenties if he had to guess.

The third was clearly younger, with a round baby face, beautiful light brown eyes and brown hair. She had a puppy on a leash and was watching as the other women played with a litter of short-legged, long-bodied dogs, but also worked basic commands into the play.

The taller of the women had a strong athletic build and sun-streaked light brown hair pulled back in a ponytail. She scooped up one of the playful puppies to observe the other woman as she worked with another little dog.

"Sit, Chipper," the second woman said with authority and combined it with a hand gesture. When the pup didn't immediately respond, she repeated the command and gently urged the pup's butt onto the ground. This time the command seemed to take, and she rewarded the little dog with a treat, squatted to rub its head and said, "Good girl, Chipper."

He couldn't avoid admiring her as she rose and raked back her long red hair with her fingers. As the puppy yipped at her, she tossed her head back and laughed, the sound pure and unfiltered.

It dragged a laugh from him and snared the attention of the three women.

The redhead went from joy to a chill as frosty as the snow on the nearby mountains, making him wonder about her abrupt change of mood.

"You must be Shane. Emma Daniels," said the one woman and walked over to shake his hand.

"Shane Adler. I'm looking forward to working with you," he said and from the corner of his eye he noticed as the redhead slowly approached where he stood at the fence railing.

"Actually, you'll be working with Piper," Emma said and tilted her head in the direction of the other woman who finally, reluctantly, held out her hand.

PIPER THOUGHT SHE'D be prepared for when she'd meet her new client, but she was totally wrong.

He was dangerously handsome, with broad shoulders and washboard abs that were visible beneath the cotton of his tight T-shirt. The soft denim of his jeans hugged long muscular legs. Intense blue eyes were framed by thick lashes any woman would wish for. A light stubble on his strong jaw and cheeks had hints of gray like those in the longer strands of hair at the top of his head.

He had been leaning on the railing and straightened to well over six feet as he said, "Shane Adler. Nice to meet you, Piper."

As he wrapped his big, calloused hand around hers, her gut clenched with awareness of his strength and masculinity. His blue eyes widened a bit before he reined in whatever emotion that had been and released her hand.

"Nice to meet you as well," she said, forcing positivity into her tone and hoping it didn't sound as artificial as it was.

The awkward exchange was luckily interrupted by the sharp yip of her puppy, Chipper, who had sneaked under the fence and was climbing all over Decoy. The older dog was calm, his head cocked almost indulgently as the puppy yapped and hopped on him, demanding attention.

"Chipper. Sit," Piper said and held up her palm in a hand signal. Surprisingly, the little pup responded, earning a treat and rub of her head to reinforce the training. "Good girl."

"She's a fast learner," said the younger woman with a laugh and held out her hand. "I'm Tashya Pratt, the DCA's vet tech."

"Nice to meet you, Tashya," he said and shook her hand.

When Chipper barked again and hopped up on his leg, Shane said, "I see you, girl. Now sit."

Chipper sat and Shane smiled and laughed as he bent to

pat the little dog's head as her reward for the behavior and likewise rubbed Decoy's head to acknowledge his calm.

That smile should be registered as a dangerous weapon, Piper thought, unable to ignore how the smile and laughter totally transformed a face that had been hard as stone only seconds before making it look almost boyish.

That hard-as-stone visage was all too familiar to her. She'd seen it on her husband's face more than once, and sadly, their time of laughter and smiles had been cut short with his death.

As Shane straightened, that hardness slipped back into place, and she told herself that was for the best.

"Are you ready to get started?" she asked, picked up Chipper and handed her to Tashya, who would care for her until Piper took her home later that day.

"I'm ready if you are," he said with an arch of a dark brow, almost in challenge.

"Great," she said even though she wasn't ready in any way, shape or form. "Let me show you around the place so you get familiar with it," she said and slipped beneath the fence railing to join him.

"I'd like that. Thanks," Shane said and trailed after her as she walked him toward the two buildings beside the outdoor training ring. The closest building had a concrete base and dark wood above and was a nice-sized structure. Piper gestured to it and, as she opened the door, said, "This is really the heart of DCA."

He followed her into the building and to the first office where a forty-something woman with medium brown hair and light hazel eyes sat at a desk. The woman looked up and smiled as she saw them. She popped out of her chair and cheerfully introduced herself, "Barbara Macy. I'm Emma's assistant."

Shane shook her hand and smiled. "Shane Adler. Nice to meet you."

"Don't let her kid you. Barbara is more than just Emma's assistant. She's the Master of All and if you need anything, absolutely anything, Barbara is the person to see," Piper said with a laugh.

Barbara grinned and did a little curtsy. "Thank you so much, Piper."

They walked just a few feet and Piper said, "This is Emma's office, but it's probably easier to find her anywhere the dogs are training."

Sure enough, as they turned to walk back out, he caught sight of Emma and Tashya. They had moved to an indoor training area right by the offices and were working with the puppies once again. Although he couldn't call what they were doing training since some of the pups were busy playing with toys while others were starting to drop off for naps.

Piper must have sensed his confusion since she said, "It's important to let puppies play as part of their training and the toys can serve as positive reinforcement as good as any treat. We also move them to different environments so they're not afraid of other surroundings."

"Good to know," he said, thinking about how Decoy seemed to be confident no matter his location, maybe as a result of all the different areas he'd been exposed to in his short life. Including the rescue foundation's kennel in Afghanistan where he'd been kept while he and the foundation cut through all the red tape to get Decoy sent to the States.

They exited and walked past doors for a climate-controlled kennel area and then large outside dog runs.

"As you can see, we have plenty of room for the dogs to stay with us and also have a place to be outside."

"Do you keep a lot of animals with you?" he asked,

impressed with the facilities and how well-maintained they appeared.

Piper stopped by one dog run to rub the head of a German shepherd who lapped up the attention. "That's a good dog, Lacey," she said, but then added, "Most trainees keep their dogs with them, but we sometimes have up to half a dozen dogs. We select some for training from nearby animal shelters while others are left by their owners for instruction. Occasionally we end up with rescues like those corgi/pit puppies."

When Piper rose, she gestured to the furthermost building, which was wooden and white and had a paddock next to it. A brown quarter horse and a black-and-white-spotted Appaloosa were close to the wooden fence, nibbling at the grass along the edges. A large orange tabby sauntered out of the barn and walked toward the horses, who ignored the pudgy feline.

"That cat is Gus. You can pet him, but he'll flay you alive if you pick him up. He's a great rodent-catcher," she said with a shake of her head.

Shane laughed. "I can tell from that belly he's good at his job."

Piper joined in his laughter. The sound was musical, bright, and it once again lightened something inside him.

He didn't have time to let that sink in since Decoy suddenly barked and lunged toward the tabby, scaring it away.

"Sit, boy. Sit," he said, but Decoy tugged at the leash again until Piper grabbed hold of it and brought him tight to Shane's side and issued a strongly worded, "Sit."

The dog sat and peered up at Piper, apparently aware she wouldn't take any guff.

She bent slightly, rubbed the dog's ears and reached into her pocket to give him a treat. "Good boy, Decoy. Good boy."

"He's usually pretty obedient, but he's still learning," Shane said and likewise stroked Decoy's head.

Piper nodded and straightened again. "How long have you had him?"

It should have been an easy question to answer, and yet it wasn't. "Decoy's been with me several weeks now in the States, and before that, we were together in Afghanistan for about four or five months. I was deployed there as an Army sharpshooter trainer and Decoy was always hanging around our complex. I started feeding him and he kept on coming back."

He didn't fail to see the change that came over Piper at the mention of his military service. Every muscle in her body tensed and a dark cloud chased away the lightness that had been in her laughter just seconds before. He should have left it alone, but he couldn't. Especially if they were going to be working together for the next month.

"Something wrong?"

A stilted shrug followed before she wrapped her arms around herself in a defensive gesture he recognized all too well. He did it whenever anyone delved too deeply into why he was no longer a soldier.

Despite her obvious reticence, something made him push. "Well?"

HE WAS CHALLENGING her already and they hadn't even really started working together, but if they were going to survive several weeks of training, honesty was going to be the best policy.

"My husband was a Marine," Piper said, but didn't make eye contact with him. Instead, she whirled and started walking back in the direction of the outdoor training ring.

He turned and kept pace beside her, his gaze trained on her face. "Was?"

Challenging again. Pushing, but regardless of that, she said, "He was killed in action in Iraq. Four years ago and yet…"

Her throat choked up and tears welled in her eyes as she rushed forward, almost as if she could outrun the discussion and the pain it brought.

The gentle touch of his big, calloused hand on her forearm stopped her escape.

She glanced down at that hand and then followed his arm up to meet his gaze, so full of concern and something else. *Pain?*

"I'm sorry. It can't be easy," he said, the simple words filled with so much more. Pain for sure. Understanding. Compassion. Not pity, thankfully. The last nearly undid her, but she sucked in a breath, held it for the briefest second before blurting out, "We should get going. If you're going to do search and rescue with Decoy, we'll have to improve his obedience skills."

Rushing away from him, she slipped through the gaps in the split rail fence and walked to the center of the training ring.

Shane hesitated, obviously uneasy, but then he bent to go across the fence railing and met her in the middle of the ring, Decoy at his side.

"I'm ready if you are," he said, his big body several feet away only he still felt too close. Too big. Too masculine with that kind of posture and strength that screamed military.

She took a step back and said, "I'm ready."

She wasn't and didn't know if she ever could be with this man. He was testing her on too many levels.

Only she'd never failed a training assignment and she didn't intend to start with Shane and Decoy.

"Let's get going," she said.

Chapter Three

Shane was pleased with how the afternoon had gone, especially considering the awkwardness when they had first begun their training.

That had ebbed little by little as Piper worked with them to determine how well Decoy responded to basic commands. Piper also instructed him on leash control and how to train Decoy to understand hand commands as well as verbal ones. In a search and rescue situation, it might not be possible to use verbal instructions, so Decoy would need to understand what to do with the hand signals.

By the end of the training session, Decoy had nailed both the verbal and hand commands for "Sit" and had started to understand "Look at me."

"That's a good boy," Piper said as she offered Decoy a treat and ruffled his golden-brown fur affectionately.

The dog rewarded her with sloppy dog kisses, yanking that bright almost musical laugh from her again.

She was beautiful when she laughed. It made her emerald gaze glitter and reminded him of the evergreens surrounding the area and blanketing the mountains in the distance.

As her gaze connected with his, he reined in his reaction and said, "I think it was a good day."

Piper nodded. "I think so, too. Decoy is a smart boy. Aren't you?"

The dog almost preened, raising his head to look at Piper and doing a quick little bark.

"He's a natural. I guess that's why he was able to find me," he said, then winced and braced himself for what the next question would be and how Piper would react.

"Labs and hounds love playing hide-and-seek. That's something we can work on as well," she said, but her tone was forced since she was clearly in avoidance mode as he was.

"Great," he said, his tone sharp.

She stiltedly repeated, "Great." She clapped her hands, wrapped her arms around herself, and said, "I think we should call it a day. Just remember to reinforce what he's learning with the leash control and treats."

"Will do." He walked with Piper out of the ring.

As they neared the kennel, Piper said, "Barbara mentioned to me earlier this morning that she needs you to fill out some additional forms."

"Okay. I'll go see her. I guess I'll see you tomorrow," he said, his tone filled with question.

"Tomorrow," she confirmed and hurried away into the gap between the two buildings.

PIPER COULDN'T GET away from Shane fast enough.

He challenged her on so many levels and she wasn't sure she was up for it.

There was the whole ex-Army thing that roused too many memories of her dead husband, David, although Shane was nothing like David physically. David had been a blond, California-surfer-dude type with a lean build and average height. Handsome with his boyish grin whose memory even now brought lightness to her heart despite his loss.

Shane was all man and anything but boyish. His stubble and short-cropped hair were painted with the first strokes of gray. His blue-eyed gaze was intense and seemingly missed nothing based on how he had noticed the emotions she had thought she successfully hid from him and others.

And he was big, well over six feet with thick work-hardened muscle. Imposing.

It had been hard to ignore that masculinity when she had to get close to him to help train Decoy. And even though she knew he'd been wounded, she hadn't detected anything while they worked together, except for possibly the occasional times he'd reached up to massage his shoulder.

She was almost home, Chipper playfully tagging along beside her on her new pink leash, when her hackles rose, and fear shimmied down her spine.

Pulling up short, she glanced around again, surprised that she was almost home. She'd been so involved in thinking about Shane that she hadn't realized how close she was to her house.

Her heart pounded in her chest as she peered at the woods surrounding the path and toward her backyard, searching for the source of her disquiet.

Nothing.

Sucking in a deep breath, there was no odor but pine scent today unlike yesterday's very obvious cigarette smoke.

You're imagining things, she told herself, and as Chipper tugged at her leash and started barking and jumping, she squatted to rub the puppy's head. "Mommy is just being silly, Chipper," she said, and the puppy licked her face with doggy kisses, relieving a little bit of her upset.

She plodded on the last twenty yards or so, but once

again skidded to a halt as she reached the alcove for her front door.

You're not imagining that those flowerpots were moved, she thought. There were obvious water rings where the pots had previously sat as well as some crushed and broken pansy stems along the edges. One plant even looked as if it had been messily replanted, and as she got closer, the loose dirt near it confirmed that something had happened to that pot.

Chipper tugged on her leash and sniffed around the pots, but Piper said, "Sit, Chipper."

The pup looked up, grinning and barking, and it took another "Sit" before she responded.

"Good girl," Piper said and offered her a treat from her jacket pocket.

After, she jammed her hands on her hips and surveyed the area again but saw nothing except a big red pickup as it turned the corner from the road for the DCA and slowly pulled in front of her house and parked. The driver's side door popped open. Shane stepped out and Decoy jumped down with him. They walked toward her, concern evident on Shane's features.

"You okay?" he asked as he approached. Decoy rushed to her and jumped up, demanding her attention until Shane gave the sit command and the dog immediately responded as did Chipper, who cuddled next to Decoy on the front step.

"Fine," she said but wrapped her arms around herself, and as his gaze tracked that move, she realized it was a tell for him that things were anything but right.

He arched that brow again. "Are you sure? You look a little…freaked."

Piper could lie again but knew it wouldn't fly with him. She motioned to the flowerpots on the cement by the path to her front door. "Someone messed with these pots, and yesterday I smelled cigarette smoke as I walked home. I feel like I'm being watched."

Shane nodded and did a slow pivot, peering all around before walking to the edge of her driveway, Decoy tagging along behind him as she kept a short leash on Chipper to keep her close.

Shane squatted by the edge and Decoy bent his head to smell the ground beside the driveway, then began to jump up and down, as if he sensed something.

"Good boy. Sit," he said and when the dog responded, he rubbed the dog's head in reward.

He straightened, looked over his shoulder at Piper, and pointed to the grass where she could see some tracks. "I'm guessing you came this way from the DCA?"

She nodded. "I did. I like the walk when the weather is nice."

Shane peered all around and the ghost of a smile spread across his lips. "Beautiful scenery," he said and then glanced her way again.

"It is. I'm probably just imagining it," she said, but that answer didn't seem to satisfy him.

He walked along the edge of the driveway, perusing the ground, Decoy beside him, as if they were searching for more footprints. With a shake of his head, he walked back to her, Decoy bounding behind him happily. Chipper strained at her leash until the little pup settled in next to her new best friend.

"Nothing there, but someone could have walked up from the road. Do you keep a key under the pot?"

She shook her head. "No. Emma has a key. No one else needs to get in," she said and bit her lower lip, well aware of what those words told him.

He nodded. "Okay. Maybe it was just someone hoping to find a key and make an easy score."

"Or maybe I'm just freaking out over nothing. That kind of stuff doesn't really happen in Jasper," she said.

"That kind of stuff can happen anywhere. Doesn't Emma have troubled teens at the DCA?" he argued.

"They would never do something like that. They're good boys who just need a little guidance," she said and poked him in the chest to emphasize her point.

He snared her finger. "Got it, Piper. But maybe you should think about putting in a security system or one of those video cameras."

Even though she wanted to again say that things like that weren't necessary in Jasper, she was still too worried about the possibility that he was right. And rather than argue with him, she said, "I'll think about it."

His nod was slow, hesitant. "Okay. Do you need me to check inside before you go in?"

She stared back toward her door, but it seemed secure. "I'll be okay."

He nodded but didn't move so she ignored him and went to her door. She tried the handle. Still locked. She opened the door and took a tentative step inside, peered around. Everything seemed as it should be, but just in case, she didn't close her front door as she did a slow reconnoiter of her ranch home, going from room to room, Chipper at her side, before returning to the front door.

Shane still stood there at the end of the alcove, solid as any rock from the nearby Idaho mountains. Decoy was at his side, patiently waiting.

She forced a smile she wasn't feeling and waved to let him know she was okay and as a goodbye.

He returned the wave and walked back to his pickup

with Decoy. The dog jumped in first, he got in, and they drove away.

Piper closed the door, double-locked it and leaned against the security of her metal door.

She peered around her home, circled around the rooms again, making sure to check that all the windows were locked, and that the sliding doors to her back deck were secured. She paused to take in the view from those doors: the nearby woods; the meadow she traversed so often on her way to get to the DCA; and the mountains with their frosting of late spring snow. A beautiful view, but today it brought a sense of isolation and loneliness.

Until Chipper jumped up on her leg, demanding attention.

"Yes, girl. I see you," she said and picked up the puppy.

The warmth of that little body and affectionate licks along her face shook off more of those feelings. She finished her walk around the house, went to her bedroom and changed out of her work clothes. To wash away any lingering negative emotions, she took a long hot shower and after changed into comfortable clothes and went into the kitchen to make herself and Chipper a quick dinner, the puppy at her side.

Stomach full, she settled in to watch a rom-com with the puppy tucked against her in bed. As the movie ended, she was feeling infinitely safer and a lot less lonely thanks to Chipper's company. Finally relaxed, she took Chipper out to the back deck so she could relieve herself. Nothing happening there. Absolutely nothing.

Breathing an easier sigh, she tugged on Chipper's leash and the pup immediately responded and followed Piper back into the house and her bedroom.

As Chipper obediently snuggled into her new doggy bed with a toy and Piper slipped into her own bed, she had only one more wish for that night: that it would be as easy for her to learn to deal with Shane and the maelstrom of emotions he roused in her.

The sound of a car engine intruded in the quiet of the night, but it didn't move on the way it would with a passing vehicle. And then the engine noise suddenly stopped.

Worry crept into her again. She snagged her cell phone in case she had to call for help, slipped out of bed and tiptoed to her front window.

A now familiar red pickup truck sat there, Decoy in the passenger seat.

That maelstrom of emotions spun ever faster, especially as Shane bent and looked out the window toward the house. As their gazes locked, she had no doubt that he'd do whatever he needed in order to make sure she was safe, including sitting there all night if it was necessary.

She'd always been an independent woman, but she had to admit that the sight of him brought…relief.

But she told herself not to get too used to it because Shane would soon be gone.

Chapter Four

She was nothing but a silhouette in the front window until she snapped on a light, illuminating her face and body. She wore an oversize brown T-shirt emblazoned with the DCA's German shepherd logo.

No worry on her face, only confusion and possibly relief as she raised her cell phone, and his phone rang.

He answered and she said, "What are you doing here?"

"I couldn't sleep and decided to take a drive. Figured I'd drop by to make sure everything was okay with you." Even though everything wasn't okay with him thanks to the nightmare that had woken him from the first semi-sound sleep he'd had in days.

"I'm…okay. You really didn't have to come by," Piper said.

She was right. He didn't really have to come by, but the short drive had helped to clear his brain of the lingering memories from his nightmare.

"I just wanted to make sure you were fine," he said, which was the truth. He really was worried about what might be happening with Piper. He'd seen no evidence that anything was going on, but Piper had been well and truly freaked out that something was wrong.

"I am. Thank you. Have a good night," she said and did a little wave.

He returned the wave and started up the car but waited until she had snapped off the light and disappeared from view before he drove off and back to the campground where his RV was parked.

"We're home, Decoy," he said and popped out of the pickup, Decoy quickly following him into the RV. He paused by the kitchen area to make sure Decoy still had fresh water and then pushed through to the back of the RV and his bedroom.

The sheets and comforter were a tangle he straightened out before stripping and climbing back into bed. A chill spring breeze, tinged with the scent of pine and fir, swept through the open windows of the RV. The breeze was strong enough to rustle the branches of the evergreens and a nearby stand of aspens.

He breathed in deeply, the scent calming. The soft whisper of the breeze and sounds of the branches soon lulled him to sleep again.

But other sounds and smells soon intruded again. The roar and heat that had filled the air when the car bomb had gone off. The rain of concrete and glass that became a deluge as the building collapsed on him and the soldiers he had been training.

The deafening silence that had followed as he lay there, his body aching in so many places he couldn't tell where one hurt began and another ended. The slow awakening of sound: the ringing in his ears; the calls of searchers; the screams and cries of the wounded. Pain sluggishly came to life as well and became focused on his right shoulder, which howled in agony.

He had been screaming. Calling out in the hopes of being found until he was hoarse and drained of energy. He'd passed out but woken to the bark of a dog. Decoy's bark. A lick on his hand and soft fur beneath his palm.

He woke up then, the sheets tangled all around him again. Decoy standing at the side of the bed, nudging his hand. Finding him once more. Saving him again as Shane moved over in the bed and patted the space beside him.

Decoy jumped up as commanded and snuggled into Shane's side, his presence and warmth comforting. Bringing him peace as he finally drifted off and slept.

THE GROUND BENEATH the tent was hard. Unyielding as he tried to get comfortable.

The only thing that made the small space of the tent habitable was the breeze blowing in through the open tent flaps.

Just a little bit more time, he told himself, only he suspected it would be longer than he would like.

He had thought he could get into the woman's home and search it right away, but so far he'd had no luck. Which meant he had to find somewhere more comfortable than the tent to stay in.

He'd been watching the place and had seen her coming and going. Pretty thing. David had been a lucky man. *Well, lucky except for dying on that mission,* he thought.

He didn't want any problems with the woman, just what he was entitled to and David had taken from him and Buck. That's all he wanted, but so far he was striking out.

And now there was a man around. He'd seen him stop and help the woman after he'd tried to find a key to get into the house. The man had been there tonight as well, damn it. He'd seen him when he'd been hiding in the woods nearby, hoping to figure out how and when he'd be able to get into the home.

Not anytime soon with the woman obviously worried something was happening and the man dropping by way too often.

He'd have to wait it out. Give it a couple of days or more for them to relax so he could find an opening for getting into the house.

David owed him and he intended to get what was his. Once he did, he'd have enough money to finally get on with his life.

He just needed to get what David had given his wife. He was sure she had it and he intended to get it back no matter what it took.

THE LICK OF a tongue along the underside of her jaw woke Piper from a deep sleep.

"G'morning, Chipper," she said and rubbed the puppy's head.

The puppy jumped up on her midsection and continued licking Piper's face. "I love you, too," she said, but nature was calling. Probably as well for the puppy.

She hopped from bed and quickly relieved herself, then clipped a leash on Chipper's collar and walked her into the backyard, where the puppy decided to nose around the potted plants, exploring.

Piper shivered in the chill of the morning air and wrapped her arms around herself to ward off the cold. "Chipper," she said sharply, drawing the puppy's attention, not that the puppy would understand.

"Sit," she said, and the pup obeyed. Smiling, she rubbed Chipper's head, earning that corgi smile in her tan-and-white face. It dragged a smile to her lips and a laugh.

She was surprised she could laugh after what had happened yesterday, but her spirit was lighter today. Not as worried, she thought as she glanced around her yard and saw that everything seemed normal.

It was a beautiful mid-April morning. The sun had just risen, painting the meadow behind her home with shades of rosy-pink and yellow light that brightened the colors of the wildflowers.

A tug on the leash drew her attention to Chipper, who had walked off the deck and was finally relieving herself on the nearby grass. She scratched and kicked up the ground in the area, marking her territory in typical canine scrape behavior.

"Come, Chipper," she said and swayed her palm in her direction, trying to reinforce the verbal command with the hand signal.

The puppy sat, ears perked up, and Piper repeated the command.

The dog immediately came to her side and Piper scooped her up, rewarding her with her attention. Once they were back inside, the sliding door locked behind them, she grabbed a treat from a canister on her kitchen counter and gave it to Chipper.

Removing her leash and letting Chipper settle into a dog bed in the living room, Piper rushed into the shower to get ready for another day at the DCA.

Another day with Shane, she thought as she washed.

It was hard to deny that maybe part of the reason she wasn't as worried was that she knew Shane was around.

But Shane wasn't going to be around forever. His training program was scheduled to last four weeks and then he'd be off for more intensive training with a search and rescue group. Not that the DCA couldn't provide that training since they often did. Emma had been working with a local group, Mountaintop SAR, and Dillon Diaz, one of the members of the Jasper PD force, to improve their SAR techniques and keep abreast of any new methods.

But Shane would be leaving, she reminded herself as she dressed, leashed Chipper and made the short walk from her home through the meadow to the DCA.

Unlike the other day, she had no sense of being watched. Detected no odors that were out of the ordinary. If anything, it was just another beautiful day, filled with the fresh scents of pine and fir, the rich colors of the evergreens and aspens in the nearby stands of trees and up on the mountain, and the wildflowers.

The ground was still moist with morning dew and wet the hem of her jeans as she walked. Luckily, she'd worn her waterproof boots to keep her feet dry and warm.

As she arrived at the DCA, she caught sight of Tashya coming out of Emma's home. Tashya was one of the young people whom Emma had fostered as a way to honor the Danielses, who had fostered her. Since Tashya's return from vet tech school in Boise, the young woman had been living with Emma. A second later, Tashya's boyfriend, Jason Wright, also came out of the house.

"Good morning, Tashya. Jason," she said, smiling at the handsome young man who had also been one of Emma's fosters and was now a rookie police officer with the Jasper PD.

"Good morning, Piper," they both answered in unison, but Jason quickly added, "I just stopped by to have breakfast, but it's time I headed to work."

He dropped a quick kiss on Tashya's lips and rushed to his car, leaving Piper and Tashya to start their morning routine. They checked in on their rescued puppies and the dogs in the kennels. Tashya remained behind with them while Piper went to check in with Emma and Barbara to see if there was anything new for the day.

As she walked out of the DCA offices with Emma, Shane pulled up in his red pickup. He parked and hopped out, Decoy following behind him.

He sauntered to them, his walk that of a man confident in his own skin. His blue gaze warmed as it settled on her. In a morning-husky voice, he said, "Good morning, Piper. Emma."

"Morning," she said and clasped her hands before her, unsettled by his attention.

"Morning, Shane. How are you today?" Emma said, looking between the two of them as if to decipher what was happening.

"I'm fine. Looking forward to today's training session since I learned so much yesterday," he said and once again glanced at her.

"Good," Emma quickly said. "I hope you won't mind that Officer Callan will be joining you today."

"Not at all. Anything for local law enforcement," he said and rubbed Decoy's head as the dog sidled up to his leg and sat.

"Then let's get going," Piper said and gestured in the direction of the training ring.

SHANE FOLLOWED PIPER into the ring, and they were soon repeating and reinforcing the commands they had worked on the day before. The "Sit" and "Look at me" commands, both verbal and hand signals.

To his pleasure, Decoy immediately responded to the commands, earning his rewards and Shane's affection as he complied.

"Good boy, Decoy. Good boy," he said, getting down on one knee to rub the dog's head and a special spot that he'd discovered behind his floppy ears.

The sound of a vehicle approaching drew their attention.

A Jasper PD police car pulled up and two officers stepped out of the vehicle along with a black-and-white shepherd dog.

Piper walked to the fence to greet them, and he trailed behind her.

"Shane. Meet Officers Callan and Diaz," Piper said.

Shane shook their hands. "Shane Adler. Nice to meet you."

"Ava," the pretty officer said. Her hair was pulled back into a tight bun as taut as her smile, clearly uneasy.

"Dillon," the other officer said. They were of a like height and build and his hazel-green eyes were filled with laughter as he gestured to the dog at his side. "This is Bentley, my unofficial K-9."

"Dillon's part of the local SAR group, Mountaintop," Piper explained.

"I understand you're interested in SAR," Dillon said.

"I am," Shane confirmed. "Decoy's very good at finding things and I'm hoping we can use those skills to help."

"Just like we're hoping that Ava can learn to work with Lacey," Piper said, clearly hoping to draw the young woman into the conversation since she'd been standing there awkwardly during the exchange.

"I hope so," Ava said, but it was obvious she was less than happy with the situation.

"It'll be fine, Ava," Dillon said, not that it relieved any of her anxiety.

"If it works out Chief Walters will be happy and if it doesn't, Captain Rutledge will be pleased, so I guess you're right," she said with a shrug of slim shoulders.

Dillon laughed and shook his head. "You nailed that right, Ava. If you'll excuse me, I have to run. Brady will be back later to pick you up," he said and walked back to the police car.

"Emma is going to bring Lacey over for you, Ava. She's a wonderful German shepherd we've trained here at the DCA," Piper explained. "You can work with her so she learns to listen to you while Shane works with Decoy and I train this little girl here," she said and bent to scoop up Chipper.

The ghost of a smile drifted across Ava's face at the sight of the little puppy. She reached out and patted her head. "She's a cutie. Is she one of the puppies Macon rescued?"

"She is. We've been training them and thanks to the newspaper article, we've placed them with various families in town," Piper explained.

"Good to hear," she said just as Emma came over with a German shepherd.

"Officer Callan. Nice to see you," Emma said and shook Ava's hand.

"Ava, please," the young woman said.

"Meet Lacey. She's a two-year-old German shepherd. Friendly. Attentive. She's good at finding things, so we hope that'll be a help to you and Jasper PD," Emma explained and rubbed Lacey's long brown-and-tan fur.

"I hope so," Ava said, but it was clear to him, and probably also to Emma and Piper, that the young officer was less than pleased at being paired with Lacey.

"Great," Emma said and handed over Lacey's leash to Ava. "I'll leave you to it," she said with a broad, welcoming smile, obviously hoping to put the woman at ease.

"Let's get to work and welcome, Ava," Piper said. "We're really looking forward to having you with us."

The young woman forced a smile but nodded and slipped under the fence railing to join them, Lacey at her side.

In no time they were going through the first commands they'd taught Decoy, reinforcing those commands for his dog. Letting Ava bond with Lacey, who already understood the instructions and teaching them to Chipper, who was a little ball of energy and those Corgi smiles that could melt any heart.

Like they were melting Ava's together with the clear affection that Lacey immediately had for the young officer. By the time the other police officer showed up to take Ava back to police headquarters, a bond had clearly been developing between the officer and Lacey, and even with Piper. The officer seemed more relaxed around her.

Unlike how he was around Piper.

He seemed attuned to every little nuance about her. The way she'd rake her fingers through her hair to pull it off her face as she worked. The flush that would sometimes paint her cheeks when their gazes collided. The gentle but firm way she had with the animals as she reinforced the commands.

When the officers left, it was just the two of them in the ring, but instead of continuing there, Piper motioned to the agility course behind the training area.

"Ready to try something different?"

He was sure her idea of different would present a challenge, but he liked that. He liked how she made him feel and as he walked with her to the course, he realized he'd follow her anywhere. He hadn't planned on that, but some said God laughed at men who made plans.

Still, this unplanned attraction was downright scary. Possibly even more scary than the dreams that came way too often.

But the military had taught him not only how to plan but how to handle it when things went south, so he'd find a way to handle Piper and keep them both from getting hurt.

Chapter Five

They spent the last hours of the day working on the agility course, letting Decoy explore the various obstacles on the course. An A-frame ramp, seesaw and elevated dog walk.

Piper was pleased with how easily Decoy handled those challenges and took Shane and Piper over to what were sometimes more difficult elements. A tunnel, chute and tire jump.

Decoy hesitated at the entry to the tunnel, but then pushed through and actually seemed to enjoy it with her at one end encouraging and Shane at the other end with a treat and affection. The chute, with its long tail of nylon where the dog was basically running blind, frightened Decoy, putting an end to the training session.

"Easy, boy," Shane said and kneeled on one knee to calm Decoy. "Easy."

Decoy settled down, especially as Chipper edged close to the older dog, demanding attention, which Decoy gave, licking the pup and placing a paw on her head to keep her down.

Piper laughed, enjoying the interaction between the two dogs. "They're so good together."

"They are. And Chipper's a fast learner," Shane said and straightened.

She was hit again by all that imposing masculinity, but

also by the tenderness he showed toward the dogs and his restraint around Ava. The young officer had clearly been standoffish, hiding behind a wall she'd built around herself.

Shane hadn't pushed, as if knowing that would only make her build that wall higher. Maybe because he had his wall as well. She'd seen it at times when they were getting too close, both physically and emotionally.

Like they were now.

"Decoy's a fast learner as well. I'm sure that by the time we're done with training, Decoy will be able to handle all these obstacles," Piper said, building her own wall so she could handle the fact that Shane and Decoy would one day be leaving.

"I think it's time to call it a day," she said. The agility course had tested Decoy and being with Shane was testing her.

"I think so, too," he said and when he met her gaze, it was obvious he was feeling much the same.

"See you tomorrow," she said and rushed from the agility course, but she could feel his eyes on her as she entered the DCA offices.

He was gone by the time she finished chatting with Barbara and Emma and started the walk home.

Her mind was filled with satisfaction as she thought of the progress they'd made with all the dogs. With how Ava had finally let her in, just a little. Of Shane and how quickly he was learning.

Shane. Shane. Shane.

Stupid to think about it since, as she'd told him, he'd be leaving once his training was done.

She drove him from her thoughts, telling herself to be on the lookout for anything out of the ordinary as she approached her home. But there was nothing. No tracks except those of her own coming and going through the meadow and the scents of pine and fir as a spring breeze swept across a nearby stand of trees.

Nothing happening near her home, she thought as she walked around to her door.

Well, nothing except Shane sitting in his red pickup truck in front of the house.

He waved at her. Decoy barked a greeting, which had Chipper straining on her leash to go visit her friend.

Piper relented. She walked to the pickup and leaned on the edge of the open door. "You don't have to do this, Shane."

"You're right. I don't. I just wanted to make sure you're okay," he said and peered around at their surroundings.

"Nothing as far as I can see. Maybe I was just imagining it," Piper said, glancing back at her house and then tracking his gaze to look all around.

"Maybe," he said and clenched his fingers on the steering wheel. Facing her, he said, "I'll wait until you get in. Let me know you're okay."

He wouldn't relent, so she nodded and walked to her front door. Unlocked it and left it open as she had the other day. Once inside, she checked all around, but much like in the meadow, there was nothing to cause alarm.

She went back to the front door and waved at Shane. Called out, "All good here."

"Good. See you tomorrow," he replied, then gave a brief chop of his hand as a wave and drove away.

"Tomorrow," she whispered to no one.

Time to grab a bite, take a shower and relax so she could be ready for tomorrow and another day with Shane.

As THEY HAD in the past, the nightmares subsided with Decoy at his side. The warmth and weight of his body brought a sense of safety, much like they had as Decoy stayed with him while his Army colleagues dug him out of the rubble of the building they'd been using for training. He had only been able to touch Decoy's nose, feel his soft breath and the lick of his tongue, but that had been enough to keep him from feeling lost and alone.

With the nightmares under control, he'd had more energy and focus during the training sessions at the DCA, and it showed as they neared the end of the first week.

"You two are learning quickly," Piper said as Shane ran through the various verbal and hand commands and Decoy obeyed. Earlier in the day they had taken a few runs through the agility course, even the dreaded chute that had so terrified Decoy on the second day of training.

"We have a good instructor," he said, then bit his lower lip, worried it sounded too much like flirting.

Bright splotches of color erupted on Piper's creamy cheeks, and she downplayed his compliment. "It's easy when I have a dog like Decoy to work with," she said, and then quickly tacked on, "and you."

The color deepened on her cheeks, and she looked away, obviously embarrassed.

Luckily, they were both saved from what could have led to even more awkwardness by Ava's arrival with Emma and Lacey.

"How's it going?" Emma asked, immediately picking up on the vibes between the two of them.

"Good," they both said simultaneously, earning an arched brow from both Emma and Ava.

"Good," Emma said and jerked her head in the direction of the agility course where they'd been working earlier that morning. "Are you done over there?"

"We are. I was just thinking of taking Shane and Decoy indoors so we can maybe work on some attack and protect commands since he's learning so quickly," Piper said.

Shane hadn't thought about teaching Decoy anything like that, but it certainly could come in handy if they were doing search and rescue in an area that wasn't secure.

"Wonderful. If you aren't going to be too late, I was thinking we could all grab a bite after the training. Shane? Ava? Are you up for it?" Emma said.

Shane glanced at Ava, who in the last week had become more comfortable around all of them. Because of that, he said, "I'd love to go."

Ava offered up a small smile before echoing his acceptance of the invite. "Sure. That would be nice."

"Great. I was thinking we could go to Bartwell Brewing. They've got some great local craft beers and the food's pretty good as well. Six o'clock," Emma said and dipped her head as if to end the discussion.

"Six o'clock," Ava said, then with Lacey on a leash beside her, followed Emma to the agility course.

"Determined, isn't she?" Shane said and ran a hand through his hair while watching the two women walk away.

Piper's gaze darkened, grew sad. "You could say that, or you could say that Emma just wants to help others."

Shane didn't think he needed help, but kept quiet, not wanting to push the issue. Tipping his head in the direction of the building where he'd seen the indoor ring earlier in the week, he said, "You mentioned something about attack and protect?"

Piper nodded. "Sure. Follow me."

PIPER AND EMMA had driven to Bartwell Brewing together as they did so often when they had a girls' night.

Shane's red pickup was parked near the mouth of the alley where the brewery was located in a huge warehouse just off Third Street and not far from the headquarters for the police department. Its proximity was one of the reasons that the brewery was such a popular place with local law enforcement. The craft beers and good food didn't hurt either.

As Emma and she walked in, Piper spotted a couple of police officers at a high-top table near the bar: Dillon Diaz and his best friend, Brady Nichols. Both Brady and Dillon had trained their dogs at the DCA and were regular visitors at the ranch. They smiled and waved as Emma and Piper walked past them to the back of the brewery where Shane sat at a table in the dining area.

He stood as they approached.

"Hi," Piper said, admiring how the dark blue Western shirt he wore accented his broad shoulders and lean midsection. The color magnified the intense blue of his eyes, which glittered brightly in the mellow light of the high-ceilinged warehouse building. Mother-of-pearl buttons barely held the fabric tight against the muscled width of his chest.

"Hi," he said, his voice slightly husky.

"Hi, Shane," Emma said cheerily from beside her and then peered around the brewery. "Have you seen Ava?"

"Not yet," Shane said at the same time that Piper's phone rang. Ava was calling.

"Hi there, Ava. We're in the back dining room."

"I'm sorry, but I won't be able to make it. Captain Rutledge wants Jason and me to work the night shift. Says we have to earn our stripes," Ava said, the exasperation apparent in her tone.

"Sorry to hear that. Sorry about Rutledge as well. I know he can be difficult," Piper said, staring at Emma and shaking her head in disgust.

"I have to learn to deal with him, right? But I am sorry. I was looking forward to tonight," the young officer said.

When noise filtered in from behind her, she added, "Have to run."

Piper swiped to end the call and blew out a harsh breath. "Captain Rutledge is making Ava and Jason work tonight. Do you think it has to do with Ava training with us?"

"And Jason dating Tashya? Possibly," Emma said and took a seat at the table.

Piper and Shane joined her, Piper at her side and Shane across from them.

"I gather Rutledge is not a fan," Shane said just as a waitress came over with some menus.

"The craft beer list is on the back, and we also have an assortment of the usual in bottles or draft. Bud, Miller, Stella and the rest," the young woman advised and took a pad and pen out of her apron pocket.

"Anything you can recommend?" Shane asked Piper and Emma.

"I love the Mountaintop IPA, plus a portion of the sales go to our local search and rescue group. I'll take a pint of that," Piper said.

"The same," Shane and Emma said.

"I'll go get your drinks and be back for your food orders," the waitress replied and hurried off to place their orders.

Emma took only a quick look at the menu and laid it down on the table. "Burgers and steaks are always good here."

With a bob of his head, Shane said, "Sounds good."

The waitress returned a couple of minutes later with their drinks, and they placed their food orders and returned to their earlier conversation.

"What's up with Rutledge?" Shane asked, pressing the issue again.

Piper shared a look with Emma and said, "He's not

a fan of the K-9 program at Jasper PD. If Chief Walters retires—"

"*When* he retires, Piper," Emma corrected. "I know Doug is looking forward to more free time."

"I GUESS THE captain is next in line to be chief?" Shane said, sensing the upset of both women over the Jasper PD officer.

Emma and Piper shared another look. One of disgust if he had to guess, which surprised him since both women were generally easygoing and friendly.

"He thinks he is, but truth be told, many of the officers have issues with him," Piper said with a wrinkle of her nose as if she was smelling something bad.

"We're hoping Chief Walters chooses someone else to take over," Emma added, and Shane understood what they weren't saying. Someone who would be supportive of the police department continuing the K-9 program and training with the DCA.

He raised his glass of beer in a toast. "To the DCA and a big thank-you for all you've taught me so far."

Both women smiled and joined in the toast. "To the DCA and to your success in an SAR group," Emma said.

Piper chimed in with "I second that," but Shane detected a momentary flicker of sadness in her gaze. As she met his, there was no doubting it from the emotion in those deep green eyes.

In their short week together, something had changed between them that had nothing to do with the K-9s or his plans to move on to possibly join a search and rescue group in Montana.

He decided a change of discussion was the best remedy for the sudden melancholy he was likewise feeling.

"How did you start the DCA?" Shane said, wondering what would have made two such bright and beautiful women dedicate themselves to such an out-of-the-ordinary life in the Idaho mountains.

Emma shrugged, but then launched into her story. "My foster dad was a K-9 officer with the Jasper PD. He helped train a lot of the dogs and officers in Jasper as well as in nearby police departments. My foster mom was very active in community affairs, including work with local animal shelters to try and get the animals rescued before they were put down. After they both died, I inherited money from an insurance payment, and it seemed right to use that money to honor them by continuing the work that they did with the dogs."

There was more to the story, he could tell, but suddenly Emma's phone rang and barely a second after Emma answered, the waitress came over with their meals.

The waitress was about to walk away, when Emma ended her call and said, "I'm going to have to take mine to go."

"I'll get you a container," the waitress said and hurried off.

"What's wrong?" Piper asked, brows knitted together with worry.

"Tashya says Gus the cat got into it with a fox. Gus won, but he got bit and Tashya needs help since Marie's busy with a horse that's foaling."

"I guess I'll get mine to go as well," Piper said.

"I can drive you," Shane said at the same time that Emma replied, "You stay."

Piper looked from one to the other and shrugged. "Okay. I can stay, that is if it's not a big deal to drive me home."

It was only about twenty minutes from his RV campground to Piper's home, but more importantly, he didn't want the night with Piper to end so soon.

"It's no big deal."

Except he could hear Gonzo's voice in his head chastising him. *Dude, it's totally a big deal because you have feelings for this woman.*

He didn't really know just what those feelings were, but he intended to take the time to find out, starting with tonight.

Chapter Six

She was alone with Shane. Great.

Except she'd been alone with him various times during the week while they trained.

But this was different. This was a potentially monumental shift in the cornerstone of the wall she'd built around herself since David's death.

You can get through this, she told herself, as Shane asked, "How did you and Emma get to know each other?"

Keep it to Emma and you, she thought.

"We met in college and became fast friends. When I wasn't in school or interning for my degree, I'd visit with Emma and her mom."

Shane cut a piece of his steak slowly, clearly thinking about what to ask next. "Emma mentioned her dad died."

Since the information was public news based on various articles that had been written about her friend, she didn't feel she was betraying a confidence by sharing it. "Her foster dad, Rick, died in the line of duty. Rick and his wife, Susan, fostered Emma after she was removed from her home because of issues with domestic violence. She loved the Danielses, and sadly, her mom passed about a year after she finished college."

"I'm sorry to hear that," he said and forked up some of the French fries that had come with his meal.

An awkward silence followed. Emma suspected what he wanted to ask and yet he didn't, maybe because then she'd ask him about his background. Much like hers, it was forbidden territory, she suspected. Still, she wanted to know more about him.

"I've met Gonzo once or twice when he brought some of his teens to the DCA to work with us. How did the two of you become friends?"

"We met in basic training. We had both enlisted right out of high school after 9/11. We just hit it off and I knew I could always count on him to watch my six," Shane explained and swirled a French fry through a mound of ketchup on his plate.

Piper chewed on her burger thoughtfully, struggling with how to phrase what to ask. Somehow her mouth blurted it out before her brain could stop her. "Were you with him when…?"

Shane paused with the French fry halfway up to his mouth, then set it down. "I was. It was supposed to be a routine scouting mission to look for a small Taliban cell that had been terrorizing a nearby village. We were ambushed and luckily we didn't lose a man, but Gonzo was seriously injured. We didn't know how bad until later."

UNTIL THE DOCTORS had dealt with the immediate emergency and then loaded his buddy onto a plane headed for the Ramstein Air Base in Germany, so he could be treated at Landstuhl Regional Medical Center.

"He was lucky to survive," Piper said, and her gaze darkened once more, to a green like that of the deepest shadows in a forest.

She was thinking about her husband. The man who hadn't survived.

"I'm sorry about your husband," he said and immediately regretted it as tears shimmered in her gaze and one spilled down her cheek.

He reached into his jeans pocket for the handkerchief his father had always said he should carry because you never knew when you might need it. Handing it to her, he said, "It must have been hard for you."

She took the handkerchief and dabbed at her eyes. "It was. I was lucky to have Emma. She was a big help because I was so lost."

He knew the feeling well and something inside him made him share. "I was an expert sharpshooter and had been offered a position as a trainer. After Gonzo was hurt, it made me realize how fragile life was and so I took that position," he said and jabbed at the steak to finish it although it would probably taste like sawdust thanks to their conversation.

She reached out and laid a hand on his, stilling his almost angry motion.

"But you were hurt anyway and now here you are. With us," she said and soothed her thumb across his knuckles, the gesture surprisingly comforting.

"I am," he said, his tone more resigned than curt.

She did a slow nod and, with laser focus, settled her gaze on him. "When David died, I asked myself time and time again why it happened. It took a long time for me to realize that I was meant to go on a different journey than the one I had envisioned for myself."

"What had you envisioned?" he asked, needing to know more about this woman who intrigued him on so many levels.

"David and me. Babies. A small house in the suburbs. Teaching elementary school. I was an education major," she admitted freely, a Mona Lisa–like smile on her face. "And you?" she added.

"In truth?" he said and paused, digging deep into his soul for the answer. "I always wanted to be a soldier. Even before 9/11. As for family, I wanted what my parents had. Laughter. Love, only... There was never enough time for that after I enlisted."

She blew out a harsh laugh, as if chastising herself. "There never is 'enough time,'" she said, emphasizing the words by using her fingers to mimic quote marks. "Unless you make time for it."

"You don't think that's what I'm doing now?" he asked because in truth, he still wasn't sure what he was doing at the DCA. When Gonzo had mentioned it and he had spoken to Emma and then the leader of the Montana SAR group, it had seemed like something to try. Something to replace being a soldier only...

Was it just another excuse to keep from really living? he thought.

That Mona Lisa smile drifted across her lips once again, filled with compassion, sadness and possibly even resolve.

"I guess we'll find out," she said.

AN EXPECTANT QUIET filled the cab of the pickup as Shane and Piper did the short trip from the brewery to Piper's ranch house.

When Shane pulled into her gravel driveway, he killed the engine and sat there, gripping the wheel tightly before he faced her and said, "Let me walk you to the door."

"No need. I'll be fine," she said, but hesitated, torn because she didn't want the night to end.

"A gentleman always escorts a lady home," he said and before she could say anything else, he hopped out of the pickup and walked around to open her door.

When he held his hand out to her, she slipped hers into his. Comfort immediately filled her from the touch of his big, calloused hand. She slid down from the high cab of the truck to the ground. He continued to hold her hand as they walked to her house, releasing it only so she could fish her keys out of her purse and open her front door.

She faced him, looking up because of his much greater height. He was so big and strong and yet so gentle with Decoy, Chipper and her. Honorable. Intelligent. Caring. All of that called to her, scared her, so she reminded herself that Shane would leave one day.

"Thank you. No need for you to stick around," she said, and gestured to the peaceful quiet of the night.

Shane did a perusal of the area. "Looks like everything is fine. Nothing new happening, right?"

"Nothing new. I guess it was just kids or someone looking to make a quick buck like you said."

He nodded, jammed his hands in his jeans pockets and rocked back and forth on his heels. "I guess it's goodnight."

"I guess," she said, even though she was conflicted.

"Good night," he said and leaned down to brush a kiss across her cheek, but as he did so, she shifted her head, just the tiniest bit. But enough that his lips skimmed hers.

A jolt like that from a live wire surged through her, weakening her knees. She had to grab hold of his arm for support, and he steadied her by laying a gentle hand at her waist.

The kiss deepened, his mouth mobile on hers for only a second before he jerked away from her with a mumbled curse.

"I'm sorry. That shouldn't have happened," he said and stepped back, giving her breathing room that she totally needed.

She sucked in a deep breath and held it, bracing herself. Expelling the breath slowly, she said, "No need to apologize. We're both adults. We know what we're doing."

He arched a brow. "Do you? Because I sure don't. I don't know what I'm doing. Where I'm going. What I'm supposed to do with the rest of my life."

Which made him a very dangerous man. After years of living with David and his absences, his death, the last thing she needed was another man who might not be there one day.

"Good night, Shane. I'll see you in the morning for training. Just training," she said, then rushed into her home and closed the door. She leaned against it, counting the long seconds until she heard the car start and the crackle of the driveway gravel as he pulled out and away.

With a rough sigh, she shook her head to chastise herself for what had just happened, and double-locked the door. She walked all around her house, checking the windows and the sliding doors to make sure all was in order.

It was.

Chipper perked up as she caught sight of Piper, and she let the puppy out of the crate. The little dog came over to jump excitedly at her feet and bark. She picked her up and cradled her against her chest, earning doggy kisses all along her jaw.

"I love you, too, Chipper," she said with a laugh, the puppy's antics chasing away her earlier upset.

With a final rub of Chipper's head, she placed the pup down, leashed her and walked her out to the back deck so she could relieve herself. The puppy did her thing quickly and they came back in, locked up and went to her bedroom, where Chipper obediently headed straight to her doggy bed.

"Good girl, Chipper," she said and patted the dog's head.

A quick look around her room and check of the windows said she was safe.

Well, at least from her imaginary intruder.

Shane was a whole 'nother problem, but come morning, she'd set things back to right.

Shane was her client and nothing else.

THERE WAS NO missing the chill coming off Piper during the last week, Shane thought. She was all business, with none of the easy smiles and laughter that had gradually become part of their training sessions the week before.

They worked Decoy through all the verbal and hand signals and the dog instantly responded, earning his treats and attention to reinforce the behavior. They'd added some hide-and-seek games, placing bits of treats and clothing in various areas around the DCA compound. Finding the treats had been a slam dunk for Decoy, the clothing not so much, but Piper had said that in time and with training Decoy's skills would improve.

Chipper wasn't as quick with the commands, but then again, she was way younger than Decoy, but little by little the pup was learning.

Decoy had also been sailing through all the obstacles on the agility course, so much so that Emma had brought in some additional tunnels and taller, less steady ramps and seesaws to challenge his dog. At first Decoy had balked at the shaky footing on the seesaw, but by the end of the week he was going up and over it without issue.

Chipper not so much on the basic course with her short legs and sometimes shorter attention span. But Piper was patient with the puppy, who did finally manage to make it up and over the ramp and through the tunnel, but not the chute or seesaw.

That warmth in her attitude was also evident when Ava

joined them to train. The young officer, who had been standoffish to start, had become friendlier and was quickly learning how to handle Lacey. It was also obvious the German shepherd had bonded with Ava and as the two of them walked away to return to the police station, Shane said, "Looks like things are going to work out with those two."

Piper tracked the officer and dog as their police cruiser drove away. "It does. Ava and Lacey will be a wonderful K-9 team. Chief Walters had a good idea to put them together."

Shane couldn't miss the note of affection that drifted into her tone at the mention of the chief. "You like him a lot, don't you?"

"I do. He saved Emma," she said and at his questioning glance, continued. "I'm not telling you anything you wouldn't know if you did an internet search on Emma and the DCA."

He did a slow nod. "I respect loyalty, Piper."

PIPER GUESSED HE was referring to more than just her relationship with Emma, but she ignored the inference to finish her story.

Scooping up Chipper, who had been growing restless, she said, "When Emma's foster dad died, she kind of lost it. She was only sixteen and she loved him. Respected him. She got involved with the wrong boy and ended up in trouble. Chief Walters helped put her back on the right path. Became like a second dad to her and to a lot of the kids that Emma has fostered over the years."

"Chief Walters sounds like a good man," Shane said and dipped his head.

"He is. He's been very supportive of Emma and the DCA. And his K-9 program at Jasper PD is one of the best in the area."

Shane smiled and rubbed Decoy's head as the dog bumped his leg, as if wondering why they were just standing there instead of training.

"You and Emma are amazing instructors. You're doing great work with the dogs and the kids you help. Gonzo couldn't say enough nice things about you," he said.

She smiled at the mention of his friend, who was a strong supporter and a wonderful man from what she could tell. "Gonzo's the best."

"He is. I guess we're both lucky to have such good friends," he said, but when his bright blue gaze settled on hers, there was no doubt the last thing he wanted for them was to be friends.

"I think it's time to call it a day," she said, and before he could say anything else, she set Chipper back on the ground and hurried out of the training ring.

In no time Chipper and she had slipped between the kennels and barn and were walking through the meadow on the way home. Beneath her booted feet, the ground was a little soft from an overnight rain. A riot of color greeted her in the meadow since the rain had encouraged even more flowers to open.

The beauty of the nature around her filled her with peace as it always did. It had been one of the things that had kept her steady in the months after David's death. Well, that and Emma. She could never repay Emma enough for the support she had provided and this new life that gave her so much satisfaction.

She loved working with the dogs and meeting new people. Seeing people grow as they bonded with the canines. Seeing others open up, like Ava and, yes, Shane.

He'd been more closed off when he'd first arrived, but during the first week he'd loosened up a little. Become more easygoing. Until the kiss, of course.

That had set them back to square one or maybe even further back, if that was possible.

As she rounded the corner of her house, she stopped short.

Her car door was ajar.

Hands on her hips, she did a slow pivot, inspecting the area all around her home.

No signs of anything else being out of the ordinary.

Chipper jumped onto her leg, demanding attention.

"Sit," she commanded sharply, and the puppy responded, her floppy ears, courtesy of the pit in her, perking up at Piper's tone.

"Good girl, Chipper," she said and bent to pat the dog's head.

Squatting there, she peered at the ground, searching the grass all around and focusing on a spot in the gravel near her car door.

Nothing.

She rose and walked over to the car. Just some fingerprints by the handle the way you might expect.

Just in case, she used the hem of her T-shirt to open the door.

The top edge of the inside door panel was slightly wet as if the door had been open during last night's light rain. She ran her finger along the weather stripping at the top of the door, which was also damp from being ajar.

Obviously, the door had been open since last night and no one had come by during the day. Which freaked her out to think about someone being out here, going through her car while she was asleep in the house.

Only there was nothing amiss inside the car. She kept her vehicle pristine and would have noticed anything.

Glancing around the area again, she ran through what she had done last night when she'd come home from dinner with Emma. She'd driven since Tashya had borrowed Emma's vehicle to take one of their dogs to the vet.

I'm sure I closed it. But her seat belt latch sometimes ended up between the door and her seat. Sure enough, the latch dangled close to the side of the seat since the seat belt hadn't retracted as it should have.

She slipped her key fob from the knapsack she usually carried to work and locked her car. Walking to her front door, where everything was as it should be, she shook her head to chastise herself for being silly.

There was only one threat she had to worry about: six-plus feet of a too-tempting Army vet.

Chapter Seven

Shane was restless after that day's training session. Well, restless and intrigued about Emma as well as Piper. She had told him about her friend's history, but not much about herself.

He needed to know more about her.

Since Piper had mentioned the internet, he jumped online and did searches to find information on Emma and the DCA. As he read through the articles, he grew even more impressed with all that Emma had accomplished at the canine academy. But buried in the various articles and blogs that the DCA posted to offer tips on training and their staff were breadcrumbs about Piper.

How she was a military widow whose Marine husband had been killed in Iraq.

That she had moved from California to Idaho to join the DCA four years earlier.

It didn't take much to find out when her husband had died and that the DCA had likely been her refuge from memories of him.

He could understand her flight. *I'm doing the same thing, right?*

Right, but when will you stop running? the little voice in his head challenged.

He shut down his laptop and grabbed his keys. Right

now, all he was running to was a nice cold pint of the wonderful IPA he'd had the other night at the brewery.

When he arrived, he noticed Officer Dillon Diaz alone at one of the high-top tables. He'd met the officer at the DCA when he'd come by to chat with Emma and Piper.

The officer waved as Shane walked in and he took it as an invitation to join him.

As he neared, he realized that the officer was having coffee and not a brew. "Officer Diaz. On duty?"

"Dillon, please, and yes. Just keeping an eye on things," the other man said.

Shane did a quick look around, but everything seemed fine.

"Problems?" he asked.

With a quick dip of his head, Dillon said, "Some. A few cars broken into. Cash taken from a tip jar here in the brewery at the end of the night. Small stuff."

Which made Shane think of the little things that had been bothering Piper and his suspicions about the pots at her front door. For a moment he wanted to share that info with the officer, but since Piper hadn't mentioned anything new in the last week, he thought better of it.

"Anything I should keep an eye out for?" he said and gestured to a waitress to come over.

"It's probably just some kids out for a thrill, but if you notice any strangers, present company excluded, of course, or anything out of the ordinary, you should give us a call," he said and sipped his coffee.

Shane smiled and laid a hand on his chest. "Glad you're not including me."

Dillon chuckled and it reached up into his hazel-green eyes. "I've seen you and your dog. Dogs are a great judge of character. So are Emma and Piper. If they're cool with you, so am I."

"Glad to hear. I understand you're part of the local search and rescue group," Shane said, and after the waitress had placed the beer on the high-top, he paid her, including a generous tip.

"I am. Bentley and I trained at the DCA and while we're not officially part of the Jasper PD K-9 squad, we help out when needed." He gestured to Shane with his coffee cup. "I hear your dog is really catching on quickly. We're always looking for new members to help out. You can't imagine how many lost hikers and stranded skiers we have."

"I appreciate the confidence," he said, but he'd already been in contact with another SAR group in Montana. Despite that, the seed had been planted and took root. After all, he wanted to be able to spend time with Gonzo when he could, and Jasper wasn't all that far away. The trip from Boise to Montana was over twice as long, nearly eight hours. Too far from Gonzo.

Too far from Piper, too? the little voice challenged.

The words left his mouth before he could rein them in. "I'll think about it. Thanks."

Dillon smiled and finished the last of his coffee. He slipped his police baseball cap on his head, tipped the edge of it with his finger and said, "I hope you'll stay."

Shane laughed and shook his head at the man's determination. "Like I said, I will think about it."

With a little salute, Dillon walked away, leaving Shane to finish his beer and consider the request.

If anyone had asked him two weeks ago if he'd even consider settling down in a small town like Jasper, he might have said no.

But after the chaos of multiple deployments in Iraq and Afghanistan, the peace and quiet of Jasper was a blessing. It was nice to fall asleep to the sound of branches gently waving in the breeze and the burble of water along the edges of the nearby Salmon River. To wake to the morning air, still chill in mid-April.

He loved the quiet, except in those moments when the nightmares came. It was in those moments that he could have used the noises of the city to drown out the memories of war. Of friends injured and lost. Of the building exploding into bits around him, pouring down on him to trap him in a grave of twisted wire, broken cinder block and smoldering wood.

Enough, he warned himself, tossing off the memories the way Decoy shook water from his fur after a morning dip in the river.

Grabbing his beer, he chugged the last of the IPA and set the glass down with a loud thump.

It was time to head back to his RV. Decoy needed to be let out one last time for the night.

But as he walked down the alley, his hackles rose, almost as if someone had a bead on him.

He stopped and looked back in the direction of the brewery. A few patrons lingered along the far side of the building, smoking. None seemed to be paying any attention to him.

He started back toward his car, but the disquiet lingered, spurred by what Dillon had told him earlier and the incidents at Piper's the week before.

Little incidents. Little thefts. But stack up all those little things and they could sometimes become bigger things. Dangerous things.

Because of that, he intended to make one quick stop before he went home.

HE DIDN'T KNOW who this guy was or why he kept on showing up. But regardless of the why, he could be trouble.

He recognized a fellow military man when he saw one.

The guy would be able to defend himself and Lambert's wife. Not that he intended to go after her. At least not when this dude and his dog were around.

Dogs were trouble, too. For some reason, they didn't seem to like him, and truth be told, he didn't like them very much either.

Since he'd overheard the police officer calling in to say he'd be doing some extra patrols around town and its outskirts, he'd have to lay low tonight.

Besides, Lambert and her little dog would be back at work in the morning, giving him plenty of time to get into her house and try to find the relics that Lambert had sent to her from Iraq.

Both he and his buddy Buck had been with Lambert on a mission when they'd found them and secured the ancient carvings and a gold bracelet. But the treasures had disappeared after Lambert had been killed and they'd gone back to get them.

He had no doubt Lambert had taken them for himself and sent them to his wife.

Now he intended to get them back no matter what it took.

But not tonight. He'd bide his time and try again tomorrow and the day after that if necessary.

It had cost him too much not to keep on trying to find them.

PIPER WOKE TO a dreary and chilly morning. It had been raining on and off all night, and a lingering drizzle and clouds made it the kind of day where she just wanted to pull the covers up over her head and stay in bed.

But she couldn't because she had obligations to Shane and Decoy. She never shirked obligations no matter how difficult it was for her to be around Shane.

Normally she'd have more of a buffer since she would only train each client for a few hours each day over the course of a month or more depending on what the client needed. But a client had cancelled at the last minute and Shane only had four weeks to spend at the DCA which was why they were training so intensely.

Because of that, both Shane and Decoy had made incredible progress over the course of the last two weeks. Decoy was a natural at finding things, probably thanks to his Lab/hound blood. But not all good searchers made capable rescue dogs, especially in dangerous conditions like those in a building collapse or finding people in the aftermath of mudslides, earthquakes or avalanches.

In those situations, a dog had to be unafraid of things like uneven ground, crevices or the kind of rubble in which Shane had been buried in Afghanistan.

Shane, she thought with a sigh.

Much like Decoy, he had shown himself to be a perfect candidate for a search and rescue group. He was calm and patient with Decoy, and the dog obeyed him without question. The bond between them was unquestionable and she had no doubt that Decoy would go into a dangerous situation if Shane requested it. But she also knew Shane would not endanger Decoy unnecessarily, and with his military experience, he'd be adept at sizing up risks and how to proceed.

As she lay in bed, her mind raced with ideas for this week's training session. They'd added more obstacles to the agility course, but with the rain it would be uncomfortable to be outdoors today so any work outside or on the trails around the DCA would have to wait. Not to mention it would be muddy in the outdoor rings.

The indoor ring would have to do for today and she

had an idea of just what to do besides some attack and protect training.

Peering at her watch, she realized she should get moving if she was going to set up that training for Shane and Decoy.

She hurried her morning routine, including a quick walk along the road with Chipper, who was almost completely housebroken.

In no time they were at the DCA and by then the rain had gotten heavier from the earlier morning mist. They rushed into the DCA offices, where Barbara had yet to arrive, but the lights were on in Emma's office. She walked over to find her friend working at her desk.

"Good morning. You're in early," Piper said and leaned on the doorjamb. Chipper settled down at her feet.

"I had some paperwork to do and figured a rainy day like today would be the perfect time to take care of that. You're here early also," Emma pointed out and leaned back in her chair.

"I thought we'd do something different because of the weather," Piper said and tilted her head in the direction of the indoor ring.

"Need help?" Emma asked, clearly eager for a break from the paperwork.

"Sure. I was going to do some more hide-and-seek exercises as well as attack and protect," Piper said.

Emma nodded and got up from her chair. "You could also think about starting to train Decoy on how to alert Shane when he finds something."

She hadn't thought about that and dipped her head to confirm. It was important Decoy learn to communicate that he'd found something important. "Sounds good. We can work on that alerting today and then test Decoy on it when we do hide-and-seek on the trails."

As they left Emma's office, Barbara hurried in, juggling a dripping umbrella, her oversize purse and a box from the local bakery.

They rushed over to help her with the items and Barbara smiled. "Thank you! I almost lost the doughnuts on the way in."

"Doughnuts? Nom, nom," Emma said and placed the box on the small table in the narrow entryway where they kept coffee and tea for clients.

Barbara smoothed the fabric of her loose shirt down and sighed. "I know I should be watching what I eat, but it's so dreary and I thought we'd need a pick-me-up."

Piper laid a reassuring hand on Barbara's shoulder. "Barbara, you are perfect the way you are."

Emma's assistant smiled. "That's what my Bob always says," she said, referring to her husband. She lived in town with him and her daughter, Samantha, who was away at college.

"And he's right," Emma chimed in, then snagged a doughnut from the box and held it up. "Thank you so much for these. They will hit the spot on this rainy day."

"You are so welcome. Time to get to work," Barbara said, then shrugged out of her rain jacket and went into her office.

"I'll text Shane and let him know we're inside today," Piper said and after she did so, they walked into the indoor ring and to an equipment locker that contained various items that they used for their lessons.

As they hauled out the long-armed glove and padded suit for the attack and protect lessons, Chipper chased after them, playfully attempting to catch the straps from the suit. "Silly dog," Piper said and affectionately rubbed Chipper's head. "Now, sit," she said, and when the puppy obeyed, she offered up a treat.

Emma bent to pat the dog's head and Chipper ate up the attention, hopping up on Emma's legs.

Emma rubbed Chipper's ears and the dog barked and continued to hop up and down on her legs.

"You're such a cutie," Emma said and laughed.

Piper couldn't argue with her friend. Chipper was adorable and turning out to be a wonderful companion. "She is a great buddy. Smart. She's caught on to all the commands so far."

"Corgis are very intelligent, and pits are friendly and gentle contrary to all the bad press," Emma said and straightened.

Chipper immediately sat at her feet, smiling, as if approving of Emma's comments.

It dragged laughs from both the women but then Chipper barked and took off toward the door of the indoor training area, jerking the leash from Piper's hands.

Shane and Decoy stood there, and Chipper was immediately climbing all over the older dog, who patiently accepted the attention.

Shane bent, took hold of Chipper's leash and walked over to them.

Raindrops glistened on the longer strands of his close-cropped hair and the shoulders of his rain jacket. "Nasty day out there," he said.

"It is, but we'll be comfortable in there," Piper said and gestured to the ring.

SHANE SURE HOPED SO. They'd been in the indoor ring another day for attack and protect lessons, but there had been something claustrophobic about it. Maybe because it reminded him of the area where he'd been training his men immediately before the IED blast that had nearly taken his life. Not to mention that in the enclosed space, it made it that much harder to ignore Piper's physical presence and how it made him feel.

Despite his misgivings, he said, "We will."

Emma gestured to the padded suit on the floor of the ring. "I guess I'll go and let you guys get started."

After Emma walked out of the room, Piper explained to Shane what they would be doing that day, finishing up with the training on alerting Shane.

Shane narrowed his gaze and glanced at Decoy, who was lying down calmly beside him, Chipper resting next to him. "You want Decoy to alert me?" he said, wanting to confirm what he'd just heard.

Piper nodded. "Yes. There may be situations where Decoy will sense a danger you might not or when he finds something. Dogs can detect gas leaks or even someone who is going to have a seizure because of their acute sense of smell."

"Seizures have a scent?" Shane asked, truly puzzled.

Piper shrugged. "There are some studies that seem to show there's some kind of smell, possibly the smell of fear."

Shane cocked his head to the side and peered at the two dogs. "Amazing. So how are we going to do this?"

"First, we do the attack and protect. Afterward we'll start by having Decoy find hot dogs and toys we hide around the ring. Once he's found an object, we can teach him to sit and bark to let us know."

"Okay. I'm ready if you are," he said, although he didn't much care for the attack and protect classes. They had involved irritating Decoy with a glove until he reacted with anger and attacked it. The irritation had been combined with an attack command.

Decoy had always been a patient animal and it had taken quite a lot to push the dog to attack. It made him wonder if Decoy would ever be able to attack if needed, not that he ever wanted to be in that kind of situation again. He'd been in enough mayhem and destruction in the military.

"Just let me take Chipper out to Barbara," she said, then snagged the leash for her puppy and walked him out. When she returned, she walked to the center of the ring and grabbed the long-armed glove. She handed it to Shane, who put it on and repeated the exercise they had done a few days earlier.

"Sit," he commanded, swinging his hand palm up to reinforce the nonverbal command.

Decoy immediately responded and he rewarded him with a treat from his non-gloved hand.

But immediately after that, he shoved his gloved hand against Decoy's nose and said, "Attack." Decoy reared back and didn't engage. He repeated the exercise, antagonizing Decoy over and over again, until Decoy finally snapped at him. But even then, it was half-hearted.

"Good boy, Decoy," Piper said, stepping in to offer Decoy a treat and reinforce the attack command.

They repeated the exercise and this time it didn't take as long for Decoy to respond and latch onto the glove. "Good boy," he said and rubbed his dog's head.

Piper provided a treat and said, "Let's try it with the suit."

When she walked over and started putting it on, he said, "No way. Let me do it."

Piper shook her head vehemently. "Although dogs can turn on their owners, I doubt Decoy would attack you, even if commanded to do it."

Shane hesitated, thinking about how gentle and patient Decoy was generally. "I'm not sure he'll attack you either."

Piper shrugged, or at least he thought she did beneath the bulk of the padded suit. "We can try," she said and motioned for him to give her the long-armed glove.

He did as she instructed, as obedient as Decoy, he realized with a strangled laugh. In more ways than she knew, Piper had him wrapped around her little finger.

He helped her put the glove on over the padded sleeve of the suit. As he had before, she instructed Decoy to sit and then antagonized the dog while giving the "Attack" command. It took even longer for Decoy to respond and even then it was clearly a half-hearted bite on the glove.

They attempted the exercise a few more times, but with little improvement.

After the last attempt, Piper shook her head and laughed. "I guess Decoy is more of a lover than a fighter."

That laugh hit him as it always did, as hard as a sucker punch to the gut, and when combined with her words, his mind spun with unwanted images of what it would be like to make love to her. Passion rose and he battled it back, laughed as she had done and in a rough voice said, "I guess he is."

Piper's green gaze darkened, picking up on his tension. "I guess," she said in barely a whisper.

He imagined that whisper as she lay in bed beside him. Voice still rough, he said, "Maybe it's time for hide-and-seek."

"Definitely," Piper said and turned away from him to remove the padded suit, almost as if by taking it off she was revealing too much. After she had put it away, she walked back to the center of the ring, arms wrapped around herself in that defensive gesture he had seen on their first day together.

With a jerky motion, she gestured to the door of the ring. "I'm going to go get some hot dogs."

She raced out of the room, leaving Shane alone with Decoy. He bent to rub the dog's ears and Decoy lapped it up, laying his paws on Shane's shoulders so he could lick at his face. "I love you, too, boy," he said, glad they were done with the protect and attack since he hated antagonizing his friend.

Decoy sat back down, but his ears perked up at the soft sound of a footstep on the floor of the training ring.

Piper was back.

He rose, his gaze fixed on her face. Such an expressive face, giving away that she was as bothered by him as he was by her. A stain of pink colored her cheeks, and she was fidgety, her hands unsure against the plastic of the hot dog bag.

He walked over, laid his hands over hers, the gesture meant to soothe, but it did anything but that. It was like being struck by lightning as awareness jolted him where their hands touched.

She sucked in a breath, and he barely had time to grab the hot dogs as she let go of the bag and stepped away.

Chapter Eight

Piper's heart skittered in her chest in recognition of his touch and all that rampant masculinity. No matter how hard she had tried to ignore her attraction to him over the last two weeks, it had proved impossible.

She was aware of him on every level. His strength. His patience. His discipline.

But she knew that his discipline would take him from her soon. In a little over two weeks, he'd be leaving, and she had to remember that.

"This," she said and gestured with a finger between them. "It can't be more than this," she said and motioned to the training ring around them and to Decoy.

His hands tightened on the bag, clearly on edge, but then he said, "You're right. We should get back to training."

The words stuck in her throat, but she got them out somehow. "You're right."

Pointing to the edges of the structure, she said, "We have small niches all here and there in the cinder block. We'll put the hot dogs there as well as some toys."

He walked to the wall of the ring, found a niche and put half a dog inside. As he bent to do so, his hand shook, and he let out a little gasp.

"You okay?" she asked as he straightened and rubbed his shoulder.

"I am," he said with a grimace. "I just never know when it will act up."

She'd told herself not to ask more than once when she'd seen that tell that said he was in pain. This time she couldn't hold back. "Is that why… Is it why you left the Army?"

His face was that stone slab she'd seen on the first day, but then he shook his head, looked away and expelled a harsh breath. "It is. When the IED exploded and the building came down, shrapnel tore through my shoulder. Damaged it so bad I couldn't hold a weapon with any precision. I guess I could have stayed stateside manning a desk chair, but I couldn't picture myself doing that. I had my twenty in and decided it was time to do something else."

"Like join a search and rescue group," she said as they moved on to the next little niche and she shoved in a toy that Decoy had taken a liking to in earlier sessions.

Shane shrugged, grimaced and rubbed the shoulder, but he pressed on to another of the niches and stuffed in the rest of the hot dog. "Actually, I didn't really know what I'd do, you know?"

She did. After David had died, she'd had no idea what to do. Besides taking things one day at a time. She'd been a walking zombie, just going through the paces of life until Emma and the DCA had given her new purpose. And a new life.

"I do know. If it wasn't for Emma and the DCA…" She didn't want to think about what might have been.

He turned and cupped her cheek. Wiped away the tear that had slipped down her face.

"You were meant for this, Piper. You're so good at what you do," he said.

His touch was gentle but wrapped in strength. She stepped into that strength, burying her head against his chest. Breathing out a shaky breath as he wrapped his arms around her and held her, comforting her.

Sensing the upset, Decoy sidled up to her and rubbed his head against her leg, trying to soothe her in the only way he knew how.

"Thank you, Decoy," she said and rubbed his head.

When she stepped back, she peered up at Shane and cradled his jaw. "Thank you."

He smiled, a ghost of a smile that she traced with a finger. "I should say thanks as well. The last two weeks…" He jerked his gaze away from her as he said, "Gonzo was right when he said this might be a new life for me."

But that new life would take him to a group in Montana, she reminded herself and took another step back from him. Distance would keep her from making a mistake that would only bring pain when he left.

"Which means it's time to get back to work."

THE SUN PEEKED out from the clouds just as they headed outside to go home after their training sessions.

"See you tomorrow," Piper said and picked up Chipper to put her in the car and secure her into the seat with a harness.

"See you," he said, but wasn't sure just how accurate that was since he planned to go in and speak to Emma about changing his training as soon as Piper drove away.

He waited, rocking back and forth on his heels, the soft rain-soaked ground giving beneath his feet. When her vehicle was out of view down the long drive, he pivoted and walked toward Emma's office, fully intending to ask for Emma to finish his training.

But with each step that he took, hesitation crept in.

He enjoyed working with Piper.

You mean being with Piper, the little voice intruded.

Yes, being with Piper, he admitted, as much as he didn't want to.

He pushed forward, knowing that he had to do it since it was what was best for both of them. But in his head, he heard Gonzo's voice this time, warning him not to be a fool. Not to throw away a good thing.

Which had him turning around and heading toward his pickup. His motion was so sudden that he almost tripped over Decoy, who was stuck on him like a fly on a glue trap.

He bent to rub the dog's floppy ears. "I'm so sorry, boy. It's just so confusing."

Decoy barked and looked down the drive in the direction that Piper had gone as if to also tell him not to let her go.

"Not you, too, boy," he said, shaking his head.

Decoy barked and once again peered at the driveway.

"Damn it," Shane said, but instead of heading toward his car, he walked toward the DCA offices.

THE SECOND PIPER set Chipper on the ground, the little pup strained on her leash, obviously intrigued by something on the ground.

A second later, she noticed the pup sniffing around the cigarette butt sitting at the top of her driveway, right near the path to her front door.

She pulled Chipper tight to her and thought about bundling her back into the car to return to the DCA, but she was no coward.

She also didn't want to be one of those too-stupid-to-live heroines in those slasher movies. She opened her car door, reached back into the glove compartment and took out the pepper spray she kept there. With that in hand, she approached her front door, but everything seemed in order.

The door was locked, and with a quick look around,

she opened it and entered, shutting and locking it behind her quickly.

Nothing seemed amiss inside.

She slowly walked through her home, but everything was in order until she got to the sliding doors to her deck. Several muddy footprints dirtied the deck close to the doors and several of them led to the edge of the wood. Beyond the deck was a trail of trampled grass leading toward the stand of trees along the edges of the meadow.

She had no doubt someone had been there, and they hadn't been up to anything good.

Shaking, she grabbed her phone and dialed Emma.

"Are you sure this is what you want?" Emma asked, fingers steepled in front of her face as she considered Shane across the width of her desk.

"No," he answered honestly because he wasn't sure. "But it might be what's best."

Emma sucked in a deep breath. Paused before she released it. "What if I'm not sure that's what's best?"

Emma knew Piper better than anyone, he suspected. He also suspected that Emma would do whatever she needed to in order to protect her friend. Her hesitation made him wonder, but he didn't have time to ask since Emma's phone started vibrating angrily on the surface of her desk.

It was only a quick look, but he could see that it was Piper calling. He wondered if it was about the same thing he was discussing with Emma. Only as Piper's voice spilled from the phone, her words clipped and a little too loud, he knew it was about something bad.

"Did you call the police?"

"No," he heard over the line and then her words grew too garbled to understand.

"Stay inside until I get there. I'll just be a few minutes," Emma said and jumped out of her chair.

"What's wrong?" he said, following Emma as she rushed out of the building and to her car.

She stopped by her car bumper and said, "Piper thinks someone tried to break into her house."

Fear gripped his gut, and his insides went cold. "She's okay, right?"

Emma nodded. "She is. Whoever did it is long gone, but she doesn't want to call the police and bother them if it was nothing."

"Let's go, then," he said, then walked to the passenger door and grabbed the handle.

Emma looked at his hand, then at him, and her blue-eyed gaze narrowed. But with a nod, she said, "Let's go."

Once they were seated, Emma tore down the driveway, the car kicking up gravel and dirt in their haste to reach Piper.

Piper's red Jeep Rubicon was in the drive. Piper was standing by the front window, looking out for them when they pulled up. Seconds later, the front door opened, and Piper and Chipper were standing there.

She had her arms wrapped around herself, pulling a hand away only long enough for her to rake back the long strands of her red hair in obvious frustration.

In no time, they had rushed out of the car and to the door. Piper and Emma shared a tight embrace, but as he neared, Piper moved away to let him enter.

"You didn't need to come," she said, meeting his gaze.

With the arch of a brow in condemnation, he said, "You think I'd let two unarmed women face a possible burglar on their own?"

She pointed to the sliding doors, where Emma stood peering out. "If it was a burglar, he's not here anymore."

Piper walked to stand beside Emma, and he followed. At the door, both dogs seemed to scent something around the edges of the door. Decoy began to scratch there, and Chipper mimicked his actions.

"Sit," Piper and Shane said at the same time.

The dogs complied, but it was clear they wanted to go back to the door and smell some more.

As he looked out at the footprints and the flattened path of grass through the meadow toward the trees, it seemed as if whoever had been at the back door was clearly gone. But he wasn't going to take any chances.

"I'm going to check outside," he said and signaled to Decoy to come with him. He hurried back to the front door, exited and walked around the side of the house. There were no footprints there, but he could see where the grass had been flattened by someone's passage. Carefully making his way around so as to not disturb any evidence in case there was a sign of an attempted break-in, he went to the back of the house and the small wooden deck by the sliding glass doors.

Someone had been there, judging from the muddy footprints. Cautious once more not to disturb the footprints, he got on the deck and examined the jamb of the door, while inside Piper and Emma stood looking at him.

There were a few scratches near one side, but they weren't deep enough to indicate that someone had tried to jimmy the door open. Trying the door, he found it was still locked, so whoever it was had not broken the mechanism on the door.

Motioning to the handle, he said, "Please open the door."

Piper went over, flipped the lock and slid the door aside so he could enter. As he did so, he said, "Someone was clearly back here, but it's hard to tell if they tried to break in. There are some scratches by the jamb near the lock, but I'm not sure if they aren't from regular wear and tear."

"I guess there's no reason to call the police," Piper said, a combination of dejection and worry in her tone.

"There is a reason, Piper. This isn't the first thing that's happened," Shane said, prompting Emma to stare at Piper in surprise.

"This isn't the first thing?" Emma said, her voice rising in harsh question.

Piper raked back her hair with her fingers and sighed. "I didn't want to worry you and we just figured it was kids or something."

"Like what?" Emma said, peering nervously from him to Piper, who seemed to be in avoidance mode, whether it was because she was in denial about what was happening or feeling stupid that she hadn't said something to her friend.

Shane raised his hands and motioned in a calm-down gesture. "Small things, but maybe Piper should tell you and let you be the judge."

THE LAST THING Piper wanted to do was distress Emma, who had enough on her plate what with worrying about Chief Walters's possible retirement and how that would impact the DCA. Sharing the info now would hopefully prevent that worrying.

"It was just some small things. I smelled cigarette smoke one night when I came back home and felt like someone was watching me. Then someone messed with the pots by the front door, like they were looking for a key. But then nothing all of last week. Yesterday my car door was ajar—"

"You didn't mention that," Shane said, lips tight with concern and possibly anger.

"I just figured I didn't close it right. Tonight, there was a cigarette butt by the driveway that Chipper found. That's what had me looking around."

"And you noticed those footprints by your sliding doors," Emma finished for her and walked to do her own inspection of the jamb.

With a shrug, Emma said, "Shane's right about the scratches, but why was someone back there? Maybe you got home when they were about to break in, and they high-tailed it out of here before you spotted them."

"Maybe, but why me? Why my house?" Piper said, worried about the various small incidents that seemed to be building toward something bigger.

Shane laid a hand on her shoulder and offered a reassuring squeeze. "It's a nice house with very little nearby. Leaving all this proof that they were here, it's an amateur thing. Maybe kids like we first thought," he said, clearly trying to make her feel more comfortable about what had happened.

"Maybe, but maybe it's time to take this a little more seriously," Emma said and whipped out her cell phone.

Piper had no doubt whom Emma was calling, which was confirmed as she said, "Hi, Chief. I hope I'm not disturbing your dinner. Can I put you on speaker?"

Since his wife had died many years earlier, the chief regularly had his dinner promptly at six at Millard's Diner. That was confirmed by the sounds of muted talking and cutlery clinking as Emma engaged the speaker function.

"You're never a bother, Emma. Theresa says hi, by the way," the chief said.

"Hi, Theresa," Emma replied.

Theresa was the secretary for Jasper PD and like a mother hen to them all. She regularly brought in home-made cupcakes and cookies for the chief and all the other officers. She knew everything about everyone in Jasper, and if you asked Piper, she had a thing for the chief, whom she flirted with regularly.

And now she was having dinner with him. *Interesting*, Piper thought, happy that maybe the chief and Theresa were a thing.

"Piper's had a few things happen around her house and we're hoping you can help," Emma said and jerked her head up, encouraging Piper to speak.

Piper shared what she had told Emma earlier and Chief Walters harrumphed and said, "Sounds like kids to me, but there's no reason to take any chances. I'll call Cal Hoover and ask him to have the men do some extra patrols in your area."

"Thanks, Chief. That would really make me feel better," Piper said. She liked the chief's third-in-command, who was an honest and dedicated man. Much like the chief, he supported the DCA's programs and Emma had helped train Cal's K-9, Ruby, a German shepherd.

"Anything for my girls," the chief said, earning a teasing, "They're not girls, Doug. They're grown women."

"Right as always, Theresa," he said with a laugh and Theresa's full-throated laugh chased the chief's.

"Thank you both. Enjoy your dinner," Emma said, then ended the call and slipped the phone back into her jeans pocket. Hands on hips, Emma gazed from her to Shane and said, "Speaking of dinner, how about some burgers and beer at Bartwell's?"

She knew Emma was only trying to put them all at ease about what had happened, and it was dinnertime after all. "I'm game. Shane?" she said, tentative about whether he would agree given what had happened earlier that day in the training ring.

With a tight smile he said, "I'm game."

Chapter Nine

Unlike the last time they'd been in Bartwell's, there was no emergency call to pull Emma away and Shane was grateful for that. She was an excellent buffer and the laughter and conversation between the two women during dinner had helped put Piper at ease over what had happened at her home.

It also helped that as they neared her house after dinner, a Jasper PD patrol car with Officers Callan and Nichols was driving by, searchlight trained on Piper's home. After they pulled into Piper's driveway, the officers parked their cruiser and came over to greet them.

"Evening," Ava said with a tight smile. Although she had gotten friendlier over the last two weeks, she could still be standoffish at times.

"Thanks for coming by, Ava. Brady," Piper said.

Brady nodded. "We got the call from Jenny the dispatcher that Lieutenant Hoover wanted us to do some extra patrols because you were having some problems."

"Want us to look around?" Ava said and gestured with her flashlight to the house.

Piper wrapped her arms around herself and shrugged. "I'm not sure that's necessary. Maybe I'm just overreacting."

Ava and Brady shared that kind of cop look that Shane

recognized well. They intended to look around whether or not Piper wanted it to happen. That was confirmed when Brady said, "If you don't mind, we'll just do a quick check."

They didn't wait for Piper's approval. Both officers headed off around one side of the house.

Emma laid a comforting hand on Piper's shoulder. "I'm sure everything is okay," Emma said, her tone soothing.

"I hope so," Piper said and gazed at him, as if seeking his reassurance.

"It doesn't hurt to take precautions. Like I said two weeks ago, maybe you should get one of those cameras and a security system."

"Maybe," Piper said, but he could tell she wasn't totally convinced.

Moments later the two officers came around the opposite side of the house and returned to where they waited by Emma's car.

"Nothing, unless you count Decoy and Chipper playing by your sliding doors," Brady said with a smile.

"Thank you," Piper replied.

"Just to be sure, we will come by again on our patrols. We have had some complaints about stealing items from cars, so make sure you keep them locked. Same thing with all your windows and doors. No sense inviting trouble," Ava advised.

"Will do," Shane said, and with that, the two officers went back to their patrol car and took off.

Emma rubbed Piper's back. "See, no reason to worry. Ava and Brady will be popping by, but maybe I should stay tonight if that would make you feel better."

"It would, that is if you don't mind," Piper said, peering at her best friend hopefully.

"I don't. I'll just run Shane and Decoy back to his car and pick up a few things."

"See you later. Shane, thanks for everything," Piper said.

He wanted to say he hadn't done much of anything, but hopefully what he had done had helped to calm her. "Anytime, Piper. I'll see you tomorrow for training."

She nodded and bit her lip, as if to stop herself from saying anything else.

Piper opened the door and called out to Decoy, who came rushing over, Chipper tagging along behind him. He whistled to the dog to come and when he did, they walked with Emma back to her car and in minutes they were at the DCA. But once Emma had parked, she hesitated, hands gripping the wheel.

"You and Piper okay now?" she said and stared at him intently.

It made him feel like one of the dogs she was trying to control, and he didn't like it one bit. But he understood it was only because she was worried about her friend, so he tamped down his alpha response to the challenge in her tone and posture.

"She's a good trainer. We're making a lot of progress," he answered, but Emma only shook her head at that.

"Don't try and kid me, Shane. Anyone can see there's more going on, which is why you were in my office earlier."

He shook his head. "It was, but I can handle it, especially now that she doesn't need any more upset. Piper needs someone who will be there for her. I'm not that guy for the future, but I will be for now."

Her gaze narrowed and she searched his features in the light from a spotlight trained on the parking area. With a shake of her head, she said, "I think you truly believe that, but I'm not so sure that's right. Just don't hurt her. She's been hurt enough already."

He understood. Losing a spouse, especially at such a young age, could be devastating. That Piper was handling it as well as it seemed was truly a testament to the strength of her character.

"I won't." He opened his door and let Decoy out of the back seat. Once they were in his pickup, he waited for Emma to enter her own home before driving away.

He slowed as he approached Piper's house and noticed her standing by the front window, probably waiting for Emma to come by. He waved at her, and she waved back. Then he drove away, but knew he'd be returning tonight.

While he trusted Jasper PD to be true to their word, he wasn't about to take any chances with Piper.

Despite what he'd said to Emma, he did already care for her more than was wise. Because of that, he'd do whatever was necessary to keep her safe.

"It's going to be a long night, Decoy," he said and rubbed his dog's floppy ears.

Decoy barked and licked Shane's hand, as if to confirm he was up for it.

Shane had no doubt about it. Decoy had tagged after him on a mission more than once in Afghanistan.

Only none of those missions were as important as this one. Because of that, he didn't intend to fail.

HE TRAINED THE binoculars on the comings and goings at Piper's house.

The on-and-off heavy rains had kept him from trying to get into her house all day. Once the sun had broken through, he'd raced down to her house. He'd been trying to enter through the sliding doors when he'd heard her pull up and had to make a dash for the nearby woods to hide.

He'd waited for the three of them to leave. The Three Musketeers he'd dubbed them. Emma, Piper and Shane, who would clearly be trouble.

When they'd driven off earlier that night, probably for dinner, he'd intended to go back and finish the job, only it had become like Grand Central Station down there.

First the cops had driven by. Then the Three Musketeers had shown up. Then it had been just Piper, but before he could act, Shane had come by in his red pickup. Barely minutes later, Emma had pulled up and gone into the house.

He could probably handle Piper and her annoying little dog. But restraining two strong women would definitely be a problem.

He'd have to wait, but not too long. He couldn't keep on doing petty thefts around town because they were already attracting too much attention. The tip jars were being watched more closely and people had started to lock their cars and doors in a town where people normally didn't do things like that.

Just another few days and he'd go in, no matter what it took. No matter what happened afterward.

He couldn't wait any longer to take what was rightfully his.

THE TENSION THAT had erupted between them in the training ring had been replaced by worry over the possible break-in at her house.

But Emma staying over that night as well as the very obvious police patrols by her home had alleviated her concerns somewhat. So had Shane's nighttime visits over the last two days. She had caught him twice when she'd been unable to sleep and had gone to her living room to watch some late-night television.

She'd waved at him and he at her, but neither had acknowledged his patrols during their training the last two days. They were all focused on Decoy and the excellent progress he was making with their search and rescue training.

"Good boy," she said, then patted his head and offered up a treat for his finding one of the toys in the indoor training area.

"He is doing well," Shane said with a smile and likewise rubbed Decoy's head, but as he did so, his hand grazed hers and they both pulled back at the instant zing of awareness.

"He is," she said and tucked her hands under her arms. "It's a beautiful day out there. Maybe we should take him out on the trail today."

"I think Decoy would like that," he said, then awkwardly added, "I would, too."

"Great. Let me round up some hot dogs and get them set up on the trail," she said.

"I'll go with you," he said, but she shook her head.

"I don't want Decoy to see where I put the food. Why don't you get yourself a coffee and a doughnut and wait for me in Emma's office. I think she took one of the horses out for a ride today."

ALTHOUGH NOTHING HAD happened in the last two days besides long stretches of heavy rain, Shane felt uneasy about letting Piper go out on the trail alone. But he wasn't sure Piper would appreciate him being overprotective.

With a nod, Shane said, "I'll skip the doughnut, but coffee sounds great."

Piper eyed him up and down and grinned. "Watching your girlish figure?"

Shane laughed and shook his head. More like he was

watching hers, but he laid a hand on his flat midsection and said, "Can't let this go to flab."

Her gaze dropped to his hand and that flush that was becoming all too familiar blossomed across her face. "I'll get the dogs and set up the trail."

She rushed out of the indoor ring, and he followed more slowly to give her space. In the hallway, she went to a small refrigerator where they kept the hot dogs as well as their lunches and snacks while he ambled to the coffee station and poured himself a cup.

Piper raced out the door with the dogs, but instead of heading to Emma's office, he walked Decoy outside and to the far corner of the building.

"Sit," he commanded, and Decoy obeyed.

"Good boy." He patted him on the head and offered up a treat.

"Stay," he said and walked around the corner of the building to watch Piper out on the trail behind the barn and DCA offices. The trail ran down the length of the open meadow, but then veered off to another section of the DCA's nearly twenty acres.

He sipped and watched, keeping an eye on her as long as he could. Counting the minutes until she had doubled back and came into view once more. She caught sight of him as he stood there and shook her head, as if chastising him, but smiled.

The smile warmed his insides as powerfully as the rays of the spring sun beating down on him.

He finished his coffee and waited for her to return. Once she got there, she flipped a hand in the direction of the door to the offices. "Let me just get Chipper from her crate. I'm sure she'd love to walk with us."

"Sure thing. Decoy loves Chipper," he said.

The dog's ears perked up at the mention of the puppy's name, dragging a laugh from both of them.

"The feeling's mutual," Piper said and hurried into the building. She returned with Chipper, tail wagging and a smile plastered on her face. The puppy immediately raced to Decoy's side and climbed all over the older dog. Decoy laid a big paw on Chipper's head and playfully tussled with her.

"I hope Decoy won't be distracted," Shane said and gave a hand command for Decoy to come to his side.

"It'll be a good test to see if he can stay focused," Piper said and started walking toward the trail, Chipper on the leash beside her, almost prancing.

Decoy was more reserved as they followed until they were on the trail. Then they walked side by side for a few yards until Piper said, "Search, Decoy. Search, boy."

Decoy immediately started nosing at the underbrush along the edges of the trail, much like he had done in the indoor ring. He hadn't gone more than ten feet when he nosed into the high grasses and came out with the hot dog in his mouth.

Piper went over to him and took the hot dog from his mouth. "Good boy. Bark," she said and much like he had been trained in the indoor ring, Decoy started barking, alerting them in much the same way he would hopefully do if he found a lost person.

"Good boy," she said and returned to offer Decoy the hot dog as a reward along with an enthusiastic rub of his head and sides.

When she was done, Piper faced him and said, "It's your turn."

He nodded and led Decoy forward on the path. "Search, Decoy."

As he had before, Decoy nosed all along the edges of

the underbrush, shifting from one side of the trail to the other until about ten yards ahead, he stopped at the edge of the trail. Decoy buried his nose in some tall grasses and then emerged with one of his favorite toys in his mouth. He dropped it on the ground and did a short quick bark.

"Tell him to bark again," Piper said.

He did and Decoy tilted his head to the side and peered at him with a seemingly puzzled look.

"Bark," he repeated, but had to do it a second time for Decoy to finally obey.

"Good boy," he said and offered up a reward again, re-inforcing the behavior.

They repeated the exercise, strolling slowly along the trail, Chipper occasionally engaging Decoy in play that was short-lived since Decoy almost intuitively knew what they were doing wasn't a game.

With the weather as nice as it was, the training was pleasant, especially since Decoy caught on quickly, earning more treats than admonishments to search or bark.

"He's doing so well. You'll be further ahead than most when you finish your lessons and go to that search and rescue group," she said, but bit her lip as soon as she said it.

"He is doing well," Shane said and tried to ignore the fact that their time together would soon come to a close, much as she had said.

But no matter how hard both of them tried to ignore it, the reality that their lessons would soon be over cast a pall over the rest of their walk. By the time they reached the end of the trail, the sun had started to drop along the horizon.

"I didn't realize how late it was," she said and instructed Chipper to turn back in the direction of the barn and DCA offices.

Shane gazed up at the afternoon sky and nodded. "It'll be dark soon. I didn't see your Jeep in the parking spaces."

"I walked," she said with a shrug.

Shane arched a brow and she looked away to avoid the reproach in his gaze. "It might be dark for your walk home."

Piper shot a fleeting look at the night sky. "It might."

Frustrated, he said, "It may not be safe for you to walk it alone."

Piper gestured to Chipper. "I have Chipper, and honestly, nothing has happened in the last few days. Plus, I can go from here and it'll be a short walk."

He couldn't argue with that. "You're right, but there are still bears, foxes and mountain lions."

"Lions, and tigers and bears, oh my!" she teased, but then nodded. "There are, but I haven't seen any scat or other signs of predators in the area."

She was being difficult, but he wasn't about to let her walk home in the dark.

"I'll go with you."

"You don't have to," she protested, glancing at him from the corner of her eye.

"I'll go," he said, and his tone brooked no disagreement.

Apparently realizing that, she nodded. "Okay, but I'm sure it's not necessary."

He did a quick lift of his shoulders in agreement but pressed on. "I'm sure you're right, but why take chances?"

As he said the words, he realized they could refer to more than just the walk to her home. Being with her, even for something as short as a five-minute stroll, made him wonder about what it would be like not to leave when the lessons were over. That was a dangerous thing, and as she lifted her gaze to meet his, he liked to think she was feeling the same way. As if it was too soon for him to leave, but he hadn't planned on staying.

He hadn't planned on meeting someone like Piper either, for that matter.

That she felt the same was confirmed as she said, "It's just a quick walk home."

"That it is," he said with a determined nod.

But as he ambled with her and Chipper across a break in the trail and the meadow, the tension built between them, warning him that it was about much, much more.

Chapter Ten

The sun hadn't been enough to dry out some large sections of the meadow. They had to slog through inch-deep pools of water, and in other areas, their feet sank deep into the ground.

"It was a lot drier by the DCA. I'm sorry," Piper said as she lifted her booted foot from a muddy patch with a sucking sound.

"You couldn't have known," he said and pointed toward one section of the meadow. "Can't we walk straight through there to the road?"

From beside him, Piper ran her gaze down the length of his arm to where he aimed. "We can. Even though it's a little longer, it might make more sense to cut over and walk along the road. It's got to be drier."

"Let's go, then," he said and took the first step, but when she went to follow him, the unsteady ground made her lose her balance.

Shane reached out to hold her arm and provide support. "Thanks."

He nodded, kept his grip on her while she pulled her foot from the mud and stepped onto steadier ground. When she took another steadier step, he looped his arm through hers and she didn't protest.

The feel of his arm tucked through hers, the slight

weight of his body as it brushed against her as they walked, was comforting.

Too comforting. It would be too easy to get used to having him beside her every day. She hadn't expected that. If anything, she had worried that his being military would be a too-painful reminder of David.

David, she thought, and guilt swept through her. She'd loved David with all her heart. She'd grieved deeply over his death. Hadn't ever thought about being attracted to another man, especially a military man.

But she was also sure David wouldn't have wanted her to be alone for the rest of her life.

She gazed up at Shane, at his strong profile, all hard lines and angles until he looked down and smiled at her. Then his features softened and his blue eyes, bright as an Idaho spring day, glittered when he met her gaze.

"You okay?" he asked, his eyes narrowing slightly.

She didn't hesitate to say, "I'm okay."

With a quick nod, they pushed on in deep dusk, shadows surrounding them as they walked along the road. But as they passed a dense stand of trees a few yards from her house, she caught sight of a blue pickup sitting in front of her home which was all lit up even though she didn't remember leaving the lights on.

But even with the lights on, it was impossible to see who was at the wheel, especially as the headlights snapped on, blinding her.

A split second later, the pickup screeched toward them, so close that Shane had to jerk her away to keep her from being hit.

"WHAT THE HELL?" Shane said, mumbled a curse and tried to get a better look at the pickup, but it was too dark and quickly too far away.

"Did you get the plate number?" Piper asked and rubbed her hands along her arms.

He shook his head. "I couldn't."

"I didn't either. I was too scared," Piper said and took a step toward her home, but he shot out a hand to stop her.

She looked up at him, puzzled. "What's wrong?"

"He was in front of your house, Piper. You don't recognize the pickup?" Jasper was a small town, and he figured most people knew what other people drove.

She shook her head. "No. I mean, there are a couple of other blue pickups only…"

He detected the unease that crept into her voice as it trailed off. "But you didn't recognize that one. You didn't see the driver?"

She once again shook her head. "No."

"Me either." It had been too dark, and the sudden snap of the headlights had blinded him.

He peered toward Piper's house, worried that whoever was driving the pickup hadn't been there for a good reason. With a reluctant nod, he said, "I guess we should go."

"We should," Piper said, but he took the lead, walking ahead of her toward the front door.

At the sight of it, they both stopped short.

The door was wide open and hanging off the hinges. Lights were on inside the house, and he could see couch pillows, papers and other objects on the living room floor.

Chipper immediately started barking and Decoy's ears perked up and he joined in the chorus, adding his deeper bark.

"Quiet," Piper commanded and both dogs stopped, sensing the urgency in her voice.

Piper walked toward the front door, but he once again stopped her with a gentle touch on her arm.

"Let me go first. We don't know if someone is still in there."

Eyes wide, pupils dilated with fear, she slowly dipped her head and said, "Don't touch anything. Just in case we have to call the police."

Shane had no doubt they would have to call the police because he was certain they were entering a crime scene. He grabbed the leashes for the two dogs from her and tied them to a post at the alcove by the front door. Striding to the open door, he paused in the entryway, examining the destruction inside the house. Piper pushed at his back, wanting to get past him, and he slowly shifted to the side to let her see.

"Oh no," she said and covered her mouth with her hand. Tears gathered in her gaze, and she stumbled when she stepped past him and into the ruins of her home.

Gingerly they stepped around the strewn papers and broken bits.

"I don't understand," she said as she stood in the middle of her living room and kitchen open space, her voice choked with emotion. Tears trailing down her face.

He wrapped her up in his arms and kissed her temple. "I'm sorry, Piper."

He held her for long seconds, comforting her. Tucking her head tight against his shoulder to hide the mess around them. Although he wanted to see if the rest of the home was as bad, his first mission was to get Piper out of the house and call the police.

With her pressed tight to his side, he walked her out and she plopped down on her front stoop, arms wrapped around herself. Tears still leaked from her eyes and slipped down her face as he called 911.

When Jenny the dispatcher answered, he said, "I need to report a burglary." He provided the information to her and then turned his attention back to Piper, hunkering down in front of her. "I'm going to call Emma also."

She nodded and swiped at her tears angrily before meeting his gaze.

"Why would anyone do this?" she said and whipped a hand in the direction of her ravaged home.

"They were looking for something," he said, peering back in the direction of her front door.

"Everything of value is right out in the open. My wedding rings. Laptop. Tablet. It's all there," she said, her tone laced with anger and disbelief.

Shane shrugged, unsure of how to answer. "We'll know more once the police arrive and take a closer look around."

After a backward glance toward her home, Piper nodded.

The distant sound of a siren grew stronger as the police car approached. When the cruiser pulled up in front, the siren silenced, but the last light of dusk was broken by the red and blue of the flashing lights on the car.

Decoy sat silently by the front step, but Chipper was cowering behind him, clearly upset by the sound and lights. Shane suspected she would have run off, but the leash tied to the post had restrained her.

Officers Callan and Nichols stepped out of the car just as Emma screeched to a halt behind their cruiser.

They approached slowly while Emma ran over to Piper, who popped to her feet and embraced the other woman.

"What happened?" she said, glancing between him and the open door of Piper's home.

"Someone broke in," Piper said.

As the officers approached, Shane explained, "We were walking home and just as we got past that stand of trees," he said and pointed to the small saplings and underbrush at one edge of the property, "a blue pickup came at us. Almost ran us over."

Ava and Brady shared a look and Ava took a small notebook and pen from her jacket pocket. "Did you get a license plate number?"

Piper shook her head. "The headlights were too bright and it all happened so fast."

Ava laid a reassuring hand on Piper's arm. "It's okay, Piper. Could you tell the make?"

She shook her head. "No. Just a pickup."

Brady nodded. "Let us go inside and take a look around. See if there's any evidence."

With a jerk of his head in the direction of the door, Ava and Brady walked inside while Piper, Emma and Shane waited outside.

Long, almost painful minutes passed before Ava and Brady came back out. They once again shared a look that brought no comfort to Shane. If anything, it brought more worry about what was happening.

"What's up?" he asked, certain he wouldn't like what he was about to hear.

"We need you to come with us. Take a look around," Ava said to Piper, her tone soothing while at the same time in command.

"Okay," Piper said, voice weak. Emma had her arm around Piper's shoulder and together the two of them followed the officers into the home, Shane trailing after them.

Foam guts spilled from the slashes in the sofa pillows and cushions. Every drawer in a nearby desk was yanked open, the contents spilled all over the floor. Books and bric-a-brac torn from a nearby bookshelf joined the mess on the floor.

In the kitchen area, cabinet doors were thrown open, one so violently the hinge was torn from the cabinet body.

Plates had been jerked from the cabinets, but luckily not all of them were broken. The fridge door was ajar, as if they had also searched inside.

"I don't get it," Piper said, gesturing to the laptop that still sat on her desk and a tablet on the floor by an overturned coffee table.

"They were looking for something specific," Ava said. "Can you think of what that might be?"

Piper shook her head.

Together they all approached the guest bedroom and Piper went in with the officers to look. There was similar destruction, but apparently nothing seemed to have been taken.

It was a different and yet similar story in Piper's bedroom. As he stood at the door watching, Piper walked around, her gaze filling with tears again, especially as she caught sight of her husband's duffel bag ripped open, his Marine uniform tossed on the floor. She went to pick it up, but Ava braced an arm across her front to keep her from touching it.

"I'm sorry, Piper. It's still evidence," she said and gestured to the contents of the room. "Is anything missing?"

ON ONE HEEL, Piper did a slow spin, looking all around the room, still reeling from the sight of David's belongings strewn on the floor.

At the sight of the empty spot on top of her dresser, her heart clenched to a stop and pain erupted in the middle of her chest. "My wedding rings are gone," she said in barely a whisper. She couldn't seem to get enough air to speak past the ache in her heart.

Emma immediately came to her side and squeezed her shoulder. "We'll find them."

"Anything else?" Ava asked, her light brown eyes filled with compassion.

Piper did another look around the room but shook her head. "Not that I can tell."

As her gaze drifted around again, it met Shane's and locked with his. It was full of compassion and caring and her heart finally began to beat again, slow, heavy beats, as if to remind her she was still alive.

"You may find something's missing once the shock wears off and you look around," Brady said with a tight smile. "But for now, it's best you stay somewhere else. You'll be safer and we need to process the house for evidence."

"You can stay with me," Emma said and rubbed her hand across Piper's shoulder.

"Thanks. I appreciate it," she said.

She took a faltering step toward the door, almost falling, her knees felt so weak. Shane was immediately there, slipping his arm around her waist to offer support. "Thanks," she said, voice as shaky as her knees.

"We've got you," Emma said, obviously forcing an upbeat note in her tone.

Once they were outside, Emma and Shane directed her toward Emma's car, but Piper pulled away from them to turn back toward her home. "I'll need some clothes."

Shane held her arms and bent slightly to force her to meet his gaze. "You can't take anything right now, Piper. Maybe tomorrow."

"I have some things that will fit you. We're almost the same size," Emma said and opened the passenger side door.

Piper looked between them and knew they were right. "Okay. Tomorrow," she said, only able to manage short responses.

SHANE HELPED PIPER ease into Emma's car and shut the door behind her.

After he finished, he stood there, Emma in front of him. "She's in shock," he said.

Emma nodded. "I'll take care of her."

"I know you will. But if it's all right with you, I'd like to move my RV to the DCA. Stay close by just in case." He looked toward the house and said, "Let me get the dogs so you can take them now. They'll help distract Piper."

Without waiting for Emma's response, he hurried to Decoy and Chipper and untied the leashes. He walked them to Emma's car and popped them into the back seat before slipping inside as well since his pickup was still at the DCA.

It took less than five minutes to reach Emma's home. In unspoken agreement, Emma took Piper and the dogs into the house. He marched to his pickup much like he would if he'd been given a mission in the Army. His mission now: to protect Piper and find out who was responsible for terrorizing her because it was about more than a break-in.

Whoever had done this had been watching her. Doing little things to make her doubt herself. To make her worry.

He needed to find out why and he needed to make it stop.

Chapter Eleven

In mission mode, he had his RV hitched to his pickup and was on the road to the DCA in record time.

When he reached Emma's, he parked his RV on a flat area where he had seen Emma occasionally park a horse trailer. As he stepped from the pickup and walked toward the house, Emma's front door opened and she stood there, silhouette limned by the light from inside.

She walked onto the porch, careful not to let the screen door bang behind her.

He jerked his chin in the direction of her house. "How's Piper doing?"

Emma crossed her arms and did a half glance toward the door. "Freaked out. I had her take a hot shower and change into pajamas. She's in bed and the dogs are in the room with her. I think they know she needs the company."

Shane was sure that Decoy sensed it. More than once his dog had climbed into bed to comfort him when Shane was having a nightmare.

"Can I see her?" he asked.

Emma dipped her head to confirm it. "Guest room is down the hall."

Shane didn't hesitate. He marched into the house and

down the hall to where Piper was lying in bed, the two dogs stretched out on the floor beside her.

She sat up when she saw him, and the two dogs perked up and peered in his direction.

"How are you feeling?" he said and sat beside her, Decoy and Chipper rearranging themselves at his feet.

"BETTER," SHE SAID, and it was the truth.

When she'd first gotten into the shower, her insides had felt like ice and she'd been trembling from the shock of what had happened. The warm shower had helped chase away the chill, and little by little, she'd been able to stop shaking.

"We're going to find out who did this," Shane said and laid his hand over hers. Twined his fingers with hers. "In the meantime, you'll stay with Emma until we can fix your place up and get a security system in place. I'll be right outside in the RV."

"You don't have to do that. Emma has a security system and maybe it was just a simple break-in. There have been others in town, I think," she said, trying to convince herself that's what it had been.

Shane grimaced and shook his head. "I think it was more than that, Piper."

"But he took my wedding rings," she shot back.

With a reluctant dip of his head, he said, "He did. Hopefully you're right. In the morning, we'll see if we can set things to right at your house."

She could continue to argue with him that it wasn't necessary, but she knew he wouldn't be dissuaded. "Thanks."

"Try to get some sleep," he said and leaned forward, hesitant. Tentative as he met her gaze and brushed a quick kiss on her lips.

"Good night."

"Good night," she said to his back as he rushed from the room.

Decoy and Chipper followed him, but he commanded, "Stay."

They obeyed and returned to lie by the side of her bed.

She reached up and gently brushed her fingertips across her lips, wondering if she'd maybe imagined it, only... She hadn't. And if she was being honest with herself, she wished it would happen again, and not just the fleeting kiss from seconds ago.

"You okay?" Emma said from the doorway, brows furrowed over sky-blue eyes.

Surprisingly, she was way more okay than she'd been just moments before.

"I'm okay. Confused," she confessed, knowing Emma would understand.

"Shane?" Emma asked and leaned against the doorjamb.

"Shane," she admitted. "He's what I expected but not."

"He's changed since he got here. So have you," Emma said.

She had changed a little. So had he. But despite that, there was one truth she had to acknowledge. "He'll be gone soon."

"Maybe," Emma said and straightened. "I've set the alarm and let Tashya know what's up. She's on a date with Jason and I suggested it would be better if she stayed with him tonight."

"That might be for the best. I get the feeling it'll be wedding time for them soon anyway." Tashya and Jason had been dating for nearly four years but had grown up together as fosters in Emma's care. Now that they were both settled with good jobs, she had no doubt something more permanent would happen.

"I get that feeling also," Emma said and smiled, obviously pleased by that prospect. "I'll see you in the morning. Try to get some sleep."

With the alarm system in place as well as Emma, the dogs and Shane nearby, she'd certainly feel safe from whoever had trashed her house.

But as she slipped off to sleep, memories came again of that fleeting kiss, warning her that her heart might not be as safe.

THE NIGHTMARE CLAWED its way from his subconscious, imprisoning him in its grasp.

Heavy weight on his chest and legs, pinning him to rough, uneven ground. He called for help, but his voice was weak, his throat dry. Dirt rained down on him from above, threatening to choke him. He drew in an agonized breath, and something rattled in his chest.

Coughing, the coppery taste of blood filled his mouth. Wet his lips.

I'm dying, he thought and fought to free himself from the rubble.

But as he did so, more concrete and dirt tumbled onto him, burying him alive.

He screamed and it pulled him from sleep.

He was sitting upright in bed, his body bathed in damp sweat. His muscles quivering and his heart beating so violently, he looked down to see if it was jumping out of his chest.

Sucking in a long, slow breath, he tried to restore calm in the hopes of getting back to sleep. It would take time, especially now that Decoy was inside with Piper. The dog's presence not only helped after a nightmare, but it also often kept them away.

But not tonight. Tonight, he'd just have to tough it out. It took long hours before he slipped off to a light sleep that didn't last for long as the first fingers of light crept past the edges of the blinds to warn that morning had arrived.

He washed and dressed quickly. Made himself a cup of coffee for some energy and hurried out, determined to put things to right at Piper's home as soon as possible.

There were no lights on in Emma's home as he left his RV and climbed into his pickup for the drive into Jasper, where he intended to pick up an off-the-shelf security system, doorbell camera, wood to repair her jamb and new hinges for the door.

But before he hit any of the stores in town for the supplies, he dropped by the headquarters for Jasper PD.

The one-story green-and-white building was located on West Main Street, just off the town square. He parked in front and walked through the large glass front doors and into a reception area and waiting room. A young Asian woman sat behind the reception desk, taking calls, and he remembered her from their visit to the brewery the other day.

As he came up to the desk, Jenny raised a finger to indicate she'd be with him as soon as she finished the call.

He examined the station as he waited. Behind the desk were doors to an open room with desks and two offices. Two officers were sitting at their desks, but he didn't recognize them.

At the far end of the room was what appeared to be a large meeting room and a break room where he spied a coffee maker, refrigerator and microwave. To the left of the reception area were four holding cells and two rooms, probably for interviews, he guessed. The furniture was a little dated, and the paint was that indeterminate institutional color that could be either gray or blue. However, the space was brightly lit, neat, clean and orderly.

As he waited, an older woman walked through the front

doors carrying in a plastic-wrapped dish holding what looked like pound cake. She had short gray hair and bright blue eyes. He guessed she was in her late fifties, sixty at most, and a bit matronly.

When she saw him, she smiled and said, "May I help you?"

He nodded and held out his hand. "Shane Adler. I was hoping to speak to someone about the break-in at Piper Lambert's home."

The older woman shook his hand and arched a brow. "Theresa Norwood. I'm Chief Walters's secretary. Are you a friend of Piper's?"

"I am. I was with her last night when it happened," he explained.

Jenny had just finished her call and piped in with, "That was Ava and Brady. They just finished processing the house and are on their way back. They should be here soon."

"Well, then. Why don't you come in and get settled in the meeting room. I'll put up a fresh pot of coffee and you can have some of this," she said and raised the dish with the confection.

He dipped his head gratefully. "I'd appreciate that. I could use a cup of coffee and that looks delicious."

Theresa got him settled in the meeting room and he could hear her puttering about next door in the break room. In no time the earthy scent of fresh coffee perfumed the room, and she came in with a piece of the pound cake on a small paper plate.

"Feel free to go next door and grab yourself some coffee. Milk and cream are in the fridge."

He had just finished making himself a cup when the sound of the door opening had him looking out into the open space where Ava and Brady had just entered.

They looked tired and he suspected they'd been working all night.

When Ava noticed him, she motioned to Brady and they both walked over to the meeting room.

"Good morning," he said and rose from the table.

"It could be better," Ava said.

Brady motioned for him to sit back down and added, "We could only get a couple of partial prints. Whoever it was either wiped things down or put on gloves."

"We did get some shoe prints from the floor of the living room," Ava said and pulled out her camera to show them to Shane.

Shane immediately recognized the tread. "Looks like standard-issue combat boots."

Brady nodded. "That's what I thought as well."

Ava swiped her finger across the screen to show him another set of photos. "We also have a partial tire tread. I may be a city girl, but even I can tell these belong to a truck and not a car."

"The blue pickup that nearly ran us down?" Shane asked, then sipped his coffee and broke off a piece of his pound cake.

Brady nodded. "Possibly, but don't get your hopes up too soon. This area is packed with pickups and it's likely this one was stolen. We'll be checking that out after we take a short break for breakfast."

"Thank you. Is it okay for Piper to go back home?" Shane asked and Ava nodded.

"It is, but we'd recommend a doorbell camera at a minimum. Simple security system would be better," she said.

He rose from the meeting room table and popped the last of the pound cake into his mouth. "I planned to work on all that this morning. Will you call Piper and let her know what's happening?"

"We will," Ava confirmed.

"Great. Then I'm off," he said, and after shaking hands with the two officers and thanking Theresa, he headed off to town to fetch the supplies he needed for all the repairs and improvements.

It took less than an hour to pick up what he needed and make his way back to Piper's house.

Emma's car was in front, so he suspected the two women were already inside, trying to straighten things up.

He wasn't wrong. They had already put things back into the desk drawers and onto the bookshelves. The overturned coffee table was back in place, together with the couch cushions, which had been turned slashed-side down.

As Piper noticed his attention, she said, "I'll have to get a new couch, but that'll do for now."

"Are you okay?" he asked as he set down the bags with all his purchases by the front door.

"As okay as can be expected. You didn't have to do all that," she said and gestured to the bags.

"On the contrary, I do. I'm sure you spoke to Ava or Brady, who recommended some upgrades around here."

Her lips tightened and she nodded. "They did. Thank you."

"I guess I'll get to that while you and Emma finish up," he said and started by fixing the doorjamb and hinges. He opened and closed the door several times to make sure it latched properly and, satisfied, he turned his attention to the doorbell camera and security system.

A little more than an hour later he'd wired up the camera and set up contact sensors on all the doors and windows as well as motion detectors in the common areas. He passed Piper and Emma more than once as he worked to install the system and they cleaned up the mess.

He had just finished configuring the base station that

connected all the devices and kept the system online when Piper and Emma came into the living room with two garbage bags.

"Almost done," he said. To complete the installation, Piper would have to establish an online monitoring account, but even without that, any entry without disarming the system would set off a siren. That was usually enough to discourage small-time burglars.

"We're finished, so I guess it's time for me to head back and get some work done," Emma said and lugged one garbage bag out the door.

Piper followed her and they both walked to the curb to place the bags there for her usual garbage pickup.

As Shane finished checking that the keypad by the front door was securely fastened, he watched as Piper and Emma embraced. Emma ran her hand across Piper's back and up to her hair. They exchanged words that made Piper shoot a quick look in his direction and nod. And then Emma strode toward her car, got in and drove away.

Piper slowly trudged back toward the house, obviously troubled.

Chapter Twelve

Don't be afraid of what's happening with Shane.

That's what Emma had said to her as they'd embraced at the curb.

Only she wasn't so much afraid as she was confused. Especially with all that was happening now.

It was just too much, and to think about any kind of relationship with Shane could only bring trouble because her emotions were too raw at the moment.

But there he was, taking care of her. Making her feel things she hadn't felt since David.

"Thank you for everything," she said and leaned a hand on the jamb, still a little unsteady with all that had happened.

"It's what…friends do," he said with a shrug that stretched the fabric of his T-shirt across his broad shoulders.

She squinted as she examined his features and said, "Is that what we are? Friends?"

Decoy and Chipper, who up until that moment had been contentedly lying together just inside the front door, hopped up and started barking.

"What's up, Decoy?" he said and stroked his head to try to calm him, but Decoy raced out the door and toward the stand of trees on the far side of her property, Chipper following close behind.

Piper and Shane raced after the dogs, who had paused by the trees but hadn't stopped barking.

"Quiet," they both said, but had to repeat it several times until the dogs finally listened and sat down in the grass.

Piper scrutinized the area where the dogs had been barking and noticed some of the underbrush had been flattened. "There," she said and pointed to it.

Shane nodded and glanced past the matted-down underbrush to the grassy area beyond. He gestured to the area. "Looks like there are tire tracks there, but are they fresh ones?"

Fear gripped Piper at the thought the burglar had returned. Determined not to let it get to her, she pushed through the underbrush to where the tire tracks were. They led to the road and were clearly from some kind of truck. As Shane joined her, Piper said, "Do you think these could be from the pickup?"

Shane squatted to examine the tracks. "Could be."

He started to straighten but then pointed to where there were a couple of cigarette butts on the grass.

"You said you smelled cigarette smoke. He was here, watching you," Shane said, then rose and came to her side. He embraced her but she remained stiff in his arms.

"It's going to be okay. I'll bring my RV around and stay here," he said and stepped away, but quickly added, "If that's okay with you."

Shane being here would be complicated. She'd certainly feel safer from the burglar. But emotionally…

"It's okay," she said with a slow bob of her head.

"Good. Let's set up the alarm for the security system and arm it while I go get my RV. We'll call Ava and Brady as well to come inspect this area."

Her nod this time was certain. "Sounds like a plan."

WITH PIPER'S HELP, he was able to maneuver the RV into a grassy space to one side of Piper's home and set up his solar panels to power it.

He put his hands on his hips and smiled. "Looks good."

Piper nodded. "It does. Thank you again."

"It's not a problem. I need to know you're safe," Shane said. A second later, a loud rumble emanated from his midsection. He splayed a hand across his stomach and said, "I've been so busy I forgot to eat. How about you?"

She smiled and shook her head. "I didn't and I could eat a horse."

"I've heard a great deal about Millard's Diner. That is if you like it and would like to go," he said just as another deep rumble embarrassed him, bringing unwanted heat to his face.

Piper laughed and reached up to brush her thumb across his cheeks. "I love their burgers, but they have lots of wonderful daily specials."

"Great. Let's go, then," he said and slipped his arm through hers. This time she was fluid against him, leaning into his side. Smiling as he helped her into his pickup.

The ride to town was blessedly short and his hunger was quickly tamped down by his first bite of an absolutely wonderful burger. "As good as I'd heard."

Piper grinned and picked up her burger. "Glad you weren't disappointed."

"I wasn't. Just like I'm not disappointed with everything I've been learning at the DCA," he said, wanting to keep the conversation to anything other than the break-in.

"Truthfully, it's been a pleasure to work with you since Decoy has so many natural skills. The two of you will be a wonderful addition to any search and rescue team," she said and took a big bite of her burger. "Mmm, so tasty."

"There's still a lot to learn," Shane said, then snagged an onion ring and took a big bite.

With a small shake of her head, she said, "There is. Working with Decoy and you has me learning as well so I can keep on challenging you."

Shane couldn't resist teasing her. He arched a brow and said, "So I challenge you?"

A becoming flush of pink painted her cheeks. "You know you do. But I think I challenge you, too."

He chuckled and grinned, admiring her spirit. "You do. I wasn't expecting someone like you."

Around mouthful of burger, she said, "Ditto."

He barked out a laugh and started eating again, enjoying the burger and the company. It was turning out to be such a nice night, he didn't have the heart to ask anything about the burglary. There would be time enough on the drive home.

Home...

When he had left California and headed to Idaho, it had never occurred to him that in just a few short weeks he'd think of it as home, but there it was. Jasper felt like home. Or maybe it was more accurate to say that Piper made it feel that way.

But in a little over two weeks, he was supposed to be on his way to Montana. Away from Jasper.

Away from Piper.

His heart did a little skip at that, forcing him to suck in a breath. The air was tinged with the faint scent of something floral. Piper's soap or maybe her shampoo.

They finished dinner with a slice of Millard's cherry pie and ice cream. A perfect ending to their meal together.

But once they started their drive home, he had no choice but to ask the hard questions. He hesitated until they were almost to Piper's. Gripping the wheel tightly, he shot a quick look at her. She looked peaceful and he hated to upset that peacefulness, but it had to be done.

"Can you think of a reason why someone would be watching you? What they would want to steal from you?"

The smile that had been on her face just moments before evaporated in the blink of an eye. "Like my wedding rings?"

He hadn't wanted to say it before, but something about the theft of the wedding rings struck him as wrong.

"The rings were right there, out in the open. So were your laptop, tablet and other things someone could pawn for quick money. No reason for them to trash the house the way they did."

Piper looked down and did a little shrug. "Kids do stupid things," she said, clearly in denial.

Sucking in a breath, he blew it out roughly and said, "It wasn't kids, Piper. It was someone looking for something they didn't find."

Piper shook her head, so violently it sent the long strands of her hair shifting against her shoulders. "What could I possibly have that's so important?"

He hesitated because bringing it up might rouse painful memories for her, but he had no choice. "Is there anything your husband might have had, that he might have given you—"

"Nothing," she shot back quickly. "He hadn't been home for months because he was on deployment and then he was killed. They sent me his things…"

A soft hitch of her breath warned him she was about to cry. He reached out and took her hand into his, offering comfort.

He said nothing else, the silence in the cab of his pickup broken by Piper's soft, hiccupping cries and sniffles.

In front of her home, he parked the pickup and swiveled to face her. "Are you okay?"

She swiped at her tears with one hand since she still gripped his hand tightly. "I'm okay. Thank you for everything."

He nodded. "Let's get you settled for the night."

PIPER SNIFFLED AND released his hand, needing to escape his proximity.

Her brain and heart were in too much turmoil to handle him tonight. "No need, Shane. I'm okay."

A harsh laugh escaped him. "There's no way I'm letting you go in alone."

She could continue to argue with him, but it was just wasting her breath. "Okay. Let's go."

Rushing from his pickup, she walked up her driveway to the path leading to her front door, Shane hot on her heels. She unlocked the door and as soon as she entered, the unfamiliar beep-beep-beep of the alarm pad warned her she only had 120 seconds before the siren would go off. At the sound of the beeping, Decoy and Chipper came running out to jump all over her legs.

"Sit," she commanded, and Shane had to repeat the command before the dogs complied.

Hands shaking, she fumbled at first, but then punched in the code Shane and she had set.

The beeping ended and Piper kneeled to rub the dogs' heads. She scooped up Chipper and the puppy licked her face, making her smile.

But that smile faded as she met Shane's gaze. It was intense and way too focused on her. "I'll be fine. You don't need to worry."

He nodded. "Just to make sure, I'll leave Decoy with

you. He didn't do all that well with those attack commands, but he's still big enough to scare someone off."

Piper hoped she wouldn't need to use any attack commands, but just in case…

"Thank you. I'll take good care of him," she said and rubbed Decoy's ears. The dog sidled up to her, happy for the attention. "Good boy."

"I know you will, but… Take good care of yourself as well. I'll see you in the morning," he said and took a step back into the alcove by her front door. He gestured to the alarm pad and said, "Lock up and set that thing."

"I will," she said, but delayed, hand on the edge of the door. Saying "thanks" seemed like so little considering all that he'd done for her in the last few days. But anything else would only complicate things even more.

"Thanks," she said, but quickly added, "We can start training again in the morning."

Her words lightened his features and a quick smile skipped across his lips. "I'd like that."

"I would, too," she said and quickly closed the door.

Chapter Thirteen

I'll settle for that, Shane thought as he ambled across her front lawn to his RV.

She has the alarm and Chipper and Decoy and me, he reminded himself. Just in case, he'd have the shotgun he used to protect against predators loaded and ready for use. But first, he did a cautious walk around her property, searching for signs that anyone was nearby again and checking to see that all the doors and windows were secured. Satisfied, he headed for his RV.

Inside the RV, he stripped down to his skivvies, but then slipped into sweats and a T-shirt and placed his boots by the front door in case he had to go running to protect Piper.

Normally he'd have a finger of scotch to relax, but not tonight. He needed to be alert and he had something to do before he went to sleep.

He swiped his phone open and dialed a friend who was stationed at Fort Irwin. A friend with lots of contacts on the base and over at Camp Pendleton. Piper had offhandedly mentioned during their sessions that her husband had trained and deployed from there.

"As I live and breathe, how are you, Shane?" his friend said.

"Living the dream, Walt," he said, repeating the joke they'd always shared when they'd been hunkering down in Afghanistan together on a mission. Like him, Walt had taken a training position, but he'd chosen to be stationed at Fort Irwin.

"But seriously, I'm doing well. How about you?" he said.

"Good. Wife and I have been talking about me finally putting in my papers," Walt said.

"It'll be a big change," Shane said, thinking about how many things he'd had to deal with the last few months since he'd retired.

"Yeah, I get it, man. It's a scary thought, but hell. We've faced scarier, haven't we?"

They had, time and time again. Walt had always watched his six and that's why he knew that Walt would help with what he was about to ask.

"I need a favor."

"Just ask, Shane," Walt said, but Shane hesitated, unsure if it would become a Pandora's box that once opened couldn't be sealed.

"Shane?" Walt pressed at his reticence.

Shane pushed on. "I have a friend who's been having some trouble. Her husband was a Marine who was killed in Iraq about four years ago. I think the trouble may have to do with his last deployment."

"What's his name?"

"David Lambert. He was with the Twenty-Sixth Marine Expeditionary Unit," Shane advised.

"If I remember correctly, they were sent into the Mosul area to help battle ISIS," Walt said and, in the background, he heard Walt's wife calling out to him. "Honey, are you coming to bed?"

"Be there in a second," his friend responded before coming back on the line. "I can't guarantee anything, but I'll see what I can find out."

"Thanks, Walt. I'd really appreciate that."

They ended the call and Shane got ready for bed.

It was a cool night, so he opened the windows in his bedroom to let in the night air as well as any sounds that shouldn't be there, like the rumble of a pickup's engine.

But it was quiet except for the hoot of an owl in the distance and the rustle of the breeze that brought with it the scent of pine and fir. A warbling trio of notes drifted in on the breeze. It was repeated a few seconds later with another trio of tones, slightly different from the first.

He smiled. A mockingbird showing off his singing skills.

He lay down in bed and closed his eyes, the night sounds enveloping him in their peace. Bringing him solace as he drifted off.

But soon his peace was shattered once again by the nightmare.

The blast of the explosion and the ringing of his ears that brought with it an unnatural silence.

His throat dry thanks to the dust and debris filling the air. Choking him as he struggled to breathe.

The weight of the concrete, wood and glass that had once been the building pressed on his chest and legs, trapping him.

He reached out, searching for the familiar touch of Decoy's wet nose and his smooth fur. The slight huff of his breath against the palm of Shane's hand, but it wasn't there.

He shot up in bed, breathing heavily. The cool breeze chilled his sweat-dampened skin, rousing goose bumps.

Wrapping his arms around himself, he slipped from bed and went into the living room area, where he grabbed a blanket, lay down on the couch and flipped on the television.

He found a channel with a program where the narrator had that flat, droning voice that soon became mind-numbing. Just what he needed.

But even that tedious narrative wasn't enough to keep other thoughts at bay.

Thoughts about Piper and who might have broken into her home. Whether they were done with Piper or if she was in continued danger.

When the first rays of light pierced the edges of the shades, Shane was still awake. He was still worried about what was happening with Piper, but for today, it was time to try and get back to normal.

SHANE WAS LEANING against the fender of his pickup, waiting for her, when she walked out of the house, Decoy and Chipper dogging her heels, happy to be outside.

At the sight of him, her heart skipped a beat.

He was so handsome. His jeans hugged a flat midsection and long lean legs. The hoodie he wore against the slight morning chill stretched tight across his shoulders.

His blue eyes were as bright as the morning sky, but there were shadows beneath, as if he hadn't slept well.

She walked up to him and laid a hand on his chest, sensing he needed soothing. The muscles beneath her hand were hard, his heartbeat strong and steady. "You look a little beat."

His shoulders went up and down in a careless gesture and he covered her hand with his. Rubbed it gently. "I'm okay. A little tired. How about you?"

Surprisingly, she'd slept better than expected. "I'm good. I slept well thanks to these guys."

She bent to rub the heads and ears of both dogs, who ate up her attention, but when she looked up, her gaze locked with his and she realized he needed her care just as much, maybe more.

She straightened and cupped his jaw. Ran her thumb across his lips, the gesture meant to comfort, but it did anything but.

Her heart pounded in her chest at the heat in his blue-eyed gaze and the way he laid a hand at her waist and drew her close. She took a step closer to him and rose on tiptoes, but the sudden sound of a car pulling up jerked them apart.

A police cruiser had stopped in front of her home, but it wasn't Ava and Brady who stepped out. Lieutenant Margaret Avery, one of the most senior officers in the Jasper PD, exited the car with rookie Officer Jason Wright. Tashya's Jason.

"Good morning," Margaret said as Jason and she approached them. Her keen gaze assessed the situation between her and Shane, bringing a smile to the police officer's face, but hot color to Piper's cheeks.

"Good morning. This is Lieutenant Avery," Piper said, introducing her to Shane.

Shane shook the older woman's hand. "Nice to meet you."

"I wish it was under different circumstances, Shane. We have good news, however. Would you like to provide a report, Officer Wright?"

Clearly this was intended to help Jason learn some of the ropes and if he was working with Margaret, he was lucky. A longtime veteran of Jasper PD, she'd earned her colleagues' respect with her wonderful investigative work and her compassion when dealing with sensitive circumstances. Normally that would mean domestic violence or special victims, but she suspected Chief Walters may have decided to treat her case as one of those sensitive circumstances, explaining the unusual visit from the officers.

"Yes, Lieutenant. We were able to get a useable partial print from one of the doors and are processing it against the various databases for a match. We likewise have solid casts of shoe prints and tire tracks and are working on identifying them. We also have DNA samples from some cigarette butts that are being processed."

"Thank you, Officer Wright," she said, having to bite back her more familiar use of his given name.

"We will find out who is behind this, Piper. And we'll be keeping up our patrols in case he comes back," Margaret said, the blue gaze beneath her bangs of brown hair filled with kindness.

But the thought that her intruder might come back sent a chill through her and she wavered, leaning back into Shane, who offered her support.

Margaret reached out and laid a hand on Piper's arm. "We will get him. And I understand you've taken precautions."

Shane was the one to respond since she was still too shaken by the thought of the intruder's return.

"WE HAVE. WE'VE INSTALLED a security system and I'll be staying here until we know Piper is safe," Shane said, but omitted any mention of his own investigations into the identity of the burglar and the reasons for the mayhem he'd inflicted on Piper and her home.

The lieutenant nodded. She was a handsome woman with chin-length brown hair and intelligent blue eyes, and she was in excellent physical shape. She looked like she could take care of herself and others, which reassured him.

"Thank you for watching out for Piper. We really appreciate what she and Emma do for Jasper PD," the lieutenant said and gazed at Piper with real affection.

"Let's get going, Officer Wright. We need to check the local pawn shops for Piper's rings," Margaret said.

Jason smiled at the lieutenant, not fazed by her order, which hinted at how much respect he had for his superior.

He faced them, touched the brim of his baseball cap and said, "See you later."

"See you, Jason," Piper said and once the two officers were gone, she faced him, her features filled with worry.

"Even if he comes back, we're ready for him, Piper. Don't worry," he said, even though he knew the words would do little to appease her. But what would help was to get her back to work and her normal routine.

"I'm ready to get back to training if you are."

She nodded and gazed at the two dogs who were peacefully snuggled together at their feet. "I'm ready. We have only a little more than a week before you go."

He winced as she said it, well aware of the looming deadline for his departure.

Her words prompted them into action and a tense silence as they loaded the dogs into his pickup and did the short drive to the DCA grounds.

The silence persisted as they walked into the training ring and resumed their exercises with Decoy, having him run through the various verbal and hand signals as well as the agility course.

Shane was happy to see him go through the paces without hesitation, even when Chipper tried to chase after him, wanting to be like her pal.

"Chipper, sit," Piper commanded but had to repeat it several times before the little dog complied. Her frustration was obvious and unusual for her since she was typically more patient.

"It's okay, Piper," he said when he thought he detected the glimmer of tears in her eyes.

She sniffled. "I'm okay, Shane. I just want you to be as prepared as you can be when you go."

And there it was again, but in a way he understood. She was preparing herself for his departure by reminding herself that he would go. Reminding him that their time together was limited.

He didn't want her to think she was failing him. Laying a hand on her shoulder, he gave her a reassuring squeeze and said, "You're doing a great job. We've learned so much."

She nodded and looked away, avoiding his gaze. "But there's so much more to learn. Maybe we can start some scent training. I'll go prepare it," she said and didn't wait for his reply.

PIPER RUSHED OFF, needing distance from Shane and the reminder that he and Decoy would soon be gone.

She was determined that when they left, they'd be totally ready to continue their search and rescue training with another group.

In the DCA offices, she went straight to the equipment locker and prepped the materials they'd need to start the scent work with Decoy.

She carefully wetted some cotton swabs with birch oil, using gloves and tweezers so that the scent would only be on the object Decoy would have to find and not her.

When she returned to the ring, Shane was playing with the two dogs, laughing and smiling as they circled him or jumped up onto his legs. She'd heard his occasional laughter in the last weeks, but nothing like this unrestrained carefree happiness.

It chased away some of the worry that had plagued her ever since someone had trashed her home and stolen her wedding rings. Besides the few belongings she'd kept from David, mostly his military items, they were the only reminders of the husband she'd loved and lost way too soon.

Well, the only reminders besides her memories of David. Happy memories mixed together with the sadness and worry she'd feel whenever he left for a deployment.

Leaving being something that Shane would do as well.

Pain filled her heart, but she sucked in a breath and pushed it away, intending to enjoy whatever moments she had left with Shane.

She walked over to the trio and Shane pushed off his haunches, still laughing and smiling. He was even handsomer when he smiled, and it took years off his features.

"Are you ready?"

At his nod, she handed him a small tin with several holes punched in the top. "Hold this in one hand and a treat in the other. Let Decoy eat the treat and after, bring another treat to the tin and let him smell it. Reinforce that by giving him the treat and then switch hands."

He did as she instructed and Decoy, good boy that he was, immediately caught on. They repeated the exercise over and over, and Decoy obeyed. They challenged him by hiding the tin behind one of the fence posts and after giving Decoy the "search" command, he sniffed all around the ring. It took a few minutes, but Decoy finally paused by the fence post, sat and started barking, just like he'd been trained.

"Good boy," Piper said, then gave him a treat and rubbed his ears and head.

"He is a good boy," Shane said, standing beside them.

"A champ," Piper said and laughed as Chipper sat next to Decoy and barked as well, copying her friend's actions.

"You, too, Chipper," Piper said and bent to reward the dog with a treat and affection.

"Are you game to try this on the trail?" she asked.

Shane nodded and said, "I'm game."

SHANE WAS PLEASED with how the afternoon training had gone. Decoy had not only been able to find the little tin box Piper had prepared, but also a pair of her work gloves and a doughnut, courtesy of Barbara, who decided the doughnut's sacrifice would help her watch her waist.

When they returned to Piper's home, there were no signs that anyone had been there, but he checked all around the grounds to make sure. Satisfied, they'd split up to shower and get ready to go to dinner together.

Shane had no intention of leaving Piper alone just in case her intruder decided to come back.

He was just getting out of the shower when his phone rang. He ambled over to it and picked up when he realized it was Walt calling.

"Good afternoon, Walt. Please tell me you found something," he said and wiped a towel across his hair to dry it.

"Something, but I'm still working on it," Walt said.

"What have you got?" Shane asked, impatient to hear what his friend would say.

"I reached out to some of my Marine buddies who were familiar with Lambert's unit. Rumor had it that some of the men found a cache of relics that were believed to have been destroyed when ISIS occupied the Mosul Museum. The relics the Marines found were reported to their superiors and were supposed to have been safeguarded and returned to the Iraqis, but somehow they disappeared again."

Shane didn't like where this was going but had to press forward to keep Piper safe. "Do you know who these men were?"

"Lambert and some others. I'm still working on finding out more. My contact was going to ask around and possibly get me some paperwork with additional information."

Shane juggled the phone while trying to wrap the towel

around his waist as a knock came at his door. "I have to go, but thanks for everything. I really appreciate it."

"Not a problem, Shane. You saved my butt more than once. It's the least I can do," Walt said and hung up.

Shane dropped the phone on his kitchen counter, grabbed the towel with one hand and opened the door.

Piper stood there, dressed and ready to go.

Bright red erupted up her neck and across the creamy skin of her face as she took in his nakedness.

"Um, um, I came over to see if you were ready," she said and gestured to his chest before mumbling a curse and shaking her head.

"I won't be long. Do you want to come in?" he said although he wasn't sure her being with him half-naked in such close quarters was the best idea. Mostly because he wanted her to put her hands on him.

Her hesitation spoke volumes about where her brain was going as well, but something made him ask again.

"So? Do you want to come in?" he said and hoped she wouldn't refuse.

Chapter Fourteen

Come in? she thought. It was like the proverbial spider inviting in the fly, but it would seem rude to refuse.

"S-s-ure," she said, but tried to avoid the sight of his naked chest and legs. Not that she would forget the way he looked, all lean hard muscle. The scar on one shoulder and another farther down on his ribs. What looked like a burn angling down one hip and beneath the edge of the towel.

Look away, Piper. Don't touch, she told herself as she stepped into the spacious RV.

Inside, he pointed to the couch in a living room area and said, "I'll only be a minute."

He turned to walk to his bedroom, displaying the perfect line of his back and the marred skin on his right shoulder: the injury that had forced him to leave the Army and had brought him to her.

When the door closed behind him, she breathed a sigh of relief. It was hard enough being around Shane while they were training. Having him close the last few days had been difficult because she was growing more and more used to having him around.

That would only bring heartbreak.

She reminded herself of that as she waited, and it didn't take long for Shane to come out, dressed in jeans that hugged his powerful legs and a white cotton shirt with dark mother-of-pearl buttons. He'd gotten some color in the two weeks they'd been working together, and the tan popped against the white of his shirt. But the tan couldn't hide the dark circles beneath his eyes, a testament to the fact he might not be sleeping well.

"I'm ready," he said.

"Good," she said and rushed to his door, eager to escape the confines of the RV, which seemed suddenly too small with his powerful presence.

She stepped onto her lawn and didn't wait for him to walk across to her Jeep. At his questioning glance, she said, "I feel like driving today. Is that a problem?"

He grinned and said, "Not at all."

She hopped up into the driver's seat and Shane joined her. "I'm a little tired of burgers and beer. There's a nice Italian place not far from the brewery and diner."

"That sounds good. I haven't had a decent plate of pasta in a while," he said and rubbed his stomach.

"Great," she said and pulled out of her driveway.

There wasn't much traffic, and Shane seemed to notice. "Not many people around today."

With a shrug, she said, "It'll start getting busier in May when the hikers and fishermen visit. People also come looking for the handmade furniture that's made in the area. But the busiest time is in July when we have the annual Salmon River Festival."

"Sounds like a lot of fun," he said.

She shot a quick look in his direction and realized he was watching her intently. Her heartbeat raced a little at his perusal. She tore her gaze back to the road and said, "It is. You should think about coming back for it."

She nearly bit her lip at how it sounded, but Shane, gentleman that he was, said, "Thanks. I will think about it."

With little traffic, they were soon cruising down Main

Street and past the diner and the alley leading to the brewery. Luck was on their side as there was an open spot just a few doors down from the restaurant. But inside the restaurant the tables were all full and they had to wait for about ten minutes before one opened up.

Once they were seated, the waitress came over to hand them menus and take their drink orders. She ordered a glass of Chianti, but Shane just got some pop. At her questioning look, he said, "Need to stay sharp."

Sharp because he expected more trouble, which dimmed her generally good mood.

She set aside her menu, knowing she would order her favorite. Shane did the same just seconds later and said, "What are you getting?"

"Eggplant parmigiana with a big mound of angel hair pasta is my go-to," she said and gestured with her hands to demonstrate just how big a mound of pasta she hoped to eat.

He chuckled and mimicked her. "That big, huh?"

She did the action again. "That big."

A lopsided smile slipped across his lips, but the waitress came over that moment to set down their drinks and take their orders.

Piper placed her order, followed by Shane, but when he did, he teased her by showing the waitress just how big a pile of pasta he wanted.

"A big man like you must get mighty hungry," the waitress said, and eyed Shane in a way that Piper didn't much like. She also lingered way too long after getting his order.

"Thanks, Brandy" she said, making it clear to Brandy that it was time to go.

SHANE KNEW IT was wrong of him, but he couldn't resist. "Jealous?"

Piper laughed, trying to hide her embarrassment, but the flush on her face gave it all away. "She's way too old for you, Shane."

Brandy was probably close to fifty and definitely not his type. He preferred intelligent, determined, barely-over-thirty dog trainers with intense green eyes and long red hair he could imagine wrapped around him as they made love.

And at that moment, he was most grateful for the table that hid his reaction to that thought. Judging from the way Piper's gaze darkened to the color of shadows in a forest at night, it was obvious she might have guessed where his brain had gone and that her brain had traveled to a similar place.

He coughed to fight his reaction and reached for a piece of bread from the basket in the middle of the table. She reached for it at the same time and their hands grazed over the slices of Italian bread.

He fought the reaction to jerk his hand back and instead steadily gestured to the basket. "Please, go ahead."

She hastily grabbed a slice and slowly began buttering it.

He did the same, taking his time because he was sure it wasn't the right time to ask about her husband. Let her get her fill of that mound of pasta and some of the red wine. Let her relax for a little bit because the last couple of days had been awful.

Because of that, he tried to keep it light. "Decoy did an amazing job today, didn't he?"

"He did. He truly was born to be a search and rescue dog. You're going to be wonderful together," she said and sipped her wine, but her hand trembled as she did so, reminding him that even this topic was a minefield.

"Again, thanks to you and the DCA, It's a wonderful

thing you and Emma do," he said, steering the conversation away from where the future might take them.

"Thank you, but it's just as rewarding for us when clients do well with the training," Piper said.

"I can imagine. I used to feel the same way when I had a soldier who excelled at sharpshooting," Shane said.

Piper hesitated, but then blurted out, "Do you miss it?"

With a shrug, Shane said, "I did, but I'm finding this new life…interesting."

Piper arched a brow. "Interesting?"

The waitress came by at that moment with their meals, placing the plates before them, and sparing him from having to explain his comment.

As Piper had indicated, the portions of pasta were generous, and the earthy scent of garlic and sweet tomatoes wafted up to him from his plate of chicken parmigiana. His stomach rumbled noisily thanks to the aromas.

"Looks great," he said and dug in, as did Piper, but he urged her to continue.

"You met Emma in college?" he asked, changing the topic of their earlier conversation.

Piper sliced off a piece of her eggplant and paused with it halfway to her mouth. "We did. We hit it off right away. Roomed together and kept in touch once we graduated."

Since he knew the rest of the story would involve how she married her husband and his death, he kept silent so they could satisfy their hunger and eat in peace.

Despite the size of the portion, he managed to eat all of it because he had underestimated his appetite. But Piper still had a good amount of pasta left and as the waitress walked by, she asked for a container.

"It's always more than I can eat, and I like to make spaghetti pie with the leftovers," she explained at his curious look.

"My mom used to make that for me." She had made the most of whatever they had because money had been tight in their family.

"Where do your mom and dad live?" she asked.

With a tight smile, he said, "They're both gone. Died in a car accident right after I graduated high school. It's one of the reasons I decided to enlist. Well, that and 9/11. I needed to get away."

PIPER TOTALLY UNDERSTOOD. After David's death she'd been floundering and coming to Emma's had been her salvation in more ways than one. It had not only let her get away from the daily reminders of her loss, but it had also given her a whole new career and life.

Sensing his upset, she laid a hand on his and stroked his skin with her thumb. "I'm sorry. I know how hard it is when you lose people you love."

The muscles of his hand tightened before he turned it over and took hold of hers. "I know you know. Losing your husband... What was he like?"

She dug past the pain, remembering David's easy smile and grace. How he could ride a wave as if he and the surfboard were one. Spending lazy Sunday mornings in bed, reading the funnies and drinking coffee before they would go for a jog together.

Her throat choked up with the threat of incipient tears as she said, "He was a good man. Caring. Honorable."

A tight smile came to Shane's lips with that last word. Focusing on his features, she said, "Is there something that you're not telling me?"

Shane did a quick look around the room, and she tracked his gaze. Chief Walters and Theresa were at a table not all that far away. In a distant corner, Lieutenant Avery sat with another police officer she didn't recognize. If it got heated with Shane, she didn't want it to be in front of people she knew.

"Maybe we should discuss this in private," she said and signaled the waitress to bring the check.

But when Brandy did, Shane snagged it. "My treat. The food was great."

She didn't argue with him, deciding to save herself for what she suspected would be a more important battle. "Thank you."

He slipped several bills into the wallet, rose and held out his hand to her, but she ignored it and hurried from the restaurant.

She restarted the conversation as soon as she was behind the wheel and had begun the drive home. "What is it you're not telling me?"

Shane rubbed a hand across his mouth and then down his jaw. "I think it should wait until we get home."

She wanted to scream that it wasn't their home, it was her home and she'd only let him park on her lawn because he was helping her. The reminder that he was helping her dimmed her anger, but only a little.

They hurried home in silence. She jerked the Jeep to a halt in her driveway and stormed into her house, Shane hot on her heels. She slammed the door shut with a resounding thud and Decoy and Chipper came running. But as if sensing that something wasn't right, they immediately rushed back toward Chipper's crate near the sliding doors in the kitchen area.

"I was only trying to help, Piper. You have to believe that," Shane said, hands held out in pleading.

"What did you do?" she said, arms crossed in front of her.

Shane dragged a hand through the longer strands of hair at the top of his head and blew out a harsh breath. Shaking his head, he said, "I reached out to a friend who might have connections at Camp Pendleton."

She wagged her head so furiously strands of hair flew across her face. She yanked them back and stalked into the center of her living room. Pacing back and forth for a second, she whirled and faced Shane. "You were checking into David? His service?"

Shane took a faltering step forward. "You heard Ava the other day. Someone was looking for something specific."

"What could I possibly have and what does it have to do with David?" she argued, not wanting to believe that the theft could have anything to do with her dead husband.

Shane motioned to the sofa. "I think you should sit down."

Chapter Fifteen

The last thing Shane wanted to do was hurt Piper or dirty the memory of her late husband. But it was possible that whatever had happened in Iraq was responsible for what was happening now in Jasper. Much like it was also possible that her husband had had nothing to do with any of it. Because of that, he chose his words carefully.

"When ISIS took over Mosul, they destroyed many relics in the Mosul Museum and after that, the museum was ransacked. Many precious artifacts were taken."

Piper peered at him, clearly confused. "What does this have to do with David?"

"My contact says that there are rumors that a group of Marines on a mission found some of the missing relics. They were supposed to keep the relics safe until they were returned to the Iraqis."

Her eyes widened as his words sank in. "You think David was one of the Marines?"

Nodding, he reached out to lay a hand on hers, but she shied away. "My friend said that it was David and his squad, but he's trying to find out more."

Piper shook her head. "David would never steal anything. Never."

"I believe you, but it's possible someone else thinks that he did. Maybe that's why they trashed your house and went through your husband's belongings," Shane said, trying to convince her, not that he could.

"If David had these relics, they would have been with his things. Those are the only things that came from Iraq. I'll go get them," she said and shot to her feet.

SHANE UNDERSTOOD HOW difficult this was for Piper. He was basically accusing the man she had loved of being a thief.

He hoped that their examination of his things would not reveal any of the relics. But if they didn't, he wasn't sure that meant Piper was safe because whoever had broken in believed that she had something of value.

When Piper returned with the duffel, he helped her place it on the sofa between them. With care she removed one item after another and laid them on the coffee table. Once the bag was empty, he examined it for any kind of hidden compartment, but there was none.

"Nothing here," he said, but Piper didn't say a thing. She only handed him David's dress uniform jacket. His medals and campaign ribbons were still on the breast of the jacket. Cautiously he examined all the seams, the lining and the pockets. Again, nothing.

Gently he folded the uniform and returned it to the duffel.

He did the same with each of the other garments, cautiously inspecting each item before respectfully returning it to the bag.

When he was done, it was clear that there was nothing hidden in any of Lambert's things.

He met Piper's gaze and it was chilly, like evergreens glazed over from a winter ice storm.

"I'm sorry we had to do this," he said and zipped the duffel closed. He grabbed hold of it and stood. "Let me put this back for you."

"I'll do it," she said and snatched the bag from him.

She marched from the room, and he heard her rummaging about in her bedroom, probably as she returned the duffel to where she kept it. But she didn't come back right away, prompting worry.

He lumbered to her door, feeling guilty that he'd put her through something that had brought her pain.

She sat on her bed, tears streaming down her face, and his heart hurt for her.

He walked over, sat beside her and took her into his arms. She was stiff at first, but eventually relaxed against him and wrapped her arms around him.

"I'm sorry, Piper. I didn't mean to cause you any pain."

She nodded and sniffled. "I know you were only trying to help, but you have to believe me that David would never do something like that."

He tucked her head beneath his chin and stroked her back, soothing her. "I do believe you, Piper. But the problem is that someone else may think your husband has these things."

Piper did an unsteady bop of her head and shifted away from him. "And they won't stop until they find it."

While he didn't want to agree with her, she was right. "They won't. But we're ready for them now. The house is secured, and you've got Chipper and Decoy with you. I'll be right outside."

She offered him a weak smile and wiped away the trails of her tears. Gazing up at him, she said, "I'm sorry I was curt with you."

He stroked her back with his hand and said, "I understand. If you had accused one of my loved ones, I'd have been upset as well."

Nodding, she said, "I guess we keep on searching for why someone is doing this."

"We do. Hopefully my friend will have more for us shortly."

He cupped her cheek and ran his thumb across her tear-dampened skin. Met her gaze, dark with emotion now. She worried her lower lip with her teeth as desire slowly replaced her upset. He lowered his head until her warm breath spilled against his lips, but then reminded himself of who she was, who he was and why this shouldn't happen.

He bolted to his feet, nearly upending her as she sat on the edge of the bed. She teetered as she rose, laying a hand on his arm for stability, and he slipped his arm through hers, offering support.

Together they tottered to the front door, Shane buoying an unsteady Piper.

At the door, he faced her, and they stood there for long moments, uncertain. But then he bent quickly and brushed a quick kiss on her lips.

"See you in the morning. Lock up," he said and rushed out the door.

PIPER CLOSED THE DOOR, locked it and then leaned against it. She brushed fingers across her lips, remembering his brief kiss. Dazed by it and the fact she wished it had been more.

Shaking her head, she pushed off the door and used the keypad to set the alarm. But she realized the dogs hadn't gone out that night yet and so she disarmed the system, walked over to Decoy and Chipper and slipped on their leashes. She opened the sliding door and took them outside, rambling around the edges of her yard while the dogs relieved themselves. She hurried back into the house and secured the doors, including slipping in the piece of wood that Shane had cut to place in the sliding door rail so it couldn't be easily opened even if the lock was picked.

Resetting the alarm, she took the dogs with her into

her bedroom, and they snuggled together on the dog bed at one side of the room.

Even though it was late, and she was weary from the weight of the emotions roused that night, sleep eluded her.

She didn't have a television in her bedroom, so she went back into the living room, Chipper and Decoy trailing after her. As she did so, she walked by the sliding doors and noticed the play of shadows and light from the back of Shane's RV. His bedroom if she remembered correctly from her brief visit earlier that night.

He wasn't able to sleep either.

She hunkered down on the couch and flipped on the television. Decoy spread out on the floor by her feet while Chipper clambered up at the end of the sofa. Their presence was calming and after a few minutes, her eyes slowly drifted closed, but then something jolted her awake again.

Had it been a shout? she wondered and listened carefully, but there was only the quiet of the night.

THE WINDOWS AT the front of the house provided a clear view into the living room.

He watched through his binoculars as Lambert's widow entered the room, the two dogs following behind her.

He lost sight of her as she settled onto the couch and soon the flashes of light and dark told him she'd turned on the television, clearly settling in for the night.

He mumbled a curse. He'd been hoping that she'd stay away at her friend's ranch, but now she was already back, and the place had been secured as if it was Fort Knox. It would be difficult to get back inside the house without setting off alarms.

He'd only just emptied Lambert's duffel bag when he'd seen them coming through the meadow and had to escape, nearly running them over in the process. At least he'd grabbed her rings to make it look like a robbery and maybe provide him some money if he could find somewhere to pawn the rings without alerting the cops.

He had to be able to get back in there and look for the relics. He was sure Lambert had sent them to his wife before he'd been killed on one of their missions. The only other person who'd had access to them had been Buck, but he'd visited his friend who had denied having the treasures. Plus, Buck wasn't living the high life, relying on his family's business to give him a clerk's job that barely paid his expenses.

He hadn't been as lucky. No one wanted to hire someone who had been dishonorably discharged, forcing him to steal to live.

But what he'd taken so far was peanuts compared with what Lambert's widow had in her possession. If he could grab the relics from her, he could sell them for millions on the black market.

Setting down the binoculars, he climbed back into the blue pickup he'd stolen in Boise. He'd have to ditch it and find another ride because he was sure the police would be looking out for it. Tonight, he'd spend the night in the abandoned cabin he'd broken into to hide when he realized he'd have to stalk Piper longer than he'd originally thought.

In the morning he'd hightail it to McCall and pick up a different a ride and then come back to Jasper and be patient. When the time was right, he'd grab Piper and get her to tell him where she had the relics her husband had sent her.

Once she revealed where the treasures were, everything would be okay in his world.

He just had to wait and watch.

Chapter Sixteen

The nightmare had raked its claws into him again last night.

He woke groggily, the weight of it dragging on him emotionally, drained physically by the lack of sleep.

But it wasn't the first time he'd gone without rest. He had sometimes spent days without sleeping while on a mission, pushing on because he had to for the sake of the assignment and his fellow soldiers.

Now he had to do it for Piper's sake.

He forced himself from bed and fixed a big cup of coffee. Stood in his kitchen watching as Piper slipped out the sliding doors and walked the two dogs.

She was fully dressed, warning him that he should be getting ready for their daily training session. Not to mention avoid another embarrassing incident like what had happened the night before when she had caught him half-naked.

He slugged back a mouthful of coffee, wincing as the heat of it burned down his throat.

Rushing into his bedroom, he dressed for the day, slipping on a T-shirt and layering a flannel shirt over it. There was still the chill of winter in the early morning, but that quickly gave way to heat as the sun rose.

He had just finished putting on his work boots and

making himself a to-go cup of coffee when a light knock came at his door.

Opening it, he wasn't surprised to see Piper at the door with the two dogs.

"Good morning, Piper," he said and stepped out onto the grass of her side lawn.

"Is it a good morning?" she said, eyeing him with concern. "You look tired."

"A little tired. I didn't sleep well," he admitted, but didn't say more, unwilling to share the reason for why it had been a rough night.

He somehow made it through the day's training and dinner with Emma, who opened her home to them. It was a pleasant dinner with no talk about the break-in, just the training. Her vet tech, Tashya, and her boyfriend, Officer Jason Wright, had come in just as they were having dessert and coffee and joined them. Luckily, Tashya and Jason had likewise avoided talk about Piper's intruder, especially since Shane turned the discussion to them.

"Have you two been dating long?" he asked, and the two twenty-somethings shared a loving look.

"About four years, but we've known each other for longer. Emma fostered both Tashya and me and that's how we met," Jason said, and Emma explained.

"Since I was lucky enough to be fostered and then adopted by the Danielses, I decided to honor them by also fostering young people who needed help," she said.

"I was fourteen when Emma took me in and changed my life. It's thanks to her I was able to finish vet tech school," Tashya added and peered at Emma with adoration.

"Gonzo told me you're helping at-risk kids now as well," he said, wanting to know more about what else happened at the DCA besides the dog training.

Emma nodded and gestured to Piper. "We do. We have

them do chores around the property and work with the dogs. It helps them learn responsibility and, like Jason, a few of them have gone on to become police officers. As for the others, most have stayed out of trouble."

But not all, he heard in her words. Although he didn't ask it, he wondered again if one of those kids who hadn't been saved was responsible for what was happening at Piper's home.

"It's an amazing thing you've done for so many of us," Jason said and shot Emma a look filled with respect and caring.

"I had to pay it forward," Emma said, obviously grateful for the people who had saved her when she needed it.

He recognized that need to help others. It was one of the reasons he'd chosen to serve in the military.

The rest of the night passed quickly, and he was soon driving Piper back home.

He said good-night to her at the front door, leaving Decoy with her even though the dog helped him chase away the worst of the nightmares. Once he was settled in bed, he flipped on the television and tried to get some sleep, but he was just drifting off when the first tendrils of the nightmare crept into his brain.

The dust and debris. Searing pain in his shoulder. This time, the sounds filled his ears. The moans of someone nearby, trapped like he was. Banging on a pipe, a call for rescue. The rumble of heavy equipment, an excavator waiting to claw through the debris.

He jerked awake, heart pounding heavily. Clammy sweat chilling his body.

Taking several deep breaths, he shoved the dream from his brain and tried to focus on the images on the television. But almost as soon as his eyes closed, the nightmare came again.

It was a pattern that repeated all night long until the first hint of morning light pierced past the edges of his blinds, warning that he had to get out of bed and prepare for the day.

Not even an ice-cold shower could drive away the lethargy.

When he opened the door after Piper's knock, her gaze traveled over his features, but she thankfully didn't say anything. At least not then.

After he'd had trouble putting Decoy through some of the search and rescue exercises, Piper stopped the training session. Hands on her hips, she eyed him up and down and said, "You don't look too good, and you've been really off today."

He rubbed the stubble on his jaw since he hadn't felt steady enough to shave, especially since the lack of sleep was also making his shoulder act up more than normal. He'd had a dull ache in it all day and his hand had been shakier than usual. Maybe because he was sitting in weird positions while he tried to get to sleep.

"I haven't been sleeping well," he admitted because to deny that something wasn't up with him would be impossible.

PIPER STRODE TO him until she was barely a foot away and had to tilt her head back to look at him thanks to his much greater height. She laid a hand on his chest. The cotton of his dark blue T-shirt was smooth beneath her hand. His muscles were tense, his heartbeat a heavy lub-dub beneath her palm. A muscle ticked along his jaw and she recognized the stance well.

Her husband could sometimes be the strong silent type, but David hadn't built up as many walls as Shane. She had seen them on the very first day because she'd constructed some of her own. She had thought that in the last few weeks together, they'd both torn down some of their defenses, but clearly Shane had put up his shields again in the last couple of days.

Wanting to restore the connection they'd started to share, she smoothed her hand across his chest and said, "You can tell me, Shane. I won't judge."

He clenched his jaw and avoided her gaze until she cupped his cheek with her other hand and applied gentle pressure to urge him to face her.

His blue gaze was as tumultuous as the Salmon River when the spring thaw on the mountains sent waters cascading down it. But as she stroked his chest again and shifted her other hand to brush back a lock of the longish hair at the top of his head, he relaxed beneath her caring touch.

"I have nightmares," he said in so low a whisper she almost didn't hear it. But the pain of it reached deep inside her.

"It's okay if you do. You've seen things none of us can even imagine," she said, recalling her husband's restless nights when he'd be home between deployments.

He nodded and, in a stronger voice, said, "I have. They're usually about being trapped beneath the rubble of the building."

"Is that why you want to do search and rescue?" she asked, surprising herself that she hadn't asked him about his motivation earlier.

With a shake of his head, he said, "No. At first I didn't know what I wanted to do or where to go. The Army had been my whole life, but I didn't want to be a desk jockey."

She glanced at the shoulder that he sometimes rubbed and remembered the scars she'd seen on his body a couple of days earlier. It clicked that his injury had forced his retirement, but before she could say anything, he said,

"When Gonzo mentioned it… It made sense since Decoy had rescued me."

She heard what he didn't say. "He saves you at night as well, doesn't he?"

"He does. He helps me get through the nightmares," he said with a nod. "But it's more important that he protects you right now."

Having Decoy with her at night did make her feel better. But for both her and Shane to stay safe, Shane had to be alert as well and he clearly wasn't.

"I think it's time we call it a day and go home. To my home. You can stay in my spare bedroom," she said, her tone brooking no disagreement.

She pivoted on her heel and marched to his pickup, giving him little time to object. At his vehicle, he did finally protest.

Laying his hand on the door to keep her from opening it, he said, "That's not a good idea, Piper. You can't even begin to imagine what my nightmares are like."

But she could, especially since it occurred to her that the shout she'd heard the other night had been Shane, calling out in the middle of one of his bad dreams.

"You'll have Decoy to help and so will I." It was the least she could do considering all that he'd done to help her in the last couple of weeks.

His jaw tightened again, but he drew in a breath and shakily released it. "Okay. You win."

Trudging away from her to the driver's side, he got in and waited for her to slip into the passenger seat.

When she did, he pulled away and did the short drive back to Piper's home. It was early afternoon because they'd cut short that day's training session, leaving plenty of time for them to pack up some of Shane's things and get him settled in the spare room.

"Why don't you try and take a nap? With everything that's going on I've fallen behind on some paperwork for the DCA and am going to try and catch up with it," she said.

He hesitated, but then nodded and went to the spare room, Decoy and Chipper on his heels, but she called for Chipper to stay with her. To her satisfaction, Chipper complied, and she rewarded the puppy with a body massage and a treat.

After the door to the spare bedroom closed, she sat down at a desk at the far side of the living room and tackled the paperwork. Some were forms intended to confirm Shane and Decoy's training. Others were schedules for future training sessions or prospective clients Emma thought Piper should handle.

They normally discussed prospective clients, which was why Shane's training sessions had been a bit of a surprise. But then again, it had been a last-minute decision on Shane's part from what she could tell, and she hated to admit it, but Emma had been right that she had learned things from working with Shane. Namely, that she was more ready for a relationship than she had thought.

Shane might have had his nightmares the last few days, but she had had dreams of Shane and what it would be like if he wasn't leaving in a little over a week. Dreams of a life she had thought was gone after David's death.

She had never imagined she'd have those dreams again, much less with another military man.

But Shane was no longer in the military, which meant they could have a steady and stable life, unlike the one she'd had with David thanks to his various deployments.

Chipper's whine at her feet snared her attention and reminded her that she'd been sitting for a couple of hours. Which also reminded her that it was almost time for dinner.

A slight drizzle had started after they'd gotten home, bringing a damp chill into the air with the coming of dusk.

They needed something warm to chase away the chill, so she got out the ingredients to make some chili and corn bread. It was the kind of comfort food her mom used to make and would do well to warm their bellies as well as possibly bring some solace to Shane.

She browned the meat with onions, garlic, some tomato paste and a chipotle pepper with some of the adobo from the can. She added beans and chicken broth and set the pot to simmer. In no time she'd mixed up some corn bread from a mix and had it baking in the oven. Inhaling the earthy scents of the chili and sweetness of the corn bread brought happy memories of her family, who were still living in California. It reminded her that it had been nearly a year since she'd seen them and that it was maybe time to visit.

Maybe with Shane, she thought in a moment of hopefulness.

After setting the table, she poured herself a little bit of wine from an open bottle and started prepping the fixings for the chili. She had just finished chopping some scallions when Shane ambled out of the spare bedroom.

He raked his fingers through his hair to smooth down the longer strands that had been sleep tousled. Although there were dark smudges like charcoal beneath his eyes, he seemed a little more alert.

"Feeling better?" she asked, although it was obvious from his posture and the easy smile that flitted across his lips.

"Much. And hungry. That smells delicious."

SHANE WALKED INTO the kitchen area and lifted the cover from the pot with the chili. Inhaling the aromas, he broad-

ened his smile as they brought back wonderful memories.
"My mom used to make chili on rainy days," he said and
glanced toward the sliding doors where a light sprinkle
fell. It was dusk, but there was little light thanks to the
clouds obscuring the last of the sun's rays.

As it got a bit darker, the dusk-to-dawn sensor light
snapped to life, illuminating a goodly portion of Piper's
backyard. He had no doubt that an intruder wouldn't risk
entry that way because they'd be too visible.

"I hope the chili will chase the chill away," she said and
laughed brightly. "Chili on a chilly day."

He joined in her laughter, grateful for the happier mood.
Grateful not to be alone in the RV on such a miserable
night.

Covering the chili, he walked to the living room windows and confirmed that the front door light had turned on
as well. It shined toward the short alcove before the door
and near the garden beneath the living room windows.
Realizing that they were totally visible to anyone on the
street, he walked over and lowered the window blinds.

Piper noticed his actions but said nothing. She continued cooking and he went over and stood beside her, laying a hand at the small of her back in a gesture that was
way too comfortable. Way too normal if they'd been a
loving couple.

Only you aren't, the little voice in his head challenged.
He ignored it, enjoying this easy time with Piper way too
much.

"How can I help?" he said.

She gestured to the refrigerator with a tilt of her head.
"There's some sour cream and shredded cheese in the
fridge. Hot sauce if you like it. Beer as well."

He walked over, took the items out and laid them on
the table she had already set. The place mats were catty-

corner to each other, which would bring them close when they ate. He didn't have time to change the setup since she walked over with a plate with some fixings and set it next to what he'd taken out of the fridge.

"Make yourself at home," she said and walked back to the stove, where she ladled chili into deep earthenware bowls. He walked over to take them from her and bring them to the table while she cut squares of corn bread and placed them on another plate.

He waited until she came to the table and sat, then took the spot next to her.

"Enjoy," she said and reached for the fixings to prepare her chili.

"I will," he said and watched as she piled her plate high with the scallions, pimentos, shredded cheddar and hot sauce.

He arched a brow. "No sour cream?"

She grinned and shook her head. "Don't want to drown the chili in too much."

Like everything she'd piled on the plate already? he thought with a strangled laugh but kept silent because the smells from the chili and corn bread were way too enticing.

He mimicked what she had done, piling his plate high with fixings. After taking a bite, the heat of the hot sauce and chili had him reaching for the sour cream and the beer to tame the spiciness.

The corn bread also provided the perfect blend of heat and sweet. He found himself eating bits of corn bread with each forkful of the chili until there was nothing left in his plate and only a little chug of beer in the bottle.

Piper had yet to finish, but when she noticed he was done, she said, "Can I get you more? Another beer?"

He held his hand up to keep her from interrupting her meal. "I can get it. Can I get you anything?"

"There's some butter on the counter if it's not a bother," she said with a smile.

"Not a bother," he replied and loved just how homey the moment felt.

He spooned himself another bowlful but skipped getting a second beer. The nap had helped improve his alertness and he didn't want to dim that with alcohol. Snaring the butter dish from the counter, he returned to the table.

While he ate his second bowl, Piper finished her first, but took another piece of corn bread and slathered it with butter.

He ate a forkful of his chili, swallowed and said, "Did you get your paperwork done?"

She nodded and chewed her corn bread. "I did. I'd fallen a little behind," she said and didn't need to explain why. The last few days had definitely taken time away from her normal schedule.

"Good to hear," he said, and silence filled the air for a few short minutes as they both finished their dinner.

When they were done, they worked together to clear the table, put away the leftover chili and corn bread, and wash dishes, standing beside each other as Shane rinsed and handed dishes to Piper to place them in the dishwasher.

They had just finished cleaning when Shane's phone rang, shattering the companionable chatter they'd been sharing.

Shane whipped the phone from his back pocket, saw that it was Walt and tensed.

As Piper witnessed his reaction, she realized who might be calling.

She gestured to her living room sofa and mouthed, "I'll leave you alone."

Worried the distance to the couch wasn't enough for privacy, he walked down the hall and to the spare bedroom.

"Evening, Walt. How are you?"

"I'm good. How about you? The woman?" Walt asked.

Shane didn't want to delay it any further. "Waiting for news from the police and hopefully you."

Walt laughed and Shane could picture his friend shaking his head to chastise him. "Always direct, but I have some good news for you. It doesn't seem like Lambert had anything to do with the theft of the relics. He reported their discovery so the authorities could recover them before he was killed in action."

"But they weren't recovered," Shane said, wanting to be sure about what Walt was saying.

"They weren't, but like I said, it seems like Lambert is in the clear there. He followed protocol, but two members of his squad apparently didn't. They went AWOL immediately after Lambert was killed and before the authorities could reach the relics."

Shane considered what Walt had said. "The Marines think that those two soldiers stole the treasures?"

"They do, but they had nothing to prove it and certainly not the relics, which are still missing. But they were AWOL and the Marines used that to dishonorably discharge them. I've got those papers for you, but they're heavily redacted," Walt said, and Shane could hear his friend tapping on keys, likely sending him the materials.

"Thank you for this, Walt. It's been a big help," he said and a second later a little whoosh on his phone confirmed that he had received an email. He took a quick look to confirm it was from Walt.

"I'm glad but be careful. This stuff they stole could go for big money on the black market. Big enough to kill for," Walt warned.

His gut clenched at the thought Piper was in such serious danger. No matter, he intended to stick to her like white on rice and keep her safe.

"Roger that, Walt. I'll keep you posted on what happens," he said and swiped to end the call.

He tucked the phone into his back jeans pocket and walked into the living room where Piper waited, green eyes wide in anticipation.

"It was your friend with info, wasn't it?"

Chapter Seventeen

Her heart pounded so hard in her chest, so loudly, that she couldn't hear what he said next. Laying her hand over her heart, she said, "I'm sorry. Could you repeat what you said?"

"The Marines think that the relics were stolen from Iraq, but that David had nothing to do with it."

"Nothing?" she said, needing the reassurance about what she had known about her husband anyway.

"Nothing. His squad found the relics while on a mission and David reported that to his superiors. They contacted the Iraqi authorities so that the items could be recovered, but they disappeared before they could get there," Shane said and came to sit beside her.

"They're still missing?" she asked and searched Shane's features while he answered.

"They went missing after David was killed in action. The Marines suspected two members of David's squad but couldn't prove it. But they were AWOL for a few days—"

"To steal the relics?"

Shane shrugged and his lips tightened into a grim line. "Possibly. Again, they couldn't prove it, but they had enough to dishonorably discharge the two Marines. My friend sent me the documents but warned that they were heavily redacted. I'd like to print them if I can."

"Sure. Send them to me."

With a few quick swipes he did as she asked and when she got them, she opened the PDFs and printed them. He hopped up from the sofa, hurried over to take the papers from the printer and came back to spread the documents on the coffee table.

Shane's friend hadn't been wrong about the redaction, Piper thought, staring at heavy streaks of black across most of the documents. As they read through what they could, the main things they could confirm were what squad they had belonged to, the leader of their squad—David—and the dates when the soldiers had gone AWOL. But luckily, they also had the names of the squad members to turn over to the police.

Piper ran her fingers over the writing on the paper. "David was the leader of this squad. And these dates," she said, running her fingers over a line in the report. "These dates are immediately after David died."

Shane nodded. "They are. It's probably when they decided to go back and take the relics."

Piper waved her hands in a stop gesture. "But someone thinks David had the relics. And they seem to think he sent them to me."

"They do," Shane said and exhaled a long breath. "We need to call Jasper PD and fill them in on all this. Maybe they'll be able to use it to identify who might be behind what's happening."

Piper nodded in agreement. "We need to do that. Maybe we should take this to them?"

"I think that's a good idea."

Ava and Brady had been working a late shift away from headquarters, but at their arrival with the information,

they'd called in Lieutenant Avery and Jason to sit and review the materials.

As Margaret had read through the materials, she'd said,
"The names will help, especially if one of them has a criminal record. If they do, we may be able to use our partial
fingerprint and DNA evidence to confirm if it's one of
these two individuals."

Satisfied that the officers were doing all they could, he
and Piper had returned home.

It was late by the time they got back, but the dogs had
needed to be walked. Thankfully the rain had stopped and
since he hadn't wanted to leave Piper alone, they took the
dogs out together. They did a short loop to the end of the
block and back and it was enough for the dogs to relieve
themselves.

Inside the house, Piper and he unleashed the dogs and
did an awkward little dance as they said good-night. When
he went to brush a quick kiss on her lips, she turned her
face and he ended up skimming her cheek. Her soft, warm
cheek that sported a bright flush of color from his actions.

"Good night," she stammered and raced off to her bedroom, taking Chipper with her. As she closed the door, he
walked down the hall to the spare bedroom, Decoy tagging
along beside him, clearly happy to be with him.

"You're a good boy," he said and rubbed Decoy's floppy
gold-brown ears.

It seemed like a hint of a smile passed across Decoy's
mouth before he barked a reply.

"I missed you," he said, but didn't close the door to the
bedroom. He wanted to be able to hear if anything was
amiss and if so, to be able to deal with it free of any obstacles.

With a quick visit to the bathroom, he got ready for

bed, and once he was settled, Decoy jumped up and settled in beside him.

He fell asleep quickly, tired as he was after two sleepless nights and the roller-coaster ride of emotions that both he and Piper had been on.

But when the nightmare came this time, it was different. There was still dust and debris threatening to choke him, but now there was something else. Piper's voice, calling to him.

He fought against the weight on his chest, using almost superhuman strength to lift the rubble off him so he could find Piper in the debris. She was yards away, trapped beneath chunks of concrete and twisted rebar.

"Piper," he called out and reached for her.

She said his name and lifted her hand. Even with the distance between them, he imagined the touch of her hand on his bare chest.

"Shane," he heard, close to his ear as a light weight pressed on him, not as ephemeral as before.

He flailed his arm, trying to knock away that weight, but her voice was louder now. More insistent. "Shane. Wake up, Shane."

PIPER BLOCKED HIS arm and took hold of his hand as he sat up in bed, bare-chested. His scars, both emotional and physical, revealed to her.

"You were having a nightmare," she said and soothed her hand across chest. His skin was damp and chilled from the night air.

"I'm okay," he said, but when his gaze focused and settled on her, he cupped her cheek, almost as if to confirm she was really there.

"You're okay. Everything is okay," she said, trying to reassure him.

Shane rubbed his head, as if trying to dispel the last remnants of the nightmare. He looked away for the briefest moment before settling his gaze on her once more.

"It was different this time," he said and ran his thumb along her chin and the slight dimple there.

She squinted, trying to figure it out, but couldn't. "How was it different?"

"You were in my nightmare," he said, shocking her.

She laid a hand on her chest and squeaked out, "Me. I was in it?"

"You, Piper. You were there, trapped. I was trying to reach you, but I couldn't," he said.

"I'm here, Shane," she said.

"You are," he said and wrapped an arm around her waist and drew her close. As he lay down, he took her with him, and she ended up lying along his length.

His body was so hard beneath hers, calling to the woman who hadn't experienced emotions like this since her husband's death. But as she inched up to meet his lips with hers, she knew it was about more than physical longing. Shane had breached the walls of her heart and she could no longer deny what she was feeling.

She kissed him, moving her mouth along his. Taking in his breath as if she needed it to breathe. Dipping her tongue in to taste him because she wanted to know everything about this strong and caring man.

As he cupped her breast through the thin fabric of her nightshirt, her nipple beaded against his palm. Her breast heavy with need, she covered his hand and pressed it to her, moaned when he tweaked her hard nipple with his fingers.

HIS BREATH EXPLODED from his chest at the sound of her needy moan and the feel of her breast against his palm, beneath his fingers. The softness of her belly cradled his erection and he wanted nothing more than to strip off her thin cotton nightshirt and make love to her, but not like this.

Not when their emotions were running high from the danger threatening Piper's life and his. He had no doubt that if the intruder needed to get to Piper, he'd kill Shane to do it.

"Shane?" Piper asked and leaned a hand on his chest to look at him in the dim light of the room.

"I… I care for you, Piper. I really do, but things are too unsettled now. We're both not thinking straight."

Her eyes widened at his words, and she scrambled off him, but stood by the bed for a halting second. "I care for you, too."

Then she burst from the room, Chipper barking and hopping up and down as she chased after Piper.

Her door slammed shut, but he could hear Piper's muffled crying, or at least he thought he did, through the wall separating them.

Decoy barked, but it almost seemed like a condemnation of what he'd done.

"Down, Decoy," he said and gestured to the floor beside the bed.

The dog didn't obey. He just sat there, staring at him.

"Down, Decoy," he repeated more sharply.

The dog barked again, but did as he said, his gaze still lifted to Shane's in accusation.

He flipped onto his side, grabbed his pillow and used it to silence Piper's crying and the sight of Decoy's silent condemnation.

Little by little he finally relaxed and tossed aside the pillow. Listened to the silence of the night, broken only by the sound of the mockingbird he'd heard days earlier.

A mockingbird mocking him and the sense of honor

that was keeping him from the only woman in his life he'd ever cared about this deeply.

But he'd lived his life with that code of honor intact and he intended it to stay that way.

When this was all over, he'd know whether or not Piper and he were truly meant to be together or if this was just a result of the danger threatening their lives.

THE MORNING WAS chilly in more ways than one, Piper thought.

Breakfast was peppered with curt one-word answers, but at least Shane looked like he had gotten a little more sleep.

They hurriedly finished the quick meal of scrambled eggs and toast, cleaned up and were on their way to the DCA. When they arrived, another car was already parked across from Emma's ranch house.

"Marie's here. She's our vet. I hope nothing's wrong," she said and quickly hopped out of Shane's pickup.

She rushed toward the DCA offices and barn, fearing the worst, but a second later Marie and Emma walked out of the DCA offices, laughing and chatting amiably.

Shane came to her side just as Emma and Marie joined her in the middle of the parking area. "Shane, this is Dr. Marie Beaumont, our vet."

He shook her hand and said, "Shane Adler. Piper's been training my dog and me."

Decoy went to Marie's side, sniffed and then sat at her feet, waiting for her attention. "You're a smart boy, aren't you?" Marie said and playfully rubbed his ears.

"Everything's okay, right?" Piper asked just to confirm.

Emma jerked a hand in Marie's direction. "Someone brought a stray pregnant dog to Marie, but she doesn't have room in her kennels so she asked if we would take care of her."

And Emma would never say no to any animal or person in trouble, Piper thought.

"We'll keep a good eye on her," Piper said, and Emma seconded it. "We'll call if there are any complications during the whelping."

"WHELPING?" SHANE ASKED, confused by the term.

Marie smiled and explained. "It's what you call it when you deliver a litter of puppies."

"She's that pregnant?" Shane asked, arching a brow.

"She's that pregnant," the vet said with a laugh, the laughter reaching up into her blue eyes. She was a beautiful woman with dark brown, slightly wavy hair that just brushed her shoulders. Of average height, she had a toned, runner's kind of body that said she was physically active.

"We've done it before, Shane. No need to worry," Piper said and laid a hand on his arm as if to comfort him.

"Good to know because Decoy is the first pet I've ever had," he admitted.

Marie peered at him, as if to size him up. "Military?"

He nodded. "Military. Hard to have a pet."

"I get it. Anyway, I have to get back. I have some patients coming in later today," Marie said and with a wave, she walked to her car, got in and pulled away from the DCA.

"Where's our pregnant patient?" Piper asked.

"The indoor kennels, only…" Emma hesitated, and it was clear something was up.

"Come take a look," she said, and they walked with her to the indoor kennel where a very pregnant dog was resting comfortably on a bed in one of the kennels.

"This is a stray? It looks like a purebred basenji. Not

the kind of dog we see around here," she said and bent to scratch the dog's ears, earning a grateful lick from the little pointy-eared dog. She had a short red-and-white coat and a tightly curled tail and even he could see that this was not a mutt.

"That's what I thought. I'm going to call Jasper PD to see if anyone has reported one that's missing or stolen," Emma said and went to her office to make the call.

"It's a beautiful dog," Shane said and followed Piper out of the DCA offices to the agility course.

Piper's brow furrowed but relaxed as she said, "Beautiful and very smart. But we have our own smart pups, right?"

"Right," he said, and Piper immediately went to work with Decoy, putting him through the paces on the agility course the first time. Once Decoy had finished, she turned it over to him and he guided Decoy through all the obstacles over and over. Decoy did each run without any hesitation or faults.

"Good boy. Good boy," he said and rewarded Decoy with treats and a body rub.

"He is a good boy. I know it's going to be a little muddy, but I'd like to take him out on the trail. Just give me a moment to hide some things."

She left him on the trail and went into the DCA's offices and he took advantage to put Decoy through another run on the agility course. He caught a glimpse of Piper as she walked between the offices and the barn to head to the trail. It made him uneasy to think about her out there with only Chipper for protection.

With a low whistle and hand signal to Decoy, they hurried to the space between the two buildings where he could keep an eye on Piper as she walked down the trail. He could see her hiding things here and there along the path and when she returned, she rolled her eyes at the sight of him standing there.

"I'm safe here," she said and held her hands wide to the area around them.

He didn't want to worry her, so he agreed despite his misgivings. "You are safe here."

One reddish brow shot upward to let him know she didn't believe him, but she only said, "Let's see what Decoy can do on the trail."

Chapter Eighteen

Decoy did wonderfully during the session, finding Emma's work gloves and knit cap as well as several other hot dogs. Except for one that Chipper beat him to at the end, possibly because by then Decoy's belly was full.

"Chipper, that's not for you," Piper said as Chipper jogged away with the hot dog in her mouth.

"Smart dog," Shane added, chuckling at the sight of Piper chasing Chipper. When she caught the squat little puppy, she hauled her up into her arms, laughing. Her green eyes were the color of emeralds and glittering with happiness. He was relieved that her upset from the night before had been chased away by the antics of the dogs. Or maybe she was better at hiding her feelings than he thought.

He liked seeing her like this, free of the worry that had plagued her during the last few weeks.

When the puppy gobbled up the last of the hot dog, Piper set him down. "Maybe I should be teaching Chipper to do search and rescue."

Although their focus had been on Decoy during their training, Chipper had been obedient and learned many of the same commands. Not as quickly as Decoy, but eventually the little pup had learned.

"She's a good dog," he said again and bent to rub Chipper's head when the puppy came over, seemingly aware that he was talking about her.

"She is. Come here, Chipper," Piper said, and the little dog complied and sat at Piper's feet, waiting for the next command. Piper rewarded her with a treat and when she straightened, she said, "I guess we can call it a day. It's almost five."

"Sounds good." He strolled beside her, their pace slow to enjoy the beautiful late afternoon sun. The dogs played together along the trail.

"They're good friends," Piper said, grinning at the sight of the two mismatched dogs tussling over a branch. Decoy was at least a foot taller, his body thicker with his Lab/hound background. Chipper had the short legs of the corgi, and her body wasn't as muscular despite the pit bull in her.

"They are friends. Or maybe it's love," he teased and wanted to bite his tongue as Piper shot a quick look at him out of the corner of her eye.

"Love, huh?" she said, her tone a mix of playful and serious. Her gaze saying her words might be more than about the dogs.

With a side-eyed glance, he said, "Maybe."

The dogs ran ahead between the two buildings and as they turned the corner, Ava and Brady were standing there.

Piper waved at them, and the two officers returned the wave and approached.

"We went by your place and when you weren't home, we figured you'd be here," Ava said.

"You guessed right," Piper said and quickly added, "Do you have something for us?"

Ava shot a quick look at Brady, who did a slow nod to confirm she should continue. As the lieutenant, he had the higher rank and was likely in charge along with Lieutenant Avery.

Ava pulled her notebook out of her jacket pocket, flipped through a few pages and then began her report. "We reviewed the papers you sent us and tracked down the two men. Buck Devare is clean as a whistle. He's been working as a clerk in his family's business. Married. One child."

She flipped to the next page and said, "The second man has a criminal record. Josh Parker. Came back from Afghanistan and a few months later ended up in county jail on a misdemeanor assault and battery charge. He's out in six months, but not long after that he's back in jail for second-degree robbery. Broke into a liquor store in the middle of the night. Got two years in prison for that one."

"All of that was in California. We got his fingerprints from those crimes and even though our print was only partial, there are a lot of points of identification," Brady added to her report.

"What about the DNA on the cigarette butts?" Shane asked, hoping that the DNA would be the final nail to confirm it was Parker who was responsible for the burglary.

"We should have our analysis back in the next few days. Second-degree robbery is a felony in California so his DNA was collected and hopefully is in CODIS so we can see if it's a match," Ava explained.

Piper glanced at him and then back to the officers. "That's all good, then, isn't it?"

"Oceanside PD went by Parker's California apartment, but he wasn't there. The manager hasn't seen him in weeks. Probably because he's past due on his rent. Until we have him in custody, we all need to stay alert. In the meantime, we've put out a BOLO on Parker," Brady said and tapped a finger to the brim of the baseball cap with the Jasper PD's emblem. "We should get going."

"We'll keep you advised," Ava said, and the two officers turned and walked back to their police cruiser.

As they drove away, Piper said, "That's all pretty good, right?" She shot a quick look up at him.

Hands on his hips, he gazed toward the cruiser as it moved down the long drive of the DCA and turned off to head back in the direction of Piper's home. "It is, but like Brady said, we need to stay alert until they can locate Parker."

Piper's shoulders slumped at his comment.

He laid his arm across her back and drew her against him. "It's going to be okay."

She worried her lower lip with her teeth and nodded, but it was halfhearted. "It will be."

"Let's get cleaned up and make it a night. Maybe call Emma to see if she's free. Try to put this all behind us," he said and playfully bumped his hip against hers.

"I like that idea."

THE BREWERY WAS PACKED, not unexpected for a Friday night in Jasper, especially with the warmer late April weather. It wasn't unusual to have the first small wave of tourists coming to see the wildflowers or head up into the higher elevations for a last blast of snow before it melted. Come the middle of May in a few weeks and they'd start to see more of the hikers, fishermen and rafters along the Salmon River.

Even with the crowd, they were quickly seated at a small table at a spot far from the bar, making it a little quieter so they could talk.

When Piper had phoned Emma earlier to invite her to dinner, she had filled in her friend on the report that Ava and Brady had provided. She had hoped that by doing so the three of them could avoid talk of the break-in during dinner and have a fun night.

The three of us, Piper thought, wondering why Shane had decided to include Emma. Granted, she was the owner of the DCA and the person Gonzo had recommended for Decoy's training. But she had been the one primarily doing the training, although Emma had dropped by on occasion to see what was up and offer advice behind the scenes.

OMG, am I jealous of Emma? she thought with a start.

No way, she thought as the waitress came over to hand them menus. It was just that she had thought that if Shane was asking her out…

Whoa, not a date, the little voice reminded.

Not a date because Emma was here and maybe that was exactly what Shane had wanted after that kiss the other night. A kiss that had rocked her and made her wish for things that weren't possible. It had upset her, but the training and the dogs had helped restore some calm to her battered emotions. But she couldn't ignore that it would be way too dangerous for the two of them to go to dinner alone, maybe have a beer and then go home to sleep in the same house.

Maybe in the same bed, she thought and felt the heat of color bloom across her cheeks.

"Piper? Did you hear us?" Emma asked, hooking a finger at the top of Piper's menu to lower it slightly.

"No, sorry," she said, and the heat ignited into a blaze, making her want to cover her cheeks with her hands but that would only be way more embarrassing.

Emma scrutinized her carefully. "You feeling okay?"

Her gaze jumped to Shane's for a split second, and it was impossible to miss the humor there. He covered his mirth by coughing into his hand and after a hot second, he said, "I guess we got too much sun out on the trail."

Emma looked from him to Piper. "Sure. Sun. We asked if you wanted to share a blooming onion."

Onion. Totally unromantic. Perfect. "That would be great."

"Great. I love onion," Shane said, and one dark eyebrow shot up in challenge.

Ignore him, she told herself, and luckily, the rest of the night passed without incident.

Burgers were eaten. Beer was consumed, although not too much since both Shane and Emma were driving. As they were exiting, they ran into Tashya and Jason, who were arriving for a date, and Brady and his best friend, Officer Dillon Diaz.

After hugs and goodbyes, Emma peeled off at the curb to go to her car and she and Shane walked to his pickup. As she was hopping up into the cab, a blue pickup slowly drove by, making the hairs on her neck rise. She tried to get a look at the driver, but the windows were tinted, and he had a baseball cap pulled down low.

She inched up, trying to see the license plate, but he was already too far away.

"Something wrong?" Shane asked when she finally sat in the passenger seat.

"A blue pickup went by, and it freaked me out a little," she confessed.

"Where did it go?" he asked and quickly started the engine.

She pointed down the street. "That way."

But as he pulled out, she could see that the pickup had already turned off West Second and was no longer visible. "It's gone," she said, dejected.

Shane did a quick look in her direction. "Did you get a license plate number?"

She shook her head. "No. He was too far away, and it was too dark."

Shane reached out and stroked her arm. "Don't worry. We will catch him."

She wished she could be as sure. The happiness she'd been feeling after their carefree dinner had been dimmed by the appearance of the blue pickup.

The ride home was quiet, the cab filled with the sound of the tires on the road and, as they stopped, the rustle of the wind through branches, as well as a mockingbird that seemed to have made her yard home.

She hopped out of the pickup and Shane was immediately there, his big hand at the small of her back. The touch was possessive. Intimate. Reminding her of where they had almost gone the other night. But she had to push those thoughts aside.

As she went to unlock the door, Shane reached around and laid a hand on hers. "Let me."

He took the key from her hand and stepped past her to open the door and disarm the alarm. "Please wait here," he said and walked into the house to take a quick look around, which she could have easily done in her small two-bedroom ranch.

"All clear," he said and came back into the living room, Chipper and Decoy chasing after him. "I guess we should take these two for a quick walk."

"Sounds good," she said and took Chipper's leash as Shane handed it to her.

They armed the alarm and locked up for the short walk, which seemed like overkill, but as Ava and Brady had warned, they had to stay alert.

The night was quiet with a slight nippiness. The mockingbird was trilling his trio of repetitive notes, making her ask, "Do you think he ever gets tired of repeating the same thing?"

SHANE LAUGHED. "Sometimes the same thing is a good thing," he said, thinking of all the times he would have wished for that while on patrol in Afghanistan. Just a moment of quiet. Of peace, like the peace he felt here, with her and the dogs, which was like a slice of heaven.

"I know what you mean. When Emma first asked me to come here, I worried I'd be bored, but there's something about the routine and nights like this... It's wonderful." She stopped as Chipper went to relieve herself by the side of the road.

Decoy joined her a second later and Shane quickly scooped the dogs' messes.

"Thanks. I always wonder if aliens came to earth and saw us scooping, they'd think the dogs were our masters," she said with a laugh.

Shane chuckled and did a little shake of his head. "Until they watched a cat and realized who was truly in charge."

Piper laughed even harder and louder. "OMG, so true. My mom had a cat that totally ruled our house."

He loved the sound of her laugh. The way her eyes crinkled at the edges and darkened to a jewel-like green. Her full lips, a lovely rose color against the creaminess of her skin.

She was so beautiful. So strong and smart and he thought he might love her, which brought him to a grinding halt by the side of the road.

She stopped as well, stumped by his action. A furrow marred the smooth skin of her brow as she peered at him. "Something wrong?"

Everything, he wanted to say, because things had gotten way too complicated. "No. Just enjoying the night," he lied and started walking again, Decoy beside him, sniffing along the edges of the road.

Piper fell into step beside him, Chipper slipping in between them to be closer to Decoy. It created space between them, which was welcome considering where his thoughts had been going.

At the door they repeated their earlier routine: disarming the alarm, checking the house, locking up and resetting the alarm. Security being paramount until they caught Parker and confirmed that he had been the one who had trashed Piper's home and stolen her wedding rings.

Side by side, they walked through the living room to the hallway leading to the bedrooms. Piper took the lead down the hall, pausing by the door to her room, where she faced him.

"Good night, Shane," she said, but her tone was hesitant. Bordering on inviting, but it brought back memories of the other night and his hesitation at taking this relationship further. But he didn't want to keep on denying that he wished there could be more with her.

He took an uncertain step closer and when she didn't back away, he bent and kissed her. Not like their fleeting first kiss or the more heated one from the other night. This was a kiss of invitation and promise. Tender at first, but growing deeper as they stood there, kissing over and over until he finally closed the distance and laid a hand at her waist to urge her closer.

Her breasts were soft against his chest. Her hips mobile when she shifted them against his erection, but as much as he wanted to take this to the next level, he couldn't until he was sure of himself and what he could offer her.

Because of that, he tempered his kiss and stepped away the tiniest bit, but it was enough.

The kiss ended as tentatively as it began, with a lingering brush of their lips and a sigh that was loud in the quiet of the night.

He moved back another step, enough to see her face. The slight flush on her cheeks. Her eyes, slightly dazed and dark. Her lips, still moist from their kiss.

"Sweet dreams, Piper," he said and didn't wait for her

reply, thinking it best to go to his own room before he made a big mistake.

Her "good night" chased him down the hall as did the sound of her door closing.

But as he had the night before, he left his open. He changed quickly and slipped beneath the sheets, Decoy at the side of the bed. Pillowing his hands beneath his head, he stared at the ceiling and mentally reviewed all the information that Walt had provided as well as that from the two police officers. Josh Parker seemed like a piece of work, and it worried him to think that someone like that might be after Piper and whatever Parker thought might be in her possession.

Relics, he thought and tried to imagine what they might be and where they could be hiding.

He'd heard his share about things like that when he'd done a short stint in Iraq. Between the American military activity and the advent of ISIS, quite a number of Iraqi museums had suffered damage and looting. But how could someone manage to slip anything like that past Customs or the other authorities? And why did Parker think that Piper had it? Was it because the relics were gone when he and Devare had gone back for them, making them think that Lambert had somehow taken them before he was killed?

Only whoever Walt had spoken to was sure Lambert wasn't involved, which left Parker and Devare as the likely suspects, even if the military investigators hadn't been able to prove it.

Piper and he had looked through everything. Whatever these relics were, Piper didn't have them.

But that didn't matter to Parker, and because of that, they'd have to continue to be careful.

Chapter Nineteen

Piper raised her face to the morning sun, enjoying the warmth of it on her face.

There was less of a chill in the mid-April air, but snow still frosted the highest elevations on the mountain. But today's warmth was a sign that in another couple of weeks, that snow would melt and send water cascading down into the Salmon River, bringing waves of rafters to enjoy the rushing waters.

"Penny for your thoughts," Shane said from beside her. They were walking the dogs before packing them up for the ride to that morning's training at the DCA.

She pointed to the mountains. "Snow will be gone soon." *And so will you*, she thought. It was his last week of training before he went off to work with the search and rescue group in Montana.

With a side-eyed glance, he said, "Sun feels great. Might be nice to go for a hike today."

She stopped and eyeballed him. "Are you suggesting we play hooky today?"

He held his hands up as if in pleading. "We've been working hard for weeks. Things have been quiet for a few days. Why not take a little time off? We could do a quick training session, get a picnic lunch and then take a hike. Maybe even dinner."

They had been working hard and things had been quiet.
It had been nearly a week since anything had happened
around her house and things between her and Shane…
Things had been good. Companionable, not that companionable was what either of them wanted.

There could be no denying the tension between them.
The desire that they'd kept banked night after night as he'd
kiss her good-night and then head to the spare bedroom.

Maybe a long hike in the woods was just what they
needed to dispel that tension and desire.

"Sure, why not?"

JOSH HAD KEPT his distance for a week, hoping things with
the cops would die down if nothing else happened. Certain that the police were looking for him, he'd trimmed
his hair to a high-and-tight buzz cut and dyed it blond to
look different from his driver's license photo.

He'd also left the blue pickup he'd stolen in McCall,
a town about an hour south of Jasper, exchanging it for
a white Jeep that might handle better in the slushy snow
surrounding the mountain cabin where he'd been hiding
out. The cabin had been in rough shape, clearly unused for
some time, but it hadn't taken much to make it habitable
and a place where he could hold Lambert's widow until
she told him where she'd hidden the relics.

Now it was time to start watching again. To wait for
the perfect time to grab Piper and get what he was owed.

Lambert had screwed everything up for him big-time.
He'd planned on selling the treasures to finally have the
kind of life most people only dreamed of.

But then Lambert had been killed, the relics had gone
missing, and the Marines had come down hard on them for
being AWOL. And unlike Buck, his life had done nothing
but go downhill once he'd gotten home.

No one in the military-oriented town had wanted to hire someone with a dishonorable discharge. A fight over some comments about that discharge had landed him in jail. That had made it even harder to get employed and he'd resorted to stealing to put food on the table and a roof over his head. He just hadn't planned on the roof over his head to be in prison.

He wasn't going to let that happen again.

That's why he was hanging back, waiting for the right moment.

As he looked through the binoculars, he watched them hiking the trail along the river's edge, looking way too happy and lovey-dovey. Especially since the big guy had basically moved into her house.

Made life way harder for him, but he'd find a way to grab her.

I just have to be patient, he told himself and continued watching them.

PIPER TRUDGED ALONG the trail, Shane right behind her. As she walked, she pointed out things along the path. "See that stand of aspens over there?" she said, and Shane followed the line of her arm to gaze at the large stand of trees halfway up a nearby hillside. "They call that stand a 'clone' because the aspens grow by sprouting from their roots so they all have the same DNA. In the fall they'll be an amazing gold color against the evergreens."

The trees were a bright spring green now, still obvious among the darker shades of the evergreens. As he watched, a bald eagle flew off from the branches and swooped down toward the river along the trail they were hiking.

"Beautiful sight," he said, but as he followed the path of the eagle, his gaze skipped to Piper and he thought, *Even more beautiful.*

"I hope to see that gold," he said, but then wished he had bit his tongue because he wouldn't be in Jasper in the fall.

She slowly tilted her head up to meet his gaze. "I hope you do, too."

But then she was quickly plowing ahead along the trail, until she held her hand up to stop them. He was about to say something, only she held an index finger to her lips to quiet him. "Shh. Mule deer."

Far ahead of them, a mule deer was slaking its thirst along the river's edge. Its black-tipped tail and large ears, similar to a mule's, were different from the white-tailed deer he'd seen growing up in Pennsylvania and around the training center in California.

The deer must have sensed them. It raised its head to stare in their direction and then bolted toward the hillside.

"They stay down in the valley during the winter but will head up to the higher elevations during the summer," Piper explained.

"Is there much hunting in this area?" he asked, tracking the deer as long as he could until he lost sight of it in a thick stand of trees.

Sadness filtered into her gaze, animal lover that she was. "The mule deer population is down in this area, so Fish and Game issued fewer permits in the hopes of building their numbers."

"Sounds like they're trying to protect them," Shane said, and Piper nodded and offered up a reluctant smile.

"They are. Idaho Fish and Game also operate nearly two dozen hatcheries to raise all kinds of fish in order to stock our rivers and lakes, including sockeye salmon, which are endangered. Luckily they've had some success with steelhead and other kinds of salmon."

"When I was growing up, we had a small pond near our house. Town used to stock it with trout and my dad and

I would go fishing," Shane said, smiling as memories of those idyllic times streamed back.

"Looks like they were good memories. We could try some salmon fishing later this week if you want. Catch and release, though," Piper said and started moving along the trail again.

"I'd like that." They hadn't gone more than half a mile when they caught sight of someone fly-fishing along the edges of the river. He waved as he saw them, and they waved back and kept on walking until they hit a section of the river that was shallow enough to traverse.

They crossed over and his storm boots kept his feet dry, but there was no denying the cold of the water streaming down the river. The rocks were slippery and as Piper wavered a little, he reached out to keep her steady. A glint of something high up on the hillside caught his eye, like sun bouncing off glass or metal.

Like someone watching, maybe? he thought and hurried Piper across the stream and into the protection of the trees and underbrush on the opposite edge of the riverbank.

The earlier happiness he'd been feeling vanished, replaced by watchfulness as they did the walk back to his pickup.

"You okay?" she asked as they neared his vehicle, obviously sensing the change in his mood.

Not wanting to worry her, he said, "Just a little tired. It's been a long time since I've done a hike this long."

She eyed him up and down and did a little shake of her head. "Not like you're out of shape."

He faked it, reaching up to rub his injured shoulder. "Acts up at the weirdest times."

Her wrinkled brow said that she wasn't quite buying it, but he wasn't going to push it because he'd never been a good liar. Actually, he'd never been any kind of liar.

"Time to go home, then," she said and got into the pickup after he unlocked the doors.

"Maybe we can stop in Jasper for an early dinner?" he said as he pulled out and drove along the road in the direction of town, heading west before then heading north toward Piper's house and the DCA.

"You're still hungry after that lunch we ate?" Piper said with a laugh.

The roast beef sandwiches, salads and cookies that Millard's had packed for their picnic had been satisfying, but if someone was watching them, a stop in a more populated area like Jasper might make for a safe haven until he could confirm if they were being followed.

"Fresh air always makes me hungry," he said and looked in the rearview mirror to see if anyone was behind them. Two cars way in the distance, but no blue pickup.

It had probably been nothing on the hillside.

They had barely gone another few miles and were still a goodly distance from Jasper when he spied a woman and dog lying on the side of the road. She started waving her hand in the air as they neared, and Shane had no choice but to pull over and see what was happening.

PIPER HOPPED DOWN from Shane's pickup and raced over to the woman and dog.

The woman's right leg was at an awkward angle and the dog was bleeding and breathing heavily.

Piper kneeled beside the dog and laid a hand on its side, trying to gauge the extent of its injuries. The dog's muscles trembled beneath her hand as the woman said, "We were hiking back to our car when someone sideswiped us. My dog took the brunt of the hit."

Shane had squatted beside the woman to check out her

leg. "It looks broken. We can try to get you in the bed of the pickup."

The woman shook her head. "My hip, too. Something's wrong there, but I can't feel anything. My leg…hip, everything feels numb."

Piper exchanged a worried look with Shane. "We'll call for help," she said, then whipped out her phone to dial 911 and gave them the information on their location and situation.

"My dog. His name is Longmire. He's hurt bad. You've got to get him help," the woman said and tried to reach for him, but screamed as she moved, the numbness possibly starting to wear off.

"Lie down and relax. We'll take care of Longmire for you," Shane said and urged the woman to lie down. He took off his jacket and placed it over the woman to keep her warm.

With a tilt of his head, he urged Piper away from the pair.

In a low whisper that only he could hear, she said, "The dog needs immediate care or he might not make it."

"We can't leave her alone," Shane said and shot a quick glance at the woman.

Piper tilted her head in the direction of his pickup. "You can load him into the bed, and I'll take him to Marie's."

He shook his head. "It's not safe for you to go alone. Let me take him."

"It's not more than ten miles and you don't know the way to the vet," she said, but he shook his head again and she narrowed her eyes to scrutinize him. "Is there something you're not telling me?"

Chapter Twenty

Shane peered up and down the road and Piper did the same, but there was no one in the vicinity.

"No, there's nothing wrong, just… Keep an eye out. We haven't found Parker yet," he said.

"I will keep an eye out, I promise," she said and held her hand out for his keys.

He handed them to her. "I'll go get the dog. There's a blanket in the back seat you can lay out to make him more comfortable."

She opened the door, reached in and got the blanket, which she spread in the bed of the pickup. Shane walked over with the dog, who was whining with pain. She ran a hand over his side, trying to calm him. "Easy, boy. You're going to be okay."

"Call me as soon as you get there," he said and brushed a kiss across her cheek.

She nodded. "I will."

Shane hurried back to the woman to take care of her, and Piper rushed to the pickup and took off down the road.

She hadn't gone more than a mile or so when she spotted the ambulance on the way to where Shane waited with the woman.

Barely half a dozen miles later, she caught sight in

the rearview mirror of a white Jeep barreling toward her quickly. Too quickly.

Slowing, she pulled over slightly to let them pass since they were in such a rush. The wheel jerked in her hand a little as the tires hit the softer dirt along the edge of the road.

The Jeep rushed past her, but when she pulled back onto the road, the Jeep suddenly veered in front of her, blocking the way across the street.

She jerked to a rough stop, hands gripping the steering wheel tightly as the driver of the vehicle got out.

He had on a baseball cap and sunglasses hid his eyes, but she didn't need to see them to know something wasn't right about him.

She put the car in Reverse, intending to get away, when his hand whipped up and he trained a gun in her direction.

"I wouldn't do that, Piper. I'm an excellent shot."

SHANE STOOD BY impatiently as the EMTs worked on the woman, stabilizing her for transport to Jasper Memorial, which luckily wasn't all that far from town. Nearly fifteen minutes had gone by since Piper had driven off, and an uneasy feeling filled his gut.

She should be in Jasper by now, he thought. Maybe she was helping the vet with the dog. Maybe Marie wasn't there, and Piper was waiting for her. *Maybe, maybe, maybe*, he thought, wanting to get to Jasper and Piper, only he didn't have a ride.

Ava and Brady pulled up in their cruiser minutes later and there was still no call from Piper.

"Shane," Ava said and both she and Brady dipped their heads in greeting.

"Ava. Brady," he said and glanced back toward the

EMTs as they finally loaded the woman onto the gurney and walked with her toward the ambulance.

"Where's Piper? We thought she was with you when she called in the accident," Ava said and looked all around.

"Lady had a dog that was badly hurt. Piper took the pickup to take him to Marie in town."

"What can you tell us about what happened here?" Brady asked.

One of the EMTs called out, "We're taking her in, Lieutenant Nichols. You can meet us at Jasper Memorial."

"We'll meet you there shortly," Ava responded.

"Shane?" Brady asked again.

"Piper and I were driving back to Jasper when we saw the woman and the dog on the side of the road. We stopped and she told us that a car had sideswiped them. We called it in to get her help. Piper took the dog, and she hasn't called me yet from the vet's," Shane said.

Brady did a quick look at his watch. "She should have been to Marie's by now."

"Can we get going?" Shane asked and pointed to the cruiser.

"Sure," Ava said, and they rushed to the police car and hurried off, Shane in the back seat, nervously bouncing his legs while Ava drove.

"How long ago did she leave?" Brady asked.

"Too long. At least twenty minutes. Maybe more," he said and then something hit him. "Didn't you pass her on your way here?"

Ava shook her head and met his gaze in the rearview mirror. "We were just coming back from McCall. We got a call that they'd found the blue pickup—"

"The one Parker was driving?" Shane pressed.

"The one we believe Parker was driving. We went to

check it out and see what other information we could get," Brady said.

Which meant Parker was driving some other kind of vehicle. Maybe even one of the ones he'd seen behind them after they'd left the trail near the Salmon River.

He mumbled a curse, but then the two officers did as well, making him lean forward to see what was going on.

His pickup. Sitting by the side of the road.

They pulled up next to it.

No sign of Piper and the dog was still in the bed of the pickup.

They hopped out of the cruiser and hurried to the front of his car.

There were signs of a skid mark across the road, as if a car had suddenly stopped in the path of the pickup.

As Shane examined the black marks, he noticed that there were some tire tracks along the softer dirt at the edge of the road. He gestured to them. "Another car. Across the road."

Ava and Brady walked over to the tire tracks to take a look and he joined them. "We saw tire tracks near Piper's house, but something's a little different."

Brady kneeled down for a closer inspection. "Pickup and Jeep might both use the same tires, but the wheelbases are different. This isn't a pickup. The wheelbase isn't wide enough. Probably a Jeep. Narrower, but we'll know once we measure and cast the tire impressions."

"But first we need to put a BOLO out for Piper and get some backup to take that dog to the vet," Ava said, then grabbed her radio and called it in.

Shane cursed, loudly and more vehemently as he raked his hand through his hair and paced away from where the two officers were reviewing the scene.

The crime scene.

Parker had grabbed Piper and he wasn't about to just sit there and do nothing.

"We need to get going," he said and moved toward his pickup, but Ava held up a hand to stop him.

"We need to process the scene and do this logically," she said, and while he knew she was right, it didn't make the delay any easier to bear.

"Okay. We do this your way," he said even though he was itching to get moving.

PARKER HAD KNOCKED HER out with the gun butt when she'd stepped out of Shane's car.

Or at least she assumed it was Parker, even though he looked different from the driver's license photo the police had shown them.

She woke up with a gag stuffed in her mouth and secured in place with a bandanna. Her wrists were duct-taped behind her back, which made it impossible for her to do anything like reach for the door handle in order to escape.

But her legs were free.

She carefully watched the scenery going by, looking for landmarks that might help her make her way back toward Jasper if she got free.

Not if, when, she told herself.

And when she did, she'd have to make her way down the mountain. That much she knew: he was taking her up into the mountains.

It was the growing chill of the air that had roused her into consciousness. The jacket she had worn for the hike was too lightweight for the higher elevations, especially since there was snow on the ground where he was taking them.

Probably one of the many vacation cabins that sometimes sat vacant for weeks, even months depending on the owner's tastes for either skiing, hiking or rafting.

Judging from the silhouette of the mountain crests, he'd kept on going north, but had probably detoured around Jasper to hide from the authorities. That meant he'd also passed by the general vicinity of her home and the DCA.

Hope blossomed that, if she could escape, she could reach either her home or the canine academy.

But as the Jeep slipped on a slushy patch on the road, it warned her that escape on foot could be treacherous. The snow would make footing precarious, and she wasn't properly dressed for any time in the cold.

Another half hour passed, and her arms and shoulders complained from their awkward position pinned behind her.

She was relieved when Parker finally pulled up in front of a log cabin. Not one of the nice vacation places. A ramshackle cabin whose roof looked ready to cave in on one side. The glass in several windows was broken, but someone had done temporary repairs by taping plastic over the holes. A small pile of firewood was haphazardly placed by the front door, but it wouldn't be enough to last the night.

Parker killed the engine and climbed out of the Jeep.

He yanked her door open and roughly jerked her from the seat. She stumbled and fell. He lost his grip on her and she figured this was as good a chance as any to escape.

Before he could grab her again, she crab-walked away from him and somehow managed to get to her feet. But she had only taken a step or two when Parker tackled her to the ground, the weight of his body driving her breath from her.

Darkness danced around the edges of her periphery from the lack of air. Pain seared the muscles of her arms as Parker hauled her to her feet.

"Not smart, Piper. Not smart," he said and half dragged,

half carried her into the cabin, where he sat her in a chair that creaked and groaned, as if ready to break. When she tried to rise, he pulled out the pistol and said, "Don't. I will shoot you."

She peered at the gun and then at Parker. Her heart galloped in her chest and a cold sweat erupted across her body, chilling her thanks to the lack of heat in the cabin. Nodding, she quieted in the chair and sat patiently while Parker duct-taped her feet to the chair legs. Then he wrapped the tape around her body and the chair, dimming any hope she had of getting free and making an escape.

When he was done, he pulled off the bandanna and took the gag from her mouth, but warned, "Scream and I'll shoot you."

Feigning a bravado she didn't really feel, she said, "If you do, you won't find out what I know about the relics."

A hint of surprise registered on his features before he squinted to examine her features. "Your husband told you about the relics before he died?"

"No. My friend—"

"The big guy. Military I assume?" he said and started pacing in front of her, the gun held, muzzle down, at his side.

Piper didn't see the point in denying it. "Ex-Army. He asked some friends who told him about the relics and your dishonorable discharge for being AWOL."

"That discharge was all a lie. Should have only been some time in the brig and loss of pay. We weren't deserters. We were only gone for a few days."

"Because you were stealing the relics," she challenged.

He whirled to face her, his agitation impossible to miss. His face was a mottled red and he tapped the gun against his thigh repeatedly. "Because your husband had already taken them, and we were trying to figure out where since he was dead."

"David didn't take them. He would never do anything like that," she shot back.

"Saint David. That's what the rest of the squad called him behind his back. Mr. Goody Two-shoes, but when we found the relics, you should have seen his eyes light up. He knew how much they were worth on the black market."

"He didn't take them," she repeated, having no doubt about her husband's character. She was sad that his men had somehow thought of him disparagingly because he had always spoken highly about the squad under his command.

"Really? You seem to have landed on your feet. Nice house even if it is out here in the boondocks. Where did you get the money, Piper?" He leaned forward and got in her face. "Did you sell the relics?"

She tilted her chin up defiantly and met his gaze, hers never wavering. "Life insurance. David took care of me just like he took care of his men, you included."

Parker blew out a rough laugh and backed away from her. "If he cared he would have let us grab the relics when we found them. But no, he had to report the find and then he stole them." He whirled on her again, the nervous tapping of the gun against his leg heightening her own nervousness since it warned Parker was on the edge.

"He stole them, and you have them," he repeated, a hint of crazy in his voice.

"I don't," she said calmly, hoping to defuse the situation. "You've got the wrong person, Josh. Maybe you should be checking with your buddy Devare. He's the one who seems to have landed on his feet."

"Buck wouldn't do that. Besides, he was looking with me. He got dishonorably discharged just like me," Josh said, leaning in until they were nose to nose and tapping his chest with his free hand. Spittle flew from his lips, some of it landing on her cheek.

"But he ended up with a nice job, a wife and a child, while you ended up in jail and basically homeless. Doesn't sound like much of a friend to me," she said and for a moment, she thought she detected a momentary flicker of doubt. But then he shook his head, as if shaking away the doubt, and stepped away. He went to one corner of the cabin and hauled another rickety chair to the middle of the room, directly opposite her.

He sat down, the hand with the pistol resting on his thigh. "Buck's the best. He wouldn't betray me, but your Saint David... Where are the relics?"

Piper shook her head. "I don't have them. I never had them because David didn't take them," she repeated, her voice steady and unruffled.

Josh looked away and did a quick tilt of his head. "Going to be a long night. Even longer days because you're not leaving until I get the relics."

While the thought of being held for days was scary and painful, since she was slowly losing feeling in her hands from how he'd bound them, she took hope in the fact that he had mentioned her leaving this hovel. Alive. But she also hoped that Shane and the police would find her long before that.

She had expected that Josh would keep on pushing her for answers, but instead he just sat there, watching her. Watching the afternoon sun dim and the shadows of dusk fill the room. She wondered if he was playing some kind of mind game with her but told herself to remain calm.

As it started to get even darker, he rose and brought in the small pile of wood he'd had by the door and placed a few of the logs in a fireplace that still held the remnants of another fire.

"Can't start a fire until it's dark. Don't want them to see the smoke and know where we are," he explained and rubbed his hand against the cold in the room.

After some cursing and muttering, the first tiny lick of flame was visible and soon he had a small fire going. Very small because it only illuminated a tiny circle of brick in front of the fireplace.

The scrape of metal against the brick drew her attention. He was placing a cooking rack over the flames, obviously intending to prepare a meal. She had no illusions he would share it with her, not that she was hungry. Her stomach was tied up in knots worrying about how long he'd keep her here and what he would do to her if she didn't tell him something about the relics he thought she had.

Despite his earlier words and his actions since taking her, things could change in a heartbeat and not in a good way.

But if she knew one thing about Shane, it was that he would never give up until he found her. He was the kind of man you could depend on. Who would be there for you and who she wanted to be there for her. She intended to tell him that when she could.

Chapter Twenty-One

Shane paced back and forth across the narrow width of the meeting room where members of the Jasper PD force had gathered together along with Emma to review the evidence they'd amassed and to formulate a plan for finding Piper.

Lieutenants Avery and Nichols, who had already been involved in the case. Officer Callan and rookie Officer Jason Wright. Lieutenant Hoover, the senior-most officer besides Captain Rutledge and the chief, was also present. Hoover was a handsome African American with a muscular build and a sharp brown gaze that seemed to take everything in although he remained silent as his officers provided their reports.

Emma sat beside Hoover, her hands laced together tightly, her fingers white from the pressure. Hoover laid his big hand over Emma's, offering reassurance as he said, "We will find her."

"It's been hours," Emma said, fear making her voice quake.

"Too long," Shane chimed in, earning a hard glance and rebuke from Brady.

"You more than most know how important it is to not go off half-cocked, Shane. There's a lot of territory to cover and we need to do it sensibly," the officer said.

He bit back a challenge, aware that Brady was right.

Injecting calm into his voice, he sat and said, "What is the plan?"

Margaret rose and went to a whiteboard at one end of the room. "We know from the tire tracks left behind that Parker's changed vehicles. The wheelbase was too narrow for a pickup. Based on the wheelbase and tires, we identified it as possibly being a Jeep."

She wrote that down on the whiteboard and Ava chimed in with, "McCall PD confirmed that a red Jeep was taken not far from the location where Parker dumped the blue pickup he stole in Boise."

Margaret added that info along with the license plate number for the stolen red Jeep. She pointed to it and said, "We have a BOLO out for that vehicle."

Lieutenant Hoover stepped into the discussion. "I think we can eliminate that Parker headed back to McCall with Piper. McCall is a nice size, but it would be hard for him to hide now that McCall PD will be looking for that Jeep. He also wouldn't head into Jasper for the same reason."

"Agreed," Margaret said, and all the officers seated around the table were nodding when another officer poked his head into the room.

"Looks like you called in the cavalry, Hoover," the man said and stepped into the room, hands on his hips. The nameplate on his black shirt said "Rutledge."

Shane recognized the name from some of Emma and Piper's earlier discussions about the man and his disdain for the K-9 programs they ran. He was a handsome man with light brown hair and a blue-eyed gaze that flitted, almost disparagingly, over the people gathered in the room.

"Piper is missing, Arthur," Hoover said calmly. "She's a citizen of Jasper, but more importantly, a friend."

When the man did a dismissive shrug, it was all Shane could do not to jump out of his chair and show the man just how important. But before he could, Rutledge said, "Just remember our resources need to be used for all citizens, Hoover," and stepped from the room.

Ava laid a hand on his shoulder and applied gentle pressure there. "Ignore him, Shane," she said in a whisper only he could hear.

He shot her a look from the corner of his eye and didn't fail to see the compassion and determination there.

With a nod, he sat back and listened to the rest of the report and the plan to review various CCTV feeds from Jasper, just in case he had come through town, as well as some from the few cameras along the route in order to pinpoint where Parker might have gone with Piper.

"Chances are he went up into the mountains, so we'll have to round up some four-wheelers and get the chains on one of our police cruisers," Hoover instructed.

Brow furrowed, he glanced at Brady, who explained. "There's still snow at the higher elevations and with the thaw started, it'll be slush, but also icy in spots. You'll need to buy some chains for your pickup at the hardware store if you're coming with us."

"I'm coming with you."

PIPER WOKE TO the crack of splintering wood and a stream of foul language.

She slowly opened her eyes, her gaze unfocused as she searched the dim light in the cabin. Based on the shadows, she guessed that the sun was only just rising over the mountains. It had been pitch-dark the last time Josh had woken her to threaten harm if she didn't tell him where the relics were. He had done it several times during the course of the night, probably thinking the lack of sleep would loosen her tongue, not that she had anything to tell him.

The room was cold. So cold that her body was trembling in an effort to warm up.

The fire must have gone out during the night. No surprise since Josh had had little wood to feed it and keep it stoked.

Pieces of the chair in which he'd sat the night before lay before the hearth as Josh tried to get the fire going again. The bandanna he'd used to hold the gag in place was wrapped around his one hand and she assumed he'd injured himself.

He grabbed a few pieces of the chair and tossed them into the fireplace, but nothing happened.

"Match might help," she said. Her throat was dry, and her teeth chattered slightly as her body fought the cold.

"Shut up," he shouted over and over and advanced on her, fists clenched at his sides. It was cold enough for her to see his breath once he was nearly nose to nose with her.

She backed away as much as she could but winced at the pressure it put on her bound arms and hands that had been numb for hours. Her feet were numb now, too, from the cold, as was the tip of her nose.

"I'm cold," she said, but he only laughed, pulled away and wrapped the bandanna around his hand more tightly.

"Hurt yourself?" she asked, surprising herself with the real concern in her tone.

His brow furrowed as he peered at her and, sensing her sincerity, he said, "Ax broke when I tried to chop some more firewood. Handle splintered and cut me."

"You should see a doctor."

"I won't leave here until I get the answers I want from you," he said, but rubbed his hands against his arms, trying to get warm. Walking back and forth before her as she said again, "I'm cold."

"Tough. No matches, no fire," he said, dragging a harsh laugh from her.

"Not much of a Marine," she challenged, not caring if she angered him. Maybe if he got angry enough he'd do something stupid that might give her a chance to get free.

"Shut up," he shouted, then drew his palm across his short-cropped hair and grimaced since he'd used his injured hand.

"You should put a proper bandage on that. But of course, you don't have one, do you? Or an ax. Or matches or food from what I can see."

That pushed him to that edge, just like she hoped. He backhanded her across the face, rattling her teeth and sending the chair toppling backward. It landed with enough force to make her scream with agony at the weight it placed on her bound arms. Black circles danced around her gaze from the pain.

She screamed again and moaned as he grabbed the chair and set it upright. His features were tight, his face red with rage, lips drawn into a sneer.

"You better mind your mouth if you want to see tomorrow."

She waited for him to strike her once again, but instead he grabbed something from his back pocket. The rag he'd used as a gag the day before.

She dreaded the thought of it and he didn't miss seeing her fear.

"We can do this the easy way or the hard way. It's up to you."

SHANE HAD AGREED to meet Lieutenants Avery and Hoover at police headquarters once he'd gotten the chains for his pickup.

But he hadn't agreed to just sit around and do nothing

after he'd left the meeting so the officers could do whatever other investigation was necessary before they headed up into the mountains.

Since their general consensus was that Parker had headed north in the general direction of the DCA, he'd packed up Decoy and gone back to where his pickup had been abandoned in the hopes that Decoy could locate some kind of scent. Unfortunately, although Decoy had sniffed around, he hadn't barked or done anything to alert him to a scent he recognized.

Although it had been dark, he'd driven around the areas near the DCA and beyond, but the roads had been fairly empty at that time of night. It had been nearly midnight when he'd driven back to Piper's house. The house seemed way too empty without Piper.

Even the dogs seemed to sense something was wrong as he leashed them and took them for a long walk, his mind racing with all the possibilities of where Piper might be. What might be happening to her.

His sleep had been troubled by those images and not even the presence of Decoy and Chipper had helped to soothe him. He'd risen before dawn and walked the dogs. Crated Chipper since he'd be gone most of the day. The puppy would feel secure in the comfortable crate.

Then he prepared, arming himself with conviction and something else: his Sig Sauer P320-M18. He also had a shotgun, but he could be more precise with the handgun if he needed to use it. Or least he hoped he could be precise.

Shane held the gun up and aimed it at a spot on the far wall of Piper's living room. His arm trembled as he did so, both from nerves and the sudden twitch of his injured shoulder muscles. It made his aim unsteady, so much so that he worried if it was more dangerous for him to be armed than not.

He hadn't held a gun in the many months since he'd left the Army. He didn't even know why he'd kept the weapon since he wasn't sure he could fire it with any accuracy. But maybe in the back of his mind he'd hoped that one day he could.

Maybe that day had come because he'd use every ounce of skill he had to make his shot true if it became necessary to use the gun to save Piper.

He loaded two magazines with 9mm bullets, slid a magazine into the pistol and chambered the first round. He slipped the Sig Sauer into his holster, tucked the other magazine into his jacket pocket and was on his way out the door when he doubled back to Piper's bedroom to grab a dirty sweatshirt from her hamper.

It would have her scent on it and maybe Decoy would be able to track with that odor if Parker and she had gone on foot anywhere.

He quickly got Decoy into the pickup and rushed to the hardware store, intending to be ready to go with Jasper PD on their mountain search for Piper. There were already a few cars parked in front of the store and he hoped it wouldn't take long at the counter.

He got out of the car and took Decoy with him. Wrapping the leash around a bollard on the edge of the parking lot, he walked into the hardware store to look for the chains. He spotted them immediately at the end of a nearby counter and walked toward it.

A man hurried past him, struggling with two large bags. The man pushed through the door, but as he did so the side of one of the handles broke, making him drop the bag right by Decoy. A few items spilled out and he rushed to pick them up and stuff them back into the bag.

Meanwhile, Decoy sat up, stuck his nose out toward the man and started to bark, surprising the man, who rushed off. But Decoy kept on barking and glancing in the direction of the man, clearly agitated.

Shane rushed out of the store in time to see the man loading the bags into a white Jeep.

White, not red like the Jeep that had been reported stolen in McCall, he told himself, but something about the man and his actions was making his radar light up, especially since Decoy was still barking and straining at the leash.

In all his years in the military, he'd learned to trust that radar.

He untied the leash and got Decoy settled in the car, keeping an eye on the white Jeep all the time as it pulled out of the parking lot and turned onto the road. Hopping into his pickup, he quickly reversed and took off in the direction of the other vehicle, keeping a discreet distance. He couldn't fail to notice, however, that the four-wheeler was heading toward the mountains, right in the direction they had discussed the night before.

It was just too much coincidence, and if it was Parker he'd need backup, so he dialed Jasper PD.

Jenny the dispatcher answered and quickly patched him through to Brady. After he explained what had happened with Decoy, he said, "He's in a white Jeep, Brady. Not a red one."

Brady immediately answered. "I'll call McCall to confirm if a white Jeep was also reported stolen. Are you still following it?"

"I am. I can send you my location to track with my phone," Shane said.

"Do that. Ava and I will catch up to you," Brady said and hung up.

Shane fumbled with his phone to send Brady the text message with the tracking to his location. He had slowed while doing that, increasing the distance between him and the Jeep. So far nothing the driver had done indicated that he thought he was being followed. But as the car pulled off onto a side road and stopped, as if to see if he would follow, he drove past, hoping that the side road only led one way: to Piper.

He didn't know why, but he was sure now that the man in the Jeep was Parker. Especially as he recalled how the man had looked, with a baseball cap pulled low and jacket collar turned up, as if to hide his features.

Which meant he had to follow Parker up the mountain.

Executing a K-turn, he headed back quickly to the side road, slowing as he neared it. In the early morning light, the Jeep's taillights were visible along the side road, halfway up the mountain.

Shane shut off his lights, turned onto the side road and hurried after Parker.

PIPER HAD BEEN DOZING, trying to make up for the night of Josh's constant interruptions, when she heard a car pull up.

Josh. She didn't know how long she'd been asleep, but it didn't feel like long. She peered through the dirty glass and plastic on the windows. A white Jeep had pulled up, Josh at the wheel. The sun was still low on the horizon, hinting at the fact that he hadn't been gone long, maybe an hour or so.

That told her that wherever they were wasn't all that far from Jasper. If she could get free and make it down the mountain, she might be able to flag someone on the road to take her to town.

She shifted in the seat again as she had been doing all night, trying to restore feeling to her hands and feet with little luck. They were still numb.

Barely a minute later, Josh pushed through the door,

carrying two bags. He walked to a small table at one side of the room and took out supplies: an ax, matches, a first aid kit and a few cans of food.

He fumbled with the first aid kit, opening it and cursing as he wiped his cut with an alcohol pad. Then he wrapped gauze around his hand, pushed the kit aside and picked up the ax. Sunlight glinted off the shiny metal as he ran a finger across the edge, testing its sharpness.

With a nod, he walked toward her, and it was clear that he had no intention of using the ax to cut firewood.

WITHOUT THE CHAINS Shane hadn't been able to buy at the hardware store, he hadn't made it past the first half a mile or so of slushy snow at the higher elevations. The car had slipped and slid until he'd lost control and almost hit a tree by the side of the road. He'd also worried that the sound of the engine would carry up the mountain and alert Parker that he had been discovered.

He needed the element of surprise if he was going to overpower Parker and save Piper.

Tucking his cell phone into his pocket so Jasper PD could keep on tracking him, he opened the door for Decoy and slipped off his leash. He grabbed Piper's dirty sweatshirt and let Decoy smell it, hoping he'd pick up Piper's scent to help guide him in case the road ahead didn't lead straight to Parker.

Together, Decoy and he trudged up through the slush, snow and patches of ice where the snow had melted and refrozen overnight. It was slow going, his feet slipping beneath him regularly, but he pushed on, aware that time wasn't on his side.

Parker had taken Piper in the late afternoon and had her overnight. He'd want her to tell him where she had the relics her husband had supposedly sent her, but he was as sure as Piper that Lambert wasn't the one who had taken them. That left one person who might have them: Buck Devare.

Unfortunately, Parker's good friend Buck had probably convinced him that he didn't have the relics. Shane wasn't as convinced.

He had gone about a mile up the road when he spotted something white through a thicket of trees. Looking more closely, he realized the road took a big bend to the left and that it was the white Jeep Parker had been driving, parked in front of a cabin that was in pretty bad shape. Broken windows, taped over with plastic. Missing planks of wood on the front porch and a gaping hole in one corner of a roof that looked ready to collapse.

He rushed up the last part of the road, careful not to make too much sound. Signaling to Decoy to stay close and quiet.

Decoy glanced at him and seemed to nod in understanding.

Creeping up the last few feet, hunched over to hopefully avoid being seen through the windows, he managed to get on the front porch noiselessly. Crouching low, he peered through the window.

Piper was duct-taped to a chair and Parker was circling her, an ax in his hand and a gun in a holster on his hip.

"You've been trying my patience all night and I'm done waiting. Next time I get an 'I don't know,' it'll cost you a toe or two," he said, slapping the ax handle in his hand over and over.

Shane couldn't delay as hundreds of scenarios raced through his brain.

The ax slicing through the air, catching Piper on the shoulder. The neck. Her lifeblood seeping from her as he stood there, waiting for the right moment to attack.

He slipped his Sig Sauer from the holster, hand trembling as he did so, but from fear. More fear than he'd ever experienced on any mission when he'd been in the Army because this time the woman he loved was in danger.

He couldn't deny it any longer: he loved Piper.

Tightening his hand on the grip, he crept to the door, grabbed the handle and threw the door open.

It bounced against the wall with a noisy thud, snagging Parker's attention.

He raised the ax and Shane issued one command to Decoy. He hoped that this time the dog wouldn't hesitate.

"Attack."

Decoy leaped at Parker, latching onto his biceps and driving him away from Piper and onto the ground with the force of his leap.

Shane rushed forward, snatched the ax from Parker and threw it across the room as the other man fought to get Decoy off him, rolling from side to side, but Decoy hung on.

Shane pinned Parker's other arm to the ground with his knee, then took the gun from Parker's hip holster and tossed it aside, well out of Parker's reach.

"Stop," he commanded, and Decoy immediately released Parker's arm.

Parker swung his now-free hand up, trying to cuff Shane across the side of the head, but Shane blocked the blow with his left arm. He punched Parker with the hand that still held the gun, dazing him.

Rolling Parker onto his stomach, he placed a knee in the middle of his back and pointed his gun at Parker's head.

"Don't move, Parker."

"She's got the relics. Don't let her kid you about that," Parker said, his voice bordering on crazy.

"She doesn't have anything, Parker," he said and looked around for something he could use to bind Parker's arms, but just then, the crunch of tires on ice and snow and a car engine told him the cavalry had arrived.

Ava and Brady rushed through the door, guns drawn, but they quickly holstered them as they realized Shane had Parker under control.

Ava immediately went to Piper to cut away the duct tape, while Brady came over to handcuff Parker and haul him to his feet.

Shane rushed to Piper's side, knelt by her and cupped her cheek. There was an ugly bruise near her temple and an angry splotch of red on her cheek. "Are you okay?"

Piper nodded but grimaced with pain as she finally moved her unbound arms. At his questioning glance, she said, "He hit me with the gun butt but right now it's a lot of pins and needles. Sore. He bounced me around in the chair and I landed on my arms."

He stroked his hand along her forearm and down to twine his fingers with hers. "Let's get you to the hospital where they can check you out."

"I'm okay. I'd rather go home," she said as she rubbed her wrists.

Shane shook his head. "We're not going to take any chances. Hospital and then we can head home and get you into a hot bath. It'll help the aches."

She offered up a little smile and reluctantly nodded. "Hospital. Home. Together. That sounds like a great idea."

Chapter Twenty-Two

Piper lazed in the hot water of the bath that Shane had graciously drawn when they had first gotten home.

Home. It hadn't felt like home when she had first come here from California, but little by little the area, dogs and people had worked themselves into her heart. But somehow deep inside she had sensed something else was missing.

But not anymore.

She swiped some errant soap bubbles from her arms and noticed the bruises on her biceps and wrists from being banged around and tied up. She ran a hand across one particularly larger bruise and winced. It was tender to the touch.

The water in the bath slowly grew tepid, her fingers wrinkly, warning Piper that it was time to get out.

Easing from the tub, she toweled down and slipped on a robe, grimacing as soreness awoke in another spot high up on her shoulder.

It would take days for all the aches to fade away, but there was another pain that would linger far longer. The pain of Shane leaving.

Their lessons were as good as over. Both Shane and Decoy were ready to go to the search and rescue group in Montana to continue their training. And now that the danger from Josh Parker was over, there was nothing keeping Shane in Jasper any longer.

Her heart clenched at the thought, felt like it was breaking into hundreds of pieces, but she belted the robe tight around her, as if that would keep the pieces from falling out of her chest.

As she walked out of the bathroom and into her bedroom, the smells of coffee, bacon and eggs snared her attention.

Hurrying forward, she caught sight of Shane at the stove, cooking. He turned and smiled as he saw her.

"Feeling better?" he said and raised the pan to tip out scrambled eggs onto two plates sitting on the counter.

She nodded. "Much. Thank you for everything."

He picked up the plates and sauntered over to the dining table near the sliding doors. Set them down and waited for her to take a seat at the table, his hands clenching awkwardly on the top rung of a nearby chair. Waiting for her to sit, ever the gentleman, although she sensed his hesitation was about more than just manners.

She sat and he finally took a chair opposite hers, his movements tentative as he reached for one of the coffee cups on the table. He filled it from a carafe and handed it to her.

Her hands trembled as she took the cup, added cream and sugar, and stirred, over and over, the spoon rattling noisily against the cup until Shane reached over and gentled her with his touch.

"It's going to be okay," he said, almost as if this nightmare wasn't over.

Narrowing her gaze to gauge his answer, she said, "What aren't you telling me?"

His lips thinned into a tight line, and he drew his hand away. She felt immediately bereft.

"Parker is insisting your husband took the relics." He picked up his coffee cup and took a bracing sip, wincing at the heat of it.

"David was an honest man. He would never have stolen anything." She grabbed her cup and cradled it between her hands, hoping the heat of the mug would help chase away the sudden chill in her heart.

"My friend had told me that the Marines didn't believe David had taken anything. He had reported the relics, which makes no sense if he intended to steal them."

"But?" she said, hearing what he wasn't saying.

"Parker's actions have forced the authorities to reopen the investigations. Since we're sure there's nothing here, they're going to visit Buck Devare."

"Josh's partner. The other man who received the dishonorable discharge," she said and finally lifted her cup to take a sip.

"Yes. They're going there today," he said and motioned to her dish. "Eat up before it gets cold."

She did, forking up some of the eggs and a slice of the bacon. She hadn't really felt hungry at first, especially with the earlier discussion, but after the first few bites, hunger kicked in, and in no time she had finished all the eggs and bacon and a few slices of buttered toast.

"That was delicious," she said and rose to pick up the plates, but Shane laid a hand on hers to stop her.

"I'll clean up. You should try and get some rest. You had a rough night," he said and again she heard what he wasn't saying: it might turn out to be a rough day as well.

She rose slowly, more aches and pains announcing their presence. As he headed to the kitchen sink with the plates, she went back to her bedroom, feeling the weight of the night before dragging her down. Closing the door, she slipped off her robe and slid beneath the sheets. They were cool against her body, but warmth soon built in the cocoon around her and the comfort of it and lack of sleep from the night before pulled her into unconsciousness.

SHANE HEARD HER bedroom door closing and laid his wet hands on the edge of the counter. Drawing in a long breath, he fought the urge to go comfort her.

She'd been through hell the day before, but he worried that whatever the authorities discovered after their visit to Devare would plunge her into an even worse hell.

His cell phone rang, and he dried his hands and checked the caller ID. Emma. He swiped to answer.

"How's she doing?" Emma immediately asked.

"She's…tired. Banged up." He had seen the bruises and abrasions on her wrists as she'd held the coffee cup.

"How did she handle the news about the investigation?" Emma said, worry alive in her voice.

"Badly, I think. She defended her husband—"

"She loved him with all her heart, and he was a good guy, Shane. I met him several times and I can't imagine him ever doing something like that," Emma said, clearly as loyal to Lambert as Piper. Even though he hadn't known him, if two women like Piper and Emma spoke for him, he must have been a good man.

"I know, but we need to let the investigation play out," he said, urging a patience he wasn't feeling. He wanted the investigation to be over sooner rather than later so that Piper could get on with her life.

"I got a call yesterday from the search and rescue group in Montana. With everything going on, I didn't get a chance to tell you. They were asking for a recommendation from the DCA for you."

A recommendation from Emma would help him continue with his training, only…

"Thanks. I'd appreciate that," he said.

"Great," she said, but her tone was ambiguous as if she didn't really believe he intended to go through with it.

"I'll keep you posted on what's happening," he said and swiped to end the call.

SINCE THE INCIDENT with Parker a few days earlier, Piper and Shane distracted themselves by working with Decoy and Chipper on the agility course. Decoy had mastered the basic obstacles as well as the more complicated chutes and tunnels they'd added. Chipper had proved herself adept despite her shorter legs.

"Maybe I'll train her for the agility course competitions," Piper said with a laugh as Chipper sped over the A frame and into the tunnel.

"She's fast," Shane said and shook his head at the little dog's antics.

But as Chipper finished the course and raced right at Decoy to play with her best friend, Piper noticed the Jasper PD cruiser parking across from Emma's ranch house.

Emma must have noticed it as well since she came out of the DCA offices and walked to join Shane and her at the training ring fence.

Ava and Brady exited the cruiser and walked over, their body postures easygoing and smiles on their faces.

"I guess you have good news," Shane said and laid a hand at the small of her back, offering support even though she didn't think she'd need it.

"We do. The authorities visited Buck Devare. At first, he denied everything, but little by little they wore him down. He admitted that he had taken the relics after your husband had reported their discovery, but before he and Parker went back to get them," Ava reported, and relief filled Piper that her husband's memory would be clear of any stain on his character.

"How did he get them out of Iraq?" Shane asked.

"They were small carved tablets and cylindrical stamps as well as a gold bracelet from Sumer. He hid them in his uniform pockets since he hoped he wouldn't be searched. Once he got home, he found an antiquities dealer who wasn't very concerned about their provenance," Brady added to the report.

"What happens now?" Emma asked and shot a relieved glance in Piper's direction.

"Devare will likely cop a deal in exchange for the name of the dealer. Apparently the last time something like this happened, the relic thief got eighteen months' probation and had to make restitution to the dealer," Ava advised.

Piper raised an eyebrow. "That's all? After everything that's happened?"

Ava and Brady shared a look that communicated they were as frustrated as Piper with the sentence. "At least Parker's going to get more. Burglary. Assault and battery. Kidnapping. He's going to spend a long time behind bars," Brady said.

"And the antiquities dealer?" Shane asked.

"They paid him a visit and got the relics back. He hadn't been able to sell them without the provenance. They'll be returned to the Iraqi authorities," Ava advised.

"So it's over," Piper said and suddenly her knees were sagging.

Shane's arm was quickly around her waist, drawing her close to offer support.

"You and Shane may have to testify at Parker's trial, but other than that, it's over. You're safe," Ava said and laid a compassionate hand on Piper's arm.

"Thank you both," she said, forcing a smile to allay the officers' fears about her well-being.

Shane echoed her sentiment. "We appreciate all you did to help catch Parker."

Brady did a little shrug. "We owe a big thanks to your quick thinking and Decoy over there," he said and jerked his head in the direction of where the two dogs were playfully chasing each other around the training ring. "You and he are going to make a fine addition to any search and rescue group."

Piper couldn't miss the way Shane's body tensed against hers with the SAR mention. They hadn't talked about it in the last few days, but both of them knew it was there, festering like a wound.

Ava's radio chirped, alerting them that they were needed. "Unit 12. We've got a 10-46 on East Crabapple about a mile from the Salmon River," Jenny said over the radio.

"On it," Ava confirmed. With a smile, she explained, "Motorist needs some help."

"We'll see you soon," Brady advised and with a wave, the two of them were off to their cruiser.

"I guess I should get back to work," Emma said and, after hugging both of them, headed toward the DCA offices.

Piper watched Emma walk away, and in her ear Shane said, "Relax. It really is all going to be okay."

Only it wasn't going to be all right and it was long past time to discuss it.

She turned in Shane's arms, but he didn't release her, bringing his hands to her waist as she looked up at him.

"Now that it's over, you'll be going soon. You and Decoy are more than ready to continue your training with that Montana SAR group. Chipper is going to miss him," she said and glanced toward the dogs, who were still happily playing together.

SHANE COULDN'T CONTAIN the laugh that escaped him. With a shake of his head, he said, "Is Chipper the only one who's going to be missing someone?"

Bright color erupted across her cheeks, and she looked away, avoiding his gaze.

He cupped her cheek, applied gentle pressure to have her face him and stroked a finger across her creamy skin. "You know I'm going to miss you, Shane."

"I'd miss you, too, Piper, because… I love you."

Her gaze widened and her mouth formed a surprised *O*. "You love me?"

He grinned and shook his head lightheartedly. "I love you and I hope you feel the same."

She answered him by rising up on tiptoes and kissing him. He could feel the smile on her lips, and warmth filled his heart with her joy.

He wrapped his arms around her waist and brought her near, her softness fitting perfectly against him as the kiss deepened. His body responded, hardening with the feel of her, bringing a reminder of where they were and that he had something else to say to her.

Tempering the kiss, he sucked in a shaky breath, and she did the same, but then she said, "I love you, but… You're going to Montana."

He once again cradled her cheek and said, "After the other night, I realized I couldn't leave you… I mean, that is if you don't want me to go."

"I don't want you to go," she said with a broad smile. Her green eyes glittered like emeralds in the bright sun.

Grinning, he said, "I'm glad because I spoke to Gonzo

and he suggested someone who can help me with the nightmares and PTSD. Then I called the local SAR group. They'd love to have Decoy and me train with them. That is if you'll have me. Permanently."

She arched a brow and her gaze skittered across his face. "Permanently?"

He nodded. "Yes, as in, I want to marry you, Piper Lambert. Train dogs together. Maybe have some kids if you want."

"I want. Really, really want. I love you, Shane Adler. I want to train dogs with you and yes, I would like to have kids someday," she said, laughter in her voice as she laid her hands on his shoulders and kissed him.

Shane joined in her laughter and her kiss, certain that he was meant to be with Piper here in Jasper. Meant to live in these mountains that had brought him so much peace and this woman who had made that peace complete.

A bump against his leg reluctantly broke them apart.

Chipper and Decoy sat at their feet, looking up at them. Chipper had that irrepressible grin on her face while Decoy's head was tilted at a questioning angle until he said, "We're home, Decoy. We're finally home."

"I like the sound of that. How about you, Chipper?" Piper said and the little dog barked.

"I guess that's a yes," Shane said, grinning.

"Definitely a yes. What do you say about us going home to celebrate?" Piper said.

Home. It sounded so nice on her lips and his as he said, "Let's go home."

* * * * *

COMING SOON!

We really hope you enjoyed reading this book.
If you're looking for more romance, be sure to
head to the shops when new books are
available on

Thursday 14th
April

To see which titles are coming soon, please visit

millsandboon.co.uk/nextmonth

MILLS & BOON

THE HEART OF ROMANCE

A ROMANCE FOR EVERY READER

MODERN

Prepare to be swept off your feet by sophisticated, sexy and seductive heroes, in some of the world's most glamourous and romantic locations, where power and passion collide.

HISTORICAL

Escape with historical heroes from time gone by. Whether your passion is for wicked Regency Rakes, muscled Vikings or rugged Highlanders, awaken the romance of the past.

MEDICAL

Set your pulse racing with dedicated, delectable doctors in the high-pressure world of medicine, where emotions run high and passion, comfort and love are the best medicine.

True Love

Celebrate true love with tender stories of heartfelt romance, from the rush of falling in love to the joy a new baby can bring, and a focus on the emotional heart of a relationship.

Desire

Indulge in secrets and scandal, intense drama and plenty of sizzling hot action with powerful and passionate heroes who have it all: wealth, status, good looks…everything but the right woman.

HEROES

Experience all the excitement of a gripping thriller, with an intense romance at its heart. Resourceful, true-to-life women and strong, fearless men face danger and desire - a killer combination!

To see which titles are coming soon, please visit

millsandboon.co.uk/nextmonth

JOIN US ON SOCIAL MEDIA!

Stay up to date with our latest releases, author news and gossip, special offers and discounts, and all the behind-the-scenes action from Mills & Boon...

 millsandboon

 millsandboonuk

millsandboon

It might just be true love...

MILLS & BOON

Desire

Indulge in secrets and scandal, intense drama
and plenty of sizzling hot action with powerful
and passionate heroes who have it all: wealth,
status, good looks…everything but the right
woman.